"Mike, tell me the Space Diver works, even if you're lying."

"It worked in Arizona."

"Right, but how does it work? How does it get from space to the ground without killing us or being detected?" Jason asked. "And I'd very much like to know how I fly the thing."

"You don't."

"I don't?"

"The inside is pressurized. Zoom! You're in the atmosphere."

"Wow, but how do I get out of the thing?"

"You don't. It shatters around you. Come on, get inside so I can take a few measurements."

Reluctantly climbing in, Jason felt as if he were entering a coffin. It was a tight fit as the Space Diver was sealed. Everything turned black. Panic began to stab at him. "Shit, Mike, I can't breathe!"

"Suck on the oxygen hose. You'll be fine after a few adjustments," assured Mike.

"If it's so fine, then you jump it. This fucker's flimsy. I can probably punch my way out of this thing!"

"Only if you're Superman. It may be thin, but it's stronger than steel. As far as jumping it, what, you think *I'm* crazy?"

Also by Michael Salazar

**DROP ZONE**

# THE
# LUCIFER LIGHT

## MICHAEL SALAZAR

BANTAM BOOKS

**THE LUCIFER LIGHT**
A Bantam Book / March 2002

ISBN 0-553-58136-8

*Published simultaneously in the United States and Canada*

Bantam Books are published by Bantam Books, a division of
Random House, Inc. Its trademark, consisting of the words
"Bantam Books" and the portrayal of a rooster, is Registered in
U.S. Patent and Trademark Office and in other countries. Marca
Registrada. Bantam Books, 1540 Broadway, New York,
New York 10036.

PRINTED IN THE UNITED STATES OF AMERICA

OPM   10 9 8 7 6 5 4 3 2 1

**ACKNOWLEDGMENTS**

I would like to thank the
following people and friends for
helping me to tell this story:
Nita Taublib, John Flicker,
Carole Bidnick, my children,
Michelle and Mike, Jr., Julian
and Jean Leek, Peter Pinto, Boyd
Lease, Ben Cadallo, Charles and
Mike Meador, Louie DeMartino,
Steve Skipper, Steve Van Meter,
Vince Sergi, John Cooper, Hugh
McFadden, Bob Bolin, Tom Vawter,
John Shiman, and Doug Warn.

To the unnamed gentleman,
next time dinner is on me.

Whom God wishes to destroy He first makes mad.

—Seneca the Younger, maxim, 911 AD

Some say all talk of nuclear disarmament is too late....
The genie, they say, is already out of the bottle. But
there's another genie ... infinitely more threatening ...
and just as unstoppable.

—David Baker, *The Shape of Wars to Come*

Deny the reality if you will. I cannot.

—Major General George J. Keegan Junior (1921–1993),
chief of Air Force intelligence

*Murphy's Law: If something can go wrong, it will.*

BATTLE WASN'T PART OF THE PLAN. A FIGHT WAS THE last thing that the Brotherhood of Death wanted, and a losing fight was unthinkable. Planned for every contingency, the mission was supposed to be smooth: Infiltrate, contact, engage, withdraw, and then extract. Assisted by every conceivable technology, the top-secret mission was designed to be quiet, clean, and fast. Instead, they stirred up a gigantic hornet's nest.

Communications were out and the team was scattered everywhere in unfamiliar territory. All the planning and contingencies had gone to hell—it was every man for himself.

The smell of gunpowder and cordite filled the air as explosions rocked the frozen Siberian tundra. Area lights and night illumination flares turned darkness into light, taking away any advantage of night vision.

The PJ, as a pararescueman is called, raised his submachine gun. Through his heads-up display he zeroed on the man sprinting up the hill and squeezed the trigger. Click! Empty. He removed the magazine and grabbed his last clip. Before inserting it into his weapon he removed two bullets, then held one out at the man bound and gagged next to him.

"See? This one is for you. Before they get me, this bullet will be in your head. It looks like I'm gonna be able to do what I came for: Against all orders, I came here to kill you."

Inserting the two bullets into the empty clip and then slapping the other magazine into his weapon, the PJ took careful aim at the man running up the hill. The man dropped without moving. One bullet. One kill. But there were thousands of soldiers everywhere he looked.

*Never directly engage an overwhelming force.*

*We messed up bad. Where did they all come from?* the PJ asked himself. Intelligence had totally underestimated the objective. *Why didn't we know? Were we set up?*

Bullets snapped over his head, and then kicked up dirt as they targeted the PJ's fight zone. "Scared" wasn't the word to describe what he felt; "anger" and "betrayal" were closer. He was beyond rage. As he ducked close to the frightened man, the PJ's teeth chattered. "You speak English? You know, I'm a PJ. I'm supposed to *save* lives, not this shit! I don't know how many men I've already shot and killed. *Now* look. The whole goddamned Russian Army's here! Where'd they come from?"

Cautiously looking over his fight site, he saw that they were about to be surrounded. Glancing at the sky above, the PJ shook his head at the irony. Who would have thought that the most important battle for space would be fought on the frozen Siberian tundra? A top-secret battle fought by secret warriors. The winner of this battle would hold the balance of world power. Out of options and low on ammunition. *The very last bullet will be for me.*

Just below him a man lay dead, his head blown almost in two. Steam rose from the blood oozing onto the cold ground. The man had been one of the most talented members of the Brotherhood of Death. Shaking his head, the PJ realized that he would shortly follow the man to his own death.

Sporadic gunfire told him that some members of the team must still be alive and fighting back—but for how long? If he could somehow rally with them, then maybe they could try and escape together. *Together?* He never felt more alone.

A shrill voice yelled, "American! American! Throw out your weapons and come out with your hands up. We will not shoot you if you surrender now."

*Buy time. Someone understands English.* "Hey, fucker, listen!" he yelled. "I got your man here. You assholes come any closer, or shoot any more of our guys, and I kill him! Got that? You got that?!"

The shooting quickly stopped.

The PJ slid to the bottom of the hole, placed the muzzle of his weapon against the temple of the man, and studied him.

The PJ forgot when he'd given up on the idea of staying alive and accepted the possibility of dying. It was strangely calming. There were probably over a hundred marksmen patiently waiting for him to poke his head over the ridge just one more time. He quit thinking about being surrounded and concentrated on the man next to him. "You're the big fish, and I got you. Everyone, even my side, wants you alive. They say you know things that can change our grip on world power. But the second I see anyone come over that ridge, I'm pulling this trigger."

Eyes widened.

"Oh. So, you *do* understand my English."

A small nod.

The PJ sighed. "You'd think I was the one with the bad luck today, but it's not just me, pal. You happen to be here with the one person who wants to see you dead.

"I guess you probably want to know who I am and

how I got here. Well, I don't see a problem in telling you, seeing how we're both going to be dead soon."

"You can call me Alice," Air Force Master Sergeant Jason Johnson told his captive. "I'm a pararescueman, and the team that I'm here with are a group of sanctioned killers. Funny, huh? Me, a lifesaver, stupid enough to wind up in this frozen hole with you, the father of Space Wars."

Jason chuckled. "I'm not sure who the bad guys are, you or the assholes who put us on this mission. You know, less than two months ago I was saving hundreds of people from a flood. Then came that Titan explosion, plane crash and all those deaths—but I think you already know about that.

"Maybe I bought some time for us, and it looks like we ain't going anywhere for the moment." Jason relaxed, but did not let down his guard. "So before your comrades come over this hill and I kill you, do you want to know how we got here?"

The man gave a small nod.

# CHAPTER 1

**0130 THURSDAY / 16 SEPTEMBER 1999**
**PATRICK AIR FORCE BASE / FLORIDA**

HARD RAIN POUNDED ON A BLUE, SIX-PASSENGER Chevrolet 3500 4x4 truck parked on the flight line. Ten Air Force pararescuemen were stuffed inside, watching as a big Hercules HC-130 aircraft taxied to a stop in front of them.

The Blue Team leader, Master Sergeant Jason Johnson, glanced at his new PJ pup, Dan Murray, a normally gregarious person who now sat oddly silent. He pressed his lips together in a tight smile, remembering himself as a young PJ. Nudging Dan, he asked, "First real world rescue mission?"

"Yeah." A shy and slightly embarrassed smile appeared on Dan's face.

"Who's your teammate?"

"Alex."

Jason tapped Alex Abbey. "Hey, Alex, if it's okay with you, I'd like to take Dan with me. You can go with my teammate, Doug."

"It's cool with me," muttered Doug Lutz.

"No problem," Alex said with a nod. "Hey, Doug, I talked to your girlfriend, and she's bummed 'cause we're both gonna be gone at the same time."

"I know. That's too bad, because her dog's in heat. You could've serviced them both."

"Work time, guys," Jason said as the HC-130's ramp and door opened.

The loadmaster guided in the truck until it backed close to the edge of the ramp, then the PJs jumped out and quickly tossed their gear onto it. In minutes all the equipment was stowed and strapped down on the airplane; then the 4x4 drove away.

Jason was the last man to climb onto the HC-130. The loadmaster closed the ramp and door, allowing the plane; to taxi back toward the runway.

Securing his gear, Jason dropped onto a red webbed seat and buckled himself in next to Mac Rio, the loadmaster and Jason's best friend. "Yeah? So what's the deal?" A phone call to his apartment in Satellite Beach had woken him, ordering him straight to the alert truck.

Mac frowned and asked, "Haven't you been watching the news?"

"I was *asleep,* thank you." Jason had known Mac for years. Together they had flown the world to famines, war, and natural disasters. Mac, with few exceptions, was the closest thing to family that Jason had.

Mac waited until the plane was safely airborne before he spoke again. "Hurricane Floyd really knocked the shit out of North Carolina. Man, day and night we've been hauling rescue gear from all over the country to Pope Air Force Base in North Carolina, but ain't nothing stopping the Tar River from flooding. It's swelled to over thirty feet—it floods at the nineteen-foot level. Now the river's become a wall of rushing water and they need all the rescue support they can get. This is our eighth and last lift for the night. We're dropping you off at Pope.

"Over thirty thousand homes have flooded and there's hundreds of people trapped in the rising water, and it's getting worse. If the people don't get out somehow, they're going to get swept away in the flood in a matter of hours and drown. Your choppers and crews are already there and are just waiting on you guys to get into the action."

Jason nodded. Hurricane Floyd, a category five storm, had come ripping out of the Atlantic Ocean and made a beeline for Florida, causing the biggest mass exodus in Florida's history. But Floyd had turned at the last minute and torn into North Carolina.

The call for help came quickly for the 920th Rescue Group at Patrick Air Force Base, Florida, as it did for every other rescue asset available in the country.

The rescue group's H-60G Blackhawk helicopters were fitted with a myriad of night vision systems, plus they had primary hoist capabilities. True to their motto, the group was ready at a moment's notice. Once again, PJs and everyone supporting them were about to put their lives on the line so that others may live.

Jason Johnson was the leader of Blue Team's ten PJs—not a lot, but knowing that they were ten of only a few hundred pararescuemen in the world made him take his responsibilities seriously.

The flight to Pope took an hour and a half. Trained for combat and calamities, natural or man-made, Jason's Blue Team methodically checked over the gear that they had brought with them. Outfitted for war or peacetime rescue, they could go into any contingency with bandages, bullets, or both and save lives.

"Hey, Mac, would you ask the navigator to call ahead and check out the weather and ground conditions at our rescue location?" Jason asked as he pulled on his lightweight wet suit. "Make sure you get the amount of lunar illumination, too."

Speaking into his microphone, Mac waited until he got the answers Jason wanted, then said, "Floyd passed through less than ten hours ago. Flying conditions not bad—scattered clouds, light winds, and occasional rain showers. The ground's something else though. From the information Jackie got, she estimates it'll be six hours or less before the Tarboro and Princeville areas are completely underwater. The river is expected to rise to forty-three feet by morning. At thirty knots constant, the river will be running over seventy knots or more in some places. Moon illumination is at thirty percent." Nodding, Jason mentally absorbed the situation. The sun wouldn't be rising for another three hours, so they would be working in the dark. Wearing night vision goggles (NVGs), he could work well in the night.

"We're on descent. The pilot says we're dropping you guys off at the Green Ramp. The Blackhawk choppers are waiting for you." Mac put his hand on Jason's shoulder and squeezed. "Be careful tonight. You better than most know that actual rescues are the most dangerous missions around. You get so caught up in the rescue that you go beyond your limits, and then you fuck up. It happens before you know it, and this one's deadly as they come. Buddy, you ain't getting any younger, so don't do anything stupid. I don't expect to be part of a mission to rescue *your* ass!"

Jason nodded. At times Mac could act like the father he never had, but that was because he cared. He called his team together and gave them their last instructions. "Don't get separated. Stay with your teammate and the chopper crew!" he yelled over the engine noise. "If you have to, use the two-minute drill that I taught you guys. Remember, rescues are the most dangerous missions around. You get so caught up in them that you start fucking up. It happens before you know it, and this one's as deadly as they come. Don't do anything stupid!"

Mac grinned over Jason's shoulder.

The two-minute drill Jason taught his Blue Team was for emergency situations: Turn the mind and body on automatic, give it everything you have for two minutes, rest for one minute, even on the move, and assess your effectiveness; then go hard for another two, rest, and so on. Don't look at the clock. It was a mental exercise to counter the temporal distortion that can happen to the mind in dangerous situations when it feels like time is slowing down.

He'd discovered the technique on his own while a PJ candidate at Lackland Air Force Base, then perfected it on rescues, firefights, and long insertion missions. Human endurance was limited to the body's four miles per hour, one-g, daylight structure. Jason found that the body could go a lot longer in short sprints, and think more clearly when not trying to do it all at once. Two-minute increments worked fine.

Mac motioned for the PJs to sit down and strap in for the landing.

## 0305
## POPE AIR FORCE BASE / NORTH CAROLINA

The HC-130 Hercules touched down and the team was up and ready with their gear by the time they taxied to a stop. Mac opened the ramp and door. Once off of the plane, they gathered around a ground controller, who pointed them to their choppers. After they'd quickly loaded up their gear on a thirty-person crew bus, the driver raced out to the H-60 Blackhawk choppers, their engines and blades turning.

Pope Air Force Base pulsated with frenzied activity. Huge cargo loaders and forklifts laden with generators, tents, and communication gear crisscrossed the tarmac. C-5 Galaxy transports, C-17 Globemasters, and C-130 Hercules planes filled with people, supplies, and equipment touched down nonstop on the main runway. Air Force, Navy, Army, and Coast Guard rescue assets staged from the base to stop the damage left by Hurricane Floyd.

Most of the rescue choppers were landing for the night.

Jason's H-60 Blackhawk choppers from the 301st Air Rescue Squadron brought two key elements to the rescue table that no one else had: night vision and PJs. The night belonged to them; they were the only ones still flying.

Jason and Dan climbed aboard BAB—the Bad Ass

Bitch, tail number 26232, always the first chopper out. Jason quickly checked out the crew complement. Chris "Sunshine" Hannon, was the pilot. Al "Hollywood" Lupinski the copilot. Brad Frizzell and Carlos Gonzalez were the flight engineers. It was a tight crew. They had been flying together for years and knew each other's strengths and weaknesses.

Hannon quickly briefed them on the mission. Call signs Tiger and Wolf controlled the airspace that they would be working in. The chopper's mission was to complete a seventy-mile box search section along the leading edge of the south-running flood line. Anyone and everyone in need of help were to be airlifted to a highland gathering center at a school ten miles upriver from the flood surge.

In a matter of minutes they were airborne and headed for Tarboro. Flying at fifty feet above the closest obstructions, and using a fully integrated display system developed for combat, the crew followed a moving map created by a constellation of satellites. They searched the ground for any movement using Forward Looking Infrared Radar (FLIR) and night vision goggles.

Jason slapped Dan on the shoulder. "Follow my lead. Take care of my back and watch what I do. When you feel like you're ready, take the lead and I'll watch your back. Plan for the worst and expect the unexpected. Stay in control and work the two-minute drill if you have to, understand?"

Dan nodded.

"I got movement on what looks to be a trailer roof," the pilot said. "But I don't see anywhere we can put down. It's all flooded, and getting worse."

"I got five body readings on the FLIR," Al confirmed. "Two big and three small."

"Yeah, I count five too," agreed Brad. "The water's about to run over the roof. We gotta get them out, and fast!"

During the short flight, Jason briefed Dan on his duties, with every intention of giving the young PJ as much

responsibility as he had the training and willingness for
and Jason filling in as necessary. "I'll be the lead on this
one, then you'll be next. After that we'll change off on
who goes down the hoist."

Attached to the end of the hoist was the Forest
Penetrator. It had been used since the Vietnam War and
was the primary mechanism used for hoisting. It had
small, foldout seats and could accommodate three people
at once. Pullout straps extended from the horse collar
that wrapped around the individual to keep him from
slipping off.

Climbing onto the Penetrator, Jason swung out from
the chopper and indicated that he was ready to be lowered into the dark, swirling water below. He had
absolute trust that Hannon and Carlos, the hoist operator, would land him safely on the trailer roof. But would
the roof hold? Would the people rush him in a panic?

There was no time to ponder these questions. In just
a matter of minutes the floodwater would be over the
roof and wash away those on it. *Here goes,* he thought.

Jason appeared out of the darkness. The people in
front of him had no idea he was there until he yelled,
"Listen to me! Listen. We got to get you out of here."
The chopper's rotor wash whipped the wind like a maelstrom. "One at a time."

Peering through the night, Jason saw a family of five:
a man, a woman, and three small children. They were
terrified. Who was this apparition who'd suddenly appeared before them?

The immediate and potential problems were obvious—the woman looked to weigh possibly three hundred
pounds, the man even more. The hoist and chopper were
going to get a real workout.

"How many of you are there?" Jason asked the
woman.

"Fi-five. Praise God, who are ya?" she stammered.

"Angels from above, darlin'. What's your name?"

"Thelma. This here's my husband, Mark. He a stupid fool."

"We gonna be fine," he said.

She hit him hard on the shoulder. "Well, we ain't fine now, are we?"

Water slapped at their ankles. "My name's Jason, Thelma, and we're out of time so we got to move! Give me the smallest kid first."

From behind her, Thelma pulled a small girl and thrust her into Jason's arms.

"What's your name, sweetheart?"

She was frozen stiff with fear.

"Her name Pat, and she six years old. I got two more girls, one ten and the other eight."

The water was over their feet. "Great, Thelma. Pat first, then the other two. We'll take you and your husband after that. Ready?"

Thelma nodded.

Jason carried the little girl to the hoist. "Pat. You have to trust me. We're going on a quick ride." He pulled opened a second seat on the Penetrator and put her on it, then wrapped the safety strap around her waist. Getting on, he held her close and keyed his throat microphone. "Okay, Sunshine, this is the first of three standard hoists. The last two will be heavy, *real* heavy."

It was a twenty-foot hoist and went without incident. The other two girls were no problem either. The mother and father were a workout, but Carlos was ready. The safety straps were too small to get around their bulk, so Jason had to use a five-thousand-pound cargo strap to hold them on the hoist. It worked, though just barely.

With everyone packed like sardines on the floor, Jason could hear the chopper's blades strain in the air to keep it flying. He looked at his watch. It had taken seven minutes to bring them up. Not bad, but there were hundreds of others who needed help.

The folksy routine had gotten Thelma and her family up the hoist; sometimes the curt and forceful approach was the ticket. The people they came across would have a choice—ride the hoist and live, or stay where they were at and chance the floodwater.

The crew stayed on night vision while the passengers sat in the dark, crying as their eyes tried to adjust to their surroundings. Through his NVGs, Jason could see the shock and loss on their faces. They had nothing but the one suitcase they'd brought up with them. They had no idea where they were going, or what they would do next. But they were alive.

*I know what you're thinking: What's next? I've been there too,* Jason thought. They had the thousand-yard stare. He had seen that look of loss many times, on countless faces in many different places around the world. *I've been on both sides.* He stroked the hair of the little girl stuffed next to him as she cried.

"Thank you, mister, thank you for all of us," the mother said as she peered toward Jason in the dark. "She lost her dog, Angel. She fall in the river, and we couldn't get her."

The little girl's eyes widened. "Angel a little black dog. She got a pink collar. If you see her, maybe you can get her. You think so, mister? Huh? I cain't see you."

Jason shrugged. "Sweetheart, I'll look, but I can't promise you anything."

They landed in a schoolyard, then Jason and Dan helped the family down from the chopper. Pat kept looking back at Jason as if her only hopes in the world rested on him.

Closing the side door, Jason stared as the family trudged away.

"Back to work, guys," said the pilot.

Everything seen through night vision was just shades of green. People were everywhere—trapped in trees, standing in water, on roofs, on top of cars.

Churches and schools seemed to be the gathering places for most of the people. The crosses acted as a spiritual beacon until they themselves were swept underwater. Still, there was no telling where they might find people—on billboard signs, hanging on telephone poles. The crews lost count of how many people they saved.

Jason and Dan took turns on the hoist, and teamed up when they were on solid ground. There was no time to dwell on the victims' personal dilemmas. Sometimes they had truckloads of personal belongings and the PJs had to make them leave it all behind. With the fast water rising, lives were more important than possessions or furniture or animals. One suitcase was all they would allow in their small cargo compartment.

When a command post and radio link was finally established, the chopper crews flew the victims to the nearest shelters.

Up. Down. People on. People off. Some people were scared, and some were mad. All were exhausted and in different stages of shock.

They continuously scanned the water, looking for bobbing heads, or bodies, fearing that at any time they would have to pull a drowning victim from the deadly river. Their luck held. All they saw were dead animals—chickens, cows, pigs, and dogs. The most surprising things they saw were floating caskets that had pushed up through the water-saturated ground from cemeteries.

Jason shuddered, remembering being caught in a raging river in Bosnia. There were five thousand dead bodies in that river. But with everything going on around him, there was no time to dwell in the past.


**0630**
**OVER THE TAR RIVER / NORTH CAROLINA**

The crew was exhausted as dawn broke. They had refueled twice; now it was time to head back to Pope to eat some chow, then go into crew rest. Line chief Vic Davis and his ground maintenance teams would get the choppers ready to go again for the next crews on Alpha Alert.

A small movement in the rushing river below caught Jason's eye. He flipped down his NVGs and scanned the water. It looked like a small animal struggling to stay afloat in the raging river. He had already seen many animals in the same situation, but with all the human rescues, they couldn't stop to save drowning animals. Peering closer, Jason made out the features of a small animal.

"Sunshine." He keyed his microphone as he flipped up his "noggs." "Do me a favor and circle back over that—I think it's a dog. Turn on your spotlight when you do."

"Roger."

Hannon made a quick turn and flipped on a powerful ten-million-candlepower spotlight.

There! It was a small black dog with a pink collar.

"Pilot," Jason said, "I got to get that dog."

"What?!" responded Hannon. "It's just a dog. No way. The river's running too fast and there's no place to put down. Sorry."

Jason leaned over Brad, the flight engineer, and looked Hannon in the eyes. "Chris, I want to try and get it. I'm asking you to do this as a favor to that first little girl we picked up. Come on, it's all she's got. Look, I'm willing to give it a go if you are."

Jason saw the reluctance in Sunshine's eyes, then the glitter of *Why not?*

"You're nuts, pal, but if you're willing, then I guess we can try. One shot. That's all I'm giving you."

The crew flew as one; a miscue on anyone's part would result in a downed chopper. The pilot raced with the river as Brad monitored all the engine data and tracked the altitude and airspeed. Staying just ahead of the animal, Carlos, acting as the hoist operator, would lower Jason toward the water and direct the pilot over the dog. Al, the copilot, scanned far ahead for unseen power lines or towers, and fiercely prayed that there weren't any. No one on the crew ever had figured that they'd be using their collective skills to put their lives on the line for a dog.

Handing Dan his NVGs, Jason strapped himself to

the hoist and dangled from the chopper. Then, nodding to Carlos, he began his descent.

"Crew, we're moving forward at thirty-five knots," Hannon's nervous voice said in Jason's earpiece. "There's a bridge coming up soon. Only one pass, Jason—one pass!"

He was just inches above the dog. "Angel. Angel, come here!" Jason yelled from the hoist seat. Leaning low, he made a grab for the animal. The rotor wash swung Jason in circles above the dog.

Angel would not come. Oblivious to everything around her, she was just trying to keep her head above the water. Timing his swing, Jason leaned farther out for the dog. Suddenly, he fell off the hoist and into the furious river.

*Oh shit! Fuck me.* Surprise and panic hit him at the same time. Caught in a raging flood, he heard Mac's warning echo in his mind. "Don't do anything stupid!" This was as stupid as it could get.

*Now what?* A yelp. The dog was right next to him. He grabbed Angel by the collar and held her head above the water. Alive or dead, the dog was staying with him.

It wasn't a matter of swimming, it was just trying to stay up and not hit, or be hit by, anything in the water. He looked up—the chopper was nowhere to be seen. "Come on, guys, I'm right here."

*Shit, I've been in situations like this before ... but never this bad.*

Eyes wide with terror, the dog tried to cling to him. Where the fuck was that chopper?

Again and again the violent currents pulled them under. Fighting back with everything he had, live or die, Jason resolved not to let go of the dog.

The situation only got worse. Sometimes just Jason's nose was above water as he was tossed and turned. His strength was waning fast.

A real bolt of panic struck him when he heard a loud roar and saw tons of water slamming into a concrete bridge at over eighty miles an hour. In a matter of less than a few minutes, he would be battered to death.

"Where are you, Babs? Come get me. I'm right here!"

Again, the water pulled him under. *This is it,* Jason thought, struggling just to get his feet pointed downriver. Doing his best to hold his breath, he waved the dog above his head like a flag and tried to break through to the surface for air. But it wouldn't happen. His breath gave out, and then everything turned black. *Time to meet God.*

Suddenly something caught Jason's wrist like a vise and pulled him through to the surface. *Breathe! Breathe, motherfucker!*

A voice from the blackness above cried, "Jason, let go of the dog!"

It wasn't God. It was Dan Murray. He was on the hoist, but Jason couldn't make out where he was at through the swirling mist and churning water.

"No way!" Jason yelled, holding the dog over his head and kicking his feet with all his might. "Take this bitch and hold on to her!"

The dog was lifted from his hand, and then Jason felt Dan's legs. They were only seconds from impacting the bridge. With all he had left, Jason pulled himself onto the hoist. The chopper rose up and away from the water, clearing the bridge by inches.

Dan's free arm guided Jason firmly onto the seat as the pilot bled off all forward motion and slowed into a hover. Jason tried slipping on the restraint belt but realized it was broken. It must have snapped when he'd reached for the dog.

Now it was Carlos's job to get them safely back into the chopper. Once they were, Dan covered the shivering animal with a blanket and Jason fell against the rear bulkhead.

There was no talking. Jason covered his face and willed himself back to reality. *Oh sweet Jesus, I'm still alive!* Shaking, he put on a spare helmet and plugged into the intercom system. "Thanks, guys," he said. For the moment it was all he could say. Looking below at the raging flood, he was shocked to realize that he'd actually made it out.

"What the hell was that all about?" he muttered to no one.

"Crew," Sunshine keyed. "I think that this save was self-critiquing and best kept among ourselves."

Double clicks on the microphones signaled agreement.

"We need to stop back at the first school," said Jason.

"Roger," Sunshine said.

"Still alive," Jason sighed off the intercom.

"What?" asked Dan as he dropped the shivering dog into Jason's arms and stripped off his wet suit.

Young and superbly muscled, Senior Airman Dan Murray was just starting his career as a PJ. It had been a spectacular start, and Jason realized he had saved his own life by picking Dan for a partner. *And* I *was going to teach* him? Jason looked down at the wet, trembling dog.

"I owe you big," he said to Dan.

Dan's shy smile crossed his face. "No problem. A beer will do."

"More than a beer—a lot more." Jason shook his head at the dog and scratched her ear. "Angel, you bitch. I ought to throw you back into the fucking river."

The chopper landed back at the collection point they'd gone to when the mission began. Jason carried Angel off the chopper and looked around for Pat. When he saw her, he put Angel on the ground and watched the animal run straight for her. The little girl cried out in surprise, delight, and relief when the dog jumped into her arms. "Thanks, mister! Thanks, mister! Oh, thank you, mister!"

Jason waved, turned, and then reboarded his chopper. He could still hear Pat calling out her endless thanks over the noise of the rotor blades.

In the dawning light, Dan smiled at him and said, "Okay. These things we do that *dogs* may live?"

"So? Credit us with a dog save. I guess they count too." Jason shrugged, took a deep breath, pulled off his wet suit, then stretched out on the cargo floor. Mac was right, and would undoubtedly give him an "I told you so" and a sound scolding after hearing the whole story. He'd gotten caught up in the rescue, and then things had gone bad. Once again, his single-mindedness had been the source of his screwup. *Maybe I'll keep this story to myself,* he reasoned. The mistakes were self-evident, and the lesson had been learned.

There would be five more days of rescues, and then back to Cape Canaveral, Florida, for a Titan rocket launch. Still breathing, he had a job to finish. As he'd done for years, he would just shake off his brush with danger and press on. He didn't know that somewhere in Texas, more danger than he could ever imagine was rolling his way.

# CHAPTER 2

A MARMON SEMITRUCK ROARED DOWN AN EMPTY Texas highway at exactly eighty miles an hour. To the casual observer the rig looked like any ordinary eighteen-wheeler. In reality it was a Safe Secure Transport (SST), the most sophisticated rolling vault ever invented. Inside the cab, the driver and passenger idly chatted.

"Do you know much about patents?" Matt Arnold, the driver, asked.

"No," answered Mike Decker, passenger and SST Transportation Safeguard Protective Service team leader, sipping from a cup of hot, spicy tomato soup while he scanned the road ahead.

They were about to pass a gold Infiniti. No oncoming headlights could be seen. Red taillights from the lead van, along with the headlights of the trailing van, assured Mike that they were the only vehicles on the road this morning. His "road warriors" were on the job.

"I do," Matt continued. "I had this idea for a humidity sensor on dryers. It would turn off the dryer when it sensed that the clothes were dry. So I filled out the proper forms, got five hundred dollars, and sent them off to the U.S. Patent Office to get it patented."

Decker peered through the windshield; they were approaching a fog bank. "It looks a little thick, doesn't it?" He leaned forward and turned on the infrared screen mounted in the dash. Through the screen he could see the infrared beacon light flashing on the lead van. A quick flip to the rearview and the trailing beacon looked normal. Somewhere overhead a helicopter gunship flew in the black Texas sky. A mobile home followed miles behind.

The recreational vehicle was really a very well-appointed armored personnel carrier that held the relief crew and enough weapons to start a small war. A little fog was no big deal.

"Go on," Decker said. Propping his feet on the dashboard, he continued sipping the spicy soup.

"I send in my money and I get back all these official-looking papers. Looks good, right? But at the end of the papers was this long list of people who already had patents on my idea."

"You just keep on thinking, Matt." Decker casually glanced at the old man driving the Infiniti as they passed. He knew that the lead van had already run the plates of the car and ID'd the man. If there had been anything unusual they would have let him know long before the SST even got close to the car.

"I have been, and I got another idea that I've been working on. You know how sometimes you can't hear car radios because there's too much outside noise?"

"Sure." Decker politely smiled. Listening to Matt's harebrained ideas usually helped pass the time. Tonight, though, the conversation was annoying. He couldn't pinpoint any particular thing, but tonight he felt edgy.

"How about a noise sensor that automatically raises or lowers the volume depending on what noise is around the car. Cool, huh? I have the schematics and everything to send."

"And you'll send in another five hundred dollars?"

"Yeah."

"It sounds like a good idea. Ford liked it so much that they even put it on some of their luxury cars."

Matt's face darkened. "Damn! I've been working on that one for three years."

Mike laughed so hard that he spilled some of the red soup on his shirt. "Damn!" Trying to clean it off, he succeeded only in smearing it more. Oh well, he had a spare shirt in the RV that he could change into later. "Look at it this way," he consoled Matt. "I just saved you five hundred dollars."

"I guess so," Matt mumbled, and then, trying to change the sore subject, asked, "Do you know anything about the load? You notice that there aren't that many documents accompanying it? Even the restricted-data block isn't signed. Everyone at Sandia seemed a lot more uptight than usual."

"A little, but it's none of your business," Mike answered. "You know the drill—sign for it, protect it until it's signed over, and then keep your mouth shut."

"Right, boss." Matt nodded. "I'm slowing down. It looks like the fog's getting thicker."

The Department of Energy Protective Service special agents picked up the SST trailer from the Sandia National Laboratories at Kirtland Air Force Base in New Mexico, to be delivered at Cape Canaveral, Florida. The highly trained team's mission was to carry sensitive and top-secret government loads around the country.

Equipped and able to handle any emergencies involving nuclear and hazardous materials, Mike's men put in endless training hours to neutralize and contain any contingency, man-made or otherwise, that might prevent them from delivering their load. A little fog was nothing to be too concerned about. The idea that anyone would actually try and attack an SST was ludicrous.

To begin with, the trailer vault had reinforced steel walls that were two feet thick. It had multiple alarm systems, including satellite location transmitters that would alert the Transportation Tracking and Communication

Center (TRANSCOM) of any emergencies. TRANSCOM would alert the gunship chopper flying nearby, the RV, and the Protective Center if anything was wrong. The vans ahead and behind carried men armed with large-caliber automatic rifles, grenades, and rocket launchers, the mission being to keep the SST moving forward at all times.

If the SST was stopped during an attack, a covered switch on Mike's dash was designed to blow the wheels off the trailer, and then a hundred nonelectrical-grounding twenty-inch titanium spikes would anchor the vault to the road. It would take a crane to move the vault.

Should anyone try and open the doors, a supersticky foam would coat the vault, disabling gases would be released, and a low-frequency alarm would make anyone close by too sick to move as their eardrums ruptured. No. To try and take the load Mike's team carried was unthinkable.

Still, if it all went to shit, the final defense was to rip open a covered and safety-wired button. Hit it, and the vault would be electrified with fifty thousand volts. Anyone touching the trailer would be instantly electrocuted.

Routine operations included certain need-to-know data of what was in the vault: net explosive weights, chemical hazards, command disabling functions, and any specific information meant only for the lead man.

Not this time, though. It was a sign-and-go deal.

*Oh well,* Decker thought. *I don't get paid the big bucks to know, just to do.* Six more hours and they would trade out watches with the team in the mobile home. *Stay tight for the watch, and then get some sleep.* It was a long way to Florida.

Matt seemed pissed off by his latest no-go idea. They'd been on the same team for over ten years, and Mike decided, *I should try and cheer him up.* "Come on, Matt, I know you have another idea."

"I do, but you'll probably shoot that down too."

"Hey, come on. You can't just give up."

They crossed over a small rise and dropped where the highway cut into a gully. Thick smoke suddenly enveloped them.

"This ain't fog!" cried Matt.

A bright light flashed ahead. Decker looked through his infrared screen. There was no lead van visible on the road. He did a double take when the van fell to the ground in flames. "Oh shit. We're in a smoke screen!" Suddenly the cab flew into the air and everything went black.


DON'T MOVE. DON'T BREATHE, DECKER'S INSTINCTS TOLD him. The passenger door opened and he felt something hard prodding his chest. Someone spoke, but it felt as if he had cotton stuffed in his ringing ears.

"He's dead, bloody dead," a voice said. "The driver's still moving, though."

"Do him. Hurry up! I reset the alarm system. We've got exactly three minutes. After that the chopper is going to show up and shoot anything that moves, then ask questions later. So let's *move*."

Even muffled, the voice sounded familiar; Decker knew it from somewhere.

The concussion of a noise-suppressed slug made Decker flinch. A smacking sound, then something warm and wet landed on his face as he listened to the fading footsteps.

Cautiously opening one eye, then the other, Decker discovered that the front end of the cab was almost blown away. A rocket attack. The cab's three-inch-thick bullet-proof glass was shattered.

His eyes flew open, and his scalp crawled when he saw Matt, or what was left of him. The top of his head was gone. Matt's brains were hanging out the side of his blown-away skull. One eye hung down from its socket and blood was everywhere.

"Jesus, Matt, oh Jesus," he whispered. "I'm sorry."

Wiping his face, Decker was surprised to see that his fingers were wet and red. *Huh?* He licked a finger. Tomato soup. Whoever was looking him over thought he was bloody dead, but it was only tomato soup. His life had been saved by a cup of tomato soup.

Frightened and disorientated, he allowed anger and adrenaline to take over. Nobody was going to kill his team and take his load! He punched the switch to blow the tires, but nothing happened. *Then we all burn!* Decker ripped off the protective cover and hit the button. Nothing happened. Either the explosion had damaged the alarm system or someone had disabled the switches. *Damn!*

He grabbed his M-16 rifle from behind the backseat, flipped off the safety catch, unbuckled his seat belt, and fell from the smoking cab. *Owww!* It felt like a sledgehammer had struck every part of his body. As far as he knew, he was the last one left. The pain no longer mattered. Even the load didn't matter. His team had been wiped out and now it was payback time!

Creeping quietly in the dark until he found the forward edge of the SST, he was surprised to find that the trailer was still upright. Decker pulled himself to the top of the vehicle and quickly crawled toward the rear.

A voice counted down numbers and commanded powerful spotlights to the rear doors.

A truck backed toward the doors.

Cautiously peering over the edge of the SST, he saw that three men on the tail of the truck were about to enter the vault. There was no time to think. The noise from Decker's automatic rifle caught everyone on the ground by surprise as he sprayed the men with lead, sending them scattering for cover.

Using their confusion as a cover, Decker leapt into the vault. Bullets ricocheted around him.

"No! Don't shoot at him. You might hit the load. We have less than two minutes left. Rush the fucking vault and hack him up!"

Now the voice connected to a face. It was Blane Taylor, the newest member of the Protective Service team.

"Blane, you motherfucker!" Decker yelled, then put in his earplugs. "Come on up here and try and take this thing." Things were about to get loud.

"That's just what I'm going to do. I'm in a hurry. Now!"

A canister rolled onto the floor. Decker had seconds to react. He kicked the canister back out and it released volumes of smoke, turning the entrance of the vault into a black curtain.

The attackers thought that they had smoke cover, but ran instead into a hail of bullets from Decker's machine gun the moment they broke through the curtain of thick smoke. The gunshots were deafening. Taylor was the last man in the trailer and went down as Decker shot his legs.

The sound of chopper blades filled Decker with relief. He wanted to signal, but leaving the vault was the last thing on his mind; the chopper's infrared system could see bodies, not faces.

Unmistakable whirling, roaring, and ripping sounds of minigun fire filled the air. The impacting lead made the ground tremble—the helicopter gunship's mission was to neutralize anything moving in the area, then wait for the backup in the mobile home.

Removing his earplugs, Decker kept his weapon trained on Taylor. Now they could talk. "Why?"

Taylor writhed on the trailer floor.

A spotlight from the chopper searching the ground illuminated the trailer enough for Decker to see the damage he had done to Blane's legs. The bullet exit wounds had almost cut off his legs. Taylor would bleed to death if help didn't arrive soon. Almost cut in half, and Taylor still wanted the load. He looked longingly at the boxed load, then at Decker.

"You couldn't even begin to understand." He grimaced.

"No, maybe not, but after they stop the bleeding in your legs I'll bet there'll be people who will."

Fighting the pain, Taylor replied, "Oh no. I don't think so." He pulled a pistol from his waistband and fired one round into his head.

Powerful Transportation Safeguard Protective Service spotlights invaded the vault, turning everything a blinding white.

Shielding his eyes, Decker saw blood wherever he looked. Ripped and bleeding bodies lay everywhere. The smell of the gore was overpowering. "What the fuck just happened? I didn't kill them all, did I?" He examined himself. Besides his hearing being faulty as a result of the explosion, he was just banged up, bruised, and covered in blood and tomato soup.

The battle over, Decker tried to clear his ears, taking time to look over the box that so many had just died for. It was just a large wooden crate chain-gated to the floor, about eight feet square and twenty feet long. There were no markings on it. No hazard plaques or biological or nuclear labels warned of its contents. It was just a plain wooden crate.

"What rotten power do you hold that people have to die for you?" he asked. "Watch. I'm going to find out."

"Verify," an amplified voice called out.

"Yeah." Decker sighed. It was the backup team.

Coded words were exchanged.

"Exit with your hands above your head."

Decker cautiously stepped from the vault, rifle and nine-millimeter Beretta raised high over his head. He could see nothing but the carnage and rifles pointed at him. "Thunderpig," he said.

"Cross," came the reply, and the rifles were lowered. "Clear."

Decker lowered his rifle and flipped the auto-fire button to safe. "Give me an assessment," he demanded. Choppers in the air with spotlights lit up the area like a macabre carnival.

"Dead," a voice replied. "They're all dead, Mike, the whole team. It was an ambush. They even had a smoke generator. It was a massacre."

Someone had known they were coming. Decker suddenly felt tired, and slumped to the bed of the trailer. Someone lifted away his rifle and pistol, then softly patted his shoulder. His body started to shake. No one but a well-connected team would know how to attack an SST.

A Blackhawk helicopter appeared from nowhere and landed. A lone figure stepped from the chopper and walked toward Decker. The black leather trench coat and slouch hat made him look ridiculous in the Texas desert.

Decker shook his head. Only a fool would be pompous enough to wear such a costume outside a dark alleyway in Istanbul or Washington, D.C. And this fool was dangerous, a fool with a long memory. Mister Black—fixer of blame and punishment. This was the man who appeared when things were bad, and he always seemed to make things worse.

Mister Black stood for a few moments looking around before turning to Decker. "What happened?"

Decker shrugged. "I don't know. It was an inside job. Blane Taylor, the newest guy on my team. Now my team is wiped out. You ask me what happened? *You* tell *me*. I didn't assign him to the team. I check out my people first. He was put on the team against my recommendation. How'd they get the SST open? *I* don't even know how to open it.

"Our routes are never known, but there was an ambush waiting for us. They had a smoke generator, for God's sake. I don't know what the fuck happened. But I want to know why."

Mister Black continued looking around at the scene and then rubbed his chin a moment before speaking. "How bad do you want to know? And what exactly do you want done about it?"

"Maybe settle the score."

"And if it's clearly beyond legal limits? Are you willing to stretch those boundaries?"

Had he heard right? Suddenly there was no question. "All the way." At that moment he'd have been willing to sell his soul to the devil for revenge.

Mister Black inspected Decker as if he were choosing

a piece of meat at the market. "You'll do. I can use you."
He took a last look at the slaughter and smiled coldly.
"There's over twenty bodies scattered around here, and
you're the last man standing. What do you get paid as?"

"A GS-twelve."

"You'll work for me and I'll pay you as a GM-
fifteen, plus expenses and personal bonuses. You're on
my clock now. Let's go."

Decker pointed at the carnage. "And what about
this?"

"It won't be here in a couple of hours, just a burning
car crash with some old man in it. He was at the wrong
place at the wrong time, but he turns out to be a good
cover for what went on here. Calculated opportunity,
Decker—it's part of the way I do business."

**0200 SUNDAY / 19 SEPTEMBER 1999**
**CAPE CANAVERAL AIR FORCE STATION / FLORIDA**

The load arrived on time, on schedule. The SST trailer
pulled into a guarded hangar and transfer papers were
signed. No mention of any unusual happenings to the
load was stated in block six remarks. Another team
would bring back the empty rig. The SST team boarded a
crew bus that took them to the Skid Strip, where a waiting company jet flew them back to Albuquerque.

Under the cover of darkness and guarded by a Cape
Canaveral Base Security team with a shoot-first authorization, the payload was moved from the hangar and se-
cured to the Titan rocket by the third shift. All functional
checks and forms were completed on two logbooks that
stated different things: One was for public records, the
other classified.

# CHAPTER 3

**0145 MONDAY / 20 SEPTEMBER 1999**
**UNDISCLOSED LOCATION ON THE EAST COAST OF**
**GEORGIA**

A SQUEAL IN THE EAR.
*Wake up*.
Froto opened his eyes.

*Where am I?* On the fifth floor in the false ceiling of a storage closet.

He'd gotten through all the security checkpoints undetected, disguised as a disabled paper collector.

Ignored and invisible. *They're not like us. Don't make eye contact with them*. No one ever takes any notice of the physically challenged moving through government buildings collecting unclassified paper for recycling, especially a midget who goes into a storage room with four retards and gimps on the fifth floor.

The Red Force Command Center was located on the fifth floor. He had gotten there two days before the exercise even started. If anyone had been closely watching the security cameras on the fifth floor they would have seen five people enter the closet, but only four come out.

Check the surroundings. All the alarms he set were still in place.

*Secure.* Get ready to complete the mission.

Work for Marine Staff Sergeant Kelly Sherwin, code-named Froto, meant infiltrating the most inaccessible and secret places on earth on behalf of the American government.

He had been abandoned at birth, and all his young life every door of opportunity had been slammed in his undersized face. He'd joined the Marines, and during basic training his fierce attitude had caught the attention of the Brotherhood of Death, a covert Marine unit under the command of the Doors, an organization so secret that it was legal to lie about its existence. Now he stole on orders, copied information, planted bugs, and killed, sometimes all at the same time.

Froto stretched his lithe frame. Tonight would be the completion of the snatch-and-grab portion of the mission.

Tonight was all a game and no one would die.

No one from the Red Force on the fifth floor knew that a mole moving just feet above their heads had already compromised their secure computers. Everything that was done on the secure computers in the "combat-secure" room was relayed to a central router located down the hall in the unlocked and unprotected storage closet. It was a simpler matter for Froto to attach a tiny receiver to the router than to try and gain access to the Red Force command post, which was manned around the clock.

The receiver was about the size of a dime. It may have been dime-sized, but worth over three hundred thousand dollars. Using a prototype photon technology and chalcogenide phase-change material (C-RAM), the bug would, on remote command, microburst the stored information to a multibillion-dollar communication satellite. Ironically, the bug was using the same Global Information Grid (GIG) used by Red Force, but on a superhigh frequency. No known bug detector could alert on the system.

Froto always worked alone, except once when he'd teamed up with a PJ named Jason Johnson on a top-secret mission, code-named Operation Furtive Grab.

Serbs using B6B, a toxin that made anthrax and smallpox look like a cure, had murdered five thousand civilian women and children in a soccer field. Their mission was to bring back a soil sample for an analysis of B6B. The mission was botched, Froto was left for dead, and then it was up to Jason to complete the mission. What had started out as an angry relationship turned into a true friendship. Froto smiled when he thought about Jason's having brought back more than just the soil sample.

During war, peace, or training, Froto loved what he did. While the rest of the military downsized, the Doors funded the Brotherhood of Death with more money for more missions, secret and precise.

Froto didn't carry any weapons with him on this mission, and he knew weapons well. To be a member of the Brotherhood was to know the tools of the trade that they dealt with. The weapons they used included guns, high explosives, poisons, and anything else that could neutralize a target, even computers.

He had already been at the Red Force Command Center for four days and set up his plan of attack. No one knew that another secret organization was also playing the game against the Blue and Red Force and that there wasn't a thing anyone could have done about it; no one had any idea that spies and assassins from the Brotherhood were spooking around. Froto read his watch: 0150 hours. Exercise Wizard Warrior, a Rapid Decisive Operation (RDO), was in full swing.

Five thousand players with all their toys "battled" at a partially closed military base. As part of the Network Warfare Simulation (NETWARS), another ten thousand "virtual soldiers" were counted in among their live counterparts. A future war waged on the streets of the base and in cyberspace. High-tech military combat warriors fought from street to street, house to house in urban warfare; the reality of this future war still meant grunts with guns. But the computer, radio, and state-of-the-art information assemblies were now classified as weapons systems that were just as vital as the gunpowder that propelled the bullets.

Wearing computer-enhanced visors on their helmets, "cyborg" soldiers appeared and mixed in and multiplied with human opponents. Bullet blanks and laser tag rigs put humans and cyborgs out of action on both sides.

It took years to bring together this clandestine exercise. American intelligence agencies such as the CIA, NSA, CIC, and several branches of the military gamed in a multimillion-dollar Red and Blue Force battle. One of the objectives of the exercise was to evaluate the ability to deploy thousands of military personnel and government agents without attracting any media attention and without anyone in the civilian world even knowing about it. Another objective was to see how advanced or retarded they were. A lot of egos and careers rode on this exercise. The war had been going on now for two days, and not one word of it had been leaked to any news agencies.

Blue Force invaded Red Force, purposely striking at the strengths of its opponent. While the infantry went at it hot and heavy from house to house, on the streets, and even in the sewers, the computer warfare in protected, shielded, and hardened buildings was just as intense.

Forget to program in a refuel supply and the vehicles stopped. Don't ask for reinforcements and you get pushed back, and watch out for viruses that could shut down the whole operation. Everything unfair was fair.

The Doors refused the invitation, and then snuck in undetected with a few of their representatives and with their own plans. The Doors always played a different game.

Kelly didn't give a shit about any of it. It was someone else's training, not his. He was doing the gig to maintain an edge. He would do his job and move on.

Red Force Command Center was six rooms away. Froto's mission was to steal the three hard drives and tape backups that ran "code word" commands and classification orders higher than top-secret. The hard drives connected Red Force to all its assets. Cop the drives and tapes. Kill the brains. The server that contained the drives and tapes were protected inside of a locked and electrically charged cage. Touch the cage and get zapped.

Normally, the diminutive insertion specialist answered to no one while prosecuting a mission. *But not today.* Froto silently grumbled while he donned his equipment line and an overgarment that absorbed light and could change color to match the background like a chameleon. The garment, called a chameleon cape, was an ultrasecret Door project.

The night vision glasses he wore were a prototype that cost over three hundred thousand dollars. Looking more like something out of a toy store, it had a heads-up display and microcameras mounted in the lenses, along with spectacular, full-color night vision and a GPS transmitter. From miles away, the Door battle staff could chart his real time progress and make suggestions. The gear he donned was worth millions. Donning a custom-made helmet with oversized ear cups, he was ready to move out.

## 0200

"Hand job," Froto heard in his earpiece.

"Blow job," he quietly responded. He wore no microphone. The words he whispered were transmitted through a pad that rested on his forehead in his close-fitting helmet. Even in the middle of a deafening firefight the helmet unit could transmit and receive clearly. The headgear was also designed to catch the bullet by decelerating its impact to seventy-five g's.

The mission was "hot," and it was time to get moving.

He traveled across the false ceiling through the bar joists using a special soundless retractable bridge. There was plenty of room to operate without having to scrunch into impossible positions. Traveling over the ceiling, he bypassed all security checkpoints, metal detectors, and locks too hard to pick.

Two thousand meters away a helicopter hovered just below the tree line. Using Ground Penetrating Radar (GPR) peering just above the tree line, it "saw" into the building and followed Froto's progress.

A voice spoke in his earpiece. "You're two grids away, to your left."

Tom Chain, Froto's controller, sat at a computer screen in a van fifteen miles away watching Froto's progress transmitted from the chopper's GPR. "Get into position and wait for the signal."

"Gotcha. On time."

Froto relaxed once he got in place over the Command Center "vault." Complacency. Red Force unwittingly chose a Command Center that didn't have a protected ceiling. Very slowly he pushed a tiny, needlelike wire through a foam tile above the room until the miniature sensor punched through just a fraction of an inch. He flipped a switch on his helmet and listened to the mayhem below, using a sound system that worked very much like a bat's sonar.

Built into the helmet were sensitive pads that, through continuous sound reflections, gave the wearer sensory awareness of what moved about in the room. He could "see" people through the ultrasonic waves bouncing back toward him. Adjusting his night vision lenses, Froto smiled, thinking about the chaos that he was going to add when power to Red Force was cut.

He checked his watch; power to the building would be cut for three minutes in exactly fifteen seconds. The moment it went dark Froto would drop to the floor, create a diversion, pick the lock on the uncharged cage, lift the hard drives and tapes, then get back into the ceiling. The only trace that he had even been there would be a sticker of the Brotherhood of Death. They wanted to leave a calling card: We can play, too.

...*three, two, one.* Everything went black. Everything stopped. Everything quit running: Computers went blank, backup generators wouldn't start, Kelly's digital watch stopped.

All power shut down—lights, air conditioners, everything; even his night vision quit working. *Good move,* Froto thought. The plug got pulled on everyone. How'd they do it? They even knocked out all his gear. It didn't bother him too much. He was flexible, and he knew that flexibility won wars when plans changed.

Froto lifted away the ceiling tile, hooked himself into his hand winch, and then noiselessly cranked down to the floor, feeling his way in the dark until he came to the server cage. In the ensuing pandemonium, there was no need for him to create any diversion. Picking locks in the dark was his specialty. With the cage open, a press of a button put the hard drives and tapes in his hands, then in his pouch. A slap of a vinyl sticker over the computer and it was time to move.

Everything was out—emergency lights, flashlights, batteries. With all power completely off he decided it would be easier to just withdraw from the scene and collect his gear later.

The confusion didn't bother Kelly. "Gas! Gas! Gas! Condition black!" he yelled for fun, adding to the quandary, causing confused people to scramble to get into their chemical warfare gear while he made his way to the dark stairwell.

Once he was outside, there was no light anywhere but from the moon. Something had happened, but no one knew what, or why. Most of the soldiers walked around in a dazed state. A fire raged just beyond the tree line. Was the Door chopper down? There was no rescue response; the vehicles would not start. He ran toward the fire in the woods.

Mission objective met, he would first see if there were any survivors from the apparent chopper crash, then would find Tom Chain and see what kind of weapon they'd used on Wizard Warrior. It had sure as hell worked, too well.

**0235 MONDAY / 20 SEPTEMBER 1999**
**8th SPACE WARNING SURVEILLANCE OPERATIONS**
**CENTER, SKY ROOM**
**CLASSIFIED LOCATION / EAST COAST**

Colonel Doug Jones walked away from the bank of computers and wide-view screens that dominated the Satellite

Imagery Complex building and into the break room. It was the Nighthawk shift, and he craved a cup of strong black coffee. His satellite hawks were settled in their chairs and poring over data and commands, after which they'd give loving care and feeding to their precious and delicate satellites.

Billions of dollars and countless thousands of man-hours put sensitive, high-tech satellites into space. The job of his hawks was to keep a constellation of surveillance satellites in good working order and to execute procedures based on messages that came to the hawks from many clandestine and military organizations around the country.

After pouring his favorite thick brew in the break room, he sat down at the counter to browse through a few morning newspapers as CNN droned on the television mounted on the wall next to him. The Balkans, Afghanistan, India, Iraq, China, North Korea, and several other hot spots around the world dominated the headlines. Jones glanced at the Sky Room behind him. A lot of stories in the papers and on the TV would probably not even be there if it weren't for his Nighthawks' mission. The Nighthawks might be only a piece of the great political puzzle, but they were a key piece to what really went on in the world.

Once the hawks finished with their preliminary "tune ups," they looked down at the world through a constellation of spy satellites, "flying" them over political hot spots as position priorities were placed on the endless classified requests they received. The whole system belonged to the National Imagery and Mapping Agency (NIMA), whose mainframe computers were sequestered at a secret location somewhere on the East Coast—the real owner was the Central Imaging Command (CIC).

Jones didn't need to perch on his team's shoulders as they processed their night's assignments. His satellite jockeys had been on the team for years. They knew the importance of their work, and he had the highest retention rate of any satellite team.

"Commander! Commander Jones!" Maria Duran, his team chief, yelled as she ran down the hall. "The Sky Room!" she cried in the hallway. Sliding to a stop in front of him, she came right to the point. "Sir, everything blacked out for a second and now all the screens are screwed up. We're getting shit for readings!"

"Impossible!" Jones dropped his coffee cup, spilling it on the counter, and ran with her to the Sky Room.

Screens flickered, faded, or blacked out while his people checked and rechecked their computers, then scrambled all over the room checking connections and cables.

"Colonel Jones, what checklist do we run?" someone cried.

"Backups, bring the backups on line!"

"No response. Negative function," Maria gasped.

Picking up the blue telephone that rang directly to the NIMA supercomputer room, the source of the problem, he waited an endless five seconds before he realized that the line to NIMA was dead. He tossed the phone, and then his heart almost stopped as all the screens suddenly went blank.

*Blank?* He was speechless. A multibillion-dollar system just doesn't crash and go blank. He picked up the red phone that connected directly to the Ground Station Command Post in Colorado, his body trembling. "Someone tell me this isn't happening!"

The phone answered on the first ring. "Ops Cap Red. This is not an exercise. Repeat. Ops Cap Red. This is not an exercise!" Jones had just declared a national classified emergency. That was it. It was out of his hands. He couldn't believe what was happening. But it was.

The eyes of the most powerful country in the world had just gone blind.

# CHAPTER 4

JASON SAT WITH HIS LEGS DANGLING FROM THE OPEN door of the H-60 chopper. Adjusting the restraint belt for maximum movement, he settled down and thought about what was bugging him. The word "routine" kept popping up.

The morning had sure gotten off to a bad start. While waiting on the fuel truck for the chopper at Cape Canaveral's Skid Strip, Jason overheard the fuel man say that someone was going to shoot the giant alligator that lived under the tunnel at the checkpoint. Hearing that, Jason sprinted across to the Skid Strip entrance and just about got into a fistfight with a guy he'd never seen before. But it didn't matter, because no one was going to kill King George.

The old alligator was sunning himself on the bank of the canal, asleep and heedless of the man in front of him with the raised weapon.

Jason jumped in front of the rifle and forcefully pushed the man away from the alligator. Standing between them, he tried to keep an eye on both.

"Touch me again and you're gonna be hurting," the man warned.

"No," countered Jason. "*You're* the one that's going to need a stretcher if you get near George. And why are you pointing your weapon at him? He's not bothering you."

"It's a danger to my boys," said the man.

Jason couldn't see the man's eyes behind his mirrored sunglasses. "Idiot, it's your taste in clothes that's a bigger danger. Are those black pajamas you're wearing? Who wears pajamas in the open at a place like this? This is tacky, very tacky, unless you're the North Vietnamese Army. Now listen, fucker, you even *point* your gun at George again and I'm gonna kick your ass and then shove that MP5 up your asshole." He stood his ground.

Over fifty years old, the giant alligator was a legend and a fixture at Cape Canaveral.

From out of nowhere, more guys in black pajamas with guns showed up, and Jason found himself hopelessly outnumbered. But he wasn't about to back down. Unarmed, the only weapon he had was his attitude.

Suddenly the chopper crew was there with him, but they too were unarmed. *Now what?*

From up the road several Cape Security vehicles raced to the scene. Sirens blaring and red lights flashing, the cars screeched to a stop, then security guards jumped out and raced to the fence overlooking George's lair. Looking relieved when they saw George on the bank behind Jason, they turned their attention toward the black pajama guys. It was clear that the Cape cops were not associated with, and didn't like, the guys in black pajamas either.

"I called them," Brad, the flight engineer, said to Jason.

"Good call," said the pilot, Chris Hannon.

"I got a call that someone wants to shoot *my* alligator?" said one of the cops. "Anybody gets near *my* gator and they're going to get an ass-whipping of a lifetime."

Jason was relieved to see that it was Colonel John Byrik, chief of Cape Canaveral Base Security. His cops loved and protected the gator.

The man facing Jason lowered his rifle. A cold smile crossed his lips as he looked at George. "An alligator with friends—who would've thought?" He turned and walked away, followed by the rest of his men.

"I think I'll stay for a while and keep an eye on George," Byrik told Jason. "Thanks."

"Thank you, John." Jason gazed at the sleeping one-eyed giant. The alligator had once been in close enough range to Jason to bite him in half, but hadn't. "Looks like we're even, buddy."

Once the chopper was fueled, the crew was glad to get in the air, away from the heavy vibes the guys in black pajamas with guns gave off at the Skid Strip. The moment they checked in on the radio, Cape Leader, the launch controller, ordered them to check out some suspicious activity near the railroad tracks that led to the base.

Flying low, they saw several men in a van setting up some sort of tripod on the tracks. When they reported back, Cape Leader ordered them to upset the scene. Using the rotor wash, Hannon created a maelstrom of dirt and wind to blind the men on the ground.

Suddenly TAC-1, NASA's armed response helicopter, swooped in, carrying black pajama guys, their guns, and their bad attitude. In seconds they had five men eating dirt on the ground, handcuffed and trussed up like pigs on a spit.

Watching the action on the ground, Jason realized that for a routine mission, everyone seemed armed but him and the crew. But that was operations normal, routine. Bottom feeders like range clearance choppers were always last in line for any changes.

"Did anyone see that?" asked Chris.

"Yeah, those were camera tripods. I think they got a bunch of reporters, not terrorists," keyed Vince Sergi, the copilot.

"Who are those guys on TAC-1?" Jason asked.

"No one from around here," Brad answered.

"Houston, maybe," said Sunshine. "A CIC tactical assault team, I'd bet. Very fast and very deadly."

Jason was curious. "Who's the CIC?"

"The Central Imaging Command. They own and operate all of America's spy satellites. They make the CIA look like a very poor relative. I once did some work for them in Texas, hauling some of their guys around. It's a good bet that's some of the same guys back at the Skid Strip."

"So why are they here?" Brad questioned.

"Ask Jason. He's our resident spook."

A halfhearted smile crossed Jason's lips. "I have no idea."

Ever since a "by name request" had taken him away on a top-secret mission in 1995, he'd had to endure innuendo and caustic remarks from the rescue community about being a spook. It was true that he was connected to some people in the black world—the most secret of them all, or so he'd thought until he heard the name of the Central Imaging Command. But then, ultrasecret units seemed to pop up all the time.

A secret unnumbered National Security Decision Directive, titled "The Legal Protection for Clandestine Killing Teams" covered a select few essentially licensed to kill. Buried deep in the top-secret attachments was a list of names that identified the Brotherhood of Death and their associates. Next to the number twenty-six on the list was the name Jason Johnson.

"So what do they do?" Carlos asked.

"Nothing *routine*," Jason remarked. He never talked about the Brotherhood of Death to anyone but Mac Rio.

Someone very powerful in the government took a force RECON unit, put them under control of the supersecret Doors, and then sanctioned them for killing on a case-by-case basis. The name of the Marine RECON was the Brotherhood of Death. Although they were officially Marines, they actually belonged to the Doors.

Bad memories of the Doors made Jason shiver. He kept away from the Door secret training base. They hadn't called on him in a long time and he hoped that it stayed that way; no news was good news. Their way of doing business wasn't his. Today's mission might be routine, but at least it wasn't life-threatening.

TAC-1 confirmed that the scene was secure, and Cape Leader ordered Hannon's chopper to continue on to clear the box.

**1450**
**TITAN LAUNCH COMPLEX 40**
**CAPE CANAVERAL / FLORIDA**

Titan-IVC, number 20B sat on its gantry, prepped and geared for liftoff. Eastern Range had spent thousands of man-hours readying the seventeen-story rocket. Across the base hundreds of launch personnel sat in front of their terminals, working together to put a highly classified payload twenty-three thousand miles into space.

**45th RANGE OPERATIONS CENTER / MISSION**
**CONTROL ROOM / CAPE CANAVERAL / FLORIDA**

Surrounded by a double fence topped with razor wire, security guards patrolled the launch facility, weapons set on fire. Security cameras rotated ceaselessly, looking for anything, or anyone, suspicious.

Inside the high-tech fortress, every safety issue had been scrutinized. The four-hour window was thirty minutes from opening. Airspace corridors were clear of all traffic. The stations at both Mission Control Room (MCR) high bays reported, "Go for launch." The weather and hazard control rooms were fully staffed, ready for any and every contingency. The 45th Space Wing was ready to light the rocket engines of the big bird.

Just offshore the H-60 Blackhawk helicopter made a low warning pass, buzzing a few spectator ships to stay outside of "The Box," a danger zone, eighty miles long, and ten miles wide, just off Cape Canaveral's Atlantic coast. It was the chopper's job to keep watercraft away from the debris fallout area in case the rocket exploded after launch.

"You see that?" said Brad.

Jason leaned out the left window, scanning the ocean. Only the fading ripple of a wake was visible. "It might be a whale, or a submarine."

"It's something, all right," agreed Sunshine. "Coming right for a low pass."

This time there was no sign of anything in the water. Everything secure, they proceeded to their holding point over the Banana River and then checked in with Cape Leader. Jason sat on the floor of the chopper with the door open, listening to the countdown on the launch radio.

For the first time in a week, he had some time to think about what was happening in his life. Six days ago he'd almost died. Today he was almost in a fistfight. In a matter of days he would turn forty, and in a few more months have over twenty-one years of military service. He could still hack the mission—maybe. He felt too young to retire—or was he?

Memories of civilian saves, humanitarian missions, classified operations, and combat rescues flooded his mind. A PJ couldn't save everyone in the world, just the ones he personally helped. Jason had countless rescues and very few "thank-yous." A small laugh escaped him when he realized that the most "thank-yous" he'd ever received at one time had come from a little girl with a black dog.

*Get out or stay in?*

He would never go home, or escape his past. Ever since the days of his childhood poverty in Washington State, he'd craved adventure. Home had been an abandoned double-wide trailer on a former apple orchard. Growing up, Jason ate so many apples that now, if someone offered him an apple, or anything containing apples, he figured they were looking to piss him off.

His mother was methamphetamine-addicted, with

five children from five men. After getting high on home-made crank, her psycho common-law husband would often beat Jason with a motorcycle chain. He'd left home at seventeen and never looked back.

*Trailer trash.* That's what everyone called him when he was young. He'd never forgotten what his mother said the day he left her to find a better life: "This is our life, boy. We go through one trial, and then a worse one comes along."

It turned out to be her curse. Getting older now, and at the zenith of his career, he had little to show for it but a chestful of ribbons.

Jason had never thought of himself as a loner, but lately he seemed to find himself in his own company more and more. Turning down several assignments to lousy locations had undoubtedly cost him a promotion, even though he was probably the most qualified PJ in the Group.

*Not getting any younger.* The body still worked, but he sometimes woke up real stiff. There was a little gray showing at the temples, but nothing Lady Clairol couldn't correct when it got worse. Wrinkles? Well, laugh lines, okay?

*Man, my life's gone by so fast. What's next?*

Jason felt a dread about the future. Caught in a midlife crisis, he felt that something was missing in his life, but he had no idea what.

A bright light caught his attention. It was the plume of the Titan.

The Titan cleared the gantry and was fifty seconds into its flight when suddenly it exploded into millions of pieces.

"Damn!" gasped Jason. It was a terrifyingly beautiful sight.

Launch radio was silent for a few moments, surprised that something had gone so horribly wrong—over two billion dollars wrong. A woman's voice spoke. "We have had an anomaly. All sections take cover. Repeat. Take cover."

Panoramically and in slow motion, what had only a moment ago been a 204-foot rocket disintegrated into a couple of million pounds of deadly shrapnel. Arcs of red, yellow, orange, and black firebrands containing rocket fuel and metal plunged to the earth, scattering over the Cape and into the Atlantic Ocean.

Like incoming artillery, Cape Canaveral Air Force Base came under attack. To be caught in the open beneath this wave of fire was sure death. Millions of pounds of metal debris and rocket fuel rained down onto the Cape. A firestorm raged on the land. Cars exploded and buildings burned. Cape Canaveral turned into a fiery hell.

Jason pushed off the Launch Radio and pulled up the Cape Leader radio just as they ordered all Response Elements into action.

"That's us," said Hannon. "Vince, get us clearance into The Box."

From their position over the Banana River, they tried to plot where the largest pieces had fallen. If some boater watching the show had entered The Box during the launch, they knew there would be little left to recover.

Jason methodically donned his wet suit and checked over his dive gear. It seemed to him as if he had spent half of his career climbing into a wet suit and the other half pulling himself out of it.

The radios suddenly came to life as several people voiced commands at the same time.

Cape Leader overrode all others. "All transmissions will cease. Only I give the orders. Jolly One, proceed to The Box and mark any large debris, then coordinate with the Coast Guard cutter *Valiant*. All teams SAM-DOT."

"Do you hear how his voice has changed?" Sunshine asked. "Someone behind him is giving the orders now." He opened the small, classified packet called a Situational and Maritime Disaster Order Tasking (SAM-DOT) and read it. "It says here that in case of a mishap, our first priority is to locate and mark the payload. The payload will look like a silver cylinder twenty feet long and seven feet wide."

A chart analysis had probable splashdown coordinates for the flight engineers to load in their moving map.

Changed from his flight suit into his dive gear, Jason continued to monitor the radios as he gauged the waters just off Cape Canaveral. The water posed no problems. The sea conditions looked fair, swells ranging about three feet, water temperature at seventy-three degrees Fahrenheit. The depths ranged from fifty to over a hundred feet.

Pieces of the Titan wreckage floated everywhere. Twisted and mangled, parts of the rocket lay on the surface of the water, coated with a reddish, toxic rocket fuel.

"Pilot," Vince keyed, "there, about eleven o'clock, about fifty yards. It looks like the payload."

They came to a hover over the object.

"Damn. It looks like it's, it's *moving*," observed Brad.

"Vince, call Cape Leader and tell them that their package appears to be moving out into the open ocean," the pilot ordered.

Cape Leader's response was adamant. "Put your PJ in the water."

"Hey, Sunshine, that water's going to be toxic," noted the copilot. "Not only that, but *who's* moving the load?"

"Good point," Sunshine agreed, so he radioed back to Cape Leader and questioned the order.

"Negative," Cape Leader answered, and insisted that their PJ go in after the load.

"Chris, they are serious," said Jason.

"So am I. Do you know what a hypergaul is?"

"No."

"It's rocket fuel that will rip the water from your body. *Yours*. It's real bad stuff, and there's a lot of it in the water right now. I have no intention of putting you in something that can kill you. We'll just drop sea dye to mark the location. There's nothing written in the

SAMDOT about putting a PJ in the water." Sunshine called back and refused the order.

"Open channel, Jolly One, return to the Skid Strip *immediately*."

Code words came fast. From countless emergency exercises, Jason knew the meanings for most of the codes. A disaster team was activated. The base was sealed, and those not under the debris or in shelter were already out collecting data and logging all the events leading up to the explosion. Suddenly he heard Cape Leader call out a secret code word. He knew the word. Damn! Someone was going "weapons hot." Someone had been cleared to shoot first and ask questions later.

TAC-1 flew dangerously close under their chopper as the coast of Cape Canaveral came into view. Tall columns of black smoke rose hundreds of feet into the air as raging fires made the Cape look like a war zone. No injuries or death codes were reported. Watching the fiery scene, Jason wondered how anyone couldn't be hurt. Looking back over his shoulder, he saw TAC-1 drop even lower over the water, a tactical move to avoid radar detection.

Jason had changed back into his flight suit and was ready at a moment's notice to give aid. The closer they got to the Skid Strip, the more obvious it became that he was wanted for other than his medical skills. They taxied to parking and saw the black pajama guys waiting with their guns at the ready. As soon as they shut down their engines, they were surrounded.

"Boy, by the looks of things you'd think that *we* were the ones who blew up the rocket," observed Chris.

The crew was herded into a dark, windowless van and driven away from the Skid Strip. The smell of smoke was everywhere. Sirens blared all around. Training taught Jason to look at his watch to try and time some of the stops and turns. He knew the base well and could figure out where they were being taken.

But something was wrong. There were no stops, just fast acceleration. Pulling out a small compass that hung from his dog tag chain, he saw that they were heading east. They were on the Skid Strip runway and headed toward the Atlantic Ocean.

The driver slammed on the brakes and made a hard right turn. Burning rubber and brake fumes filled the rear and the crew was thrown around the van. Dust poured in from everywhere as they raced down a dirt road.

In less than five minutes the van stopped and the doors opened.

"Get out!" an angry voice commanded.

Jason was last to step from the van. Looking around, he saw that they were in a small stone hangar of some sort. It was musty-smelling and mildew peeled the paint from the walls. Several large green mobility containers were stacked against a wall. There were no windows. It was a big holding area, probably hidden underground, and the men facing them weren't regular Cape Security.

"Over there," a man in black pajamas ordered. Wearing mirrored sunglasses, he stood about six feet, with greased-back black hair. Muscles bulged everywhere.

"Christ," Jason muttered. It was the guy who'd been about to shoot King George.

Four documents were spread out on a table.

"What are those?" Sunshine asked.

"Nondisclosure statements," said the man. "Sign them."

"Why?" Sunshine was getting hot.

A short, fat man, dressed in a black trench coat and slouch hat, pushed past the men in black. "Because you questioned valid orders, refused the SAMDOT, and discussed classified information over an open channel. You want more?"

Jason did his best to suppress a laugh. It was a silly scene. The man's overall appearance reminded him of Boris Badenov of the Rocky and Bullwinkle cartoon. The man would have been hilarious, if it hadn't been for the menacing troops behind them.

Sunshine had had enough. "Who are you? You can't force us to sign anything!" He put his hands on his hips and stared Boris down.

Boris threw open his trench coat and put his hand on the pistol in his shoulder holster.

"Oh man," Jason said under his breath. "We're about to get caught in an Old West shoot-out, and we ain't got guns."

Outgunned twenty to zero, Jason felt his temperature rising.

On closer inspection, they looked well equipped, with all the latest toys; MP5 machine guns, Ray-Ban mirrored sunglasses, and Danner boots—polished, with no scuff marks.

He tried to eye each man, but there was no read behind the sunglasses. Jason concluded it had to be some kind of mind game. Testosterone. Well, he could play the game too. Besides, he owed Sunshine.

He stepped next to Sunshine and assumed a relaxed, but very obviously fighting, stance. No one was going to fuck with his pilot.

The man who'd ordered them out of the van stepped forward and stood nose to nose with Jason, his fists balled. It was Boris's boy.

He looked to be in his early or middle thirties.

"Anytime you're ready, alligator man," he sneered.

Suddenly a door opened and Brigadier General Alan Daniel, the 45th Space Wing commander, came rushing in. "Everyone, stand at ease!"

"Later, *old* man," Boris's man nodded.

Jason was bewildered. *A fistfight.* For the second time in one day, he found himself in a situation that he hadn't been in since high school. One thing he knew for sure—he wanted to trade blows with Boris's boy.

General Daniel rushed over to Hannon and pulled him to one side of the room, where they conversed for a few minutes in hushed but intense tones.

Jason knew that the crew was out of luck when he

saw Sunshine's shoulders sag and his head drop as he nodded.

The general rushed past the crew and was out the door in seconds.

Sunshine trudged back to them. "I tried telling General Daniel that we saw the payload moving, but he wouldn't listen. He says that we have to do whatever these guys say. *Orders*."

They walked over to the table and signed the Sensitive Compartmented Information Nondisclosure Statements, promising not to discuss with anyone anything that had happened or was going to happen.

"Empty your pockets, and then strip!" Boris barked.

Jason reached into the sleeve pocket of his flight suit.

A brass coin resounded on the table. Boris scooped up the coin, scrutinized it, then tossed it back onto the table. Boris's man picked it up, studied the coin for a second, and his jaw dropped open. He whispered in Boris's ear as he handed it over.

A look of surprise registered on Boris's face. "Where did you get this thing?"

"Where do you think?" Jason smiled. It was a numbered coin. The coin belonged to the Brotherhood of Death. Number twenty-six was stamped on it. The best point man and infiltrator in the world, Kelly Sherwin, had given it to him when he made him an associate member.

Boris blanched. "Yours?"

Lightning-quick, Jason reached out, grabbed the coin, and then narrowed his eyes at Boris's man. "We can finish this anytime."

"What are you people doing here? You're standing on your own grave." Boris glared. "You should've identified yourself the moment you got here—unless you're trying to hide something."

Casually reaching down and scratching his scrotum, Jason smiled. "Do you have a need to know?"

Boris stepped close to Jason and bared his teeth.

"You think you Doors can infiltrate anywhere, but not here on my turf. Get nosy and you'll get burned. You better back the fuck off!" Leaning closer, so no one around could hear, he hissed. *"You Brothers better have not had anything to do with this. This is the place where people are never heard from again. I can make you disappear right now, understand?"*

"The only thing I understand is that your breath stinks, and that your men look out of fashion in their black pajamas. It's fall—they should be wearing brown or red pajamas. By the way, is that hat you're wearing government-issued?" Jason blinked and rested his wrist on his hip. "I think that we can do better than this, don't you think?"

Someone behind Boris snickered.

"This *isn't* a place for humor," Jason admonished.

Everyone started laughing.

Like discovering a dog turned rabid, the deadly look in Boris's eyes told Jason that he had made an enemy. *Uh-oh, I fucked up,* he thought. This was Boris's place and Jason had just pissed in his territory.

"Shut up! Shut up!" Boris snarled.

A black pajama guy burst into the room and sprinted over to Boris, then whispered in his ear.

Boris blanched, then yelled, "Get them the fuck out of here, NOW!" His eyes bored into Jason as the PJ climbed back in the van.

As they rumbled down the dirt road, Chris asked, "Jason, what in the hell was that all about?"

"Sorry, Sunshine, but if I tell you, I gotta kill you. Just be *real* glad we made it outta there. And thanks for refusing the SAMDOT."

The second the van stopped at the Skid Strip, the crew jumped from the van, and their chopper was off the ground and back at Patrick Air Force Base in record time.

"Remind me not to do these 'routine' range clearings anymore," the pilot said, adding, "If I were you guys I'd remember that no one saw anything—we signed our names to that fact. Avoid everyone and just get lost for a couple of days."

Back at the PJ unit, Jason stowed his gear in his locker, then got in his car and drove off, rather than hanging around for the obligatory beers and shop talk at the King's Club. Boris and his men had gone way out of their way to shut up the chopper crew. Maybe they recovered their own payload. But that didn't make any sense. *Forget about it. Just do what Hannon said,* Jason thought. Rockets blew up; it was part of the business. It was just a routine launch gone bad. Whatever had happened today was best forgotten.

**1715**
**45th RANGE OPERATIONS CONTROL CENTER**
**CAPE CANAVERAL AIR FORCE BASE / FLORIDA**

Within minutes of the explosion, the Disaster Control Group (DCG) had assembled at the Command Room. Their purpose was to minimize loss and protect assets. Men and women, mostly in blue Air Force uniforms, sat around a U-shaped table. A phone and placard, identifying unit and position, sat in front of each person. The phones stayed busy as contracts and logbooks from the Titan were gathered and impounded, if they hadn't burned somewhere.

Pacing in the space between the tables, Colonel Dana Beach asked questions of the group. "Has weather verified that any toxic clouds are moving away from any population centers?"

"Yes, sir," Lieutenant Colonel Tina Welch, his second in command, answered while she listened into a green phone. "Hazard Control tells me that the computer model and weather's Doppler radar has the big red cloud going straight out to sea."

"Is the Initial Response Element on scene?"

"They can't get in yet," Tina answered. "Too hot."

"I want the Crash Net and Notification Checklist

completed, now! Double the cordon and airspace restrictions."

"Yes sir," Tina answered.

A thousand questions had to be answered and taken care of, fast.

Who had jurisdiction? Was the mishap a component malfunction or a criminal act? Terrorism? Plus, there was a lot of ancillary damage to cover.

Several arguments broke out as fingers pointed and old wounds got picked at. A few in the room already had their mishap paperwork finished—they just changed the date from the last Titan explosion.

Colonel Beach called the room to attention as the door opened and General Daniel entered, accompanied by a man wearing a black trench coat and slouch hat.

"Everyone here, including your subordinates, is under general order fifty-six," Daniel began. "This is a highly classified incident, but you will say that it's a routine AFI-101A investigation. You will deliver any and all information to the Central Imaging Command. That is all. *Anyone* who breaks the general order will be immediately terminated and subject to immediate arrest by this man next to me." Daniel put his hands on his hips. "Folks, just comply with our visitors, and Mister Black assures me that they will be gone in a week. Now please leave."

As the DCG members left the room in total confusion, men in black suits entered from a side door and began gathering up every piece of information about the disaster.

All leaves at Cape Canaveral were canceled. Hundreds of light carts were brought out from the Air Ground Equipment (AGE) storage hangar. Tents went up, and for seven days, twenty-four hours a day, Cape employees combed the fallout area for wreckage. Special divers and salvage ships pulled up Titan wreckage. Contractors were called in to fix roofs and make any repairs that the Titan had caused. Damaged cars were towed away and melted into metal bars. Insurance claims were processed the same day as they were received. Everyone connected directly to the rocket explosion was signed to secrecy.

Within the week the withdrawal phase was completed and the recovery to restore the site done. Only burned patches of vegetation testified that anything had happened at all at Cape Canaveral Air Force Base.

The 45th Space Wing's public affairs official news release was that a classified satellite had been destroyed when the Titan malfunctioned and began a self-destruct program forty seconds after liftoff.

Nowhere was it reported that shortly after the blast, the TAC-1 helicopter disappeared. The call for rescue never went out. The next day a salvage ship quietly retrieved the remains of the anonymous chopper crew members, and then disappeared.

The payload was not recovered.

# CHAPTER 5

**2355 TUESDAY / 21 SEPTEMBER 1999**
**OVER THE NORTH ATLANTIC OCEAN**

NEW YORK CENTER CLEARED ENGLISH AIR 943 FROM London for a gradual descent from thirty-five thousand feet toward its final landing at New York's La Guardia Airport. On board the 747 was a crew of twenty, and three hundred and fifty passengers.

All the screens in the cockpit suddenly went blank for a moment. When they came back on, all the readings went haywire. The flight controls became stiff, slow, and unresponsive to any of the pilot's input. Smoke began to pour out from the flight panels.

"Oh damn." Captain John Cooper gulped. "This is bad. Radio New York Center and declare an in-flight emergency," he said to the copilot.

Without hesitation the copilot got on the radio. "New York Center, New York Center, English Air nine forty-three heavy is declaring Pan Pan Pan. We need an immediate diversion for a landing at...at Halifax."

"Roger English Air nine forty-three," replied the air traffic controller for New York Center. "Descent to flight level three-one-zero. Please state the nature of your emergency."

"New York. Stand by, stand by short," said the copilot.

New York Center cleared them direct to Halifax International Airport, and again asked the nature of the emergency, but the call was never returned.


**2359**
**CANADIAN FORCES BASE / GREENWOOD / NOVA SCOTIA**

The moment English Air 943 went off the radar screen, the supervisor of the air traffic controllers called the Rescue Center at Greenwood. After all, 747 commercial passenger jets just didn't vanish from radar screens with a total loss of communication.

Joe Christ, monitoring the alert desk at the 413th Transport and Rescue Squadron, reached for the ringing scramble phone.

"Joe, this is Red Connock down here at New York. Every second counts, so I'm passing Rescue Control Center and callin' you direct. A 747 passenger jet just went off our screens near Halifax. I just faxed you the points of the last reported location. Now I'm callin' RCC."

"Right. I'm on it."

Hanging up the phone, Joe turned the Launch key and grabbed the paper from the fax. Rescue claxons echoed throughout the base, the loudest of them at the Rescue Alert Quarters (RAQ) just behind him.

"Ah shit," yawned forty-seven-year-old Tom "Toby" Wiler. "This better not be another false alarm or exercise." The Search and Rescue Technician (SARTech) had just nodded off to sleep. "Oh well," he sighed, "rescues while on rescue alert *are* part of the job." Still, twenty-seven years on the job and countless rescue alerts made him feel a little annoyed to be roused from his precious sleep. After rolling out of bed and sluggishly pulling on his orange flight suit, Toby reached for his boots.

SARTechs, the Canadian equivalent of American PJs,

trained like their counterparts and were regularly called upon to perform a multitude of rescues in the Canadian wilderness and the cold North Sea. Their motto—"That Others May Live"—was the same as the PJs'. They were truly brothers in arms.

The RAQ door flew open. Troy Arce, Wiler's partner, stood in the door. "On the move, Toby. This one's for real. A passenger jet has gone down off Sable Point."

Sleep fell away as Toby went on automatic, his many years of rescue experience guiding his moves. In fifteen minutes he was aboard his yellow CH113 Labrador helicopter, number 301, sitting inside Hangar Ten, ready to go wherever the pilots flew. Rescue gear had been prepositioned and stowed. Like American PJs, whether on water or land, SARTechs were ready to act at a moment's notice.

Sitting at his crew position, Toby listened to the rescue talk as it filtered from the planning room out to the flight line. A 747 jet from London to New York was diverting to Halifax for unexplained problems. At thirty-five thousand feet it had just gone blank on the radar screens.

Toby thought about calling Vivian, his wife, to let her know that everything was all right, but decided against it. A phone ringing in the middle of the night only meant bad news.

The pilots came running from the command post. Jumping into their seats, they explained that they were headed to the last reported location of the jet, and then began the Before-Starting-Engines checklist.

## 0200
## SABLE POINT / NOVA SCOTIA

Whatever hopeful anticipation the crew felt crashed the moment they saw the water through night vision and Forward Looking Infrared Radar (FLIR). This was not going to be a search-and-rescue mission: There were no signs of life. The closer they got to the water, the grislier it became.

There was only silence on the intercom, because there was nothing to say.

Taking a deep breath, Toby unrolled a body bag. "Okay, pilot, get lower so I can begin."

**0830 WEDNESDAY / 22 SEPTEMBER 1999
920th RESCUE WING / PJ SECTION / PATRICK AIR
FORCE BASE / FLORIDA**

The rescue community is a small world. Many things go through a rescue specialist's mind when a disaster pops up on the television. What's the location? Are there survivors? Who's on the job, with what equipment? Why wasn't *I* called?

The PJs collected in the main briefing room and watched CNN on the TV with rapt interest, anxious to be called and a little envious of those already on the scene.

"A Labrador chopper from Greenwood," observed Alex Abbey as an aerial camera panned on a yellow chopper hovering over the ocean. "Four-thirteenth. That's Toby's unit."

"Hey look, it's the Long Island Guard out of New York, Jack Brehm's boys," added Justin Ivie when the same camera caught the fin flash of a C-130 Hercules circling overhead.

"Looks like they won't be needing us," Jason said. "They got all the help they need."

Lance Supernaw peered closely at the screen. "I wonder what happened."

"Who knows?" Alex responded. "Terrorists maybe, or mechanical, like a blown engine."

Suddenly all the news channels had their "experts" voicing various opinions about the calamity. Search and rescue was the "hot topic" on TV. It never failed to amaze Jason how the media clamored like vultures for the best action shots as the search-and-rescue teams did their best to bring a little dignity and respect to the dead and dying.

"It's not search and rescue. It's search and *recovery*," Abbey corrected the screen. "Man, those really suck."

"Especially after all the body parts turn into strainers floating in the ocean," said Jeff Curl, the chief PJ.

"What's that?" asked Rob Carcieri, the newest PJ member on the Green team.

"That's when the flesh and guts strain out through our litters," Jason said.

No one laughed. It wasn't meant to be funny. It came with the job. It was grizzly and repugnant work, but someone had to do it.

Working a mass casualty was the worst. Jason knew downed jets; he'd worked Swiss Air 800 and several jet fighter crashes. Guts and body parts—he'd done the toe-tag body drag many times. He knew the smell and feel of the dead. Wrap them, stack them, and then put them in order. The toughest pain was seeing the family and friends who came to claim and grieve over their loved ones. The screams of loss, anger, and denial always split Jason's heart in two.

Touch it, feel it, live it, go home, and then try sleeping through the nightmares that followed. Confide the fear and fright only to a friend who understood, like Mac Rio.

Jason would give Toby a week or so before he called. Toby used Jason to talk things out the same way Jason used Mac. Over three hundred people had gone down in the explosion. There would be a lot to talk out.

# CHAPTER 6

**0420 TUESDAY / 28 SEPTEMBER 1999**
**SATELLITE BEACH / FLORIDA**

"RUN OR DIE!"
*Black, black all around. Run, fool. Run away from the light! Go into the dark. It's behind you and it's gaining. RUN! Run like you've never run in your life!! If it gets you, you're dead, gone.*

*Tripping and falling. Get up! Get up. It's on you!*

*Time to die.*

"I KNOW YOU'RE AWAKE, SO DON'T MOVE."

Jason felt the unmistakable feel of the muzzle of a gun at his temple. His mouth went dry and he couldn't swallow. Shadows glided about his bedroom. "What's going on?" *I'm dreaming.* Turning his head toward the pistol that was in his drawer, his face was forcefully pushed back by the muzzle of the gun. A pillowcase had been pulled over his head.

"Shut up. Next time you move, you're dead."

Jason froze. He wasn't dreaming. He was awake, and this was real.

"Just answer yes or no, quietly. Was the Brotherhood of Death involved in an attempted hijacking of an SST?"

"What's an SST? Who's the Brotherhood of Death?"

"Don't fuck with me, asshole, or I'll put a bullet in your head. You won't hear it, but you sure as fuck will feel it."

The sound of the trigger being cocked echoed off the walls.

"I don't know."

"Does the Brotherhood have anything to do with the downing of Titan 20B?"

"I don't know."

"Does the Brotherhood have anything to do with the downing of TAC-1?"

"What?"

A nudge with the pistol. "Just yes or no."

"I don't know."

"Does the Brotherhood have anything to do with the downing of English Air nine forty-three?"

*"I don't know!"*

"Quiet, asshole. Does the Brotherhood have anything to do with the crash of the Canadian Labrador over the English Air recovery area?"

"What crash?"

The pistol pushed again, but Jason pushed back. "What is this, a deposition by gun? What Labrador crash?"

Trying to sit up, he was pounced on by several people. He struggled, but the more he moved, the tighter they held, so he quit moving. "Look, I ain't working for the Brothers! I haven't worked for them in years. I have no idea what they have working, but it's sure not conducting international terrorism. Who are you guys?"

The hood was pulled back, and he saw a face. It was the face of the man in the hangar with Boris.

"I think I actually believe you. You're just a fucking flunky, alligator man. So if they ask, I want you to pass a message on to the Brotherhood for me. Tell them to stay out of this. We're handling it on our own. Be grateful I'm not leaving you with lead in your head, gator man."

Then they backed out of the bedroom and were gone. Jason turned on the lamp and ripped open the drawer of his nightstand. His nine-millimeter Ruger P95DC was still there, but the clip had been removed and ten bullets were neatly arranged in a row next to the clip.

*Oh shit!* Jason started to tremble, and then realized that he was still drunk, or something. His head spun, but it didn't feel like alcohol. Looking at his clock, he saw that it was four in the morning.

The phone rang and he about jumped out of his skin. "Hello?"

"Jason. This is Jeff Curl. Have you heard?"

"Heard what?"

"The Four-thirteenth Rescue Squadron out of Greenwood, Canada, lost a Labrador chopper. Jason? Jason, are you there?"

"Oh God." Jeff didn't have to tell him. He already knew. Toby was on the chopper.

"There's an American flight from Orlando to Halifax leaving in three hours. If you want I'll book you on it. I can reserve a room for you at the Prince George Hotel. I'll turn in your leave slip for you, too."

"Yeah. Thanks, Jeff." Jason hung up the phone and covered his face with his hands. Taking deep breaths in an attempt to slow his booming heart, he tried to put together what was happening.

*One question at a time.* What malevolent powers had conspired to land him right back in the middle of another hellish existence?

"When did it start?" he asked aloud. Jason sat up in bed and picked up his watch. He suddenly realized that he'd somehow lost forty hours. He slid back down onto the mattress and discovered that his sheets were sopping wet with his sweat. What happened forty hours ago? *My birthday! Yeah, that's right.*

He was sitting by himself at the Cove nightclub in Satellite Beach. It was his fortieth birthday. Mac couldn't celebrate with him because he was out flying on a local night mission. Then some Asian girl came on to him. She looked hot, really hot. She said that her name was Lisa and asked why he had no date.

When he told her why he was alone she said that she knew Mac and that he'd told her to be Jason's date. He'd invited her to sit with him, but aside from having had a few drinks he couldn't remember anything—except waking up with a gun pointed at his head. He couldn't even remember how he got home.

Picking up the remote control, he turned on the TV to CNN. The newscaster announced, "A Canadian Labrador helicopter has been lost over Sable Point, Nova Scotia. Details of the crash are not being released, and names of the crew members are being withheld pending notification of next of kin."

Staggering out of bed into the kitchen, Jason opened the refrigerator and poured himself a glass of cold water, then vainly tried to shake off the effects of whatever that bitch had slipped him.

The apartment was turned upside down. The safe in his closet was open. What were they looking for?

Uprighting a kitchen chair, he sat on it and tried to figure out what was happening. *A rocket blows up and little is reported.* "But *I* get into trouble." Something happened to TAC-1 but nothing's reported. A 747 jet blows up, killing over 350 people. "Now Toby's dead," he voiced aloud, a cold, hollow feeling gripping him as he said the words. A woman dopes him, and then thugs wake him with a gun to his head. "What the fuck is happening?"

There was just one way to find out. There was only one man he knew who could possibly uncover some of the answers. But calling his number had its own consequences. Favors asked meant favors had to be returned. Still, there was no one else he could turn to; he was in deep shit. Killer shit. And nobody dealt with killer shit like this guy. Picking up the phone, Jason dialed the number.

Four rings. *"Leave a message."*

"This is Alice. There's some really weird shit going on here and I need help, now!" Jason hung up the phone and stared at it for a long time. "Man, did I fuck up," he gasped. He should have never shown the coin to Boris, or given the creep any reason to suspect that he was connected to anything. He should have just let it all go. How many times had his attitude and screwups put him right in the middle of situations he wanted no part of?

He jumped when the phone rang. "Hello?"

It was Mac. He had just heard about Toby's death. Toby knew a lot of people.

"Mac, I'm going absolutely FUCKING CRAZY! We gotta talk, but not on the phone. Can you come over? Uhm, like NOW!"

"I'll be right there."

Jason ran outside the moment Mac pulled up in his new cherry red Mustang. Opening the passenger door, he tossed his rucksack in the backseat, then dived in the passenger seat and closed the door. "Drive! Fast!"

The streets were empty, and they burned rubber in the morning sun. Jason's head turned like it was on a swivel as Mac raced over the Pineda Causeway.

"Get on Highway ninety-five and go to the Beeline."

"Mind telling me what is going on?" Mac asked. "We're acting a *little* too paranoid this morning."

Once they were on the Beeline Expressway and Jason had assured himself that they weren't being followed, he relaxed. He sat back, closed his eyes, and ran his fingers through his wet hair. "Try *a lot* paranoid—and most of it real, I think."

"Tell me about it."

"No. Not now. I don't want you involved. You know how things can get for me."

"No shit, pal," Mac said with a laugh.

"It happened again tonight," Jason said. "*Another* goddamn dream!"

Mac was startled. "The same one?"

"No. This one's different. But it felt real. And then I got woken with a gun to my head. It really shook me up. You know what I'm saying."

"Oh no! Not again." Mac remembered his family's

Indian practices, in which, through extreme physical and mental rituals, they'd push the body and mind into a mystic trance. Mac would never do it. "Man, you're cursed."

Mac sighed. He knew Jason's dilemma only too well. Jason had been plagued earlier in his life by another recurring nightmare. It had almost destroyed his mind—but it had turned out to be a premonition, one that dropped him right into the lap of danger. He was physically and emotionally damaged, and lost, after the event.

Mac, was part Yaqui Indian who held religious family beliefs, and understood the journey Jason had endured on a mission named Operation Furtive Grab and he had helped his friend to recover his sanity. The ring Jason wore was a talisman he'd gained from the experience. It took many months for Jason to understand and accept the pain that he suffered, leaving him with what Mac called a Sacred Scar, something only a chosen few received.

Jason looked at his ring. "Can you take me to a good witch doctor?"

"Not around here."

"Then mind driving me to the Orlando airport? American Airlines."

"Sure, but running out of town, trying to get away from a nightmare is crazy!"

"No, no. I'm trying to avoid the bad guys that invaded my dreams." Jason grinned, then dropped his head and rubbed his forehead. "I'm on the first plane out to Halifax to do what I can for Toby's family."

"Yeah, I'm hip. How'd it happen?"

"No idea." Jason wanted to change the subject. "Hey, tell me about this girl you set me up with at the Cove."

Mac looked confused. "What girl?"

"A hot Asian chick, just the way you like 'em."

"A real slut, huh? Hey, I didn't set you up with no chick. I can, but you never let me. Jason, I *never* set you up with any broad. What's her name?"

"Lisa."

"Describe her."

Jason did, then told his friend how she'd drugged him.

"Yeah, I'm pretty sure I know her—I know a lot of sluts. As you're all too aware, they're my passion, but they're *nice* sluts, see. Not Lisa. Not this one. She's a bad girl. Been married and divorced six times that I know of. I know where she lives. I'll tell you what: While you're gone I'll go and see her and find out what really happened." A lusty laugh escaped him. "It kinda gives me an inspiration to find out how bad she really can be."

Mac pulled up to the empty American Airlines departure curb at the Orlando International Airport terminal.

"Thanks for coming to my rescue again, pal. Don't wait for me." He pulled out his pistol from the small of his back and handed it to Mac. "Here. They won't let me take this into Canada."

Mac was about to speak, but Jason cut him off. "I know: 'Don't do anything stupid.'"

## 1030
## HALIFAX INTERNATIONAL AIRPORT / NOVA SCOTIA CANADA

Jason had the cab drive him directly to Toby's house in Dartmouth. Several cars were parked in front of the white two-story home. The door was open, so he walked in and dropped his ruck inside the doorway. The house was full of people he hardly knew, and he went directly to Vivian, Toby's widow, who sat in a chair wearing sunglasses. Surrounding her were her three sons: Toby Junior, twenty-one; Easton, eighteen; and Seth, fifteen. They looked like clones of their father.

Toby's five dogs, mostly retrievers, sniffed at Jason and then tried to get reassuring pats from him as they continually trotted back and forth to the front door, nervously waiting for the master who would never return.

Slowly kneeling, he waited until Vivian looked at him. "What can I do for you?"

"Oh, Jason," she whimpered, "please make them all go away."

"Are you sure?"

She nodded.

Looking at her sons, he asked, "Is that okay with you guys?"

"We'll help you," Easton said.

Toby lived in a big house. Going from room to room, Jason graciously but firmly directed everyone to leave. The dogs took the hint and started growling at everyone. There were a lot of people to eject. Jason wrote a Please Do Not Disturb sign and then posted it on the door.

Vivian hadn't moved from the black chair. Jason recognized the recliner as Toby's favorite. She softly stroked the chair's arms, as if for comfort. "Okay, they're gone. What else can I do?"

She had cried herself tearless. "Make the pain go away...."

Jason kneeled down to her. "Has a doctor taken a look at you?"

"One came but I sent him away. I didn't know him."

"Can I examine you?"

Wordlessly, she nodded.

He went and got his bag. Pulling out his medruck, he began a thorough examination of her.

A pararescueman, like all lifesavers, learns early how to recognize trauma and shock, both physical and mental. In many cases the physical trauma is pretty much self-evident. But there are many different types and severity of shock that affect the body—hemorrhagic, metabolic, anaphylactic, cardiogenic, and so on. While Jason knew better than to make the kind of professional diagnosis that only a doctor could, he knew what Vivian was going through, and his heart went out to her.

Psychogenic shock—which has other names, such as shell shock and the thousand-yard stare—affects the mind. No one symptom can characterize it: lethargy; slow, fast, or weak heartbeat. Combined with physical trauma, it can be the fatal blow. The trauma Vivian was going through was mental.

Gathering her boys, Jason explained the situation. "I think the best thing to do is to sedate your mother in order to let her mind and body get back in sync. I'll help you take care of all the memorial details for your father. It'll be military. Your mom wakes up, goes through the memorial, and boom, move on to the next step."

"It sounds bloodless, Jason," Toby Junior said.

"True, but I think it's the best plan we have at the moment," injected Easton.

"We want to help," Seth added.

"Let me take care of your mother first." Life and death were part of a PJ's job, but this was the first time Jason had planned a memorial. *Stay neutral. Keep the objectives in mind.* His friend was dead and it was his duty and honor to help the family.

Fixing up a sedative in a syringe, Jason was suddenly struck: *Weren't you just recently on the receiving end of one of these?* He helped her to bed, then injected her.

Vivian went out, her vital signs stable.

After writing out the memorial details, he gave the boys their assignments. Boys? They were men now. Jason remembered how scared he'd been when he'd first struck out on his own. At least they had each other and their mother to help keep them strong—and the help of one PJ.

Jason made a few phone calls to Toby's unit, put on his PJ uniform, borrowed the family van, and then drove flat out to Greenwood Canadian Air Base. The uniform got him past the reporters and spectators. He drove to the 413th squadron, parked the car, and went directly to Darrell Cherry, chief of SARTech operations. They were old friends.

"Jason, it's good to see you, even if it's on such a sorry occasion," said Cherry, quickly ushering the PJ into his office. He then locked the door and drew the blinds closed. "Sorry for all the secrecy, but it's been very strange and sad around here."

"I'm here for Toby's family."

"I understand. And I'm glad that you're here. I knew you would come. Vivian and the boys need you."

"Has anyone been through Toby's gear?"

When a crew member goes down, a discreet inventory of his locker is always made by a close friend, in case it's necessary to purge anything that had nothing to do with the crash and that might prove embarrassing to the deceased, his crew, or his family members.

"Me. There was nothing. You know Toby—he was as clean as they came. No black books or anything questionable. Nothing. I'm glad I checked when I did, because these guys in black suits were right behind me and took away everything."

"American?"

"Yeah. The day after the jet went in, all these guys showed up in dark suits, mirrored sunglasses. Real spook stuff. Never totally identified themselves, just implied serious consequences if we didn't give in. Our unit commander told us that they have full authority. And on *our* base! Flamin' assholes with colored names: 'Mister White,' 'Mister Green,' 'Mister Black.' "

Jason got a jolt. "Mister Black? Does he look ... *odd*?"

"Oddest one of the bunch, I'd say, with his black trench coat and hat. I think he's in charge. It's been *strange*. They come in and run us as if we're their servants, having us fly them anywhere at any time. Then they put us under classified orders—no one says anything. I'm sure you're probably not supposed to even be here, and I shouldn't be talking to you."

Jason felt his hair rise. "Maybe I should go."

"Yeah, before one of them shows up and demands to know who you are."

"Darrell, I've never been here."

"I haven't seen you. Jason, do you know what's going on?"

"No, but I'm trying to find out. Where have they been taking the English Air remains?"

"Halifax International. What's left of the bodies are being kept in three refrigerated trailers just outside D hangar. The jet wreckage is being assembled in that hangar, too. You know, the Maple Air Ambulance has a pretty good view overlooking the trailers and hangar."

"Thanks, man."

"You just be careful, Jason, real careful. Don't do anything stupid."

"It seems like I've heard that before."

"Then you should listen to the advice."

## 2230 / TOBY'S HOME / DARTMOUTH / NOVA SCOTIA

The house was silent, so Jason let himself in with the house key. He checked on Vivian, who was sleeping soundly, her pulse strong. Everyone in the house was asleep, so he made his way to Toby's game room to sleep on the foldout couch.

Opening the closet to pull out a blanket, he saw the fishing gear that they used when he came up for Toby's annual fishing trip with the boys. An envelope was taped to his pole. *JASON* was written on the envelope. It was in Toby's handwriting. Sitting on the couch, he read the letter.

*Jason,*

*If you are reading this, then something's happened to me and I'm probably dead. So here I am talking to you from the "other side." Funny, huh? The reason I'm gone will probably be connected to what's been going on around here.*

*Hours after the crash every safety organization in the world started showing up, but then these "secret squirrels" showed up and took over the whole show. They act as if we aren't even here. They're looking for something from the plane wreckage. I know it's small because I hear them talk. I overheard one of the guys say, "It's smaller than he thinks. We're looking in the wrong direction." I don't know what that means, but I have a real bad feeling about all this. I think they're scared, or hiding something.*

*Jason, from the first day we met at the Maple Flag search and rescue exercise, you have <u>always</u> been my brother. I know that you'll help Vivian and the boys get through this. Hey, I'm too fucking young and good looking to die, but like you, I have been living on borrowed time.*

*Vivian knows how much I love her and what she means to me. I've taught the boys all I can and hope that they will become (with your help) fine young men. I'm not rich, but all my insurance, stocks, and benefits should set them up well.*

*I have to go. They are arming us for tonight's flight. Odd again, guns on a recovery mission? Damn, I don't know what's happening. Maybe you can find out for me.*

*I know you, friend, and don't do anything stupid. Take care of yourself and please keep an eye on my family for me.*

> *Your rescue brother,*
> *Toby*

Toby was his friend.

Jason froze. Toby's death was no accident. Nor were the other things that had happened. *Do I get involved?*

He realized that it was not a matter of *getting* involved; he *was* involved. It would be wrong to just walk away. He had to try and do something—but what? No doubt something stupid.

It appeared that Boris was looking for something from the crash. The jet wreckage and what was left of the bodies were being kept at Halifax Air Base. It was late, but the car and his uniform would get him access to it.

He looked at his bag and understood why he had packed a few "extras," for "just in case."

## 0245 WEDNESDAY / 29 OCTOBER 1999
## MAPLE LEAF AIR AMBULANCE SERVICE / HALIFAX INTERNATIONAL

The air ambulance alert crew slept soundly and the night duty officer was hypnotized by the television screen. From the roof of the building, Jason peered across the tarmac through his night vision goggles. No one had come or gone from the three white trailers in over an hour. All security faced away from the space that separated him from the trailers. He'd been watching for three hours. It was time to move.

*Wreckage or body trailers?* Pieces of the plane had come in almost nonstop; it was a twenty-four-hour operation. Nothing had come to the trailers the whole time he'd been watching. It was his guess that they must be gathering the human remains in something like a fish locker until they had enough to make a truckload. But no one was keeping a close eye on the trailers.

There was no choice. *Body trailers. Shit!* It had been a long time since he'd used the skills Froto taught him.

Minimum hindrance, minimum gear. Dressed in black coveralls, Jason carried only a miniflashlight, a Spyderco knife, and a multiplier tool.

From shadow to shadow, Jason edged along the tarmac until he was parallel to the trailers. Sneaking up the stairs, he discovered no locks on the doors and stepped inside—to a horror chamber.

There was the constant whine of an air conditioner. Overhead fluorescent white lights highlighted an eerie, surreal, grizzly scene. On a steel table about fifteen feet long and three feet wide, body parts lay exposed, or in packages. Just a short while ago the pieces had been whole, filled with vibrant life. An unknown force had ripped them to shreds, turning them into pulpy red meat.

Jason had seen the dead many times, but he wasn't immune to the creeps while looking for something out of the ordinary—though what could be out of the ordinary among all this gore?

The cold held down the smell of the dead, but not all of it.

The table was split into sections. An overhead camera was set up at the far end of the trailer, positioned to take pictures of every body part. Crude signs—Dental, Blood Typing, DNA Match, and Explosive Tracing— identified several steel trays filled with bones and flesh. A rack of plastic bags, tags, and a box of latex gloves hung on the far wall.

Slipping on a pair of latex gloves, he took a deep breath and picked up the tray closest to him.

## 0450

Jason snuck into the last trailer. Frazzled, he wondered how much more he could take. He prayed that the spirits he disturbed would understand that he was doing this for a reason. He had to act fast—the morning crew could arrive any minute. *Come on. What's out of place? What doesn't belong?*

Suddenly he noticed a complete right arm, clutching something. A dark suit sleeve covered the arm, and the hand was holding on to its sleeve cuff. *Odd.* He picked up the arm and examined it. It took effort, but he pried open the hand. A cuff link. The hand was gripping its own cuff link. Why? It was a silver cuff link monogrammed with an encircled black letter Z.

Suddenly he heard noises outside. Voices.

Someone was coming, and there was nowhere to hide. A mostly empty body bag lay in the corner. They were close, too close. Pocketing the cuff link, he dove toward the body bag.

The door opened.

"MI6 assures me that he was on the plane. Something left of him *has* to be here."

*Voice one.*

"Is Mister Brown here yet?"

*Voice Two. Oh shit! It's Boris!*

*Voice Two.* "Yes, sir. Just landed at Halifax. He should be at the gate any minute."

"Decker, he comes straight here and doesn't go anywhere until he's through."

"Yes sir."

*Voice Two. Two is named Decker. I know that voice. Decker's the asshole that put a gun to my head!*

"Where'd we stop? Anything new come in?" Boris asked.

"Just that body bag and two fifty-five-gallon drums," Decker responded.

"Let's start where we left off."

Jason wanted to throw up. Whatever was in the bag with him was putrid. He stayed still, trying not to think about what it might be.

"If it wasn't the Brotherhood who took out my chopper, then who was it?" Boris asked.

"The six CIC men on board meant more than that chopper, sir."

"Decker, in the past two weeks someone has taken out over three hundred people and countless millions in assets. Right now our spy satellites can barely see anything, anywhere. Who did it? *How* did they do it, Decker? How?"

"I don't know, sir."

"Neither do I, and it's my job to find out—who, how, and why. Decker, you're useful, but replaceable. I got a lot of people working this thing, but they only have pieces of the puzzle. Keep up with me or you're gone."

"I'm right with you, sir."

"And don't try and get ahead. Bring that body bag to me. *Someone* took my reflector, and I don't know of any world actor with the talent to do that. Any guesses?"

"The Chinese?"

"That's stupid. I have so many moles in their government they can't even scratch their collective asses without my knowing."

"Islamic terrorists?"

Boris chortled. "Don't be so lame! It's beneath discussion."

"The Russians?"

"A possibility, but why? How? They're peasants with nothing. Why would they nab the reflector? And what would they do with it? They don't have the sophistication to operate it. No. I think it's someone on our own side."

"Mister Black, that can't be. Our own side doesn't go around killing each other. Rough 'em up a little maybe, but no killing."

"You know where it's written that we can't?"

A long silence.

"Did you have a look at this arm? It looks like it held something. The sleeve. It's a good cut of material. Decker, I asked you a question."

"I've never seen it. This is the first time."

"Put it in our container for Brown and get that body bag over here."

Jason fought an overwhelming desire to cut open the bag and run for it. *These guys got guns,* a voice of reason cautioned. *What do you have?*

A hand grabbed the bag. Jason froze. If discovered, he knew, he would be breaking a whole host of laws, most of them international.

The door opened.

"Mister Black?" a voice asked.

"What?"

"Mister Yellow is at the gate with Mister Brown."

"And?"

"Mister Brown is not logged anywhere as having access to this base."

"So? *I* give him access," Boris said.

"No sir. You may be an important man where you come from and I might be just a low-level security guard, but I do a good job, sir, and you have only just so much authority here. You have to come to the main gate *personally* and do the paperwork, probably call the base commander. He's not happy with the idea that you're here. I'm sure he'll be less happy knowing that more of you are coming onto his base."

"Damn! Decker, come with me and help with Mister Brown's gear."

The body bag was dropped. The door closed, and Jason was out of the bag and through the side door in seconds. Inching between trailers, he got close enough to hear Boris talking to Mister Brown.

"He's here?! Where? Decker, did you hear that? Your goddamn fucking PJ is here in Halifax and registered at the Prince George Hotel. WHAT THE FUCK FOR? Brown, get your ass into those trailers and find what I'm looking for. The rest of you spread out and search for any trace of that fucker! Put some people on the hotel, now! I want him found. Now go!"

This was Jason's exit cue. He was gone in seconds, and had everyone by a mile. The Prince George Hotel was the last place he would go to; the first place was somewhere he could dump these putrid clothes and find a shower!

### 0900 THURSDAY / 30 SEPTEMBER 1999
### SAINT MARK'S CHAPEL / CANADIAN FORCES BASE
### GREENWOOD / NOVA SCOTIA

The memorial for Toby was held at the Greenwood chapel on a cold, drizzly morning. Hundreds of people filled the chapel and more spilled out onto the sidewalk. Carefully scanning the crowd, Jason did not see Boris or Decker, but the crowd was so huge it didn't mean that someone from the CIC wasn't there.

There wasn't a dry eye anywhere. Vivian was unreadable behind her dark sunglasses; Jason had sedated her just enough to keep her awake. The boys held the dogs, which sensed the somber mood of the crowd and lay quietly on the floor.

To Jason, it seemed death was everywhere he stepped. He'd showered for an hour after getting back to Toby's house, but still couldn't get rid of the smell that clung to him from the body bag.

The grief was as close as a stab through his heart. He felt useless sitting there, because there wasn't a thing he could do to erase the sorrow.

The priest began Toby's eulogy, and soon Jason wanted to run out of the place. A husband, father, lifesaver, and so on. Was there anything that his friend had not been, and done?

Whatever was left of Toby's body was scattered in pieces with the rest of the Labrador crew across the cold Atlantic Ocean. The living gathered to remember the life of an exceptional man. Slowly wringing his hands, Jason fought the overwhelming urge to get up and leave. *Toby, pal, I hate fucking funerals and memorials, even yours.*

Standing in the rain after the services, he barely remembered shaking anyone's hand or offering solace. It felt as if someone was watching him. He clenched and unclenched his hands.

## 1330
## TOBY'S KITCHEN / DARTMOUTH / NOVA SCOTIA

Vivian sat at the kitchen table, numb, but her eyes were focused. She ate some soup Jason had made. It was a good sign. She didn't need any more drugs.

"Thank you, Jason," she whispered. "I don't know what I would've done without you."

"Your boys did it all—you have good sons. I'll call you in a couple of weeks." He gave Vivian a hug and a kiss. There was nothing more to do. It was time to leave.

The boys sat in the living room. The dogs slept.

"Listen, guys, let me ask you a question: If it turned out that someone had a hand in your dad's death, what would you do? Think about it." Picking up his travel bag, he walked to the front door toward the waiting cab.

"Uncle Jason?"

"Yeah?" Jason turned around to find Easton facing him. The boy had called him "Uncle" as soon as he'd learned to talk.

"My dad told me that saving lives isn't all that you do. I know that you're a special operator. The best."

"Your father could tell *some* stories. . . ."

"He told me about it on the last night he, he . . . It was like he *wanted* me to know."

Jason cocked his head as he looked at the boy. "Okay."

"If someone really was responsible for my dad's death, and you could do something about it, then revenge, is that so bad, or too much to ask for?"

Jason searched the boy's eyes. "In some countries they have this thing called vendetta. It's a private thing where the family of the murdered gets revenge. It's vengeance. Is that what you mean, a vendetta? Are you sure you know what you're asking for?"

Easton nodded. "If you can do it, a vendetta is what the Wiler family wants. I think that's what my dad would have wanted, too."

Jason rubbed Easton's head and nodded. He climbed into the cab and did not look back as the vehicle drove away.

Toby had had the life that Jason hoped to have one day, but now it was gone. It was gone for Jason too. Until he had some answers, there would be no normal life for him.

Settling into the backseat of the cab, Jason tried to find the missing link between him and his dead friend. He came to a conclusion. "Well, Toby, if I can find what's behind your murder, and I can get to the top man, then I'll get your revenge," he vowed.

"What, sir?" the cabby asked.

"Nothing. I'm just talking to myself."

# CHAPTER 7

JASON WAITED FOR MAC AT THE AIRPORT DEPARTURE curb, but he didn't have to wait long before Mac pulled up in front of him in his red Mustang. Tossing his bag in the backseat, Jason climbed in.

"How'd it go?" Mac asked as they drove. He reached under his seat and handed Jason his pistol.

"Not good, but I know more. And the more I uncover, the more twisted it gets. I need some serious help in finding answers."

"Anything I can do?"

"This shit's pretty deep, buddy. I'd hate to see you get fucked up in it."

"It looks like I'm already in. Remember Lisa?"

"How could I forget—or remember?"

"I went and saw her. Of course, she thought I just wanted to boink her." Wistfully, Mac smiled. "So I played along. Anyway, I asked her what the deal was with her drugging you. She told me that someone put her up to it for a couple hundred dollars. The guy who did it told her that he knew you and it was just a joke to get back at you for something. I believe her. She may be a bad slut, but she

ain't no killer slut. She played you good, buddy—she
didn't know you knew me or that it was your birthday.
You told her that, and she used it against you like you were
some kinda rube. Some operator you are.

"She didn't know what was in your drink because
she picked them up off of the table from the guy who set
you up. She got you home in a taxi. You passed out with
her in bed and she left. You're lucky, I hear she usually
cleans out a john's place."

"So who put her up to it?"

"From the description, it sounds like the guy you ran
into during the Titan explosion."

Jason nodded, understanding more. "His name is
Decker. Works for a guy named Black, whom I call Boris.
They're with the CIC and connected somehow to all
this crap that's been happening—I don't know if they're
responsible for what's going on, or covering it up, or
both. Now I want to know. Hey, they could've asked me
for my help anytime. Instead they treat me like the opposition."

Raising his eyebrows, Mac asked. "So, *who's* the opposition?"

"Beats me, buddy, but I brought back a little something that might help."

"Me too. A couple of visitors showed up at my
house as I was leaving to pick you up. They came in real
secret-like. One doesn't even know the other is already
there. They're looking forward to talking to you.
Apparently my place is going to be your safe house for a
few days."

## 2230
## JAMES LANDING / MELBOURNE / FLORIDA

"Tom! Man, am I glad to see you," Jason said as he rushed
over to shake hands with, then hug, the man sitting in the
oddest wheelchair that he'd ever seen. They'd had some
telephone conversations, but he hadn't seen Tom in a few

years. He'd hardly changed. With Ken-doll looks–perfect blond hair and huge arms developed from years of pushing a wheelchair, he was a match for Jeff Bridges.

Jason had first met Tom Chain in 1995 when he was ordered to the Doors' secret headquarters. Though Tom was confined to a wheelchair, his brains drove the Brotherhood of Death. It was said that he had connections everywhere in the world. Jason liked the way Tom worked; he was cool, methodical, and logical. If there was anyone in the world who might be able to shed light on what was going on, it was Tom.

"Uhm, that's no ordinary wheelchair, is it?" Jason asked.

It looked like an old person's personal scooter on steroids.

"Like it?" Tom smiled. "It's not a wheelchair at all. Watch."

Tom flicked a joystick, and he and the chair suddenly stood.

Jason's jaw dropped and he stepped back as he watched Tom balance on two wheels.

Spinning around Jason, Tom grabbed the PJ's legs from under him so fast that Jason didn't have time to react. Before he could hit the ground he was cradled in Tom's arms, and then he was back on his feet in an instant.

"Damn," Jason gasped. "What the hell is that thing?"

Tom was still balanced on two wheels. "See, I can do jujitsu again." Pulling on the joystick, he elevated himself to over seven feet. "I can do seventy on the highway, faster with a few more adjustments."

"Can it fly?"

Tom furrowed his forehead. "Not quite yet."

"Like I said, what is it?"

"It's called an IBOT. The Doors got me this from DEKA research. There's nothing like it. I can climb stairs, outrun anything on two feet—and I have the balance of a gymnast. Of course, I had a few modifications made after I got it."

The IBOT was not so much a mobile chair as it was a command center. With Tom's added modifications, it was really a communications platform. Self-propelled by powerful batteries, it used gyroscopes and microprocessors to give it its incredible balance. At any moment, or at any time, Tom Chain could get just about anything, or reach any person in the world, from his IBOT. Press a button and plasma screens would flip up from the side panels and present any media he might want. It was also armored and could shoot back if attacked.

Jason slowly took a seat at the kitchen table and tried to regain his composure. Tom had been a formidable man in a wheelchair, with a mind second to none; now, with the IBOT, he was a superman.

No classified American secrets had ever been denied to Chain. His security clearance had its own classification: Top Secret—Directorate / For Waiver / Termination Group (DFWTG). Loosely translated, it meant, *Don't Fuck With This Guy.*

Tom rolled next to Jason and reclined the IBOT. "So what's this that you need my help? Mac's filled me in on the kind of women you pick up in bars."

For the first time in weeks, Jason breathed a sigh of relief. Help had arrived. He was with family.

It might have been argued that the Brotherhood of Death existed to kill, and kill they did, but that was no reason to think that they couldn't hold sentimentalities. A family love existed among the team's members.

"Somebody call for the services of the U.S. Marines?" asked a small man who had appeared in the kitchen doorway. "I see that Tom's still showing off his toy."

"Damn, Kelly!" Jason got up and embraced him. Now, with the pint-sized Marine here, Jason was energized, ready to take on the world.

The little guy was unstoppable, even one on one. The size of the fight in this dog was giant.

"Kelly," Tom said. "I didn't realize that you were responding to Jason's call, too. How'd you know to come here?"

Kelly just smiled and turned beet red. "I think we should hear what's up with Jason."

"It's like this," said Jason, then he went on to fill in Tom, Kelly, and Mac on all that had happened—as well as he could recall, anyway. The moment he finished speaking, he slumped onto the couch, exhausted.

"This Mister Black—describe him," Tom said.

"Slimy," "sleazy," "shady," and "sinister" were some of the adjectives he used to draw the man. "I call him Boris."

A slim keyboard slid across Tom's lap and a paper-thin, twenty-inch screen unrolled from the right side of the IBOT. Tom's fingers flew over his keyboard. A matrix of fifteen Department of Defense intelligence agencies appeared on the screen, including the CIA, NSA, Air Force Intelligence, the CIC, and others.

"Different command structures overlap and intersect to make up the overt and covert protection of America and her allies. Each guards its own territories." Tom pointed to the top of the screen. "The Central Imaging Command. They run our space reconnaissance and intelligence. We have a lot of different kinds of satellites in space, and a shitload that measure anything and everything, in almost any media. The most valuable are the spy satellites, and they belong to the CIC." Then, pointing toward the bottom of the screen at the Doors: "That's who we work for, of course. As the Brotherhood, we take care of the really touchy missions, but I think that we're about to cross paths with the CIC."

The screen dropped away.

"Of course, you know Mister Black is not his real name. From what you tell me, he could be operations control for the Central Imaging Command, or maybe the deputy director. I'll find out. He's probably very tough to have gotten where he is. And you tell me you got us involved with him?" he asked Jason.

"Not on purpose...well, not intentionally. I'm sorry, Tom. I screwed up."

"It doesn't matter now." Tom said. "I think you

might've stumbled across something well worth investigating, and I have a very bad feeling that this probably relates to a classified exercise Kelly 'n' me were recently on—Wizard Warrior."

Tom leaned close to Jason. "What I'm about to tell you is the closest-guarded secret we have today: Something's shut down our key satellite ground computers. They didn't go after the satellites—they did something to the computers that interpreted the data. Smart. Somehow the Wizard Warrior exercise got zapped. Right after that we lost the computers of the National Imagery and Mapping Agency that process our satellite reconnaissance and surveillance imagery; they're still badly degraded. Essentially, our spy satellites are out. No one outside the American intelligence community has been told that we lost our detailed overhead imagery capability. It would give all the bad guys a green light to do a lot of bad things."

Tom sucked air through his teeth. "I'm damned if I, or anyone else, has figured out what happened. It could be a computer virus, a jamming system, or even some kind of zapper. Believe me, everyone in the intelligence community is looking full-time for answers, including me. You know we lost a contract chopper crew on the exercise, and I want to know why.

"The CIC's been more tight-assed than usual with their information, and now I have to go on the assumption that they're probing us. But I don't know for what. I do know that the Titan launch was part of a deep black project of theirs, whose specifics are well hidden. Now I'm going to bring in our ferrets to find out what that operation is all about. I'm surprised that Black even mentioned anything to you at all. Even *I* don't know about the details of the program—but it's time we started digging."

"So how are you going to find out in what way the CIC is connected to these incidents?" Kelly asked.

"I'm going to start everything in motion by putting one of our big guns on it. Kelly, go outside and see if Jason was followed, and then check his car for bugs." He looked at Jason. "I'm not doubting one word of your story, but I need anything you can give me that I can go on. Some tangible evidence or something."

"Sure." He reached into his pocket, handed Tom the Z cuff link, and told him how he came into possession of it.

Tom's mouth fell open. "You really hid in a partially full body bag? Yuck!"

Jason nodded.

Taking out a jeweler's loupe from his folding armrest, Tom inspected the cuff link. "It looks like the letter Z, in Cyrillic, maybe."

"Or a design, perhaps," Jason added, then glanced at his ring. *Or a talisman.*

"That someone's last act before dying was to put a death grip on this while they got ripped apart tells me that it's something worth looking at. I'm going to have this analyzed to the nth degree. Whatever it means or contains, we'll find out." Tom looked up at Jason. "Right now you've seen too much, and that makes you a security liability to the CIC. If they're not above intimidating you in bed in the middle of the night with a gun, then they might be willing to go further, even though they're not sanctioned to kill. Going back to your apartment might be a mistake. I'd advise you to get a room on base at Patrick, and then to go back to work—and don't tell anyone what's happened. Like you, I'm starting from square one, but I do have a few assets at my disposal that I can use."

Tom handed the cuff link to Mac, who looked at it for a moment, then handed it back. "Nothing."

Kelly returned to the room. "Clean all around."

Tom handed Kelly the cuff link. "Kelly, I want you to hand-deliver this to the Doors, now. Have it looked at under my code authorization. I want something back ASAP."

"Now?"

"Any reason why not now?"

Kelly turned red.

"Uhm," Mac cleared his throat. "I'll tell her to wait for you, Kelly." He scratched his head and smiled at Tom. "See, Kelly just happened to be here. He comes to visit me every so often to 'meet' with some of the girls I know."

Jason laughed. When Kelly was seventeen, he was horribly scarred across his face in a suicide attempt. After that, no woman ever looked twice at him, but the disfigurement was recently corrected by a plastic surgeon. Kelly and Mac were introduced by Jason, then the two became fast friends, and Kelly quickly learned from his pal what it took to attract women. The little man said that he had a lot of lost ground to make up.

"It's all about the pussy," Mac explained.

Tom spun his IBOT. "I don't hear anything...."

## 1755 FRIDAY / 1 OCTOBER 1999
## JAMES LANDING / MELBOURNE / FLORIDA

The front door was open and all the lights were on—normal for Mac. It was just a front. With the Brotherhood of Death around, Jason knew, the house and property were probably filled with all sorts of security devices and alarms that had been set by Kelly and Tom. Wherever the Brotherhood went, they *always* covered their trail. Anyone coming within gunshot view of the house was probably recorded and ID'd before even stepping on the lawn.

As Jason cautiously stepped through the front door, a great aroma wafted to him from Mac's kitchen. Walking into the room, he saw a laptop computer sitting on the kitchen table, surrounded by stacks of paper and books.

A woman stood at the stove stirring a pot of delicious-smelling spaghetti sauce. She spoke without turning around. "I see Tom has you working his hours."

Jason wondered who she was.

"Hello, Jason. My name is Jean Fawcett. Tom will be back very shortly. I sent him to the store for a bottle of cheap wine that I like—it's the secret of my famous spaghetti sauce. Don't tell anyone else, though."

She put down the spoon and faced Jason. He felt as if he were standing in front of June Cleaver with glasses.

Jean calmly walked over to him and took his hand in both of hers. "Tom thinks the world of you, but don't let him control you. Please, sit down."

Jason was enchanted with her. "Are you Tom's girl-friend?"

Jean laughed. "Oh, we do have our moments."

"Moments of what?" Tom asked, rolling into the kitchen with a bottle of Verdi wine in his hand.

"I was sharing some dark secrets about you with Jason," answered Jean, taking the bottle of wine from Tom and going back to her pot of sauce.

"Don't listen to her," chided Tom. "Well, listen to her, but nothing about me."

Jason saw a casual relationship between two people who seemed very comfortable with each other. A thought creeped in. "Wait a minute. You're not the 'big gun' Tom was talking about, are you?"

"Is there any reason why I shouldn't be?" Jean looked at Tom, who nodded.

"Jean worked in government procurement for twenty-three years. A while back she was outsourced."

"Outsourced?" Jean tilted her head. "Tom's being nice. I was fired. I was ordered to send night vision sets to a huge Army unit deploying to Desert Storm. The problem was, they didn't have the double-A batteries that powered them. They weren't available anywhere in the supply system, so I cut a five-thousand-dollar check and bought them at a local store.

"I was fired for funds mismanagement." Jean smiled. "I've been known to do as the situation dictates, which pissed off the brass. So I was out for helping our boys. No benefits, no retirement."

"I've known Jean for a long time," Tom took over. "She's worked for enough four-star generals to fill a galaxy. There isn't a budget or government contract for which she can't find out the source of the money. There's not a government-procured item that she can't find out who the manufacture is, who bought it, and for how much.

"More important, she knows just about every general's secretary in the DOD. The day after she lost her job, she was working for the Doors." Tom rubbed his legs. "The Brothers of Death aren't discriminatory. Jean, tell him what you found."

Jean walked over to the table, sat down in front of her computer, and plugged a cable into one of Tom's portals. Inserting a DVD disk into her computer, she began. "First, let's look at several views of the explosion captured by the NASA cameras."

Tom's screen came alive with fantastic shots of Titan 20B's last moments.

"During the launch a special calculations program ran to plot the probable splashdown of the payload if the rocket exploded." Quickly sampling the disk, she continued her narrative. "Although everything appears to be normal at the Cape, the Titan anomaly is under special investigation, run by the CIC. General Daniel is furious that investigation control has been taken away from him and that a gag order has been put on him, but a promise of a second star has been made if he keeps his mouth shut.

"A helicopter did go down just after the rocket explosion, and no one at the Space Wing is talking about it, except for one secretary I know. She tells me that it wasn't the NASA chopper TAC-1 that went down—it was a CIC chopper and crew. That's all she knows about it.

"English Air and the Canadian Rescue Service are under a similar gag order not to discuss the crashes with anyone," she concluded. "No word back on Black yet. Decker either. Give me another day."

"Why was the CIC in Halifax?" Tom pondered. "You've raised some almost unbelievable questions, Jason. The silver cuff link was just that—no hidden devices, nothing. The letter Z raised plenty of red flags with the ESCHELON and the CIA Seven Dwarf supercomputers, but they're not giving out any details to us. That's really pissing me off. It's too bad you couldn't bring back the arm." Tom grinned. "I've gotten word that some very powerful individuals want us to back off of the CIC and their investigation. Fortunately, *our* top dogs tell me to press on.

"Something big is going on, and I want to know what. I've got people shadowing the CIC's people, who're shadowing ours. Our assets are out digging up leads, bomb experts, legal, Internet, satellite telemetry, but nothing's breaking. You should see the combat going on up at NIMA.

"Without the regular flow of high-grade surveillance photos and video, every secret agency has to wait in line for degraded pictures. Try telling the CIA that they have to wait in line for grainy pictures of the latest Chinese weapons program. The only good side of this is that we still have manned reconnaissance, DSP satellites, and other systems to back up our spy satellites. Even civilian satellites. I've been looking at getting the Doors an alternative overhead source, but it's not easy, or cheap.

"Right now there's a lot of stress in the American intelligence community, a *lot* of stress, and everybody's suspect." Pointing at Jason, Tom said, "I think that hanging your ass out there for the CIC to take more shots at is a real bad idea. Face it—your life might be in danger. You got to disappear for a while." Tom tapped his lips. "Jason, when was the last time you had a by name request?"

"To go back to the Doors? You're crazy! I don't want to do that. Shit, I told you a million times that I'm not a spook."

For years Jason had resisted Tom's efforts to recruit him full-time into the Brotherhood of Death. While thousands would have jumped at the chance to be a part of the spook world, Jason's mission was to rescue. He had seen more than his share of death and had had enough of killing. Besides that, the price he'd paid for going to the Doors the last time had almost cost him his life, and had about ruined his career as a pararescueman.

Jason tried to walk out of the kitchen, but Tom

quickly cut him off. "Spook or not, you could stay here. I could leave, and you could deal with Boris on your own. Are there many more options I'm missing here? Remember, *you* called *us*."

Tom was right. He'd called on the Doors for answers, but had forgotten that getting answers might also mean doing something about what he found out. He'd opened a *big* can of worms. Even though he remained friends with several of the Brothers, he'd made it a point to never ask about what went on in their world. Besides, they hadn't called on him since the first mission. Suddenly a horrible thought struck him.

"Is that asshole Kyle Kneen still running the Doors?" If he was, Jason *really* didn't want to go back. Thoughts of the inconsiderate, self-important asshole officer who'd almost killed him by "following procedures" made Jason shudder.

"Oh no. He didn't last a year. We got rid of him, kicked him upstairs, a two-star job with the NSA, thank God. You know Kneen—he can bob and weave, a total politician. I'm surprised that no one told you about his departure." Tom held out his hand. "By name request. I promise you, you'll get much better treatment this time, at least from me. Come on, Jason, you started this thing—don't you want to see where it will go?"

"Go? I know where it will go. Go to more meetings than I can stand. Go and get up at all hours to train, lose sleep, and live like a vampire. Sure, I'm ready to go."

There really was no choice. If he wanted all the answers, he had to go to the Doors to find them out. "You weren't so bad the last time," Jason said as he shook hands with Tom. "But tell me, why do I feel like I'm shaking hands with the devil?"

Tom gave Jason a wicked grin. "Who says you're not?"

# CHAPTER 8

THE BY NAME REQUEST FOR JASON CAME TO THE 920th Rescue Group bright and early, just as they opened for business. It was delivered by a courier, who then passed it from hand to hand, and by the time Jason signed for the orders, he knew that he'd made another mistake. His own command was totally pissed off at having to give up operational control of a valuable PJ to an unnamed secret agency. Normally there were specific rules, regulations, and limitations on how long one agency could have control over another agency's asset. Not this time—the Doors' classified order stated that they would release Jason when they were done with him, and not a minute sooner.

There were costs for stepping out of the system.

It was a strange experience. It felt like he was being frozen out for jumping from rescue to special operations. He wondered if it was envy, jealousy, or both. A lot of people he had known for years all of a sudden turned their backs on him. With the exception of his PJ brothers and Mac, most people in the group treated him like a traitor. But knowing better than to make a scene, he just signed the orders, grabbed his medruck, and left. Jason wondered if his team leader position would still be there for him upon his return.

HE WAS ALREADY BILLETED AT PATRICK FOR THE DOORS assignment. A black jet would come and carry him away in a couple of days. Then he would be gone until the mission was completed, or he was dead, or both.

Relieved of duty, and with plenty of time on his hands, Jason worked out endlessly at the base gym.

*Pull up. Hold. Release. Pull up. Hold. Release.* Jason didn't count his pull-ups. Too many things were on his mind, vague questions with no solid answers. Pull-ups were his way of doing something about a situation he had no control over. *I know that the Brothers don't have anything to do with what's going on, so what does the CIC have to do with all of this? There's more than Tom says about letting me in on this.* There was a connection somewhere. Someone had killed a lot of people to keep from being discovered. All he really knew was that his friend Toby was dead and that he'd promised the family revenge. *But how? Why? There's a key somewhere. Find it.*

"Fifty-two, fifty-three," a woman's voice counted.

"What?" Jason opened his eyes. "Oh, hi, Rita."

Captain Rita Meine, twenty-eight, stood looking at him. She was six-foot-three, with short red hair and blue eyes. She was something to look at, especially in her pink spandex. She was good-looking, all right, but she wasn't his type. An officer.

Dropping to the floor, she tossed him a towel.

"I got a lot of shit on my mind. I just can't seem to make things connect."

"Yeah, tell me," Rita responded. "I know what you mean. I got the same thing at work. I tried to get my boss to look at some data I had, but he laughed, and then he tried to make a pass at me. I told him to cut the crap, and now he's pissed."

"Want me to kick his ass, Rita? Right now I would enjoy giving someone a good ass-whipping, especially an officer."

"No," Rita said, chuckling. "But it does bother me that he won't look at my work."

"You know *I* don't know anything about your work. It's *way* out there."

Rita worked at the Air Force Technical Applications Center (AFTAC) as a nuclear analyst. She'd tried explaining what she did to him once, but lost him after the first sentence. She worked with seismic measurements of some sort. The best Jason could figure out was that she worked with satellites that scanned the earth for explosions.

He liked her company at the gym because she was always fun to chat with. He listened with amusement to her story.

"I tried again today to get him to look at my data, and this time he threatened me with a letter of counseling. He said that my data was minor and came from the wrong direction. That I was stupid, looking the wrong way."

Jason froze. "What? Say that again. What was the wrong way?"

"Chirps. Electromagnetic chirps. That's what I call them, anyway."

"Tell me about these chirps. How do you know about them?"

"Well, I told you about my job before. I interpret satellite imagery for anything that gives off an electromagnetic force—lightning, volcanoes, nuclear explosions, junk like that. All this comes from Earth, in the air and space, underground and underwater, so we use satellites that measure the signals—acoustic, radiochemical, seismic, and electromagnetic."

"Right. Keep it simple, *Captain*. Ah don't know nuthin' 'bout satellites."

"Asshole." She grinned. "All explosions give off heat and light. One of my jobs is to monitor our DSP satellites and measure the electromagnetic spectrum when things go boom."

Jason frowned.

"Look, I'm *trying* to keep it simple."

"Sorry."

"Electromagnetic pulse, EMP, is traceable through backscatter signals. A volcano has its own signal; so does TNT, or a nuclear explosion. It's one method by which we can identify what made the explosion. You follow?"

"I think so."

"Okay, EMP backscatter chirps. A couple of weeks ago I was taking my turn at the tube. It can be *really* boring. All I have to do is listen for a bell and then read and record the data. Good explosions never happen on my shift. The only thing happening was the Titan launch, remember?"

Jason nodded. How could he forget?

"About forty seconds into the liftoff I get a bell, but a short one. I read the data. The explosion signals read right, but some of the backscatter was coming from *that* way." Rita pointed up. "I tried telling Colonel Mark that, but he said it came from the Titan itself. He's such an asshole. It didn't happen the way he said. Jason, I recorded the exact time it occurred on our atomic clock, and the self-destruct sequence began a moment *after* the chirp."

Jason looked around. "You know that what you're talking about is undoubtedly classified."

Rita shrugged her shoulders. "I know, Jason, but who else can I talk to?"

"I know someone, but let me throw this at you: There was a chirp a couple of hours after the explosion and you lost some of your imagery capability."

She nodded. "The chirp? Yes, but we don't use the same system as...." Her eyes flew open. "Jason, that's a *big* secret."

"And you got one the night English Air went down."

"Are you psychic or something?"

"No, better than that, and I bet that there's been

other chirps from the wrong direction too." Jason felt fire and ice in his heart. There probably was a chirp the night Toby went down. "Rita, I'm going to have a friend of mine come see you today. He'll be in a cool-looking wheelchair."

"Jason, a guy in a wheelchair can't just go rolling into AFTAC."

"This one can. He's one of the good guys. Also, tell him about your beef with your asshole colonel. He can make some changes." He stood, said good-bye, then ran out of the gym toward the Intelligence Shop and a secure phone. At last, he had found something that might shed a little light on what was happening.

## 0600 THURSDAY / 7 OCTOBER 1999
## A1A HIGHWAY / PATRICK AIR FORCE BASE / FLORIDA

Jason sat on a sand dune watching the sunrise over the Atlantic Ocean. There were just enough clouds to make it a gorgeous sunup for the start of a perfect day on the Space Coast. The wind was offshore and the waves were three to five feet high, with flawless form.

"I'd rather be surfing," he mumbled to himself. He'd rather have taken his chances on the unseen sharks in the water than on land sharks like Boris.

A small black jet had its wheels down for landing. "Shit," Jason muttered.

He got in the passenger side of Mac's car and they pulled out of the parking lot and drove to the front of Base Operations, making small talk until the jet touched down on the main runway.

Jason chewed on his thumbnail.

Mac looked at Jason. "Are you sure you know what you're getting into? I mean it's not like you're mission essential—or are you? What's your part in this? These guys are killers. Do they want you to grease people for them again?"

Jason sat in silence. Killing for the Doors was not an

issue, not yet. He wasn't about to let his friend in on his own plan to go after Toby's killer. Plan? It was more like just a harebrained idea, and looking more and more ridiculous the closer the jet came.

"Okay?" Mac asked, knowing that Jason wanted to say something. He waited for an answer.

Reaching into his pocket, Jason handed something to Mac.

Mac looked at the white envelope. "All right, a blank envelope, and taped closed, too. Thanks! It's something I've always wanted. Gee, I got you something too." Pulling his comb from his pocket, he grinned. "It's a little used, but you have to consider that it's already broken in." He saw that Jason wasn't smiling, and pointed to the envelope. "What's in this?"

"I, uhm, want you to... You know those Indian vibes you get?"

"Yeah? Tell me about my 'vibes.' "

"While I'm gone, if you get one of those vibes that tells you something's wrong with me, then open it."

"Come on, man, is this your will or something?" Mac was incredulous.

"I have this bad feeling that I'm not coming back."

"Bad dreams again?"

"That, and other things. It feels as if everyone in the rescue community has turned their backs on me." He wanted to tell Mac to point the car in the opposite direction and to take him as far away as he could get from the black jet that was turning off the runway.

"Jason?"

"What?"

"Look at me." Mac smiled at Jason for a moment, then smacked him in the mouth.

Grabbing his mouth, Jason cried, "Fuck, man, why did you do that?"

"Hurt, huh?"

"Enough to kick your ass!"

"Tell you what. You can kick my ass when you come back." Mac put his hand around Jason's neck. "Man, you have more heart and determination than any ten guys I know. You can't count how many people are alive today because of you. You've spent your life helping everyone else. But who helps you?

"There's this thing you can't see, but it's there, pal, and I think it's what's missing in your life—hope. Better than anyone else, I know things with you are fucked up. But you gotta have hope. If you give up hope, pal, then you *ain't* coming back.

"You, Mister PJ, are about to get on that jet, and if you don't come back it will be because you gave up hope of finding what you're really after." Mac released his hold on Jason and then studied him for a moment. "You know, my grandfather used to say that the gods can drive a man crazy with their love."

The black jet taxied to a stop in front of Base Operations, and the crew door opened.

*Hope.* Jason rubbed his lips. They didn't hurt that badly. Mac hadn't hit him that hard, just woken him up a little. "Right now the only hope I have is to get back. If I do, I'll tell you all about it—*after* I kick your ass."

Mac got out of the car and helped Jason with his bags and medruck. They shook hands, then hugged as only brothers can.

"You better come back, asshole," Mac said through tight lips. "Besides, who's gonna tell your story if you don't?"

Jason walked up to the crew door and then turned around to wave at his friend, but he was gone. *Mac must be taking disappearing lessons from Kelly,* he mused.

Climbing aboard the jet, Jason couldn't tell exactly what kind of plane he was on, but it was *nice*. The young airman didn't even check his papers, just smiled at him with an almost starstruck look and motioned him to an overstuffed leather chair. "My name is Airman Michelle Thomas."

Buckling his seat belt, he reclined in his chair as the young lady closed the door and they taxied back onto the runway. As the engines wound to a roar, Jason sat up straight, suddenly remembering that he almost died the last time he worked for the Doors. *Oh fuck me, is it too late to get off this ride?*

Once they were airborne he relaxed, and then the airman came up to him with a trayful of peeled shrimp and a cart selection of beverages. Handing Jason a menu, she said, "The flight will be less than two hours. There is every convenience here. It's my job to see to your needs. Mister Chain welcomes you."

Jason laughed loudly. "I see that Tom's budget isn't hurting any." Looking out the window, he decided that Patrick Air Force base looked like a better place to be than to leave. As he thought about his destination and the people there, a queasy feeling tugged at his stomach.

He knew the drill all too well. He had done it before. It was called going behind the Door. It was time to start covering his ass by playing it cool, keeping his eyes open and his mouth shut.

Unconsciously patting the medruck next to him, he suddenly remembered that he had left his PJ beret in his locker. Now the medruck was the only reminder that he was a lifesaver and not a killer. He promised himself that no matter how deep the shit got, he would always remain a pararescueman in his heart.

There was never telling why the Doors did anything. It wasn't like he was mission essential, but here he was being treated like a principal player. Well, if that was how they wanted to play it, he'd dance to their tune, as long as he could play his own tunes as well.

**0800**
**DOOR HEADQUARTERS / CLASSIFIED LOCATION**
**FLORIDA**

The plane landed and taxied to a stop, then shut down its engines. Airman Thomas opened the crew door.

"Mister Johnson!"

"Hey, Bob, you look as ancient as ever. How are

you?" Jason was glad to see Bob Gitthens, his driver from the first tour. For security purposes it was less complicated to assign drivers to Door visitors than to have them wander around the base unescorted. Gitthens had acted like a bastard at first, but turned out to be a nice guy, for a retired Office of Strategic Services (OSS) agent.

"I'm fine, Mister Johnson. When I heard that you were coming back I insisted that I be your driver. They were just going to give you a car to drive. 'Oh no,' I told them, I was your driver the first time you was here, and I'll do it again."

Jason laughed. "Bob, you do know how to flatter me."

"No flattery at all, no sir. There aren't too many people around here who don't know that Alice is back. Shoot—I'm the one that told 'em!"

*Alice.* It was a stupid code name that Kelly had pinned him with, and much to Jason's chagrin, it had stuck. "Okay, Bob, just knock off all that 'mister' and 'sir' crap with me—you're a bud."

"You bet, Mister Jason! Oh, Mister Chain wants me to tell you that you've already been cleared onto the base. Also that there's an important meeting at the War Room at eleven that I'm to drive you to. I already got you checked into the VIP quarters. Here's your key. Is there anyplace you need to go before I take you there?"

"No." *Damn, I barely step foot on this base and the meetings start.* Jason climbed into the spacious Dodge van. This rig was *plush*. With its television, fully stocked bar, DVD player, computer, and radios, the van was exceptional.

To the casual visitor, it was a neat and very clean base. Nothing really stood out. But if you looked closer, in certain areas you could see rotating surveillance cameras mounted on light poles, recording the comings and goings of everything and everyone. Even though the base looked perfectly manicured at all times, there always seemed to be teams of gardeners and grass cutters working around the perimeter.

Very few people walked. A lot of passenger vans and buses came and went. It also seemed like a big portion of the cars on base were compact Fords.

If a casual visitor got lost in the area, military police kindly directed him or her out. If the visitor got past the nice military cops, double chain-link fences topped with razor wire and warning signs told the visitor he or she was in the wrong place. Get past that and a shoot-first, ask-questions-later policy existed.

The grass cutters had a seven-two response time—seven men in two minutes. Armed with more than just mowers, the special guards were on duty twenty-four hours a day.

Show the false. Hide the real. It was a tenet of everything about the base.

Plain unmarked buildings dotted the base. Jason knew that behind the walls, secret plans and operations took place that no one would ever read about in a newspaper or see on television. He wondered how much of a stir his information had caused. In which unmarked building was his information being discussed, and by whom?

Gitthens drove past the cameras and stopped in front of a small but elegant two-story house next to a river. They were quarters for a flag officer. Entering the house, Jason was stunned by the accommodations. "Opulent" would have been an approximate description, but "overdone" would have been more accurate.

The furnishings were not the standard tacky prison-made crap that went into most government quarters; an interior designer seemed to have had a go at the house. Leather living room sofas, plush green velvet curtains, hand-tied rugs—and was that a real antique Civil War saber hanging on the wall?

He felt a twinge of resentment that the big brass could live so well while enlisted scum like him usually got the scraps and qualified for food stamps. "Rank hath its privileges," he muttered. Of course, some general had made up that line. Another line came to mind: "Live well, for tomorrow you may die." Jason dropped his bags and began exploring the house.

A loud knocking on the front door brought him downstairs.

Jason blinked, put his tongue in his cheek, and slowly came to the most rigid and formal attention he could muster. He then snapped a crisp, sharp, textbook-perfect salute. "Master Sergeant Jason Johnson, reporting for duty, sir!"

Marine Brigadier General Ben Cadallo filled the doorway. The only change Jason could see in him was that he'd been a colonel back then and didn't have gray hair at his temples. He was a black god, with sculpted muscles packaged perfectly in a tailored and creased Marine uniform. Power emanated from the general like a force field. He was frightening. Nothing escaped his eyes.

Ah, there was something else different: silver-framed glasses. *Well, we can't stay gods forever.*

Cadallo eyed Jason, and then slowly paced around him as he inspected his uniform and military bearing. Standing back in front of him, he put his hands on his hips and leaned forward. "It's good to see you, Alice."

Jason smiled, but inwardly cringed. *Alice* again.

Cadallo gave Jason a bone-crushing handshake. "Right now there's secret emergency meetings happening here and at the Pentagon. Tom's tight-lipped, but tells me you've brought us something unlike anything we've ever seen. True?"

Jason couldn't help it. "If I tell you, sir, I'll have to kill you."

"Boy, bring it on anytime you think you're tough, or stupid, enough to try." Cadallo laughed. "Besides, I'm on my way to find Tom and *make* him tell me what's going on so I don't look like a fool at the meeting. It's not healthy to keep the boss in the dark."

"You're the commander here?"

"Any reason why not?"

"Nothing, nothing at all, since Kneen's gone."

Cadallo's face soured. "Other than using us as a fast track to a promotion, the bastard had no reason being here—but that comes with the territory. Like your quarters? It was Tom's idea. I went along. The Doors are trying to treat you a little better than the last time you were here. You know about the meeting?"

Jason nodded. "Eleven sharp, sir." On base less than an hour and even General Ben Cadallo was trying to pump him for information. He was back in the spy-versus-spy world. Not letting the right hand know what the left hand was doing seemed to be official policy. He suddenly realized that formulating his own plan was going to be harder than he'd thought.

"Then see you there." Cadallo turned to leave, but stopped. "Oh, before I go. Here, I stopped by to give you this," he said, handing Jason a credit card. "It's a government credit card. We've gone to plastic. Charge all your gear, food, billeting, and ancillary expenses on it. Keep it within reason and turn it in when you leave."

"And when will that be, sir?"

Cadallo smiled. "Why, when the mission is done." He closed the front door behind him.

# CHAPTER 9

I T WAS CALLED THE WAR ROOM. ACCESS CODE TO THE cipher lock was 1369. Jason punched in the numbers and entered as the door automatically locked behind him. Normally a raucous place, today it had all the somber trappings of a funeral. A recall of the Brothers only happened during national emergencies or a world crisis.

There was no need to run through warnings, cautions, and all the other preliminaries that normally began a top-secret meeting. It was an engagement attended by people who held the highest security clearances in existence. The casual dress exhibited by the people in the room did not belie the seriousness of the situation. Indeed, long hair and tattered clothes was the required costume for some.

Conversations in the War Room were secret, and could deal with anything up to infiltration and assassination. No holds were barred and any question was valid. This was an invitation-only affair, a gathering of the most covert operators in the world.

There was no table, just an assortment of chairs

arranged in two loose circles—thirteen inner chairs and twenty-six on the outside circle. Six men sat in the inner circle. Seven of the chairs were empty, those of operators on active missions. Jason took his place just behind Kelly, signifying his connection to the group as Kelly's partner.

Jason quietly observed the Brothers' inner circle. He knew the six men sitting there. Some wore their hair long and were dressed in jeans and T-shirts, others were in military dress. There was no tighter group of men anywhere.

From Vietnam to the present, of the billions spent on Special Forces only a tiny fraction of the funds went to actual missions; the rest of it went into pay, training, and materials.

There were Special Forces units that trained endlessly and could only hope for a chance to be called on to exhibit their skills. Overblown egos, bragging, and arrogantly bad attitudes usually marked these prima-donna operators who had never logged a minute of combat time. The men in this room had nothing to prove. Each had been on enough secret operations to fill volumes of mission logs.

The Brotherhood rarely got involved in counterterrorist operations or hostage rescues—they were America's hit men. But call one of them an assassin to his face and you could wind up with a busted jaw.

Team leader John Lucas, code-named Rabid, hadn't changed at all. He was bald, skinny, six-foot-five, and had eyes that could freeze molten lava. Lucas never got excited, never got mad, and never yelled. But to cross him was a *big* mistake. His kills were rumored to be in the hundreds. Even he did not know how many lives he had taken.

Sitting next to him was his partner, Nicholas Pia. No code name, just Pia. Compared with Pia, Arnold Schwarzenegger looked like a Cub Scout. Heavy weapons, the garrote, and mantraps were his specialties. When mayhem or cover fire was required, Pia was The Man.

Kevin "Z-Man" Zimmerman, code-named Ming, was the communications specialist. Radios and frequencies were his life. He was five-eight, one hundred and seventy pounds, with short blond hair and owl glasses, and had an unlit cigar that always hung from the corner of his mouth. Jason had never seen Z-Man out of uniform or without his survival vest.

Strapped to his back was a machete whose handle protruded menacingly from behind his neck. As scary as he looked, Z-Man had a wacky sense of humor with an unrestrained laugh that had a sinister side tone that could make your soul shiver.

Julio Lopez, code-named Zorro, a former gangbanger from East Los Angeles, was a numbers and gadget wizard. A master fencer, he was great with bladed weapons and had a penchant for switchblades. He was also a natural with computers, and had a gift for getting the most out of an electronic device.

Lopez tasted blood early growing up in the public housing projects of Ramona Gardens. Knowing he would either die at an early age from gang violence or wind up in prison, he joined the Marines and quickly caught the eye of the Brotherhood. He traded drive-by shootings for front-line assassination.

Rusty Bradshaw, code-named Puma, looked like a puma and spoke eight languages, among them Russian, Chinese, and Spanish. Interrogation was his gift. He had never been to college, but had learned the different languages by traveling through, or living in, various parts of the world. He knew a lot of people. Next to Lucas, Rusty probably had the most kills on the team.

The Brotherhood took on high-risk missions that sometimes were considered just short of suicide. They didn't scare. Collectively, their talents were unstoppable. Their combined skills made them the deadliest fighting group in the world.

Though covertly they were warriors, the skill that the Brothers valued above all others was silence. In and out, unseen and unheard, undetected. As with Death himself, nothing heralded their arrival or departure. Immersed in their deadly trade, they never, ever took deaths for granted. Having dealt it many times, each death made them value life more, knowing that it could touch them at any time.

Jason had yet to learn the ability to disappear as quickly as the others. *You're only as good as your last mission.* It'd been five years since he had been called on as an operative team member. *I may not have your killer instincts, but at least I can outlast you guys in the survival arena.*

Behind Tom sat his associates, Jean Fawcett and Mike Dennis, and another man.

Jason waved at Mike. They would talk later.

Mike Dennis was a discovery of Jason's whom Tom had quickly scooped up. He was the owner of Oregon Aero, an aviation company located in Portland. He was also an inventor, and so good that he now ran the Door Fabrication Shop (DFS). He was what Q was to James Bond.

The other man Jason did not know, but there was something very odd about him.

Tom started the meeting. "Thank you all for making it here on such short notice. Usually, we're the ones kept in the dark about our missions, until we get the tasking, and then more often than not it's only a tiny piece of the puzzle. This time it's *their* turn to play catch-up. Okay, let's get down to business. I've already talked with some of you about your reasons for being here. Those of you who are hearing this for the first time, try and keep your jaws off the floor.

"Master Sergeant Jason Johnson has full sanctions as an associate member of this group. A number of days ago he came to me and told me about a series of events so fantastic that I felt compelled to check them out. I believe them all to be connected, and that the CIC is involved." Tom then related the events surrounding the Titan explosion and all the other incidents Jason had uncovered.

"The CIC? Are you sure?" Rusty pointed toward the ceiling. "That ain't our turf."

A cold look crossed Tom's face. "It is when a Titan rocket explodes and multibillion-dollar packages are stolen. It is when someone takes away our ability to see what our enemies are up to. It is when American, British, and Canadian aircraft are mysteriously shot down and the CIC covers up official investigations. It is when the Doors lose a contract chopper crew on an *exercise*!" He took deep breaths to calm down before speaking again. "Now the latest information Jason has given me *really* fucks with my head." Tom went on to explain all the events that had convinced him to make a recall of the Brothers, something done only in a national crisis. Any Brother or associate not key to an operational mission had been required to attend.

"Oh come on, Tom," Pia chided, "why would the CIC want to steal their own load by exploding a Titan? And what does the CIC have to do with shooting down aircraft?"

"And that's why we're here, darling." Tom smiled sardonically.

"Oh."

The lights dimmed and a hologram of a man stood at the center of the room.

"Tom, how do you get these things?" Jason asked. He was shocked when he recognized the hologram.

"Patrons, Jason. Friends in high places." Tom rolled to the center of the room and next to the hologram. "Mister Black of the CIC. Jean?"

Several different shots of Boris beamed around the room.

Jean Fawcett read from a notebook. "Mister Black. Director of internal security for the Central Imaging Command, his real name is Frank McCone. Former assistant to CIA director William Webster, he left the company in 1985 under unreported circumstances and took over the National Photographic Interpretation Center (NPIC), which he then put under the National Imagery and Mapping Agency. In 1987 he was appointed as the CIC's security chief—NPIC is actually controlled by the CIC. There've been few documented activities by McCone since he's been connected with the CIC. Like us, he covers his trail well."

Jean looked up at Tom for a moment. "I checked with my sources and they tell me that McCone is an autocratic hatchet man. He's become a power unto himself."

"The enemy within?" Lucas asked.

Jason didn't care about the name "McCone." Mister Black would always be "Boris" to him.

The hologram dissolved and was replaced by another.

"This is one of McCone's chief lieutenants, Michael Decker," Tom said.

"Can't be," Pia interjected. "Lucas and I know about him. He's former Delta, but now he's with the Department of Energy's Transportation Safeguard Protective Service as an SST team leader. A guy like Black would never get involved with a guy from an SST courier team."

"Yeah he could," Tom counted. "Jean uncovered the chain of command and found out that the CIC actually funds the Protective Service—even the PS operators don't know that. Jean."

Jean continued reading from her notes. "After his military duty, Decker was hired by the Protective Service in 1980." She looked up. "From what I've been able to find, something happened to one of their SST loads and several large sums of cash were paid out to the families of Decker's team, but not insurance money. Each one of his team has turned up dead, with the death certificates claiming natural causes."

"Finally," Tom said, "there's this." He explained in layman terms what he had gotten from AFTAC about the "chirps" he had found and the Z cuff link. "Now I open the floor for all your questions and theories."

"How do you shoot down aircraft without explosive residue?" Lucas asked.

Zimmerman raised his hand. "And why? Political?"

For the next hour the conversation bounced around the room, with ideas, arguments, and rebuttals. Tensions and stress rose with the realization that they were onto something really big.

"I think that we might be way out of our league here," mumbled Kelly.

Julio summed up the feelings in the room. "Tom, what's the point of this discussion? There's no mission-tasking, and a tasking isn't ours to make. Anything that we might come up with is just speculation and conjecture."

"Mister Jason—Alice?" The odd-looking man behind Tom looked at Jason.

"Sir?"

"If you don't mind, I'd like you to answer a few more questions for me."

"If I can."

"I understand that you were doing the range-clearing mission the day that the Titan exploded."

"I was."

"Did you see any submarines?"

Jason was startled. "I think maybe a submarine, or a whale."

"All the Navy subs were in their pens at Port Canaveral that morning," Jean added.

An instant detail sprang to Jason's mind from that fateful morning. The wake he had seen in the water—a whale's isn't symmetrical like that; only a sub could cut that kind of wake. "Now that you ask, I'm pretty sure now that it was a sub, sir."

The man's body twitched as he worked the keyboard on his laptop computer. The screen exploded with data. He stopped, then scanned his work and nodded in agreement with what he'd done.

With concentration and effort, he stood up and walked to the center of the room. "I want to try and offer some possible explanations."

The room became silent. He had a nervous tic on his shoulder and his face would occasionally make very gnarly grimaces.

"I think that the connections to the explosions and Mister Black, while steeped in subterfuge, don't involve any direct sabotage by the CIC. As a matter of fact, after studying these 'chirps' and checking with all my sources, I think that the CIC is actually trying to solve these explosions and the loss of their load. I believe that the CIC was trying to keep their situation secret and Jason just got caught in their path."

"Why do you say that, General?" Jean asked.

*General?* Jason was astounded that the twitching man wearing faded jeans and a white T-shirt could be in the military at all. He looked and acted more like a short-haired Joe Cocker. His body stayed in constant spastic motion.

"As you know, there's black projects, and then there's *black* projects, projects so dark that even the President doesn't know about them. They're invisible. The CIC is running one of those programs. It's called the Godspeed.

"It was a pet project of Reagan's secret Star Wars program that he hid from the public and his political opponents. He formed a small group of experts, and then issued a top-secret presidential directive that made it legal for the group to lie to anyone about Godspeed. He funded it through the CIC, and his objective was to make a working directed energy weapon. But now I find that there's enough evidence to prove that someone else has beaten us to the punch."

"Sir, how do you know this?" asked Jason.

"I'm the one who edited the directive. I think now's the time to let all of you in on a few things."

The man smiled at Jason and unsteadily pulled out a pen-sized object from his back pocket, pressed a button on it, and then jerked the red beam around the room. "Laser light and microelectronics. A few years ago this little laser highlighter didn't even exist. Now we're testing lasers to shoot down missiles with a bigger version at Kirtland Air Force Base. Researchers at Sandia Labs are making a big to-do about it to the news media." His face spasmed. "It's a front! Sure, the lasers can work, but on the worldwide stage they're not dependable. Today, the best we've got is the Directed Infrared Countermeasures—DIRCM. It's an in-theater tactical weapon.

"Now think big, *real* big. What if someone could harness the power of a thermonuclear bomb? They get billions of watts of power. If they can contain it, they could then direct its power around the globe to wherever they want. Think of the kind of forces that they would be dealing with. Think about what they could do by focusing the electromagnetic power of a nuclear explosion on a tank, plane, or rocket launch. How powerful a beam could they make? How wide? What else could they do with that beam? You see, ladies and gentlemen, it's already here. It's produced from a method called magneto-hydrodynamics—MHD. It's an electromagnetic-pulsed generator—EMP—and the Russians appear to have it first. I have good evidence that they stole most of their high technology from our side."

The room was coffin-silent.

"It's not so surprising when you look at the history of our rivalry with the Russians in space—they've always been first. We've spent trillions in sophisticated technology while theirs has always been basic simplicity and reliability, basic.

"Let me add this to the floor: There's a research program in Gakona, Alaska, called the High-Frequency Active Auroral Research Program—HAARP—that's beaming incredible amounts of energy off of the ionosphere. Pure research. Really? So was the Manhattan Project, until it exploded the atom bomb. I know for a fact that the CIC was putting up their first fighting reflector and was going test it out using the HAARP generator. So Titan 20B was launching Godspeed. It was supposed to be our first active directed energy weapon.

"Here's my speculation: The Russians used their EMP to blow up the Titan, then stole our reflector. Then they blacked out NIMA's mainframe computer network. They also pulsed the Wizard Warrior exercise. Why

English Air? I think that it was taken down to kill someone on that plane. But who? That I will find out.
Whoever it was, he was important enough for someone
to also down out a Canadian chopper to keep the CIC
from finding out.

"How'd they do it? The sub Jason saw has to be
Russian, and most likely acts as the targeting platform
for the EMP, or floats a team in with a targeting device. If
I'm right, it's quite simple. The sub targeted the Titan
and CIC chopper, stole our reflector, and then moved up
the Atlantic coastline. It was just a matter of staying in
hiding until it was time to surface and target the English
Air jet and the chopper. Even though our own media
missed it, I'm not so surprised that they got the time and
place of Wizard Warrior. NIMA's mainframe is where?"

"Within range of the sub's targeting system," Tom
replied.

"But who are these people?" He nodded to Tom,
who pressed a button on his panel, causing an eight-foot
hologram of the Z cuff link to appear. "I believe that this
is the Russian organization behind the EMP. I have no
idea what this Z monogram means. Anybody?"

The shock of dealing with a concept so bizarre kept
the room in stunned silence.

Pointing toward the ceiling, the general grimaced.
"Something up *there* is whacking things down *here*.
Right now our researchers are using telemetry, spherical
trigonometry, and high school geometry to plot positions
of the Russian satellites that fly over the East Coast. I
believe that whatever we're looking for is not a conventional satellite. Most likely it's a sort of reflector
disguised to look like something else.

"All right, calculating the optimal position of their
angles, it's very possible that the generator originates
from somewhere in Siberia. Anybody know anything
about a secret facility in Siberia?"

Silence. Many secret cities had been constructed by
the Soviets during the Cold War. So far only ten had been
detected. Many more were still hidden across Russia's

vast continent while they further developed their nuclear program.

Tom broke the silence. "Come on, people. Someone is taking down our assets and killing hundreds of people. I want some answers!"

No one in the room spoke, but the sounds of people squirming in their chairs made more than enough noise. Jason watched the intense concentration on Cadallo's face; like most in the room, he was hearing all this for the first time.

The general's face turned red as he shook. "How is it that this could happen in this day of instant global communication? I'm in a roomful of intelligence elite who can't tell me a damn thing! Come on, tell ol' General Twitch whatcha know."

Silence. Who knew from secret Soviet cities and nuclear directed energy weapons?

Twitch relaxed a little. "Jason has brought us what could happen to be the most important secret event I've ever witnessed—and I thought I'd seen it all. Now we have to start somewhere to solve a situation that promises to get nastier the longer we sit here with our heads up our asses."

"Hey, Jason, couldn't you have found something a little easier for us to handle? Like a dose of the crabs, or Jimmy Hoffa's body?" quipped Z-Man.

Cadallo rubbed his chin. "Folks, we're the shooters. I can't ever remember generating our own ops. Can anyone else?"

More silence. This was new ground for this group of killers, and it made them nervous. It wasn't in their job description to act as an operational intelligence agency.

"Well, folks," Tom said, "this meeting wasn't pretty. We have a lot of soul-searching to do. This stuff is so deep, I expect to take a lot of flak for even finding out about it. The CIC is hiding this information from the intelligence community, and they were doing a great job until Jason came along. I've studied Black, and can see now that he's creeping out of line. *My* next step is to get an up-channel coordinator for our findings. I'm gonna verify this data, and then I'm going point on the political trail while General Normandin cuts the technical road, and I expect it to turn into a war zone. I want each of you to treat what you learned here today with the highest sensitivity. This really is one of those 'If I tell ya, I gotta kill ya' numbers."

Tom closed the meeting. "Folks, we're the shooters. Leave the political bullshit to the politicians and strategists. I expect that once this information runs up the ladder, a mission-tasking *has* to come back down to us. My bet is that the EMP generator, wherever it is, has *got* to go down. This time we're the ones making the rules. Start thinking about your plans and get in shape for a mission to the ends of the earth. You know the rules of the game; only volunteers on this mission. We've taken on the impossible before. This time I'm asking you to tackle the unheard-of."

Jason noticed that while everyone rose to leave, General Cadallo remained seated, lost in thought—the leader left in the dark. Strange.

Tom followed Jason out the door.

"Now what?" Jason asked.

"It'll take three working days for General Normandin to get on the National Foreign Intelligence Board (NFIB) docket. That's where the CIC is going to know we know something, if they don't already. I think that we'll uncover a lot more before the general presents our case."

"Hey, what's up with all those twitches? Who is that guy?"

Tom stroked his chin for a few moments. "General Brian Normandin has one star, but he should have four. He ran Air Force Intelligence forever, until his tremors got too bad for him to appear in public. Bad public image. There're four-star generals whom he brought up who now avoid being seen with him—the twitches bother people. He's one of the most brilliant minds I've ever met. You can call him Norm, or Twitch, if he lets you. He's a visionary. It's a long story how he became my associate; suffice to say his added connections are the best in the world. Satellite imagery, intelligence codes, everything."

"What about me?"

"What about you?" Tom quizzed.

"You're the one who requested me here. Am I a consultant or an operator? I need to fit in somewhere." A million combinations and possibilities swam in Jason's mind.

"Listen, Jason, this ops is mine, but I can't do this thing alone. You brought it to me. I need help, but mostly I need people I can trust. Can I trust you?"

Jason nodded.

Tom smiled. "Then where you fit in is something you have to figure out for yourself, but I think that you'll know soon enough. In the meantime, all our facilities are at your disposal. You have full Door privileges, charged to your Blue Door credit card. Tell me, how do you like your quarters?"

"Fabulous!"

"Things here at the Doors are different now. With the way world politics have changed, the Doors have become much more valuable. We've proved that we're sometimes cheaper to send into a politically sensitive area than American troops. Nobody even knows who we are. Hence, some argue that our budget is excessive, but it's millions cheaper than funding an air wing or Army division for some of our operations. I've owed you for a long time. This is my chance to make you feel welcomed. Besides, Boris can't touch you here.

"Jason, have you given any thought about what you've uncovered?"

"Yeah, if I would have kept my mouth shut *I* wouldn't be here."

"And things would have been worse. You don't want to be here?"

Jason thought for a few moments. He had to keep his agenda to himself. "I'm not sure. I'm not sure about a lot of things these days."

"Then let me give you a few things to chew on. Do you know what defensive measures we have in place if some foreign country launched nuclear missiles on us?"

"No."

Tom smiled. "With all the bazillions we've spent on high-tech gadgets, we would know who launched it, where it was launched from, how fast it was moving, where it was headed, when it would hit, and what kind of rocket fuel propelled it. We would even know how many warheads were coming at us. But we haven't got a goddamn thing to stop them. Nothing!

"We've been living under the threat of nuclear devastation since the day we invented the atom bomb. The political posture and power we hold throughout the world revolves around the thousands of nuclear bombs and missiles that we have in our inventory.

"Mutual Assured Destruction—MAD. You launch on us, we launch on you, we all die. It's been the cornerstone of all our nuclear treaties since the Cold War. You would be amazed at all the politicians who think that a balance of terror is the best answer we have to avoid a nuclear conflict.

"During the Cold War we pumped billions and billions into American nuclear strategy and treaties. Today, right now, with what you brought, that's all changed, and our intelligence agencies and defense measures haven't caught up with the changes. *Now* we're vulnerable.

"You know, the Internet holds more technical and classified information than all our intelligence agencies combined. The CIA, CIC, and NSA can't keep up with their own data. Are we derelict? It seems like we've become dinosaurs in a mammal world. We've got to change or go the way of the dinosaurs.

"Our opponents have developed a weapon based on pure energy. Do you know what that does to the whole game? Think of how the balance of power would shift if a Communist or third world country could stop incoming nukes. I mean really stop them. A real missile defense. Not this bullshit missile-defense pipe dream that's on the news. A beam that can shoot down anything in the air at the speed of light a continent away. No more MAD. Who would want a weapon like that?"

"Everybody."

"And if I knew I could stop your incoming nukes, what would I do with mine?"

"Shoot 'em off with impunity."

"There it is. It's all changed. Changed like the guy who invented the shield to stop the sword. Then look what gunpowder did to the sword. Jason, we're sitting under the Sword of Damocles. We've gone from gunpowder to the ray gun, and very few people know it."

Jason looked up at the sky. "What if the information leaks out?"

"The sword falls."

# CHAPTER 10

**T**OO MUCH WAS ON HIS MIND, SO JASON ROLLED FROM his bed, stumbled downstairs to the kitchen, and opened the refrigerator. Pulling out a Corona beer, he opened it and downed it in two swallows. "All this shit's just not right," he mumbled as he grabbed another beer and walked out to the patio. It was a beautiful night. Regardless of what situation he might find himself in, he always tried to remember to take a moment and drink in exquisite surroundings. Falling into a chaise longue overlooking the river, he propped up his feet and sipped his beer.

It was a clear and warm night. The moon wore a crescent smile; Venus and Mars bejeweled the grin. *What does it look like on the Siberian tundra?* Someone on base nearby was probably dealing with that question, and more.

He had to find his place on the mission, and that was all there was to it. He had a very short time to learn all he could about Siberia and an unknown enemy. Everyone was making plans. Every plan had a high priority.

Jason tipped his beer to the moon. "Well, I can make my own agendas with my own priorities, too."

**0730**
**WAR ROOM / DOORS / FLORIDA**

"Those sons of bitches!" Twitch fumed. "I brought them the evidence. It's as plain as their asshole noses on their faces."

Jason walked into the War Room. Tom and the general were the only ones in the room. He just stood near Tom and waited and watched Twitch rage.

"Those arrogant bastards! They actually believe that they own the right to think. '*There is no way Russian peasants could possess a directed energy satellite.*' That's what those sons of bitches actually said. Can you believe it? Can you fucking believe it?" His hands and arms flew through the air. "It's a reflector. An EMP reflector is not that difficult to make." Twitch spasmed hard. "M-m-motherfuckers!"

"He having a problem?" Jason whispered to Tom.

"I'll say," Tom quietly answered. "We went to the NFIB in Washington and he presented our case. It was something to see, me rolling around on my IBOT and him twitching up a passionate storm. He was beautiful. There were no leaks in his case. It was tight, brilliant." Tom's eyes looked at the ground. "And then he had a real bad spasm, and they ridiculed and laughed at him." A twisted smile crossed his lips. "A gimp and a twitch in front of the National Foreign Intelligence Board, trying to present the biggest secret anyone's ever come across in history. We got laughed right out the door. You should've seen it. I should've taken you."

"Was Boris there?"

"Right in the middle of the whole thing. Ever been to an inquisition?"

"No."

"Neither have I, not until yesterday. Man, we were

preaching *heresy:* We knew what they didn't. We spoke blasphemy in front of the gods. I was waiting for them to bring out instruments of torture to get us thinking their way. But we got them scared. They know we know more than we let on. We were after an unseen enemy, but this meeting also identified our adversary, if you can call the CIC the opposition."

"Boris. I could've told you that. So now what?"

"Watch," Tom whispered, and then rolled over to Twitch. "Well, General, we tried. I guess we should fold up the show."

"Fold? Hell no, we don't fold! Jason!"

"Yes sir?"

"I'm going down to see your nuke chick with Jean. What's her name?"

"Rita Meine."

"Right. I'm going to nail the *exact* discrete points in space of that reflector, then I'm going to pinpoint the *exact* location of the fucking beam from Siberia, verify the evidence, and then ram it up the NFIB's ass!

"People like to laugh at ol' General Twitch. That's good, because it keeps them off balance." Twitch smiled coldly. "The NFIB has fucked with me once too often. I was sure they would forget their politics for once and want to deal with reality. Okay, we followed the rules. As soon as I confirm what I know is true, I'm heading straight for the Veil Committee. I know what's out there. I know the game. And I'm changing the god-damned rules!"

## 2330
## DOOR GYM / FLORIDA

Remove the ring. Put it on the necklace. Stretch the hands. Pop the knuckles. Unroll the wrap. Start with the right hand. Make the pad, four folds. Lay them across the impact zone. Now wrap the hand.

Jason had done this countless times. It was a ritual

he relished. Well-wrapped hands in leather bag gloves were almost invincible when you connected against a heavy bag, or skin. The impact felt good. You could let out your rage.

The empty Door gym was beautiful: mirrored walls, chrome free weights, every piece of Nautilus and fancy exercise machines in place. There were saunas, Jacuzzis, massage rooms, and an Olympic pool. There was nothing the Doors did not have, or wouldn't get for their killers for mission enhancement.

But you don't just show up at the Doors and not be ready to perform. *I'm back, so let's get on with it.*

"I'm here looking for answers and revenge," Jason muttered to his reflection in the mirror.

A spark of anger began to burn in him. At the same time anxiety pricked at his mind. He could blame only himself for the situation that he was in. The mission was probably suicide. *Been there. Done that.* Once again, anywhere else was looking better than where he was at and headed at that moment. "I'm not a bad guy, so why does this shit always happen to me when I least expect it?" he asked himself aloud.

The bag he stood in front of was an Everlast two-hundred-pound heavy bag, anchored with very little give. But to Jason it was Boris that was in front of him.

"You son of a bitch, if it wasn't for you, I wouldn't be here."

He exploded onto the bag with savage rage and fury, driving perfect killing blows. For two minutes every strike he made was meant to end the life of Boris.

Two minutes could be an eternity. Jason fell away from the bag drained. Looking at the clock on the wall, he saw he had one minute to get his act together for another two-minute attack. In his twenties he couldn't wait for the minute to pass. Now, at forty, it seemed as if that second hand moved just too goddamn fast.

To get at Boris he would first have to get by Michael Decker. He shuddered, remembering the feel of Decker's gun against his temple in the night. The bastard taunted him. Now it was Decker that was in front of him.

This time his attack was methodical, timed, and focused, with low kicks and blinding eye gouges designed to maim. He wanted to hurt Decker first. A few more strikes and Decker disappeared.

But in reality Boris and Decker were a minor problem. Attacking the bag as if it were his frustrations and fears, he tried to piece together what was happening.

Two minutes. Three minutes. He forgot about time.

Jason fell against the mirrored wall and slumped to the floor. "Can't somebody else be the hero this time?"

An unseen enemy had taken the Godspeed reflector. The enemy's initial was Z. It was the real fight. It was where his life was leading him to fulfill a vendetta. Jason pulled himself up off the floor. "Mission first. I can't help myself," he said to the reflection in the mirror. "But when this is over, I'm gonna find me a woman and get laid, and it'll be a *lot* longer than two minutes!"

The gym door opened. It was Gitthens, his driver. "Mister Jason, Mister Chain asks that you be at the Pentagon for a meeting on Friday morning. All the transportation's been arranged. I'm gonna drive you to the jet. He'd like you to be in dress blues."

---

# CHAPTER 11

**0730 FRIDAY / 15 OCTOBER 1999**
**PENTAGON / ARLINGTON / VIRGINIA**

*Climates of secrecy.*

**F**OR A PERSON TO EXIST AND OPERATE INSIDE THE Pentagon—also known as the Puzzle Palace—requires many security classifications, and to get inside this room required the highest of them all. In an unnumbered room just down from the Joint Chiefs of Staff (JCS) known as the Vault, an Ultra Sensitive Compartmented Information Facility (USCIF), members of the Veil Committee convened to take action on a forced meeting called by Mister Bruce Davis, chairman.

The luster of brass travel and protocol did not affect Jason. The plush jet rides out of Florida and the limousine security service from Andrews Air Force Base in Maryland to the Pentagon was just what Bob Gitthens called it: transportation. The amenities were more of an insult to an enlisted guy while serious shit was happening.

A mirror in the car caught his reflection and Jason did a last uniform check. He smiled for the first time he could remember since the mission had started. Wearing an Air Force Class A uniform paid for by government credit card, he looked *good*!

A chestful of silver qualification badges, decorations, and awards covered his dress blue jacket. Been there. Done that.

Falling back on the seat, Jason adjusted his new maroon beret. He'd preferred his old one but that was back in his locker, a long way away.

The limousine passed through a side gate and disappeared underground. It took a couple of lefts and rights, then stopped at the base of some stairs. A young one-striper in an Army uniform guided him up four flights of stairs, past three checkpoints, to a huge windowless conference room, and into a plush leather chair.

Jason sat in the room at General Normandin's invitation. Tom sat next to Jason. Twitch was talking quietly to a man at the other end of the long table. Cadallo was absent from the meeting.

"This is where we get the green light, or not," Tom whispered. "We gotta play our cards right; the stakes have never been higher. Twitch is pissed. He's best when he's mad. No one dares disagree with General Normandin when he's mad. No one. For a brigadier general, no one can ruin careers like him. Watch him in action when this meeting starts."

Jason had been in this room before. Back then Kelly and he were just meat for inspection. Now he was the Door "rescue consultant."

The two chairs at opposite ends of a thirty-foot-long table belonged to the brokers behind *real* political power. Politician puppets came and went, but whoever sat in these chairs held the strings. Bruce Davis sat in the blue chair. The red chair was empty.

"Tom, where are the old crones who run this thing?" Jason whispered.

"Dead—old age. Our man died last month. Their man died just three days ago. Old age finally caught up with both of them. It's a good thing, too, because this meeting would probably have put them in their graves anyway. There's a pretty nasty fight going on for control of the red chair, so that's definitely going to work to our advantage. I think we'll get a better reception from Bruce Davis. He sits on lots of committees. He's secretly known as a Bilderberger, a key member of the trilateral commission, and he sits on the Council of Foreign Relations, and most important for us, is successor of the blue chair. He reports directly to the President."

The room had changed little except for the furniture and the screens on the wall. The top-secret-briefing luster had also worn off. All Jason wanted to do was hear a yes or no from the committee—then he could commit to the fight or go home.

The Vault door opened. Boris and Decker walked in and were seated at the far side of the table near the red chair. Jason looked at his watch. It was two minutes till the start of the meeting. He couldn't wait. Standing up, he walked over to where they were sitting.

Heart racing, he leaned over and eyed each man, then tapped Decker's shoulder, hard. "Like to break into people's homes and put guns to their head, asshole?" Then, narrowing his eyes, he hissed at Boris, "Motherfucker, you want to make a play for me, go ahead. But if you *ever* go near Toby's family or my friend Mac, I will come after you, and there won't be a thing your lapdog can do to stop me from killing you. Do you understand me?"

Jason stood back, ready for anything, but Boris put his hand on Decker's arm, whose face was white with rage. There was a look of fright in Boris's eyes. Satisfied, Jason strolled back to his chair.

"What was that all about?" Tom whispered.

"Just clarifying a couple of things."

The lights slightly dimmed. *Showtime,* thought Jason.

"I'd like to say something before this meeting begins," Bruce Davis said. "If anyone here briefs me using a

PowerPoint presentation, I am going to get out of this chair and *kick your ass*. I hate those things. Make your points without the Hollywood slides crap. I'm in a hurry, so let's get on with it."

Several people scrambled to reconfigure their boring, special-effects-to-make-a-vague-but-useless-point brief. For Jason, there was no worse torture than trying to figure out some unbelievably complex computer-based slides made by overachieving bench sitters.

By the time the overview briefer was done with the mandatory warning formalities, Jason was already nodding off. He couldn't help it. After his having endured years of them, briefings by goobers triggered the sleep mode in him. Tom nudged him back to consciousness.

General Twitch nodded to a young Tom Cruise look-alike. The young man stood up and, using just notes, gave a letter-perfect version of what Twitch told the NFIB.

"So, gentlemen," General Twitch took over, "to summarize, a Russian group known only as Z has a directed energy weapon in Siberia, and it works. They have also stolen our EMP reflector that the CIC was putting into space."

"A secret Russian organization with a directed energy weapon? And how can we put a reflector into space—it's against *all* our treaties with Russia. Mister Black, is this true?" Davis asked.

Jason couldn't help but grin at the way Boris squirmed.

"I can't talk about it, sir," Boris mumbled.

"What, classified?!" Davis asked.

"Yes, sir."

Davis eyed Nate Morrison, the CIA director. "You know about this?"

Looking at the ceiling, Morrison nodded.

He stared down David Marfin, the NSA chief. "You?"

"I do," Marfin sheepishly answered.

"I see—everyone in the intelligence community seems to know about this directed energy reflector that was stolen but me. So why didn't *I* know?"

"Godspeed is a deep black research project that was hidden during the Reagan years," Boris said.

"So, the President has been kept out of the loop for *TEN YEARS?*"

No one in the room spoke.

"This is supposed to be the Veil Committee. The most secret agendas in the world are handled here, only here. And now I find out I've been stonewalled. Who the hell do you think you are? I have to have the Doors, a special operations field group, come here to tell me that my own members have been hiding secrets from me. *ME!* What's next? Am I going to find out from someone other than this committee that we're holding space aliens?"

Davis fumed. "Everyone except for the Door people get out of this room until I call you back. And while you're out, start thinking about replacements for this board."

The three men facing Davis remained quiet for a long time, waiting while he tried to calm down.

"General, is there really a, a *ray gun* out there? Has someone really built one that works?"

Twitch opened his briefcase and passed a map of Siberia to Davis. "Someone's got something, Bruce. As you know, I have access to more than just the CIC and the DSP spy satellites. I've had hundreds of people working compartmentalized pieces of my puzzle. There's only a few pieces left to complete the picture. Here's what I have."

"You are going to keep it simple, aren't you?" Davis asked as he studied the map.

"Of course, sir. No PowerPoint slides, graphs, or charts, and nothing up my sleeves. Just that map and some pictures." Twitch opened a notebook. "As you know, the NFIB refused to accept my information and followed their usual political policy of denial and ridicule.

"First, the facts of a Russian reflector. We used telemetry, spherical trigonometry, and good ol' high school geometry to plot potential positions of Russian satellites that have been orbiting over the East Coast. There's one that's supposedly dead and flying in a Russian Molniya orbit. We list it as satellite number SSC-2-14-08196, inclination 68.8, 67.1, 73-74, and 82-83.

"That son of a bitch was launched in 1985 and we forgot about it—space junk. The incredibly corrosive nature of atomic oxygen in space should've corroded it to nothing, but it didn't. It took *a lot* of called-in favors to have one of our own reconnaissance satellites repositioned to have a closer look at it. It's not a conventional satellite. It's a reflector. It's a sleeper Mylar reflector that was disguised to look like a communications satellite until the nuclear-pulsed generator was up and running. From our calculations it's a reflector that can handle *a lot* of power.

"All right. Triangulating the position of each pulse when it happened, we've come close to estimating where in Siberia the beam originates."

He passed over a small stack of photographs, each one stamped TOP SECRET at the top and bottom. "These are spy satellite pictures and manned observations of the northeast region of Siberia taken over a ten-year period. The first ones, taken in 1980, show nothing—a supposed diamond mine fifty miles from two frozen lakes close to one another. Now look at the second series of pictures, taken in '81. No activity at the mine. Abandoned? But look at those towers. Well, someone is boring through the permafrost tundra and right into solid granite. Another mine shaft? Nineteen eighty-two. A road has been cut, but to where? For what? Nothing's going in and nothing's coming out. No ore trucks, no railroad to carry away any minerals or diamonds that they might be digging for, only a few trailers. I'd bet that they knew when our satellites were overhead. Who told them? Our geologists at that time said that they were probably working worthless ground and gave up on the project.

"Nineteen eighty-five. Now look at the trenches being dug—big trenches. *Huge* pipelines were laid, then buried. Notice the circular pattern? They aren't pipes for gas. Sir, by that time they had us. We thought that they were after diamonds or gas and no one cared what they did in their godforsaken land.

"A few days ago my high-energy physicists went back over all the data and estimated and calculated the amount of ground they dug and *how* they dug during the placement of the pipeline, and other things that take a while to explain. They concluded that right here,"—Twitch pointed to a spot on the map—"a closed core fission reactor has been built, with the capability of generating over thirty billion watts of power."

"Wow! Can you explain how this reactor works?" Davis asked. "In *simple* terms."

"Of course. It's a magnetohydrodynamic, or MHD, reactor that makes contained nuclear explosions. In one chamber you make the explosion, then you direct the energy into a second chamber; a draw-off from a supercooled magnet in between the two chambers turns the heat from the explosion into electromagnetic power."

Davis's eyes widened. "Is this possible?"

"Very. We ourselves are still in the experimental stage."

"And it's been done on the Siberian tundra?"

"Yes, sir, it has. On several occasions over the years, early warning satellites detected large amounts of hydrogen with traces of tritium in the atmosphere, originating somewhere over the Soviet Union, but the amounts were so small that they thought it was just poor control of their nuclear generators. The thermal sensors on our early warning satellites pinpointed the Soviet Semipalatinsk weapons development plant. Just research, right? That was over ten years ago."

Twitch fought to gain control over himself. He went through a series of wild gyrations. "Damn! This can happen when I get to the good parts."

Taking a few deep breaths, he continued. "Three weeks ago we got five radiation readings uncharacteristic of any known nuclear detonation or natural explosion. They appeared to be microexplosions. There were these 'chirps' on all our sensors at the same time we got the readings. Until the last chirp, we had been looking at our systems thinking it was a glitch or a virus. We looked at it very close when Wizard Warrior was blacked out, but couldn't fit anything together.

"Then Master Sergeant Johnson here brought us startling information about the Titan explosion, the CIC chopper crash, the English Air 943 flight, and the Canadian Labrador crash. We looked at the exact time NIMA lost control of their spy satellite mainframe. Going back over the data and examining other sources, we found that they all match to the nanosecond when our sensors chirped. Sir, the system *was* working.

"The early warning system also detected a chirp the moment Wizard Warrior blacked out. An area the size of six city blocks had all its electrical-powered units fried—relay stations, computers, car ignitions, radios, lightbulbs, everything. The pulse is so fast that even systems shielded against EMP burned just like NIMA's imaging system. The EMP also killed three people when our contracted helicopter crashed because the controls fried.

"A Russian stealth sub off the coast acted as the targeting system." Twitch fidgeted and gyrated as he made his final points. "I can bore you with the technical details, but it will still lead you to only one conclusion: There is an operating directed energy weapon, and it doesn't belong to us."

Davis put his head in his hands. "Oh my God. If what you say is true, then the balance of power will change. What about all our nuclear arms?"

"Under a new Russian leader who wants to get back their stolen destiny, they could fire all the nuclear warheads they want at us and stop all of ours with their EMP beam, or they could use their beam as an offensive weapon. Sir, the Cold War is over. We're supposed to be the winners, but the reality is that they can beat us to the punch at will."

Tom spoke. "The Russians don't know that we are onto them. All preliminary investigation shows that President Yeltsin isn't even aware of what they have. We have to stop this thing before it becomes an uncontrollable monster, and it will be if they launch the stolen reflector. They'll have us hostage."

Davis looked surprised. "But how? Only the KGB could keep a secret like that operating, and they're disbanded."

Tom handed a cuff link to Davis. "The Godspeed project was hidden from our presidents for ten years, and you just found out about this stuff right now."

"Point made. What's this?"

"A cuff link with the letter Z on it, sir. Jason recovered it from the English Air crash. It has to be *deep* KGB to remain hidden for so long. We highly suspect that this Z organization is behind the weapon."

Davis studied the cuff link for a minute, then handed it back to Tom. "I would bet that this is how they identify each other. Tell me, what does Z mean or stand for?"

"Unknown at this time, sir," Tom said. "We have *every* resource we have looking at that. But some agencies aren't being very helpful."

"Gentlemen, please don't take this wrong, but I couldn't more flabbergasted if you'd come to me with space aliens. How can this be?"

Tom pointed at Jason. "Master Sergeant Jason Johnson. You ask him, sir."

Jason turned red. *I'm gonna kill you, Tom.*

Davis wrote something on a scrap of paper, got up, walked next to Twitch, and put his hand on the general's shoulder. "Master Sergeant Johnson, I have known this man for a long time. I majored in political science and military intelligence at the Air Force Academy. General Normandin was my professor. I hope you can imagine my astonishment over the situation, because I believe what this man tells me. Something like this has never happened. My God, can you imagine the panic this could cause if it leaks out to the public? This weapon has got to be stopped, but how? Do we hit it with a nuke, or a cruise missile?"

"No good, sir," Tom answered. "You know as well as I that hitting it with a nuke would be an act of war; besides, the reactor is buried too deep. The only way to get at it is with a hand-placed thermonuclear charge, a Special Atomic Demolition Munitions. A SADM, sir."

"The Doors are willing to accept this tasking?"

Tom nodded. "Yes sir. At the President's command."

Davis looked around the room for what seemed like an eternity, then at his aide. "Call back everyone."

To Jason, the Veil Committee members looked like schoolboys about to be punished by the principal for a misdeed. He took extra pleasure in watching Boris squirm almost as much as Twitch did.

After everyone had assembled, Davis spoke. "I don't know what bewilders me more—the existence of a secret enemy with a ray gun, a secret American directed energy program hidden from the President, or you assholes sitting in front of me!

"What a shame it is when the board chairman of the Veil Committee is kept in the dark by his own board members. We spent over *sixty billion* dollars on Reagan's Star Wars program. Can any of you tell me how much we really spent on what, or what programs were actually funded? Some of your agencies have become so secret and powerful that you think you can keep me in the dark forever. Shame on me. Well, let me tell you something: I don't know who is going to remain with me on the Veil Committee, and who isn't. Your actions in the next couple minutes will tell me."

Davis stood and walked around the room. "There are those who say that the Soviet empire has fallen. I think 'stumbled' would be a better description. And it looks like if they get back up they could be a lot stronger than us." He searched the eyes of each Veil member.

"This, Z—they have a generator and one reflector. The way I understand it, if they put up a second reflector, ours, then they'll be able to hit anything we have anytime they want. That's unacceptable."

He stopped in front of Mister Black. "Is what General Normandin telling me true?"

"Parts..."

"Most parts?"

"Possibly."

Jason couldn't keep the grin off his face. Watching Boris squirm made his day.

"What does Z mean?"

"Zond. It's the name of the Soviet's first space program. Zond funded many other Soviet programs under the directions of the KGB. Hidden in the program was their first directed energy tests."

"Who's the head of Zond?"

As if on cue, Boris opened a folder and produced a picture, giving Jason a cold stare when their eyes met. "Oleg Kurgan, former chief scientist at the Baltic State Technical University, pioneered Soviet high-energy physics. He disappeared ten years ago and triggered a covert worldwide manhunt, but we turned up nothing. The CIA surmised that he was either in Iran, Iraq, North Korea, or China. He's undoubtedly at the Zond fortress in Siberia, with at least five thousand men."

"Weak," whispered Chain. "He's tap-dancing using *our* music."

Twitch nodded at Davis. "It makes sense. I read Kurgan's paper on mercury-enhanced-plutonium energy propagation. It was revolutionary, but in our own arrogant way our physicists dismissed it as undoable, nuts. I'll be damned. He did it. He's got to be the brains behind the EMP. *Now* I'd like to get a second shot at the NFIB."

The picture was passed from hand to hand along the table until it finally reached Jason. The picture was a black-and-white, eight-by-ten glossy photo of a stereotypical Russian. Oleg Kurgan. Jason burned the face into his memory.

"You have been sitting on this information," Davis said.

"Privileged information under order number—"

Davis cut Black off. "Jam that order. It won't do you any good where I could send you. Anything else?"

"No sir."

Davis stood up and sighed. "Gentlemen, the way I see it, the genie is out of the bottle. It's our job to put him back or kill him. How do we do that?

"For the record, no one agency will run this entire mission, not this time. I don't trust you! I expect that the President will approve the mission as I see it." Pointing at Boris, Davis said. "CIC, your job is to monitor the Russian launch. At the same time the Space Command will assault the Russian reflector, and the Doors will take out the EMP generator. The issue of what to do with Kurgan needs a closer look.

"Is there anyone here who sees fault in my reasoning? Not that I trust any of you."

Jason smiled when no one answered. Keeping a steady gaze on Boris, he felt the desire to put a knife into him, at the least to catch him in bed the same way Decker had caught him.

Davis sighed. "My God, how did this happen? And can we stop it?" Picking up his scrap of paper, he studied it for a moment. "I'm calling this mission Operation Lucifer Light. Start filling out your operation plans and submit them directly to me for funding. This meeting is over." Bewildered, he walked out of the room.

Jason walked toward the head of the stairs. He had a name: Oleg Kurgan. *Elevators. You'd think they'd put more elevators in this place.*

"You just wouldn't leave it alone, would you? You seem to be forever fucking up my plans."

Spinning on the balls of his feet, Jason automatically went into a defensive position, and found himself facing Boris and Decker.

Decker snickered at Jason's surprise. "What? You

think I'm going to take you down right here, alligator man? Here in the Pentagon?"

Jason kept up his guard, looking around for any escape route in case he had to make a hasty exit. "Leave what alone?"

"The whole fucking thing," Boris hissed. "Who are you? You're no one from nowhere, *trailer trash*. You think that Davis is The Man? You don't even know. You can't remove my safeguards. I don't have to share my information with Davis's oversight. And I won't! Space dominance is too big for the politicians, too big for civilian reconnaissance or commercial spy craft. And way too big for Twitch and the fucking *Air Farce*."

Boris was on the offensive. "Space warfare, asshole, that's what this is all about, not using space to support *ground* warfare. My job is to deliver Space Power, and my backers don't give a fuck how I do it. They're stronger than any group that's ever been, understand?

"You Doors aren't invulnerable. You can be gotten to. Chain has his weaknesses. You have no idea the trouble you're causing, and you don't know what you're getting into. The Doors can't hide you forever."

"Maybe not," Jason said. "But you remember what I told you back in the Vault, or this trailer trash is going to fuck up all you think *you* are."

Jason backed toward the stairs, then stopped. "You ain't no keeper of the Big Secret, or forbidden knowledge; you ain't so superbad. You're just a big asshole, that's all. You're such a creep you could've given Hitler mean lessons." Sniffing the air as if he smelled shit, he descended the stairs like a king, but he knew that his situation was just getting worse and worse. *Momma, you bitch, you cursed me.*

---

# CHAPTER 12

**0900 MONDAY / 18 OCTOBER 1999**
**DOOR HEADQUARTERS / FLORIDA**

J ASON'S VAN WOVE THROUGH THE MONDAY MORNING
traffic. Nothing seemed different or out of place
about the base, except for the long line of heavy-
equipment trailers loaded with road graders and
front-end loaders. But that wouldn't draw anyone's attention; there was *always* construction on military bases.
The van came to a stop in front of an unmarked building.
There was very little that gave away the fact that the
Doors were on full alert for a clandestine mission.

The room Jason stepped into was full of activity.
Numerous people concentrated on the large screens that
surrounded the walls or buried their face in computer
screens. The room was filled with laptop computers,
notebooks, printers, dry erase boards, and plenty of
paper.

Through an open door he could see a small army of
technicians and engineers stringing computer cables
and wires leading to everywhere. Tom had called him
over to see the Door nerve center of Operation Lucifer
Light.

Controlled bedlam was probably what Jason

would've called it. Someone in the room passed him a laptop computer, assuming he would know what to do with it. He got only as far as turning it on. Everyone was too absorbed in tasks to tell him that the computers, cell phones, faxes, and Internet were connected to XMAT, a multibillion-dollar secure communication system that accessed the most sophisticated intelligence computers and spy satellites in existence.

But the weak link was the NIMA supercomputer that processed and delivered overhead imagery. Some people looked at Siberian photos under equipment that looked like a microscope or some other magnifying instrument. With everyone thrown back into the Stone Age, old imagery tools reappeared from storage and were dusted off.

Jason pushed away the laptop, found a seat, and then quietly sat at the back of the room, mesmerized by all the computer action going on around him and listening to the intense conversations. His world involved muscle and hardware, guns and medicine, and death. Stepping into cyberspace and satellite telemetry was beyond his reasoning. He hated computers.

From an amateur viewpoint, he could only guess that the picture on the front screen was a view of Siberia as a spy satellite flew overhead. The front screen remained the same while the side screens changed every few seconds.

"Stay on your toes—we only got ten minutes of linger time," someone said. "Let's see what we can see."

"Look here, the high oblique. See those two lakes?" A cursor zeroed in, highlighted a section of the screen, then bracketed it. "Screen two. The vertical shot. Is that an air shaft?"

"Got to be. There are no vectors of wind around it. But is it an exhaust vent or intake?"

"Can we get a radiochemical analysis done on it?"

All heads turned. Jason saw only squiggly lines and colored blobs. Whatever they could see had taken them years of practice to discern.

"I can't rely on the flight path. Let's concentrate on the primary forward and aft shots."

"I still can't get a clear view of it. Fucking shit! When are they going to have the system all the way back on line?"

"Screen two. Look, it's two lakes, about thirty miles apart. I'm going wide-angle, and check out the temperatures. One is almost frozen over; the other reads thirty-eight degrees. Look, all other lakes are frozen for a thousand miles around. Explain that one."

"Geothermal?" someone asked.

"Thermal imagery says no. It's got to be natural gas at best. Do we have any satellite in the area that can get us a read on radioactivity, or get a spectral?"

"Steve, do you see all these little heat spikes? They aren't *on* the surface of the permafrost."

"You're right. Bingo! Any-money bet says that they're heat pipes that draw heat from the ground, the same kind we use on the Alaska Pipeline to keep the ground from thawing. But why? What's underneath?"

"Is that a road?" Highlighted, bracketed. "Screen three. Oblique and convergent shots."

Heads turned.

"Got to be. But what kind of vehicles do they use on permafrost?"

"They would have to be similar to the ones we used on the Alaska Pipeline."

Jason was getting dizzy. It was like watching an out-of-control tennis match.

"The screens are still too fuzzy. Bad reception. Want to change the channel?"

Jason jumped. "Tom! How do you guys just show up? I've been trying to learn how to do that since I met you guys."

Tom merely smiled. "I'm glad you made it." Everyone in the room quickly mobbed him and plugged into the open portals on his IBOT like piglets to a sow.

Chain turned into a machine, asking questions and giving orders. It sounded to Jason like they were speaking a foreign language, which they were.

Tom finally unplugged the leads and then spoke to his imagers. "No more! Let me take a break a moment while I talk to Alice here."

There was a sudden silence as many stole looks at Jason.

"Screen four. Let's try some more filters," someone said.

"The code name Alice is legendary around here," Tom said. "I've been using this team for a few years now. They just about found everything that Twitch is looking for. That guy over there is Steve Leath. He's a geodesist from NIMA. He's the one who correlated Rita's data and helped Twitch to find the location of the EMP generator."

"A geowhatist?"

Tom chuckled. "He measures shapes, curvatures, and dimensions of the earth. These people have spent years learning to see things on the ground that untrained eyes can't. Collectively they're called blobologists. I got a Siberian environmentalist putting together a report on the area the team's going into."

"Oh." Jason started laughing. "What's going on here? I thought you already knew the location."

Tom put his finger to his lips, then looked at his watch, then at Screen One. "I do, but from what I've been gathering the land might be radioactive." He swept his hand across the room. "Photogrammetry—that's what this room is all about. It's like constructing an octopus, but now we're getting all the help we want, thanks to Davis. We'll build the mission plans in the next room from the developed imagery right here. We are going to turn the impossible into just a difficult challenge.

"A lot of bright people are here—a senior sensor analyst from the CIA, an imagery specialist from the National Photographic Interpretation Center, a nuclear and particle physicist, a thermodynamicist, a geologist, and satellite scientists. Brains, you know? Twitch by-name-requested Rita Meine to be a part of this team. She should arrive here anytime.

"I'm bringing in a Russian photographic interpreter,

but I'm still waiting on a Siberian interpreter of that region. There's only a couple of them in Japan."

Peering closer at the main screen, Tom asked, "You know anything about Russian camouflage?"

"Not a damn thing."

"I do. They're a lot better at it than we are. They even have a name for it—*maskirovka*. Concealment has always been their forte. Finding the Zond generator by imagery and telemetry is hard, but nobody in the free world ferrets better than Twitch. He contracted a CIA SR-71 spy plane that carried a Hyperspectral Imaging Sensor and had it fly just off the coast of Siberia. The HIS can distinguish camouflaged and partially hidden objects on the ground. He found it! That's the area this group is working on: ground zero.

"We still have a ton of stuff to uncover before the Brothers go in. How deep it is. How big it is. *How* to blow it." Pride showed in his voice. "We hit a home run at the Veil Committee. Watch this."

Tom flipped open his laptop and his fingers flew over the keyboard. "I got the main screen."

The room silenced.

"Who's looking at that two-lake issue?"

"I am, sir," Steve answered.

"Good work. Now start looking for the ventilation shafts. They're the key to this thing. If there's ammonia traces from the heat pipes, then you nailed the location I'm looking for. When you find them all, get me data on what's coming out of the rest of the pipes. Look for radiation. Compare it to the rest of the region. See that depression? I'd bet that's a main air vent for their filtration system. Go back over it with narrow angular coverage and build your mosaic from that. Be ready to tell me more about everything on my next visit."

"But sir, we still can't get the definition we need," Steve lamented.

"I've got some people coming here tomorrow to try and correct the situation." Tom left the details hanging. "Also, run an image history of a thousand square miles since 1980 and deliver them to the ground analysis team. At least those photos will be diamond-sharp. The rest of you do the best you can with what we're getting until we have the better system up and running. Be happy knowing that you don't have to wait on NIMA's Central Imagery Office like the CIA, NSA, and even the CIC do to get their crappy imagery pictures.

"You're all doing great." Pointing at the main screen, he added, "There's something going on down there. I want facts, speculations, irrefutable conclusions, and wild-assed guesses. I want them now!" Tom slammed shut the lid of his computer and looked at Jason. "Do you mind accompanying me out to my van?"

Jason followed Tom out the door. "Nice effect, Tom, but how are you gonna make the details any sharper?"

Tom looked around, then spoke in a low tone as he rolled along the hallway. "I contacted the worst people possible, a civilian concern called Universal Images in Raleigh, North Carolina. They run their own satellite system. It cost the Doors a cool two million, but I've arranged overhead imagery time on one of their satellites that comes close enough for us to get a good look at the Zond installation. I just hope they don't catch on to why I'm using them, and that the other intell groups don't suddenly start doing the same thing and let our cat out of the bag."

When they were by the van, Tom spoke. "You've probably been wondering why I've been dragging you around to the bigwig meetings."

"Yeah, I've given it some thought."

"For my own reasons, and they're classified, or if you figure it out, I want you to know all I know on this project. On the President's authority, Davis reorganized the Veil Committee about an hour ago. He fired some high-powered people, so we can be sure to expect a lot of fallout over that. We got the green light and funding for our mission. Ben has been named the operations manager. I kept him in the dark to keep him from being compromised in any way by Boris and his web.

"The CIA assures Davis and the President that Boris

Yeltsin knows nothing about the EMP generator; he's too preoccupied with the war in Chechnya. But how dependable is the CIA's information? Especially now. They speculate that someone very close to Yeltsin is actually in control of the generator, one of his successors, Primakov or Putin possibly. They tell us that if we are successful in taking out the generator the Russians will have nothing to say about something that officially never existed.

"My liaison in the CIA also told me that they know something of Zond, but as usual they aren't handing out any hard facts. They're just one source I use."

"So where do the Doors stand?"

"In a better position than everyone else, which has the CIC on a rampage, since by design they should have been the ones to bring what you did to Davis's attention. All that we have uncovered is too classified for even the Presidential Daily Brief, or any of the other daily intelligence reports.

"Bruce Davis is going over the bridge to bring the President the bad news at the White House, but he's also presenting him the good news: a plan to take out the gun."

"How?"

"It's going on even as we speak. I want you to be part of the planning cell."

A cold arrow pierced Jason's brain. Like a sky diver who, frozen in the door, realizes that there's no turning back and suddenly makes his commitment and propels himself into the void, Jason spoke. "No. I want in on the ops."

Wide-eyed, Tom looked at him for a moment, then frowned. "No. I need you here."

"I asked what my position here was and you told me that I'd find out. Now I know. I have a reason to go on the Lucifer Light. Tom, you know me. You know what I can do. Now, I help you all I can before the mission goes, then go on the mission, or I will refuse my orders and go home."

"Jason, that move could ruin your career. You've reached your twenty years. You'd lose your retirement. Are you willing to walk out on your retirement and benefits?"

"I gave my word to a kid. Tom, I may not be the most daring guy in the world, but I gave him my word that I would honor his request if I could. This is the only way. I go on the mission or go home."

"Care to talk about it?"

"Can't. Classified, need-to-know." Jason grinned.

"Are you sure you're in shape for this? You *don't* need to go on this."

Unexpectedly, Tom seemed different. Usually he was a straight shooter. Now he was acting as if he was hiding something. "I didn't show up unprepared. Besides, I've got a promise to keep."

Tom pressed the lift lever and then got behind the wheel of his van. "Blackmail, Jason—you're using a kid against me. That's low," he said in an agitated voice. He started the van and drove away.


**1130**
**WAR ROOM / DOORS / FLORIDA**

Tom, Ben, and Twitch sat at the front of the room facing the insertion team. The doors were locked, the No Admittance. Classified Briefing in Progress sign was turned on, and the building was sealed.

From under his seat, Tom pulled out seven folders. "Come and get them, guys. They're your operations orders and log plans. Just twenty-two pages, but once you sign for them they'll be the most secret documents in the Doors' possession. They'll be with you day and night, or checked in to me. Do not discuss the material with anyone other than your teammates. You're authorized to use immediate and lethal force if anyone tries to take the folders from you."

Jason got in line, took his folders, and sat down to look it over. He was a little disappointed. They were copies of copies, and poor-quality.

"Okay, sign your name in the lower-right-hand corner of the page. See the number just below it? Sign just below it," Tom instructed. "Good boys. Now tear off the corner with your name on it and pass it to me."

After he got the scraps, he smiled. "You've just acknowledged that the ops plans are in your possession. I will be collecting them once they're filled out and you deploy."

"Why the scraps?" Pia asked.

"The paper's treated with its own DNA. If anything happens, your copy will only match these scraps. If there's no more questions, we'll start building this thing."

Pictures began appearing on a screen at the front of the room. Several angles of a low building on a flat white field were highlighted.

"For your logbooks, at 0515 hours the Doors received classified orders for Mission Identification HGT-DMLY9279, code named Lucifer Light. Gentlemen, once you get past all the general headings in your logs, you'll find your specific tasking. Right now to simplify, the Brothers of Death have been assigned to take out the Zond EMP generator, located one hundred miles inside northeastern Siberia.

"The secondary mission is a snatch and grab of Oleg Kurgan, to include interrogation and, if necessary, elimination or retrieval. That's it in a nutshell."

Jason shuddered. Kurgan was being handed to him on a platter.

"How do we attack an enemy we don't know?" asked Puma.

"How do we insert undetected one hundred miles into Siberia?" questioned Pia.

"Are you done asking questions you yourselves must answer? Because if you are, I'd like to continue," Tom chided. "The operation plan is yours. The mission specifics, measured response, and operations support have a blank check approved by Davis. Anything to get the mission done is yours."

"Can I get Jennifer Lopez?" asked Zorro.

"Not today," answered Cadallo. "The training mock-up will be finished today, so have your mission profile ready to roll and operational, like yesterday. Any problem with that?"

Everyone but Jason spoke at once, voicing perceived obstacles and advantages, until the magnitude of the objective stunned them all into silence.

Jason sat quietly thinking about Oleg Kurgan. The man he wanted to kill would be in his hands if they could figure out a way to get to him. His mind wandered, thinking of ways to take out the man, until he too became overwhelmed by the mission.

With all the high-zuit equipment and technology at their disposal, no one could even tell them what kind of toilets the people at Zond used, let alone perimeter security, weapons, or anything else. Satellites in space were only so good, and shit when blind.

A nuclear bomb hit on Zond was high-risk, the snatch and grab all but impossible. But these were the kinds of missions the Brotherhood specialized in.

Chain closed the meeting by agreeing to make it a two-part assignment. Kelly and Jason would plant the nuke and then blend into the snatch and grab.

Timing and flexibility were everything. Timing and flexibility would keep them alive. Now that they had objectives they could build the rest of the mission. They would practice, research, and rehearse until their actions became automatic. There was no room for egos. One mind. One team. They were a well-defined group with a mastery of their environment. This was how the Brotherhood of Death operated and stayed alive. Distractions were deadly. They would train for the mission first. Everything else came last.

## 1400
## WAR ROOM / DOORS / FLORIDA

While technical specialists and political strategists scrambled to assemble technical data and agenda, the seven men in the War Room prepared for the impossible. If anything went wrong, these were the men who would be left holding the bag on the Siberian tundra, denied by everyone.

This was their first nuts-and-bolts assignment meeting.

They studied amazingly detailed maps of the Siberian tundra, trying to figure out the quickest way in and, more important, how to get out. Plan after proposed plan was discussed, argued, and then scrapped. Tensions ran high. Without all the hard details, it was like trying to write in the dark. Tom's support team would be ready with all the facts and answers to questions, having used every available resource. The Brothers never showed up at payoff time without having done the preparation.

Lucas began. "We've been assigned to take out the EMP and do a snatch and grab of Oleg Kurgan, both targets at the hidden Zond base on the Siberian tundra in Russia. If Kurgan becomes a liability, we do him. Nobody sees us arrive. Nobody sees us leave."

Jason wanted to shit his pants. He couldn't believe how calmly everyone was taking it, like it was no big deal.

Julio tapped his lips, "So how do you infiltrate into Siberia in the middle of fall? Has it ever been done? This is fucked-up."

"So? We'll unfuck it when we get there. We've been on hundred-mile marches a shitload of times. This march will just be a little colder and faster, that's all," assured Z-Man.

Lucas sniffed, looked around the room, and then stood up. "We're on the clock. Let's get to work."

Using reams of maps, photos, and videos of Siberia, the team went at it for three hours before settling on a preliminary plan.

The fundamental strategy they finally concluded could work was for the mission-tasking to be based on their backing up the sapper team, which would plant a thermonuclear satchel bomb on, or very close to, the reactor. Kurgan's snatch would be secondary.

For practical purposes everyone agreed that part one of the plan should begin as a two-man operation. Kelly would be the sapper and Jason would be the backup. For the secondary mission, the rest of the team would act as support or be the diversion unit until the primary objective was met.

Tom's photogrammers estimated the depth of the EMP's exhaust vent at between one and two thousand feet.

Kelly didn't even bat an eye when he learned the news.

"How do you climb down a shaft like that?" asked Jason.

"You'll see." Kelly rubbed his hands together with glee.

*And how do we get out?*

"So much for simple strategy," Lucas said. "Now for tactics and assignments."

"Since I'm the sapper," said Kelly, "I have an insertion idea that I've been working on. And it's a Mike Dennis design."

"Of course," everyone said in unison.

Looking at Jason, Kelly said, "And if you don't want to go, I'll understand."

"Okay. Go," said Lucas.

"I have to get there first, and I don't have time to lug the nuke all the way in."

"Yeah, that could be a problem. There might be a good chance that they have some sort of device that could alert on the radioactivity in the bomb before we even got close enough to use it—*we* have units that can detect it. Kelly, how would you beat that?" Z-Man asked.

"I'm gonna free-fall with the bomb from a hundred and twenty thousand feet. The shaft itself will be my drop zone."

The room burst into laughter. A High Altitude Low Opening (HALO) jump from that height had never been done. It was unthinkable.

Everyone in the room laughed but Jason, who watched the glimmer in Kelly's eyes.

The room settled down.

"He's not kidding," Jason said.

Now everyone was stone silent.

"Yeah?" said Lucas as he crossed his arms.

"It's already been done, a long time ago." Getting up from his chair, Kelly passed out some photocopies of a magazine article. "Sorry if I'm so low-tech, but a couple of years ago I read this *Airman Magazine* article and took it to Mike. It's about Joe Kittenger Junior, a guy who jumped in a space suit from over a hundred thousand feet. It's a good article. So I talked to Twitch, and then got Mike and the DFS to make me something that we call an SD, for Space Diver."

"Wait," interrupted Lucas. "You already have one?"

"He made me four. I got two left."

"What happened to the other two?"

"I used them."

Lucas was surprised. "What? How come I didn't know?"

Kelly started laughing, then the whole room laughed.

"Twitch told Mike 'n' me to keep our mouths closed. He outranks everybody. Hey, just wait," Kelly said, "even Tom doesn't know about it. So Mike and me took the Space Diver out to our test-jump place in Arizona. It worked. He made three more and I got two left. They're a onetime-use unit."

"I don't understand. How do they work?" questioned Lucas.

"Now that would take too long to explain. The drop is as undetectable as it gets. Nobody can see it. Nobody. Not radar or anything else."

"Okay, but answer me this: How are you dropped?"

"From a modified SR-71 spy plane. It can drop specialized payloads like mine at up to one hundred and twenty thousand feet moving at Mach Three."

"Mach Three." Jason whistled. "It'll rip us apart!"

"Not really. The air is so thin up there that we won't even feel it."

"You little fuck," said Lucas. "I can't believe you've actually done it. Why didn't you tell me?"

"You think *I'd* cross Twitch?"

"Yeah, you're right. Go ahead."

"Wait," interrupted Rusty. "There's only three Blackbirds still flying, and NASA has all three. A certain Air Force general had a real bad grudge against the SR-71 because they wouldn't let him in the program, so he chopped up the engines. He took the planes and stuck their carcasses on top of poles in front of air museums around the country. Makes you wonder what the replacement is."

"Or so you think. The NSA has at least one active Blackbird that I know of. Oh well, the cat's out of the bag. See, this little dude can have his secrets too." Kelly chuckled for a few moments. "So the moment we brought in the SR-71 the NSA took it over and dropped a classified curtain on it. They told me I couldn't do any more jumps except under their authority; you know the drill. So, is the drop on?"

"Man, Froto, you never fail to astound me. This is a little wild, even for us. I don't have a problem with it as long as the NSA stays out of the rest of our business, but I'm sure that Twitch will cover that square." Lucas was getting back to being Lucas. "Anyone?"

"Maybe we should jump too," Rusty said.

Kelly raised his finger. "Time. The SDs aren't completely tooled yet. They're prototypes. Each one took months to make—you can't do a rush job on these things. A malfunctioning SD at one hundred and twenty thousand feet is instantly fatal. Lose pressure and without a pressure suit your blood would boil in seconds."

Rusty raised his eyebrows. "I take back my comment."

"You said *two* left," said Jason. "You and me?"

"They were both made for me, so it'll be a tight fit for you, but I'm sure it will hold you."

Lucas stood and stretched his frame. "I will attach a copy of questions we want answered and use it to build our ops plan. As of right now we are in training until we get our tasking order."

Groans filled the room. They all knew how hard a taskmaster Lucas could be when training for a mission.

"Yeah." Julio smirked. "By the time we're ready to insert, 'Zond in Siberia' is going to be a vacation spot for us."

"We'll do the mission as fragged," said Lucas. "Now, last order of business—who wants out?" His eyes settled on Jason. "This is your chance."

Jason got pissed. "Look, I said I want in on this ops! Why do I get the perception that I should stay out of it? Does anyone here doubt my ability to do this job?"

An uncomfortable silence followed, until Rusty spoke. "Jason, even though you're counted one of us, you might not understand the politics behind this. Lucas is just trying to be nice."

"Something he's not good at," offered Pia.

Kelly zeroed in on Lucas. "I don't know about the rest of you, but I *want* my partner with me."

"All right. When I leave this room I'm going to submit the team list to General Cadallo to get our orders cut," Lucas said. "And, unless you die in training, you're mine. So, I'm saying for the record, anyone who wants out, speak now."

Silence.

"This is our ops. Go do all that admin stuff to get it out of the way. Tom says to get your mobility folders and shot records up to date by tomorrow. No exceptions."

Jason folded his arms across his chest. He watched as Lucas leaned over a table and wrote down names on a piece of paper. Then he stood up and left the room. A space dive into enemy territory to set off a nuclear charge? *Shit, I've done stupid things before, but this takes the cake!*

# CHAPTER 13

TO JASON IT LOOKED LIKE A MINIATURE VERSION OF the High Bay Launch Control Center at Cape Canaveral. Everything in the room would be moved to a forward location when the mission was prosecuted. Jason guessed that he was looking at at least forty thousand pounds' worth of electronic equipment. Tom said that his support team could break it all down, including antennas, and have it loaded into Individual Storage Units (ISU), ready to deploy, in less than three hours.

Several people stood around a huge screen wearing 3-D glasses. He stepped closer and saw the blurry Siberian tundra landscape. Picking up a set of glasses from out of a box and putting them on, his mouth fell open when he looked at the screen. It was almost as if he could reach out and touch the land.

Someone punched him on his left shoulder. "Oww!" His arm was still sore from all the shots he'd taken at the shot clinic that morning. One had left an especially nasty welt.

"Hello, Alice. I thought you were so tough."

"Oh hi, Rita. Not tough enough, I guess." He rubbed

his shoulder. "How's it goin'? They told me you were here. Hey, what fuck ratted out my code name?" Jason had his ideas.

"Oh, I have my secrets too."

"You having fun?"

"Jason, I can't tell you how much I've dreamed of being involved in something like this. I even have a certain status."

"How so?"

Rita beamed. "I know *you*, Alice, and I'm a by name request too. Are the rumors true?"

"What rumors?"

"That you are one of the greatest spies in the world."

Jason erupted in laughter. He made a mental note to tell Gitthens to tone it down a little. "No, it's not true. It's just that everyone else is so bad. Enjoy all this while you can. Hey, what's this 3-D thing? Man, it's amazing!"

"Isn't it? This is for your team to study the land that you'll be working in. It's an Onyx2 VPW on HDTV."

"A what?"

Rita chuckled as she typed on a keyboard. "Visual Presentation Workstation on High Definition Television. A U-2 took spectral images and recon photos of the area five hours ago. We've fed the SR-71 data into a supercomputer. Now look at the terrain through 3-D."

Jason looked back at the screen, awed at the clarity and detail he saw there.

"Do you want me to tell you what we found?"

Jason nodded.

"It was the cleanest area around for thousands of miles."

"Yeah?"

"Radiation."

Jason waved his hand over his head. "You've already lost me."

"There's more secret facilities in Siberia than the one we're after. After the start of the Cold War, Stalin created them to make the nuclear and radioactive materials that went into his bombs. There is no such thing as environmental protection in Siberia. For over fifty years nuclear waste has poisoned their lakes and rivers." Rita leaned back and swept her hand over the screen. "So what we did was eliminate the known from the unknown and calculate Twitch's data. The result was this location."

Her enthusiasm drifted into technical terms.

Most of what Rita spoke about was over his head— hyper- and multispectral images and panchromatic views. Tom's imaging team had split out thousands of ground cubes and then sliced them like bread. Each slice showed the ground to about two hundred feet deep. The Zond stronghold was much deeper than that, but they'd reconned enough data to construct the entrance and build a scale model mock-up.

Comparative measurements of the Zond area had made many things obvious. Hidden roads were detected. Tire tracks became visible in gravel. With the commercial imagery, the resolution was so good that the image specialists could tell if a truck had passed and if it had come back, even where it had turned.

"There's two roads that lead to...*here*." Rita electronically highlighted the 3-D computer image. "They're winter roads that stay frozen even in the summer." She pointed to one of the maps on the wall. The map was dated and changed every thirteen hours to keep up with every satellite pass. "One leads to the abandoned diamond mine and the other one goes north, but to where? We're still trying to see if there are train tracks or anything else that lead in from the north and go to the landfill also. We're using current imagery and going as far back as ten years ago. We measured the activity and position of the topographic changes using Ground Penetrating Radar. Estimating how much heat the heat pipes radiate to keep the ground frozen, plus the volume of airflow in the air vents, we think at least five thousand people could be living underground there, maybe more.

"Mister Chain brought in a company that will use this system and Ground Penetrating Radar to model an underground city blueprint.

"And see these thermal images of the area? Look at how the heat readings climb and dip. Comparing them to the chirps, they peak exactly when the EMPs fired."

Jason removed his glasses and walked around the room, amazed at all the electronic wizardry. Millions of dollars were going into learning all there was to know about a speck of land thousands of miles away from where he stood, all to put him there with a nuclear bomb. It was crazy!

High tech, high zuit, and high resolution, all for two sappers with an SADM. Jason figured that millions more would be spent on "high" things before he found himself at the bottom of a thousand-foot radioactive hole.

**0615 WEDNESDAY / 20 OCTOBER 1999
DOOR EXERCISE FIELD / FLORIDA**

Jason ran wind sprints along the river. Two minutes fast as he could go, then stop and walk normally for a minute, then run, then walk, then run, again and again. His mind was way ahead of his body. How to get one on one with Kurgan?

"Jason, you look like a demon's on your tail! Isn't Lucas running you enough?"

Huffing, Jason trotted over to Tom's van and bent over, putting his hands on his knees. "Yeah? What's up?"

"Listen, another change. We've got to get this thing operational sooner than we anticipated."

"Shit," he huffed.

"Get in."

**0700
WAR ROOM / DOORS / FLORIDA**

"Listen up. I got this brief together as soon as I got the news a couple hours ago," Twitch said. "On September twentieth of this year the CIC attempted the launch of an electromagnetic pulse reflector. Frank McCone is the project manager. The Titan rocket, 20B, was destroyed and the payload has been determined to have been stolen by a Russian submarine that was in the area at the time of the explosion."

Tom took over. "In virtually all nuclear war games, the attack always begins with an EMP laydown by a one-megaton nuclear bomb burst at five thousand feet to knock out command and control systems.

"Information warfare conducted by an electro-magnetic-pulsed attack has always been a standard tactic in war gaming. Davis cleared me to reveal that we do have an operational EMP bomb, but not to the scope or scale of the attack on exercise Wizard Warrior. We're in-fantile by comparison." He sighed. "Currently, the fifteen billion dollars we spend in the shielding of high-value military electronic material is based upon enemy nuclear weapons detonated three hundred and fifty miles above the United States. Under the guidelines we were given, a low-end EMP shielding was the solution."

Twitch spoke. "Irrevocable evidence leads to the conclusion that the directed energy weapon we are deal-ing with can overpower all our shielding. At present we have nothing in place to protect ourselves against this beam. Nothing. We're running our labs on a twenty-four-hour schedule trying to assess the damage caused by the recent concentrated EMP attacks on us." Twitch stopped for a moment to gather his thoughts. "Our nuclear gamers have operated under the assumption that the first attack would be a nuclear airburst. This EMP weapon put us all back at the drawing board."

"Hey, this is all nice and good for the bench sitters, Twitch. What's it got to do with us?" Julio asked.

"I'll tell you," Twitch answered. "A short-notice launch schedule has been made for the Plestesk Cosmodrome in Russia. It will lift off on November third. The rocket itself is capable of launching a twenty-thousand-pound payload. Enough evidence exists that they have reprogrammed, and are launching the Godspeed."

The room erupted in pandemonium.

Twitch silenced the room. "Gentlemen, the way I see it, our two objectives must be met. We can't stop the launch, but if we can destroy the EMP generator it would make the stolen reflector useless. For the record, our act, by definition, is an act of war. Is there anyone here who has reservations about the course of action we're taking?"

Silence.

"Then we speed up our mission. This thing is driven by the Russian launch date. We're being tasked to make the hit on the launch date sooner than expected. Can we do it?"

"Yes sir." Lucas spoke for the team.

They were ready when any mission showed up. Preparation was the key, but now they had to pick up their game.

## 1435 THURSDAY / 21 OCTOBER 1999
## DOOR TRAINING FIELD / FLORIDA

Having tried, then abandoned the cumbersome and expensive Land Warrior system as impractical for clandestine warriors, they turned to Mike Dennis and pleaded for advanced battle gear that was light, strong, and effective.

Dennis outfitted the team with a revolutionary customized integrated battle uniform made for the freezing temperatures of the Siberian tundra.

The first layer of protection was called a Zeta suit. It was made from spun Kevlar, conforfoam, and a cotton/wool outer shell. Impregnated into the suit was a layer of Vivarex. The Vivarex, when ruptured by a high impact, acted as a coagulant, stopping any bleeding that might have occurred. The suit, while keeping the wearer warm, diffused heat and reduced infrared signature to almost nothing. It also acted as a nuclear radiation barrier.

But it was Dennis's headgear, custom-molded for each man, that was years ahead of the standard soldier's helmet. He showed up one morning and pulled out a shiny steel helmet that looked to be of alien design.

"What planet did you get that from?" Julio asked.

"This one, in the fifteenth century, from Germany. It's called a close helmet."

The helmet was passed around.

As he held the helmet, the batlike mask seemed to stare at Jason. "It's heavy. We're supposed to go to battle in this? It must weigh at least ten pounds."

"No. This."

A flat black helmet appeared in his hands.

"I based this one on the steel one." Mike went on to describe the almost unbelievable innovations it possessed. Three head-mounted tubes had night vision and thermal infrared imaging. They overlapped and were projected on the shield visor, giving 180-degree color-enhanced vision in the dark that could see a temperature difference of two hundredths of a degree. The system could see the heat left behind by hand- and footprints. A bullet-resistant polymer visor offered a heads-up targeting display that was slued to the forward sights of their weapons.

Powerful silent microblowers and filters kept the helmet slightly overpressured to keep out chemical agents. An echolocation device was woven over the visor into the bat like a face mask.

"Don't any of you try putting it on. It can do bad things if it doesn't know you—like seal around your neck and suffocate you," Mike said. "It belongs to Kelly. They're custom-fit. I'll show you how they work as we go along. You're going to love 'em."

Dennis passed around the revolutionary helmet.

"Goddamn, it's light. Strong?" Rusty asked.

Mike nodded. "You'll see."

Lightweight, molded, and layered with Kevlar and patented conforfoam, it could decrease a 300g impact to no more than 50. The clear screen built into the helmet gave the wearer heads-up information and targeting possibilities with or without the night vision visor.

For weapons they decided on the Heckler Koch MP5SD, sound-suppressed, fully automatic rifle, and the Springfield Ultra Compact 1911-A1 pistol with silencer. The two weapons fired the same forty-caliber bullets.

The rifle and pistol sights were fitted with magnetic trackers that allowed the bore sights to be displayed on the face screen so that targeting could be accurately achieved and fired from any position—prone, hip, around corners, or on the run. Move the dot on the visor over the target, and pull the trigger. It made unerringly deadly shots every time.

A flat, pressure-sensitive microphone placed in the helmet so it rested on the forehead was so sensitive that wearers could communicate with just whispers, eliminating the need for a boom microphone. Small horns took the place of earphones. The horns were attached to an amplified hearing unit that gave wearers the ability to "see" an ultrasonic picture.

Jason studied the helmet. He could see similarities to the fifteenth-century steel helmet, but this one was ultralight. To him the head covering looked like something out of a Japanese space cartoon. The black protective covering felt almost pliable.

Their body armor was made from the same ultralightweight material and had a Class Three body protection rating. Velcroed to their arms, legs, and torso, and fitted over layers Gore-Tex, they could move in relative comfort in minus-ninety-degree weather.

The boots were the most important item and were left to each man's particular desires. They had to last over two hundred miles in the rigors of a freezing land.

Though the battle dress uniform they wore was revolutionary, the material contained in their small fanny pack was the most astounding thing of all.

At a moment's notice they could pull a cord on the pack and just disappear. Contained in the pack was a material that ran on two double-A batteries. Energized with charge-coupled cenospheres in the fiber-optically woven material, it had the ability to absorb any color it was near and, like a chameleon, change color. It was also able to absorb infrared and thermal imagery, making it almost invisible to night vision and radar detectors.

Outfitted in their stealth gear, the Brotherhood of Death became a whisper in the dark.

Enhancing their navigational and scouting abilities was the Dragon Eye. It was a portable unmanned air vehicle (UAV). A small battery-operated remote-controlled plane weighing just a few pounds would almost noiselessly fly ahead of the ground team's route. It was capable of taking off and landing by itself.

Equipped with a daytime camera, infrared camera, and a low-light camera, the UAV would relay images to the team as it scouted the waypoints for any intruders or ambushes.

---

# CHAPTER 14

**0815 FRIDAY / 22 OCTOBER 1999**
**ZOND MOCK-UP / DOORS / FLORIDA**

**D**UST FILLED THE AIR AS HUGE EARTH-MOVING MA-
chines dug deep into the earth and filled up an endless procession of dump trucks. Road graders
and tractors crisscrossed the training field, scraping the
ground to exact specifications. At the same time the director of exhibits from the Air Force Museum at Wright-
Patterson in Ohio directed his artisans from a central
tower, creating a close approximation of the Zond objective. Of course, he and the workers were just following a
blueprint, with no real idea what they were making. They
liked their jobs, and were well paid for their labor, especially considering the huge bonus check they'd get if they
completed the work ahead of time. It wasn't part of their
job to ask questions.

Seven men sat on field chairs facing the training field.

"Gentlemen," Cadallo said as he paced in front of the
raiding team, "we have no time to waste. Once this set is
built, you will have ten hours to familiarize yourself with
the grounds here and then devise your strategy and tactics.
Today we will be bringing in Special Forces units, contract
security teams, and anyone else who can provide the

possible security measures that Zond may use. These units know nothing of your mission, so there will be no discussion of specifics with whomever you go against. They're there just so we can iron out tactics that worked for us, or didn't. Playing dirty counts on *both* sides.

"As in incentive for a good defense, there's a three-hundred-dollar bounty on each of you 'dead,' five hundred and a three-day pass if they bring you in alive. Instead of our usual laser tag gear, we're going with something new. We're going with real guns and gunpowder." Lightning-quick, Cadallo unholstered his pistol and fired, point blank, at Pia's chest. Pia flew over his chair and landed flat on his back.

The team scattered as Cadallo emptied his weapon at anyone else in his sights until his clip was empty. "At ease! Get your asses back here," he commanded, and waited for everyone to reassemble as he stood in the gun smoke. Pointing at Pia, Cadallo sneered. "*That* was a kill. Pia knows it, I know it, and so does any-fucking-one else with eyes. If you get shot in a vital area, just stop what you're doing and go back to the neutral area. If you don't wear your armor these little doozies can really fuck...you...up. Z-Man."

"Sir?"

"Come here."

Z-Man got out of his chair and walked toward Cadallo. He suddenly shuddered and fell.

Cadallo walked over to Z-Man and stood above him. He kicked away some dirt beneath the unconscious man, revealing a metal pad. "This field will also have interactive traps and things that can shock you and disable you for thirty seconds or so." He waited until Z-Man gained consciousness, and then reached down and pulled him to his feet. "You okay?"

"Yeah, but could someone pick up my dick? I think it's still in the dirt."

Cadallo released Z-Man and continued speaking. "The effects will be completely gone after two minutes. There will also be disabling gases and other nasty tricks that will give away your position. But, you will get a few tricks of your own to use.

"I caution you: You can get badly hurt here. At no time will you remove your headgear or body armor while the game is on." He put his hands on his hips. "Now you got the field, but you also have to have your first drafts of plans, scenarios—resupply, escape and evasion, all that shit—on your folders by the end of today.

"Every Door asset is at your service. Mike Dennis is on his way here to listen to your concerns, outfit you as needed, and check ops gear."

Pia got slowly to his feet. His chest was covered with blue paint. "Fuck! That hurt," he moaned.

"Zeta bullets. They have about the same impact of a rubber bullet." Cadallo tossed a handful of the bullets to the team to inspect. "Talc embedded with iron ferrous fibers. Superheated by the gunpowder, the bullet shell remains resilient, but the inside of the cone turns into liquid paint, like a paint ball.

"The teams you'll be going against are practicing Russian Special Forces defensive perimeter measures. The first team you go against will be in place and ready tomorrow. So you better be ready to go too." Cadallo strolled away from the field as they surrounded Pia.

Z-Man fingered Pia's chest, then looked at the paint. "Man, this is as close to being a blueblood as you'll ever get. Nice demo. Does it hurt?"

Pia narrowed his eyes. "Not as bad as how you're gonna feel after I kick your ass."

Lucas smiled. "I think we're all going to be seeing a lot more blueblood if we don't stay focused. Zorro, start building us an inventory based on all the shit we've covered. The rest of you start figuring out just how the fuck we're going to stay undetected one hundred miles inside of Siberia."

The logistics of the mission would come later; the tactics came first. How were you supposed to hit a command center and snatch one man when a nuclear bomb was set to go off?

The Zond operations center was as flat as the landscape. Using Ground Penetrating Radar, Doors Imagery was able to build four lower levels of the Zond command center to accurate dimensions. The ground floor contained the control center and was the target objective of the ground team—providing that Oleg Kurgan would be there during the Russian rocket launch.

*He'll be there,* Jason willed. He had to be.

## 1245

Kelly told Jason to meet him at the insertion point. A huge tower stood close to the Zond mock-up. It had been constructed almost overnight. Inside was a steel tower about one hundred feet high, with big fans attached to it. Hanging at the bottom of the tower was a parachute harness connected to several cables. On closer inspection Jason could see that it was Strato Cloud Delta rig, a sophisticated unit. But the chute was missing.

"Ready to jump, Jason?" Kelly called from the top of the tower. "Come on up."

He climbed a ladder until he was on a platform next to Kelly, and then was unsure of what he was looking at. It looked like a simple line stretched around a few pulleys and double-wrapped around a pole. Connected at the end of the line was a parachute rig, minus the parachute. "What is this thing?"

"It's a Systems Technology parachute flight simulator, virtual reality stuff. A place called On the Edge in Florida designed me this free-fall system. We 'jump,' then move out to the mock-up."

"How's it work?"

"Suit up—you're about to find out. Hey, C, help me out," Kelly cried out.

A young man stepped out from behind a bank of computers on the far side of the platform. C, as Kelly called him, was the programmer for the simulator.

The rig fit well, and Jason stood placidly by while C

slipped on virtual reality lenses and a Gentex lightweight parachutist helmet. C asked Jason's weight and then walked to his computer.

"Now what?"

"You're about to see," Kelly intoned. "Look over the edge."

The VR lenses came on, and Jason could see the ground.

"See it?" Kelly asked.

"Yeah."

"It's our drop zone in Siberia. The image is taken from a satellite, then fed into the computer. See the shaft?"

A spot on the ground flashed. Jason had to admit that the picture appeared real. Looking around, he could see the horizon and the sky. So far so good.

"Now what?"

"Jump."

"What? You're nuts!"

"No I'm not, and we can't go any farther until you get this unit wired."

"So this is a leap-of-faith kinda thing?"

Kelly put his hand on Jason's shoulder. "I've done it lots of times already. It's safe, pretty much. Ready? I find it easier if I get back a little and take a running jump."

Jason shook his head and cringed for a few moments. Then, backing up a few feet, he took a deep breath. "Oh shit," he said, and flew over the edge.

Falling, he could hear the wind rushing past his ears and feel the air from huge fans blasting his body. The Earth got bigger as the altimeter ticked off the height.

"Pull!" yelled Kelly.

Jason pulled the ripcord and felt a shock as the chute opened. Looking up, he saw that he was under a virtual full canopy. Reaching his arms overhead, he grabbed the riser extensions and maneuvered toward the landing zone. "Man, this is great!"

"Too easy, buddy! Let's make it more challenging," Kelly yelled down. "C, give him fifty knots at altitude and twenty on the ground."

Jason had to *work* to stay on track. It quickly became obvious that making the landing zone wasn't going to happen. Just trying to make a smooth touchdown occupied all his attention.

"Twenty feet. Flare," advised Kelly.

Jason pulled as hard as he could on the risers to flare the chute, but was out of control. He slammed down hard on the crash mat and began to drag in the wind. Rolling to his back, he pulled parachute releases and lay flat on his back. He pulled away the helmet and VR lenses.

"Damn!" was all Jason could say.

"Damn right!" cried Kelly. "Works good, real good. By the time we get into Siberia it'll be like nuthin'."

Jason had to agree. It was as close to a real jump as it could get.

"Wanna do it again?"

"Yeah, man, but this time let's cool it on the winds a bit."

**1915 SATURDAY / 23 OCTOBER 1999**
**DOOR VIP QUARTERS / FLORIDA**

It was just a few hours until the first insertion rehearsal. Gitthens patiently waited outside in the van. Jason paced the bedroom. Uncontrollable thoughts and feelings poked and stabbed at him. *There I was, about to figure out what to do with the rest of my life. Find me a woman. Fall in love. Get married. Have a bunch of kids. And, and, let the rest of the fucking world go by and live the rest of my life happy for once, like Toby.*

Something began to gnaw at him, again, something that had bothered him since he'd landed at the Doors: Everyone seemed cavalier about a mission that any sane PJ team would've analyzed and rejected as suicide.

He was involved in probably the blackest operation ever designed. The Brotherhood knew, but didn't care, or wouldn't admit to the dangers. Maybe that was why Lucas was so reluctant to have him be part of the team.

Suddenly he knew that the nightmare he was having was real, and only getting worse. "How can I get on with any life if I don't even know what I really want, or where I'm going?" Was he there for the mission, the vendetta, or both? His life always seemed to be racing ahead but on hold for the things that mattered most.

Pulling his coin from his pocket, he studied it for a few moments and then hurled it across the room. It struck the wall with a resounding thud. Jason shook his head. *Fuck me.* He felt a chill as a thought struck him. *I'm going a long way just to kill a man. A man I don't even know. Why? Because he killed Toby, that's why.*

And who could tell him best how to murder a stranger? There was only one man to talk to.

## 2030

Room 666. *It figures.* Peering closer, Jason saw that someone had added an extra vinyl 6 to the room number. Jason knocked on the door and waited.

The door opened. Lucas stood in the doorway in a hooded black robe. A scythe would have completed the picture.

Jason pointed at the number on the door.

Quickly rubbing the sleep from his face, Lucas smiled. "My boys can be clowns. With all the misdeeds I've done they think there should be signs around me that say I'm going straight to hell, with no appeals. I was sleeping pretty good, and we're going to be very busy in a couple hours. Can this wait?"

"I don't think so."

"Well then, come on into hell's waiting room."

It didn't look like anything but standard enlisted quarters. Jason lived palatially by comparison. No books, magazines, computer, or anything that said that any person occupied the room. Lucas's clothes and toiletries were stowed in a green bag. Jason guessed that Lucas could grab his bag and walk out of the room at a moment's notice, and leave no trace that he had ever been there.

"Sit down. What's on your mind?"

Jason took a few moments to gather himself. "I'm on this mission for a reason."

"Okay."

"Did you ever know my friend Toby Wiler?"

"No."

"I loved him like a brother."

Jason watched Lucas's cold eyes flicker for a moment, then said, "Well, I gave my word to his family about something I would do if I were given the chance. I might have given my word in anger, but I gave it. See? It's a vendetta."

"A vendetta?" Lucas smiled. "Isn't that a little archaic?"

"Look, so I screwed up again. I gave my word."

Lucas began to laugh. "Ah, Jason. I know you, and you did screw up. Who's the vendetta on?"

"Oleg Kurgan."

Lucas stopped laughing. "*Oleg Kurgan?* Be serious. That could cause . . . *problems.*"

"I *am* serious."

Lucas's face suddenly became hard, unreadable, and cold. "You know the orders: You and Kelly set the bomb, and then we do the snatch and grab. Once Kurgan is in our possession we keep him alive until we flush his brain. We transmit what we get out of him, and then we whack him if he don't behave. Hey, maybe you want to be the one to waste him."

Jason slowly nodded.

"Execution—you think so? Jason, in this business you got two things going against you: honor and pride. The Brotherhood delivers death, no more. You don't know it, but I've followed your career for a long time. You would've gone farther here, but being a PJ and saving lives is more important to you, and now look where it's gotten you: an execution. Look. We have to deal with your vendetta before you leave this room.

"You want to kill him? Jason, I know you—you would never purposely go out of your way to kill someone. Is it so personal that Kurgan ceases to become merely a target?"

"What can I tell you? I don't know the word that describes it."

"*Giri.*"

"What?"

"The word that describes it. It's a Japanese thing that's usually connected with vendettas, and you're just the kind of guy to carry it out—full of 'honor' and 'pride.' So I got to tell you something you don't know about this mission."

"So?"

Lucas clasped his hands together. "The Lucifer Light orders are our death warrant."

Did he hear that right? "I don't understand."

"Let me ask you something. Haven't you figured out that this mission is a rubout?"

"A rubout? Whaddaya mean?" A bad feeling clutched at his gut.

"There's other politically correct words for it. But I call it what it is. Chum, this is *worse* than a suicide mission. Once you blow the reactor and we pump Kurgan, everyone connected with the operational mission disappears. It's the only way to make sure that a mission like this stays buried. I tried to let you bow out gracefully, but you wouldn't listen to what I was trying to get across."

Jason suddenly felt a cold sweat. "How do you know all this?"

"I've rubbed out operators before in similar circumstances," Lucas stated simply. "I've got inside information that no one knows about. No one." A small laugh escaped him. "As it stands, you're the only one I can tell this to."

"Come on, man, who's going to take out the Brotherhood?"

"Maybe one of our own."

"What?! Man, why are you telling me this?"

"Because I know you're not the traitor."

"Why?"

"Because you're a primary target. If you make it back, then someone will be waiting to take you out. See, there ain't no laws in this game, not really, not for the players, just agreements and understandings. Of course there are *dis*agreements and *mis*understandings."

The face of Michael Decker flashed in Jason's mind.

"If we can get the information out of Kurgan before we extract, then both you and Kurgan will be liabilities. We could get abandoned in Siberia and freeze or starve to death, or maybe the guys who come to extract us waste us, or—my bet—one of our own takes us all out. Then there's the possibility that maybe the nuke is remote-controlled and will blow early. The possibilities are endless, but to think that one of my team might be the hit man . . . well, that's pretty ironic."

"Are Tom and Ben in on it?"

"That's a great question. If either one is in on it—or Twitch, or any other fucking principal—I wouldn't know how to tell. Would you? Shit, we took on this mission like good Boy Scouts and then someone turned the tables on us. Haven't you noticed that all of the team is single, with no family, wives, or girlfriends?"

"They are?"

"That's right. That's one reason why you were so desirable for the mission. You die and no one knows, or cares. We're expendable, *especially* you. A rubout decision for the team has already been sanctioned."

"Come on, man, this has got to be a joke."

"No joke. Look, we're the bottom feeders, small fish. Those fucks in the suits meet at real nice places to make the big decisions, sign the papers, and then put us out there to do their dirty deeds. Now we're going to do the *big* dirty deed, the biggest ever. After we do it, if we're successful, we die, the papers disappear, and then any connection between them and us are gone. Easy. It always goes like that, but not this time.

"This time there can't be *any* connection to a nuclear weapon blast and the suits. None. Shit, man, we haven't used a nuke against anyone since World War Two. No. It's too hot an issue. Some suit decided that anyone this closely connected to the mission has got to go, even heroes like you. No smell left. Fucked-up, huh?"

Suddenly it became clear to Jason why Lucas had offered him an out and why Tom wanted him to know so much about the operation. But were they helping him out or setting him up? A grunt like him sitting on a shitload of top-secret information made him a most delectable target for a lot of people. One thing was for sure: There was no one to go to for protection, because it would tip off everyone else.

Jason's head spun. Suddenly there were bogeymen everywhere he turned—spy versus spy. *Damn!*

His left hand slowly slid to the ring on his right hand. A target had been put on him. A chill shot through him when he realized that being at the Doors, a fatal "accident" could happen to him with no one being the wiser. "Lucas, you aren't going along with the deal, are you?"

Lucas's smile almost scared Jason silly. "No. Ol' Rabid hasn't stayed alive this long by being stupid. I have my own plans, and Kurgan's the key. If we live through the infiltration and make it to the extraction point, then Kurgan's our passport home. By the time we have him word will get to the right people and we'll be his escorts home. So I hope you see why I need him alive while we're in Siberia."

"I come here to tell you that I want to kill a man, and you tell me all this. What the fuck?"

"Now you know what the rest of the team doesn't know. You keep this to yourself. You know what they say: 'If I tell you, I got to kill you.'"

"Yeah. I know." Jason felt like bolting for the door.

"It applies to you and me, for real. Your vendetta will have to wait. I'll help you with your vendetta as long as you play along with me." Lucas reached out to shake Jason's hand. "Do we have a deal?"

Jason nodded. *A handshake with the devil got me here; another handshake with another devil will seal the deal.* He gripped Lucas's hand with everything he had.

# CHAPTER 15

**2100 / 23 OCTOBER 1999**
**ZOND MOCK-UP / DOORS / FLORIDA**

JASON ENTERED INTO THE MOCK-UP OF THE ZOND control room and watched Kelly fumblingly try to strap a small case to his back.

"Trouble?" Kelly was his friend, but now doubt had entered his mind. Was Kelly the one detailed to kill the team? If it wasn't him, then who? He watched Kelly's back, but would Kelly be watching his through a sniper scope? *Fuck!*

"You try carrying this thing."

Kelly seemed the same unconcerned professional, his friend.

It was heavy. "What is it?"

"A miniature nuclear bomb. A real one. Small, ain't it?" Kelly smiled. "The munitions guys just delivered it to me a little while ago. We got a class tomorrow with a guy from the Chicago Police Bomb Squad on how to plant and set it."

Jason's jaw dropped. "No. Come on. I know one man is *never* allowed to be alone with a nuke. It's policy. No Lone Zone and all that crap."

"Oh, yeah? Whose policy?" intoned Kelly, trying to sling the satchel onto his back.

"How's it work?" Jason suddenly felt himself become more cautious.

"It's a version of a limpet mine," Kelly grunted as he made some adjustments, then took off the case, set it on the ground, and opened it up. "It comes in two parts." Holding up a small silver ball, he explained, "This is the core: plastic explosive, plutonium, and tritium. When I'm ready, I slip it into the mainframe, like this." He dropped the ball into a tube. "Then I attach it to the generator, or as close as I can get. Set the remote code, and then we get the fuck out of Dodge. All of us get the fuck out or fry." Satisfied with the fit, he held it toward Jason. "Here, help me."

It weighed at least a hundred pounds. "I can't believe that we're actually gonna carry this thing in."

"By the time we finish our training you're going to know as much about it as I do."

"You're the sapper, not me! Bad enough I'm following you down a thousand-foot hole."

"You're the backup. If I can't get to the generator, then you'll take it in the rest of the way. Tom's nuclear guys figure that the generator's at least a thousand feet deep. I think it'll be deeper."

"Straight down."

"All the way to the bottom."

"How big is the bang?"

"Big. It has different settings—low, medium, high. Pretty cool, huh? The charge is designed to punch a hole in the shell of the generator. If the generator's up and running, it will amplify the blast. Look, this is the trigger." Kelly flipped a switch. "Oh shit! It's live." Kelly dropped the satchel charge and raced out of the building, closely followed by Jason.

"What? What?" Jason yelled as he got up alongside Kelly.

Stopping, Kelly looked at Jason for a moment, and then started laughing uproariously. "It's not *real*. It's just a training aid. But you should see the look on your face. Come on, let's go get my toy and have a look at the mock-up of what we're blowing."

"Kelly, you little fuck! That wasn't funny," Jason gasped.

"Oh yeah it was. Lighten up, man, no one lives forever."

They climbed down seven floors, then Kelly stopped. "This is as far as the Ground Penetrating Radar could go."

The size and dimension of the construction made Jason's jaw drop. It looked like a giant twirling baton, four hundred feet long.

"We got scientists and physicists directing DEA nuclear reactor constructing specialists, and the numbers they come up with told munitions how big a nuclear limpet charge to build." Kelly took off the satchel. "Damn, I hope it's not as heavy as this one."

Jason sensed a change in Kelly. "Why are we really here?"

Kelly sat on his haunches. "To ask you why *you're* here."

"What do you mean?"

"We're great friends. Jason, you're not getting any younger."

"I've already heard it."

"So tell me the real reason you're here."

"I came here to kill Oleg Kurgan. But I found out something." He couldn't hold back from Kelly. *Fuck the paranoia!* Assassin or not, Kelly was his friend. "This mission is a rubout."

Kelly was astonished. "Who told you this?"

"Are you the one that's supposed to take us out?"

Kelly looked around as if searching for the right words. "You're gonna have to figure who you think the traitor is on your own. But it ain't me, Jason. I'm not going on this mission for God and country. It's this: When you've been at this business as long as I have, you get addicted to the thrill. A nuke, man—I'm going to set a nuke and pop it! No one's done it since World War Two."

Jason jumped. "Oh fuck, Kelly. You're as crazy as Lucas is!"

Kelly stood, then tapped his finger on Jason's chest. "Hey, dude, you're the one who started this thing. We're the expendable stiffs, the small fries who have to clean up everyone else's shit and then get bleached ourselves. Call me insane, but *someone* still has to climb down that shaft and plant that nuke. Tell me, buddy, what sane fucker would be willing to do that? *You?* You're coming with me. Or are you backing out now 'cuz you know that it's a rubout?"

Kelly sat on the floor.

Jason sat next to Kelly. "I keep asking myself that. How far will I go to kill a man?"

"And?"

"To the ends of the earth. Siberia." Everyone else had an agenda, so did he. Lies, half-truths, and threats of death wouldn't scare him off Operation Lucifer Light and killing Kurgan the first chance he got.

"So tell me, who's the fucking lunatic, you or me?"

Jason raised his eyebrows. "It's pretty stupid when I think about it, but now I'm in too deep."

"Have you talked to Lucas?"

"He's the one who told me."

"I figured that. Well, now that you told me your secrets about Kurgan and the rubout, you got to know my secret before we go down the shaft: If I get compromised, I'm going to detonate the bomb. You won't have to worry about Kurgan, a rubout, or anything else, because I'm going to take out everything, including us. Look, I think Lucas is wrong. My brothers wouldn't take me out."

Somehow, knowing Kelly's intention made him feel better. It would solve a lot of problems. "So you gonna confront them with this information?"

Kelly took a deep sigh, and then grimaced.

"What if it's true?" Jason asked. "It'll kill the mission."

"No nuke." Kelly put his hand on his chin and rubbed it while he thought. "No. I won't say anything. But I can't see how they would get to one of us without getting to someone in the Doors."

"So what are you gonna do?"

Kelly rubbed his forehead, then shook his head clear. Smiling at Jason, he said, "The way I see it, it's you and me again. Just like old times. I watch your back, you watch mine. If we get rubbed out, it will be because we screwed up somewhere." A determined look crossed his face. "Nothing's changed. I'm gonna plant that bomb and explode it."

There was no question that the little man meant what he said. Jason only wished that Mac had hit him harder back at Patrick. The Doors was a mental rat maze. He seemed to be walking into dead ends and twists wherever he turned. This was it. There was no hope. No, he was wrong: He had a hope. But it was a nightmare.

"Now let's go check out our shaft, Alice."

## DROP ZONE POINT OF IMPACT / DOORS / FLORIDA

They stood looking down at the deep shaft. Kelly wrote on a notepad as Jason dictated the equipment they would need while in the shaft. They listed ascenders, carabiners, pulleys, line—plenty of line—silent drills, and drill bits. The list looked endless.

"Damn, buddy, a thousand feet–plus. We're gonna need a *ton* of gear." Jason felt dubious about all the extra weight they would be space-diving with. There was no way it would fit in the capsule.

Kelly crumpled up the paper and tossed it down the shaft. "Nah, forget all this bullshit. All we need are just a few magnets. Tom verified it's a steel shaft. We can use magnets to climb down and then back up."

"What?"

"The SEALs use these climbing magnets to get on ships. Jean made a call for me. We should have two sets here this afternoon."

"Waaait a second. I'm not planning to climb down a thousand-foot shaft using *magnets.*"

"A thousand feet–*plus,* and yes you will, 'cause we'll

be old men by the time we make it to the bottom if we use conventional climbing gear."

"Kelly, have you ever used these magnets?"

"No, but I told Jean to make sure they include directions with them. We'll figure it out. Look, I gotta go get our stuff ready. You got a little time before the fight, and our Space Divers are here. Have Gitthens take you to check them out."

## 2225

A black pod rested on a cart.

"Mike, tell me that this thing works, even if you're lying."

"It worked in Arizona."

"Right, but how does it work? How does it get from space to the ground without killing us or being detected?" asked Jason. "And I'd very much like to know how I fly the thing."

"You don't."

"I don't?"

"Well, let's see." Mike pursed his lips and squinted.

Jason knew that he was trying to figure out a way to explain a complicated issue to a simple mind and was "dumbing down" his choice of words.

"In 1961 the B-58 Stratofortress bomber had an escape capsule. It was named the High Speed High Altitude Ejection System. The bomber had individual ejection seats that safely ejected at seventy thousand feet, moving at over twice the speed of sound. I designed mine using the original blueprint, but modified it a little bit. You'll be lying down instead of sitting. The life-support system is close to the original.

"You don't fly it. You just hold on to the handgrips and it's flown by a flight system guided by our GPS constellation." Mike held his palms out. "You just get in and hold on."

"And we can't be detected?"

"You mean, 'How does the stealth system work?' "

"Right. That's what I meant to say."

"It would have cost us millions to try and use the same stealth technology as the F-117. So, I made some calls to friends and we came up with a garage invention for a lot less.

"If you were to get a magnifying glass and look at the Space Diver hull, you'd see millions and millions of tiny holes. Those holes will create a cooling cushion as you enter the atmosphere, even though the temperature will be more than a thousand degrees. The hull is a glass and ceramic composite. Watch." He took a blowtorch, lit it, and then held it against the hull for about thirty seconds. He pulled the torch away and immediately put his hand on the hull where the intense flame had been.

Jason was stunned.

"See? Now you try." Mike repeated the process. "Feel it."

Jason gingerly touched the hull. It was warm, but not sizzling.

"The inside is pressurized. Zoom! You're in the atmosphere. Why don't they see you on radar?"

Jason shrugged his shoulders.

"Top-secret coal dust."

"What?"

Mike chuckled. "Burn coal at a high enough temperature and you get these particles called fly ash. The scientists call them cenospheres. It would take a Ph.D. dissertation to explain what it does to radar and thermal detectors, but they can't see it, or anything coated with it. Think of cenospheres as little round balls that spin together and never let radar signals bounce back, but spin off and go around like it was never there."

"Wow, but how do I get out of the thing?"

"You don't. It shatters around you."

"What?!"

Mike let out a belly laugh. "It'll be fine. It's stress-designed. Once it goes through a hundred thousand feet it becomes flawed, but trust me, it's still harder than steel. As it comes back down and passes through five thousand feet, the internal stress created by the heat during your descent will be ready to explode the pod into a billion pieces, each piece no bigger than a grain of sand. Pressure-sensitive bolts will start the reaction."

Jason had to trust that Mike knew what he was talking about.

"So come on, get inside so I can take a few measurements."

Reluctantly climbing in, Jason felt as if he were entering a coffin.

"All the way in," Mike said, pushing on Jason's legs.

"All the way? Damn! I'm already in all the way."

"Well, suck in your gut!"

It was a tight fit as the Space Diver was sealed. Everything turned black. Panic began to stab at him. "And how long am I going to be in this thing? Shit, Mike, I can't breathe!"

"Suck on the oxygen hose."

Barely able to move his arms, he felt around until he found a small hose. Sucking on the flowing oxygen, he felt relief but was still very cramped. It seemed like forever before the Space Diver was opened and he could squeeze out. "And I'm supposed to carry all my gear in this, and my parachute?"

"*Plus* a pressure suit. You'll be fine after a few adjustments," assured Mike.

"If it's so fine, then you jump it. This fucker's flimsy. I can probably punch my way out of this thing!" exclaimed Jason.

"Only if you're Superman. It may be thin, but it's stronger than steel. As far as jumping it, what, you think *I'm* crazy?"

**0130 SUNDAY / 24 OCTOBER 1999**
**ZOND MOCK-UP / DOORS / FLORIDA**

It was time to go up against defenders. The Door gear was about to be tested. Coupled to their helmets and body armor, the Brotherhood of Death were ready for anything that came their way.

The first couple of defense teams were cake. The insertion team took no hits and stumbled into no traps. With their Zeta suits, chameleon capes, body armor, amplified hearing, full-view night vision, enhanced targeting, and silenced weapons, they were a formidable crew. Who could stop what could not be seen? They were men who cast no shadows.

The plan was to wait until Jason and Kelly planted the bomb and exited the shaft, then to meet up with the team and go after a two-hundred-pound dummy that simulated an unconscious Kurgan, protected by the defenders. Having no intell on the number of defenders or their opponents' defensive capabilities, the team had to adjust to every surprise while maintaining their own tactic objectives.

Moving in the dark was almost too easy for the team. It had taken them no time to adjust to the amplified hearing. From two hundred yards away they could sense any movement and could hear their opponents' whispers and breathing. Kelly said that if he got close enough, he could hear heartbeats. And there was a bonus to the helmet that they hadn't known about—they could "hear" the electrical crackling of the stun traps and reset them against the defenders.

The battle visor made the field of night vision almost unrestricted. They did not have microphone booms. The communication pad was set in their helmet foreheads and could sense the vibration of their speech through their skulls. Even a whisper was crystal-clear.

Mike Dennis taught the entire team how to use his chameleon cape. Attached to their backpack was a fanny pack that had a quick release that let the wearer completely drape himself in three seconds. It blended into the landscape, and with their heads-up visors down, they could bull's-eye any target without having to raise their rifles any higher than their hips.

Infiltrate. Using state-of-the-art communication devices, defenders and aggressors crawled over and under trenches and berms.

Contact. Once contact was made on the mock Zond operations center, they identified their targets.

Engage. The team was in and out in seconds. They hit their targets with deadly accuracy, then carried away the two-hundred-pound dummy.

Withdraw. Diversions were needed. Sometimes they were explosive, other times they were quiet, but they were always deadly.

Extract. For all involved, this was the most difficult aspect of the mission. Only through numerous trials and failures could the team evolve the best solution. So they got better with each assault they made. The defenders never caught on to the real mission, never detected an eighty-pound mock nuclear bomb planted on the mock generator.

Only when the bright field lights came on and the rehearsal was over could the observers see how intense the one-on-one battle had been, as defenders covered in paint chased ghosts.

**1700 MONDAY / 25 OCTOBER 1999**
**DOOR HEADQUARTERS / FLORIDA**

The classroom wasn't much bigger than a closet. A small satchel covered by a blue towel lay on a wooden field table. As Jason and Kelly sat quietly, a man walked in.

He appeared to be in his late forties, had curly gray and black hair, and looked a little disheveled.

Jason and Kelly introduced themselves.

The man seemed a little hesitant, but then shrugged his shoulders. "My name is Greg Bronsberg—Greg to you guys. Some grumpy old driver drove me here. I'm with the Chicago Police Bomb Squad. I got pulled off the job to come here." Glancing at Jason and Kelly, he shook his head. "I got no idea why I'm here, who you guys are, or where this place is. Damn, I don't even know if I'm still in America. My captain calls me into his office. He tells me to expect to be gone a couple of days. I get driven to the airport. Hell, I couldn't even go home to get a bag and say good-bye to my wife.

"A black jet shows up with blacked-out windows. I land here—wherever 'here' is—in the dark. In the morning a guy in a wheelchair meets me, has me sign some papers, then tells me what I'm supposed to do, and here I am. Man, is this real or a game?"

"Very real, Mister Bronsberg," Kelly answered. "No game. The guy in the wheelchair tells me you're the most knowledgeable person in the world about what's under that towel in front of you. He also tells me that you are one of a few people in the world qualified to teach how to detonate the M-188 Special Atomic Demolition Munitions."

Jason watched as Greg's eyes grew wide; then he quickly tried to assume a relaxed position.

"Man, that kind of information's secret stuff. What're you guys trying to do, blow a hole in Fort Knox?"

"Don't worry," assured Kelly. "You can speak freely here in this room—and *only* in this room."

"Understood." Greg sighed, resigned now that he understood what he was here for. Lifting away the towel, he involuntarily gasped. "Is this live?"

"Inert," said Jason. "So you know the thing?"

"I helped design these little beauties. It's a block of enriched uranium that's activated by a chemical explosive trigger." He inspected the weapon for a few moments. "So, what do you want to know?"

"Do you know what an MHD generator is?" Jason asked.

"Yeah, it's a big word that does big things. It's only theory, though."

"So in theory, how close does an SADM have to be to blow up an MHD? Theoretically speaking," Kelly quizzed.

Greg whistled, then thought for a few moments. "Air, surface, or subsurface burst?"

"Subsurface."

"Well, you'd have to know a few things—depth, the construction of the reactor chamber. Then you'd dial up the size of the charge and set the code decoder and firing unit. Placement of the SADM would depend on several things also. Just how much time do you have before you sap a real one? Or are we still dealing in theory?"

Jason smiled. They had found their man.

# CHAPTER 16

**0145 TUESDAY / 26 OCTOBER 1999**
**ZOND MOCK-UP / DOORS / FLORIDA**

THE BROTHERHOOD HAD SOMEHOW LOST THEIR EDGE.

"Alice, who are these guys?" Froto asked.

"Look, I've been shot in the ass. Goddamn, it hurts! I've *never* been hit in the ass! It's like they already know our moves."

Goons were everywhere they turned. Loud and flashy, they shot at anything that moved. It was well-orchestrated chaos.

The goons were all over the place. There was no way to slip past them to plant the nuke. All the insertion routes were blocked. The sons of bitches even rolled in stolen light carts and had the training ground lit up like high noon.

Kelly looked over a berm. "Think we ought to send out a retreat code?"

Jason shook his head. As bad as things seemed, it was only training. It was better to see how things played out.

There was something familiar about the defenders, but Jason couldn't put his finger on it—at the moment, he was too busy scooting for cover. Checking over his body, Jason grinned wide. He was clean. "Froto. Check me out."

"Lucky."

"Damn straight!"

"Or we're getting set up."

Jason quit grinning. Whoever they were up against was good. Almost too good. All they had to do was stall the Brothers another fifteen minutes and it would be over. The Brotherhood of Death would lose. The linkup with Rabid wasn't going to happen. Turning on his communicator, he whispered, "Reach." The code word meant that they were blocked or pinned down.

"Reach, Delta, Bravo," Lucas responded. The entire team was in a bad situation, and Rusty and Julio had been taken out.

"Damn," whispered Kelly. "Who are these guys in black pajamas?"

Black pajamas. Now Jason knew. "Froto, do you think you can plant the nuke by yourself if I divert them?"

"Just try me."

"Good." Jason keyed his radio. "Broken glass."

"Affirmative," Lucas keyed.

"Broken glass" meant that Jason was going to draw away the defenders by exposing himself. "Here goes."

"Good luck, pal," said Kelly.

Jason removed the silencer on his rifle, stood up, and fired his weapon toward the light carts, blowing out several lights.

Dirt kicked up around Jason as the defenders returned fire. Forgetting stealth, he sprinted in a zigzag over the mounds and berms toward the Zond operations center. Stopping and sliding into a culvert, he pulled out his bayonet. Time to play rough.

Yelling and screaming, they came at him. Jason got a quick peek over the berm. *Damn!* It was three against one.

As they got closer he saw them spread out to avoid being hit at the same time by one sweep of an automatic gun, a textbook small-unit assault maneuver.

Looking around, Jason saw that there was nowhere

to run, so he lay low until they were almost on top of him. Then he kicked out the legs of the first man and jumped at the second. Knowing that the third man would get the shot on him, he drove his blade into the second man's thigh about an inch, and then turned him around to use as a shield.

The man howled as Jason twisted the bayonet. Suddenly the third man was down and the first attacker had jumped up and run away. Great! His boys were close by, providing cover fire. Tripping the man he was holding onto his back, Jason punched him in the mouth and then took off in the opposite direction, not caring if anyone was on his trail. He heard the man howl. Jason had just "pinked" him bad enough to scare him, not kill him.

"He stuck me! The fucker stuck me! Medic! Medic!"

The defenders forgot about the fun they were having and went to the aid of their comrade.

"Page," said Lucas. The Brothers were on the move, diverting attention away from Froto.

*Playing dirty counts. Do the drill.* Jason sprinted, and then ran for a full two minutes before slowing down to get his bearings. No one followed him. *What next?* Grab the dummy, wait for backup, and then finish the mission.

Jason slithered and crawled slowly toward the control center. The closer he neared the entry point of the building, the more he sensed that something was wrong. Amplified hearing and visuals through the NVV told his senses that the control center appeared to be almost deserted.

A man with his back exposed stood at the entrance of the low building.

Jason took aim, but did not fire when the man stepped into a light from a light cart. Turning off his radio, Jason lowered his weapon, unsnapped his heads-up visor, and then walked to the edge of the entrance. "Hey, asshole, I still owe you for waking me up with a gun to my head. Are you the one who set those goons on me? And hey, after this is over I want my bayonet back from the man I stuck it in."

"Alligator man, *you're* the legendary Alice?"

"Michael Decker, Boris's bootlicker. Did Boris send you here to keep me off this mission?"

Slowly, Decker turned around. "Boris?"

"Frank McCone. Mister Black."

"Boris?" Decker thought for a moment, then chuckled. "Boris, yeah, it fits. And no, I'm here for me. I know that you've got to get through that door and get your 'man' or you lose. My team's outmatched the *famous* Brotherhood of Death. We know your moves, thanks to someone very close to you guys."

"This might be just a game for everyone else, but not for you and me, asshole. Let me see you stand in front of the door and try to stop me, fist to fist, boy." Jason had never thought of himself as a legend, but this punk thought he was real bad and still owed from trying to shoot George and rudely waking him up with a gun to his head.

"Sure. Take off the rest of your headgear and let's do it."

Jason holstered his gun, unstrapped his helmet, removed it, and then took a step toward the light.

Lightning-quick, Decker brought up his gun and shot Jason's helmet out of his hands. Jason dived after it as Decker fired wild shots.

Grabbing the helmet, Jason raced to a ravine and crawled away. The helmet was trashed. *Shit.* It was an operational helmet, worth thousands of dollars. How long would it take Mike to make another one?

"That's right, Alice. This is *just* a game," Decker called out. "Four minutes more and you lose. I'm not going to fistfight with you—right now I'm just going to outwait you. I just got a report that your boys are pinned down again." Decker laughed derisively. "This is worth dollars to me. Bounty! Right now that's all you are to me."

*Stupid. Stupid. Stupid!* Decker had played him like a fool. Jason looked over the rise at entry control, then at his watch. Three minutes. Now the game didn't matter.

All he wanted to do was beat the shit out of Decker. *Breathe deep. Let everything go on automatic. Ten seconds. Five, four, three, two, one.*

A roar caught Decker off guard. He didn't have a clear shot at Jason because the PJ was zigzagging as he ran. Just when Decker finally got a bead on him, Jason threw something into the air.

A brilliant flare ignited and washed out Decker's night vision.

The gun came flying out of Decker's hand as Jason tackled him and they both fell to the ground. They scrambled to their feet, and Jason threw a left jab, followed by a right cross. Decker stepped into the cross and grabbed Jason's wrist. Jason was off his feet and onto his back, instinctively kicking toward the grip on his right hand. He connected with Decker's head. He kicked again. Decker dropped to the ground.

Now there was nothing between Jason and the door entry.

"Shoot him!" cried Decker.

Jason was only feet from the door when he was stitched in the back with about fifty Zeta bullets.

"Oh shiiit!" yelled Jason, falling through the door. He was stunned, in pain, and couldn't move or get up.

A taunting voice behind him hissed, "So you made your time. So what? You still lost. Boris just wanted to see if you had a chance in Siberia. I'll be seeing you later, Alice the alligator man, I have to go and pick up my bounty for tonight's work."

Jason groaned. "I'm gonna get you, fucker." Is that how it was going to happen? He would complete the mission and Decker's boys would be waiting to shoot him in the back?

"No, Alice. If you want to 'get' me, you better 'get' better."

Then there was nothing. It seemed like an eternity before the area lights came on, signaling an end to the exercise. Jason lay in pain and did not move. There would be bruises. He was also exhausted, and there seemed to be no reason in the world to get up. He lay in the dirt until he heard footsteps.

"Jason, are you all right?" Froto asked.

"You set it?"

"Yep."

"Are you the only one around?"

"As far as I know."

"Then we won and I'm in a lot of pain."

The rehearsals were over. Ready or not, it was time to go operational.

Kelly helped Jason to his feet. Walking stiffly away from the training ground, Jason had never dreaded the future more than at that moment.


## 1200 WEDNESDAY / 27 OCTOBER
## WAR ROOM / DOORS / FLORIDA

Tom Chain and General Twitch were working endlessly to root out any American connection to Zond. Tom gave the predeployment brief, but was still unsure of the forward operating location. This morning he drew a Z on the dry erase board.

"Before we deploy, I want to share this with you guys, the last piece of the puzzle. A big question we've been trying to uncover is how Zond paid for such a monumental undertaking. It had to be a multibillion-dollar program."

Z-Man folded his arms across his chest. "And how much did we pay for our directed energy program? And what did we get for it?"

"Ask Boris," said Jason, gingerly sitting on his chair, his back a series of welts and bruises, compliments of Boris and the CIC.

"A reported sixty billion dollars," Lucas said. "But it's probably twice that."

Ignoring the comments, Tom continued. "In 1980, a diamond cartel called the Golden ADA opened up in San Francisco, selling flawless uncut diamonds mined from a deposit they said was discovered in northeastern Siberia, in Zond's region. It supposedly rivaled the DeBeers diamond mines."

A picture appeared on the screen. "Look where they claimed the mine was located."

"Damn!" gasped Rusty. "Did Zond dig out their place while they mined diamonds?"

"Close, but no cigar," Tom said. "Millions and millions went through the company. Tons of uncut diamonds, gold, and jewelry showed up at the center. Suddenly San Francisco was about to become the world center of the diamond trade, usurping South Africa's DeBeers. The worldwide diamond market was about to plunge, and several governments like South Africa were about to destabilize.

"DeBeers put its own investigators onto the Golden ADA. The investigators found that the heads of that Russian cartel didn't know shit about the retail diamond trade or diamond mining. Something wasn't right. Not only did the ADA sell diamonds, they also started moving gold, emeralds, antique Russian artwork, and jewelry, by the *ton*.

"Looking at the reputation and background of the management, they found out they were major league criminals and scumbags."

Julio raised his hand. "You mean like us?"

"Can it, Zorro," motioned Lucas.

"DeBeers turned the info over to the FBI, and then things finally got rolling. The ADA management got greedy."

Pia interrupted. "Hey, what Russian mobster ain't greedy these days?"

"Major Victor Zhirov."

"Who?"

"He worked for the Financial Crimes Division of the Russian Interior Ministry. The man's a bulldog. He followed the trail to the Russian Treasury. The cartel was looting it. The FBI and the IRS busted the Golden

ADA. All of a sudden a lot of people started showing up dead.

"Well, we looked at all the data and it was very disturbing for us—the diamonds turned out to be only the tip of the iceberg. A whole other operation was going on, and the people running it knew what they were doing.

"The mobsters were the front. Zond used the profits to set up their Siberian EMP. They exported tons and tons of American high-tech material back to Russia."

"Enough to make an EMP?" Rusty asked.

"You win the cigar! They paid for everything in cash and then disappeared without a trace the day after the Golden ADA was raided. No suspicions were ever raised, because all accounts had been settled.

"One last item: A Russian mole was bringing information to the CIA. Zond is a powerful Russian organization, dealing in everything—organized crime, espionage, chemical weapons, terrorism; everything. This Zond mole supposedly had details of an unbelievable directed energy weapon. That mole was on board English Air 943, but it never made it to New York."

"Ahhhh, fuck me!" Jason spit. "The CIC made the Canadian Labrador choppers search for the remains of that mole."

Tom nodded in agreement.

"So the CIC already knew about Zond?"

"Yeah." Tom pressed his lips together.

Something began to crack inside Jason. A pain like that of an animal caught in a bear trap howled in his soul. Politics and intrigue had killed a good man, a loving family man—a man who saved lives. Now he was part of an elaborate betrayal and, as with Toby's murder, he couldn't do a damn thing about it. Weariness washed over him like a crashing wave.

"Now you know the whole story," Tom said. "Are you ready to deploy?"

"Fuck, Tom, we haven't even picked our forward operation location," Z-Man said.

"Do we have all our gear on hand?" Kelly questioned.

Lucas scratched his head. "We haven't even worked out who's moving us to our insertion point."

"One thing at a time," Cadallo said. "Tom's was first. Are you guys ready to deploy?"

"We're always ready," Lucas said. "But the real question is, will the extraction be there for us?"

"They'll be there," assured Cadallo. "Is the bomb ready?"

"Done," replied Kelly.

"Then everything else is secondary," injected Tom. "So now the only thing we're missing is the forward operation location."

Maps were brought out. Classified operations orders were delivered, and like monkeys picking lice, the team combed over all the possible operating locations within a few thousand miles of the Zond stronghold.


## 1620
## WAR ROOM / DOORS / FLORIDA

"Anyone ever remember when a lack of a forward location canceled an operation?" Z-Man asked.

"Shit, we're going in even if we have to travel to Siberia by rubber raft," countered Julio.

Jason was determined that the mission would not be aborted. He scanned the maps, slowly following the Siberian insertion point backward until he came to masses of land. Northern Japan appeared to be the closest. Stopping at one point of land, he smiled. "You know, the Forty-fifth Fighter Wing at Misawa is having their Operational Readiness Inspection (ORI) in five days."

"How do you know that?" Cadallo asked.

"The Nine-twentieth Rescue Wing is going there to provide rescue support for the fighters during the inspection."

"Input," said Tom.

Twitch looked at the map. "One of my first commands was the Three hundred first Intelligence Squadron at Misawa. Yeah, I know the place well. They've got a very secluded part of the base called Security Hill that sits over a bay leading out to the China Sea. Very nice."

"An ORI. We could blend in and work the mission without anyone being the wiser," mused Cadallo.

Tom rubbed his hands together. "Okay, we got a primary; let's keep looking and see if Misawa is the best place."

Secure phone calls were made. Dates and mission itineraries were checked. The more information the team received, the brighter things looked.

An ORI tested an Air Force wing's ability to fight a war. Many other different organizations were called in to add valid support to the testing: RC-135W Rivet Joint airborne warning control, EC-130E Compass Call electronic jammers that also acted as an Airborne Battlefield Command and Control Center (ABCCC), and AWACS.

Tom gazed at Jason.

"What?"

"You came to me with a wild story and looked what it has turned into. Now you give us this. I can't help but wonder how you did it. Where would we be without you?"

"You would've uncovered it anyway."

"I don't think so. This thing's been hidden for a long time, deep. No, I think that we might've lost, but you keep giving us an edge. Right now there are some very powerful people sitting on pins and needles. What happens in the next days will tell them where they stand and what the future holds. Operation Lucifer Light has only a slim chance of succeeding—are you sure that going on the mission is what you want to do?"

"No." Jason sighed. "But now I'm a part of the team, and like I told you, I got my reasons." *What do you want, Tom? You're fishing for something.*

"Okay. Then let's get this mission on the road."

"Right. Misawa it is."

# CHAPTER 17

**1630 THURSDAY / 28 OCTOBER 1999
MISAWA AIR BASE / JAPAN**

THE C-17 GLOBEMASTER TAXIED TO THE NORTH END of the tarmac, far away from the passenger terminal and curious eyes. It came to a stop in front of a large hangar. The engines shut down, the doors opened, and the ramp lowered. At the foot of it, three trucks and a passenger bus met the team.

Bags and cargo were quickly loaded and the team was on the streets of Misawa in minutes. No one stationed at the base bothered to notice that the elite team had arrived.

Z-Man opened his window. "Look. They drive on the wrong side of the road here." Pointing at a parking lot, he cried, "Hey, transportation!"

"Pull over," Lucas ordered the driver.

The team swarmed over the Nissan cars and vans parked in neat rows. They were contract cars provided for the Headquarters Inspection members. The keys hung over the visors.

"Don't get greedy, just take what we need," Lucas called out. "Hey, dibs on that silver Nissan convertible!"

A startled lieutenant came running from the adjacent

Wing Headquarters building. "Just what do you think you're doing?"

Ben Cadallo stepped off the bus and intercepted the young officer. "Look," Ben said, pointing to his red Inspector General (IG) badge. "You got one of these?"

"No, sir."

"Then your job is to attend to the needs of people wearing these. If you have any questions, you walk your happy little butt back to your headquarters and call your boss. I'm sure he will enlighten you, or anyone else not wearing a red IG badge."

The young man shriveled under Cadallo's glare, did an about-face, and turned to leave.

"Wait."

"Yes sir?"

"Who owns that building over there?" Cadallo asked, pointing to a three-story building on the flight line.

"Units on temporary duty use that building, sir. It's reserved for the IG team."

"It is? Who's got the keys?"

Tom's Imagery Team already had the front door opened and was moving in their gear in an antlike fashion. In less than one hour they would be up and running.

"The fighter unit right next to it, sir."

"Good. You go and get me the keys, then let your wing commander know the Red Badges are here. Tell him, 'Don't call us, we'll call him.' What's your name, son?"

"Lieutenant David Wolff, sir."

"How long have you been at this base, Lieutenant?"

"Three years."

"You fly?"

"Not enough, sir."

"Is that right? Well, *Lieutenant* Wolff, I like you and could use you. It looks like you're gonna be my liaison while we're here. You let your commander know that, got it?"

"Yes, sir."

"You're gonna like working for me. I might even pull some strings to promote you before we leave."

"Yes sir!" Wolff said, and smiled.

## 1730
## BUILDING 625 / ROOM 305 / MISAWA BILLETING / JAPAN

Kelly walked into the Kanto billeting quarters, followed by Jason. A door was opened. "Pretty nice."

Jason agreed. It contained a bedroom, dayroom, kitchen, and *private* bathroom. There seemed to be a party going on, as several men sat around drinking beer and whisky. They looked like they'd been at it a while.

"Yeah? Whaddaya want?" someone spit out.

Kelly smiled. "Do all the billets look as nice as this?"

"They do if you're an officer, little boy. Now what do you want?"

Kelly's smile got wider, but it was not a friendly smile. "I want you to get out of my room."

The man stood up, towering over Kelly. "You get out of here, boy. You're in IG quarters. The children's day care is on the other side of the base."

Everyone started laughing, including Kelly. "Hey, you got an IG badge like this?" He pulled out his badge. "See? See this pretty red color?"

"So?"

"So it says that *you're* in the wrong motherfucking building. Maybe they have room for *you* at that day care center. Whaddaya think?"

The man became indignant. "I'm not going anywhere."

"Oh, I think you are." Kelly handed the man the phone on the kitchen counter and wrote down a number off his badge. "Here, call that number. The man on the other end will be even funnier than you. Go ahead, call it." Kelly went cold sober. "Consider it an order, *sir.*"

Jason watched as the man dialed the number and explained his situation to the person on the other end, and then as the man's face changed from arrogance to astonishment.

"But sir, I'm a *lieutenant colonel*!"

"Hey, tell your boss for me that I'm a *Marine*. See? No day care for me—maybe for him," Kelly said to the men in the room.

"Sir? Yes, sir. No sir."

"Three bags full sir," said Kelly.

Except for Kelly, the men in the room grew frosty but worried as they watched the demeanor of the man on the phone change from arrogance into submissiveness. The man hung up.

"You need help packing?"

The man glowered at Kelly, then stomped into his bedroom and slammed the door.

"Hey, who are you guys?" Kelly asked kindly.

"We're with the IG team," said one of the men through narrow eyes.

"No shit? Are all you guys *officers*?"

"As a matter of fact, we are." The man pulled out an IG badge.

Kelly looked closely at it. "Wow, but do you have a red one like *this*?" Kelly pulled out his badge.

"Uhm, no."

"Oh. I see," Z-Man said as he barged into the room. Puffing up a smoke screen with his cigar, he rested his right hand on his machete and growled, "Then you got the wrong stinking badges. Go get your shit, and like your friend get your collective asses out of my building."

Pia entered the room, machine gun at the ready. The members of the IG team were out of the room in seconds.

Jason felt a little sorry for the men. Selected for their experience and seniority, they'd arrived at Misawa to evaluate the base's ability to mobilize and conduct simulated war with their F-16 fighters. He who held an IG badge was god. But not today. Bigger gods with better badges had descended on them and kicked them off their cloud.

"Kelly, Jason, don't get comfortable yet. I want

to show you the country," Lucas said as he dropped his room key into Pia's hand. "Take care of our gear, please."

## 2045
## NORTHERN JAPAN

They tried to be inconspicuous, but their size gave them away. Three hours into a drive to the north coast of Japan, Kelly was at the wheel of a small Japanese car, Lucas was stuffed in the passenger seat, and Jason was crammed in the back.

"Fuck me," muttered Lucas. "How do they drive on these *tiny* roads? And the wrong *side* of the road!"

"Got a problem?" asked Kelly. He was happy with the little car. It had everything a stateside car had and more. He flipped up a six-inch TV screen on the dashboard. Japanese baseball was on.

"Yeah, small cars, small roads, and *small* people," Lucas shot back.

"Yeah, but it is a cool little car," Jason observed. It was equipped with a digital map display.

Following the map's blip, signifying their car, they pulled onto a side road that wound up the side of a mountain, then drove until they came to a dirt road protected by a chain. Kelly turned off the ignition as Lucas and Jason struggled out of the car. They massaged themselves vigorously.

Jason looked at the trees. "What're we doing here?"

"Lucas's associate is here. This guy don't travel—he doesn't even exist in anybody's records," said Kelly. "It's lucky that we came to Japan because what we need for Kurgan can only be gotten here from this guy."

"Where?"

"Up that road, but I wouldn't just skip up there because people are watching."

As they stood quietly by the car, a lone man appeared on the road, then turned around and started walking away.

"That's our signal to follow," Lucas said, stepping over the chain.

"Even hear of the ninja?" Kelly asked Jason.

"Sure, in kung fu movies. They're not for real."

"They're not?"

They walked through a forest that soon opened up into a small meadow. A house with a thatched roof sat at the edge of a small cliff overlooking the ocean. A cottage sat to the side.

The Japanese man pointed at the smaller house and then disappeared back into the forest.

Lucas walked to the paper door, slid it open, then took off his shoes and went in, followed by Kelly and Jason.

Inside the small house a man worked with clay over a bench. Jason watched with rapt fascination as the man nimbly cut away clay tiles and inscribed them with simple but elegant designs.

"Yes, *origato,* come in. Please come in and sit. I will be done in a few moments," the man said with his back to the men.

They sat quietly until all the clay had been cut into four-inch-square tiles. The man then kneeled in front of Lucas and gave a formal bow. "Please excuse me, but there are times when the clay requires my full attention. You and your friends are welcomed here." His English was clipped and precise, easy to understand.

Lucas introduced Tami to his friends as "a pottery maker and sword sharpener."

Trying to be polite, Jason bowed, but as usual could not get the act to appear natural. Looking at the man, he could not guess his age. His hair was jet black, but his eyes were wrinkled like a gnarled tree. Jason felt the man's penetrating gaze.

A door opened and a woman came in with tea and coffee on a tray. She set it down and left.

"Mister Jason, I suspend the tea rituals with my tall friend here. He is a *gajin* with Asian attitudes." A small smile crossed Tami's lips. "You usually come alone, Mister Lucas. Or you send Mister Kelly."

"This is a special time," Lucas whispered.

"How can I help you?"

Lucas leaned forward. "I—we—have a mission. I need one of your potions. I must make a man tell me all he knows in a very short time."

Tami smiled. "*That* is a potion many would like. Not easy to make."

Lucas nodded. "The usual arrangements."

"Yes. But there are things you should know about this potion. A man under its influence may go insane. While he's under it he will feel that death is close. He will look for a savior, and that is when he will tell you everything he knows. But you must be careful of the amount you give or his brain will be damaged for life. Are you sure this is what you want?"

"*Hai,*" Lucas answered.

"It is introduced into the body by injection. Do you have someone who knows how to do this?"

Lucas put his hand on Jason's shoulder. "This guy."

A chill shot through Jason's body.

"I will make what you ask and it will be delivered to you."

"Then our business is done."

They bowed and were soon on their way back to Misawa.

"You couldn't just call?" asked Jason.

"This guy doesn't talk on telephones. Consider yourself special. Most people who've seen him are dead," Lucas replied.

"Oh, thanks."

"Okay," said Lucas with gravity and meaning. "Once we grab Kurgan in Siberia, you will inject him with the stuff. Depending on what we get out of him, you will kill him. You will have executed your part of the mission."

"But be ready for any changes," Jason added. Lucas just peered back at him.

## 1335 FRIDAY / 29 OCTOBER 1999
## SECURITY HILL / MISAWA AIR BASE / JAPAN

The team sat quietly in the briefing room reading their operation orders and notebooks. No one spoke. This was the quiet time—the premission briefing before they went into the forty-eight-hour grubdown isolation period. Then the mission began for real.

Jason was the last man to enter the room, and took the empty chair.

Looking at his watch, Tom spoke. "You're going to hear this one last time, so that no one misunderstands what we're doing here. We are clandestinely infiltrating into sovereign territory to destroy a foreign government's secret asset with a nuclear weapon. We are kidnapping a foreign citizen and we are also destroying Russian life and property. Any one of these actions, by law and international agreement, is an act of war. BUT, we are not going to war and the American government at all levels will refute any verbal compromising of this mission."

Z-Man rolled his eyes. "Another suicide mission."

"This here meeting is for you guys," Cadallo said. "Are there any last-minute concerns or 'what-ifs' that we haven't looked at?"

The only "what-if" Jason had was: what if someone was out to kill him?

"Well, at least I know where I'll be for the next few days," moaned Z-Man. "In fucking SIBERIA! Shit, they don't even have whorehouses there, or do they? I should've found out."

"Thank you." Tom smiled. "Turn in your mission folders before you leave here. The next time we'll get together will be at the insertion brief. This time is yours to tighten up any loose strings. I will see you at the appointed time." He rolled out of the room.

Tom seemed changed; running the mission looked to be getting to him. Jason felt sorry for him, but at the same time knew that he must be having the time of his life. Like the rest of the team, he had to trust Tom with his life—even if he turned out to be the traitor.


**0410 FRIDAY**
**SPACE WARNING SURVEILLANCE CENTER /**
**SCHRIEVER AIR FORCE BASE / COLORADO**

Colonel Doug Jones made a call to his wife, Manette, and let her know that he wouldn't be coming home. He used a code word between them that told her there was a reason behind his absence.

"How long?" she asked.

"You know the drill, sweetheart."

"I know. I love you," Manette said softly as she hung up the phone.

He looked at the armed guards in front of the white steel vault door as he placed the phone back onto the receiver. The room was known to only a few on the base, its location classified.

Presenting his ID card to the guard, he placed his hand on a laser scanner and looked into a retina viewer to verify that he was the person on the card. Doug couldn't help but notice that the guard's pistol was set on fire position.

A man in a black suit silently waited near the door. Avoiding direct eye contact, the man waited until the guard nodded after the verification check. Then the man in black turned, faced the door, and spun the battery-operated combination dial at the center of the door. He turned the chrome lever, and the door opened with a thick cranking noise.

Jones walked through the door and watched the suit pull out a cellular phone, dial a number, whisper one word, and then slam the door shut.

"Fuck me," Jones mumbled. He had been through the routine just once in his career, and then it was only a simulation.

The FLASH message came through the moment he walked into the Sky Room that night. The Emergency Message came directly from CINCSPACE, the big man himself. Chosen for what he knew, rather than whom he knew, Jones was one of only a few "birdmen" in the world, ready at any time to go behind the steel door and disappear until a mission was completed.

Walking to a safe on the wall, he spun the dial to the memorized numbers—and to his surprise, it opened. He pulled out the plain brown envelope and read the time penciled on it: 0430. Looking at the atomic clock set in the wall, he saw he had twenty minutes before he had to get to work, so he immediately began checking out the small room.

Spartan, it had a toilet with a shower and three towels, and a bed too small for his six-foot-five frame. The refrigerator was filled with water, sodas, and microwaveable food. The walls were white-painted concrete, three feet across, and encased in steel. A nightstand and a table and chair were the only other things in the room, besides a computer. It was the computer that made him nervous.

Pulling the chair in front of the computer, he turned it on and entered his password, then sat back and looked at the clock until it read 0430. Doug opened up the envelope and began to run the checklist that was inside. He had never run the real article before, just the simulation. The checklist was pretty mundane, but his hands still shook with a nervous anticipation.

"Establish communication," he read aloud. He punched in the hexadecimal code on the keyboard, a green light flashed on the screen. "Communication checks good; check power." Looking at the screen for a green light, he smiled. "Checks good too."

He ran down the rest of the checklist, and when he saw there were no negative responses he turned the page and began the Orbital Element Sets by plugging in the data. Jones had no idea what the data meant; he just had to get it right, perfect. Someone else had programmed the computer; he just hit the keys. After all the data had been plugged in, he turned the page and saw a time on the clock: 0530. Following the command on the last page, he closed the checklist, put in back into the safe, and shut it. Now he had nothing but time to wait for the clock on the wall—the most accurate clock in the world—to roll around for thirteen hours.

The Satellite Inspector (SAINT) program was a secret space project proposed to President Kennedy in 1962 and approved in 1965. Under the program, highly maneuverable satellites were to be mounted with cameras, X rays, and a host of other sensing devices. The program was soon canceled when it was leaked to the public that the SAINT was actually an antisatellite weapon.

Brought to the attention of the architects of Reagan's Star Wars, SAINT was revived, made a black program, fully funded, and in operation by 1988. Few outside of the CIC knew of its existence.

In an area of unused space, a small, stealthy satellite woke up on Jones's commands after five years in a secret Russian Molniya orbit and relayed at light speed that it had checked its system and that all systems were operative. The SAINT was ready for more commands. It was ready to kill.


**2145 SUNDAY / 31 OCTOBER 1999
SECURITY HILL BEACH / MISAWA AIR BASE
JAPAN**

Fifteen thirty-foot fishing boats were beached on the calm shore in the bay. Japanese fishermen loaded their nets and line into their boats in the night. Absorbed in their tasks, no one paid any attention to the Americans loading boxes into the last boat.

"Here," Jason said, handing Rusty a footlocker containing high explosives that they might need to blow through doors or walls. Other boxes contained supplies such as the ammunition they would use and cases of Meals Ready to Eat (MREs).

The fishermen began to push their boats from the shore, start their engines, and move slowly into the bay.

Jason shook hands with each Brother. He saved Lucas for last. "Did you get the stuff from your ninja?"

"Don't you know?" Lucas smiled. "There are no ninjas. And yeah, you're the man when it comes time. Don't you lose this, because it cost us a fortune." Handing Jason a small vial, he climbed into the boat. "Good luck, Brother. See you in Siberia." He waved as the boat pulled away and mingled in with the fleet.

The fleet entered the Sea of Japan and turned north. One boat, however, turned south to rendezvous with the SSN *Jules Verne*. Secretly assigned to the Pacific Submarine Force and based in Yokosuka, Japan, it was the newest stealth submarine in the Navy's inventory. The sub would submerge and not reappear until it was just offshore of Siberia, then a second, smaller sixty-five-foot submarine would detach from within the mother hull.

At their forward destination the small sub would cut through the ice floe, and then the boat would disembark the team, who would disappear into the frozen tundra.

The small sub would return six days later and wait for a short and very specific time. If no one showed by departure time, it would return to the *Jules Verne* and they would leave.


**0745 MONDAY / 29 OCTOBER 1999**
**MISAWA AIR BASE / JAPAN**

"Hey, Jason. Jason!"

Recognizing the voice, Jason went from a jog to a flat-out sprint. Past the chow hall and through the Navy barracks he ran, stopping only when he came to the train tracks that led off base. Breathing hard, he rested against the chain-link fence.

"You ain't that fast."

*Shit!* "Dan, what are you doing here?" Jason gulped.

Dan Murray wasn't even breathing hard. "What're ya trying to do, lose me? I didn't even know you were here."

"I'm not, okay?" A chameleon cape would've helped. Jason would never be able to perfect the knack that the Brothers had of disappearing at will. He had spent his entire time at Misawa avoiding his PJ team. Not that he wanted to, but the mission dictated that he avoid contact with anyone but mission operatives.

Dan smiled, and Jason realized how much he missed his fellow Blue team members. It seemed like ages since he had seen someone from the "free" world. Living in the black world wasn't for Jason.

"But why?" Dan asked.

Sliding down the fence until he was on his haunches, Jason crossed his arms. "If I tell you, I got to kill you."

"You're kidding."

"I wish I were."

"Boss, the whole team is wondering what's happened to you. Alex Abbey says you're probably dead."

Jason's heart jumped. "Maybe he's right. I'm serious, don't tell anyone that I'm here. Okay?"

"Yeah, sure. But..."

"But what?"

"Are you a part of the weird shit that's going on around here?"

"Any IG inspection has weird shit. It's part of the design."

"No, not like this. This is different; something else is going on. Us PJs just can't figure it out. Lance even said that some guys in black suits came around asking about what we were doing here."

Jason pressed his lips together for a moment. "Don't

try and figure it out or you might find yourself in a situation like mine."

"I don't know. I've heard stories about some of the things you've done. Tell me how I get to do those kinds of things."

Jason shook his head. "Dan, you *don't* want to know."

"Yes I do! I want that kind of adventure."

Jason stared at Dan, who had a look that reminded him of himself, twenty years ago: fresh, naïve, willing to face any danger in the world for "adventure." *If he only knew.* "You could get killed and no one would ever know."

Dan looked wonderingly at Jason. "So Abbey's right?"

"I'm gonna do my damnedest to prove him wrong." Standing, Jason took Dan by the collar. "Look, kid, you haven't seen me, understand?"

Dan nodded, but looked confused.

"Look. You got a great career as a PJ ahead of you. I know. You started out with the perfect save: me. You became a PJ to save lives, remember that. Don't give me that hurt-puppy look. Now get lost."

It almost broke Jason's heart to see Dan trudge away with his head down.

Back in his room, Jason slowly inspected, then packed his gear. Checked over the operation of his helmet and guns. Fitted the silencer on his rifle. A lot of people were already signing him off as dead, while others were probably planning his death. The odds were against him, but that was nothing new; it was his life's story.

# CHAPTER 18

**T**WO MEN WALKED FROM THE SHOGUN BILLETING AND climbed onto the blue crew bus. Past the base exchange and shopping mall, the small bus took a left in front of the Bob Hope Elementary School and headed down toward the flight line. A right turn just before Base Operations, a brief check at a security gate, and the bus was on the flight line driving past the KC-135 and C-130 parking spots.

Jason had been through this section many times, but never beyond it. Highly restricted, it was once used for the comings and goings of Blackbird support. Even though the spy plane no longer flew, he knew that there were Army sharpshooters hidden somewhere and ready to fire at anyone trying to make off with a nuclear weapon.

All their equipment had arrived on a C-130 Hercules in the middle of the night. The weapon was now stuffed inside one of two small black experimental units designed to break apart while plummeting to earth at three times the speed of sound.

*And I'm gonna be inside of one of them!* Jason thought.

Kelly sat quietly reading his ops manual, committing to memory every last piece of information he might have overlooked. He looked like a little boy on a school bus studying his homework, but no schoolboy ever brought the kind of apple he was carrying to his teacher.

The bus slowed down in front of the Hush Hangars and stopped in front of one of them. Stepping off the bus, the two men hesitated, then turned around in a slow and deliberate circle. Jason knew that he was in the crosshairs of several sniper scopes, and that so was Kelly. Words were being exchanged as they were ID'd before they entered the 39th Life Support unit connected to the hangar. If either was questionable, a bullet in the head would restrict them from entering.

Rather than go directly into the life-support rooms, Jason and Kelly took the first door, which led to the massive hangar.

The black spy plane—the SR-71F12B Lockheed Blackbird—sat silent in the hangar. In this part of the world the sleek plane was called Habu, after the deadly island viper. Built by Kelly Johnson's Skunk Works in 1962, the Delta wing titanium-alloy spy plane was still ahead of its time.

Flying at the edge of space, and traveling at over Mach 3, it was considered untouchable by any enemy. It was an awesome plane by anyone's standards. This particular plane had been modified to carry payloads in its fuselage belly. Able to drop monitoring or reconnaissance devices, it could overfly enemy airspace and release packages weighing up to one thousand pounds. Tonight Habu would release its most unusual load ever.

Sophisticated as they were, it wasn't the plane's electronics that had Jason awed, it was the plane itself. At over a hundred feet long and fifty-five and a half feet wide, it was straight out of a Buck Rogers dream. It looked like a black javelin in flight. How could something so big and beautiful be hard to see as it raced across the heavens?

Tonight's mission was just an illusion. Here we are. Have a look at us. Everybody! We're right here.

Show the false. Hide the real.

Touching the big spy plane, Jason felt like the ball in the ball-and-cup game, palmed at the last instant.

Fantastic as the plane was, it was the two small black pods that sat on bomb-loading carts that had Jason truly floored. For the first time since the mission began, Jason felt his stomach become queasy. "Fuck, Kelly. It still looks so, so *small*. I can't see how I gotta fit inside *that* carrying gear and a nuclear bomb."

The Space Diver looked like a miniature F-117 jet without wings. The only modification it had undergone since the last time Jason had tried to fit inside of it was a small rod that had been added to the nose.

Kelly walked around his pod and admired the work, touching the diver as if it were a work of art. "*I'm* the one jumping in the nuke. Alice, trust me, it'll work."

"Where's the nuke?"

Kelly made big eyes. "Coming."

"It's a mistake, pure and simple. Peer pressure and all that shit. Froto, man, this is *fucking crazy*!"

"Not so crazy, Jason," a voice said.

"Mike, how'd you get here?" He hadn't been on the plane ride to Misawa, or the jet trip to Kadena.

Mike Dennis stood in a doorway of the hangar.

"Someone has to make sure you get off safely." Mike smiled.

"So explain to me one more time what's going on, because my partner here actually thinks that *that* will drop *this*." He pointed from the Blackbird to the SD.

"That's right. Moving at three times the speed of sound, you will be ejected from the plane into space, glide down to your insertion point, and your SD will dis-integrate into a billion pieces. I told you that before."

"You also told me I'm supposed to survive this," Jason said.

"We'll survive," assured Kelly as he put his hand on Jason's shoulder. "I've done a couple of these drops before—classified, of course. This is the first time for a two-man drop, but the ballistics remains the same."

"NASA is pitching a bitch over *lending* the Doors two pressure suits," Mike mused. "But we got to have them in case you lose the pressure in your pods."

"So?" quipped Kelly. "You're the genius. Make some."

"Not these things. They're custom-made with special tools. I could, and probably make them better, but you'd have to give me a year and you don't have that kind of time. The reason NASA's having a cow is that they each cost over a quarter-million dollars—and you'll be leaving them behind, so they won't be getting them back. But NASA doesn't know that yet."

"Oh," said Jason.

"I don't care. I didn't sign for it. And neither did you," Kelly said.

"Don't even ask how much the SD costs," said Mike. "Well, let's mosey over to life support and get you suited up and start your prebreathing. Chain is waiting for you two there."

"Hey, Tom," Jason said as they walked into a room filled with oxygen bottles, hoses, and two black pressure suits. The place looked more like a doctor's office than a preflight room. Under orders to say nothing other than what was necessary, four airmen stood next to two leather lounge chairs, waiting to get Jason and Kelly ready for flight.

Jason hadn't seen Tom in a while, and he had changed. Dark circles under his eyes told of the too many sleepless nights he had spent coordinating Operation Lucifer Light. His normally tight upper body looked slack and neglected. The pristine image he liked to present was gone, replaced by a seven-day-old beard and unkempt hair.

"You look like shit," Kelly said as he handed Tom their mission folders.

Tom smiled. "I can always count on you for moral support. I've been busy while you two have been jacking off. I just came to see you on your way. The team is already in-country and about one day out from their mission point. You guys are next." He reached into a side compartment of his chair, pulled out an apple, and offered it to Jason.

"Fuck no!" Jason said. No bad omens!

"Sissy," Kelly said as he took the apple and bit into it.

The crunching sound had the same effect on Jason as a pair of nails scratching a slate blackboard would have. His stomach heaved.

"I got more, if you want one." Another apple appeared in Tom's hand, and Mike took it.

As the sounds of apple carnage filled his ears, Jason turned his back on the others and looked through the glass window at the black jet. Suddenly a small hand gripped his shoulder.

"You're gonna love it! It's a ride like you've never had before. Shit, it's worth doing the mission just for this ride." Kelly's eyes were filled with an almost childlike excitement.

"Brother, you're as nuts as they come."

"Come on, let's not keep these life-support folks waiting. We got to be on the drop zone on time."

They opened the A-3 bags that contained their gear and donned Zeta suits and overalls, and then stepped into the pressure suits. Jason turned down the technicians' offer of a urine tube that wrapped around the penis like a condom. It was a customized pee bag, in case he needed to go in flight. "No. I won't be in the plane long enough to need it, so I think I'll pass on that."

As they lay on the long couchlike chairs breathing pure oxygen, the life-support technicians worked wordlessly around them attaching the various pieces of their pressure suits. Adjusting hoses. Putting on the helmets, the technicians inflated the suits three times and checked them for leaks.

Jason didn't have the heart to tell them that he would be using a knife to cut himself out of the costly suit, and would leave it in shreds in Siberia.

Jason lumbered off the chair and toward the hangar with the oxygen unit attached to his suit. It would be the air that he would breathe during the drop.

"The mainframe clarity of our spy satellites is just about resolved. We're down to two-foot resolution," Tom said. "Cadallo's been following the team's progress back in Misawa, and we'll be following yours once you've inserted." Tom stopped in front of Jason. "I know what you're thinking. And I'll tell you that I think this operation has a high probability of success."

*Success? Sure. The question I want answered is, Will I come back?* Jason looked down at Tom as a thought occurred to him. "Hey, Tom, how did you get in that chair?"

Tom turned red for a moment, then smiled. "I'll tell you when you return."

"Let's do it," Mike said.

Kelly put on his helmet and parachute and then crawled into his Space Diver. "See, room to spare! Hey, Mike, where's the nuke?"

"It's on the way. Start sucking on your oxygen." Mike looked at Jason. "Your turn."

"Oh shit." He pulled himself into the Space Diver, which seemed a lot tighter than the first time. He had little room to move; it felt as if he had stuffed himself into a fifty-five-gallon drum. Claustrophobia gripped him.

"Comm check," keyed Kelly.

"Checks good. Goddamn it, Kelly, this is tight!"

"Makes you horny, don't it?"

"No! This sucks. How long you say we got to be in this thing?"

"First we have to suck on pure oxygen for one hour to get rid of the nitrogen in our bodies so we don't get the bends in space, then from takeoff until we are over the drop zone, not including air refueling, a little over three hours. But it's good we're on oxygen because when

the Blackbird has been fueled, the fumes will be everywhere. Come on, you can handle it."

"Thanks for telling me now, asshole." He was used
to long waits on the ground breathing pure oxygen in order to make high-altitude jumps. But he'd never, ever
been closed up in a tiny coffin.

"Your nuke's here," Mike yelled into the Space
Divers.

Jason could hear only scrapes and snaps as Army
specialists positioned the SADM into Kelly's pod. *This
mission is hot.*

"You guys ready to be sealed?" Tom questioned
through an external intercom box.

"I don't like the way you said that, Tom."

"Don't like what, Jason?" Mike asked, methodically
clamping closed the shell around the PJ.

"Any last questions?" Tom asked.

"Can I quit now?" asked Jason. Everything was
black around him. Feeling claustrophobic, Jason just
wanted to scream.

"Good one, Jason," Tom answered. "You didn't listen to me. I can't help you over there—you're on your
own. Be careful."

*Don't say it! Don't say it!*

"And don't do anything stupid."

*Fuck. He said it.*

Suddenly it was dead quiet.

"Kelly?"

"I'm here."

"What next?"

"We get loaded by the bomb loaders. They have no
idea that we're in here, so stay quiet. This bird has to refuel seven minutes after takeoff."

"It uses that much fuel?" Jason asked.

"No. It leaks through the skin of the plane until the
heat expands the plane and seals it up."

"No!"

"Yeah, and shut up. After that we will climb to cruising altitude and get this drop going. Any more questions?"

"Why wouldn't you tell me this before?" After all he'd been through, this part wasn't shit, just tight and uncomfortable.

"It would have taken all the fun out of it for you. I wanted to keep you hyped for the jump."

"You little fuck. You owe me."

They became quiet as a door opened and closed, and then they heard a noise of some sort—the whine of a small engine.

It was an MB-1 bomb loader, nicknamed Jammer. Two muzzle fuckers, as bomb loaders are known, entered the hangar with their bomb loader. They were unknowingly loading the most secret and first operational space dive.

"Hey, chief, you got the loading manual for these things?" a voice asked.

"Yeah, the guy in the fuckin' weird wheelchair gave it to me. Creepy guy, huh?" Chief Master Sergeant James Baarda answered. "It's a standard bomb shackle unit. But these things are fuckin' strange, aren't they? I wonder what they do."

"Don't ask me. You're the big dog on this shit, not me."

"So let's get to work, okay?"

"Hey, you see the new banana show on BC Street?"

"You mean the one where the broad takes some fuckin' ice cream and chocolate syrup, spreads it on her shaved pussy, shoves a banana up her snatch, and then serves it up to a GI like a fuckin' banana split. That one?"

"Yeah. I ate it last night, and it tasted great."

At first it sounded to the muzzle fuckers like each of them was laughing, but then they looked at each other and saw that they weren't. The "laughter" was coming from one of their loads.

"What the fuck?" Baarda exclaimed.

"I don't fucking believe it," his partner gasped.

They loaded the units in record time and were gone.

"Jason?"

"I'm sorry, but I couldn't help it."

"Don't worry, I was laughing too. I'm really jazzed about this drop."

"Man, I'm just glad I got to piss and shit everything out of my system. I can't believe I'm doing this. And this is only the start!"

"Hey, just wait until it happens."

The sound of an opening door quieted them.

The pilot and support personnel had entered the hangar. Jason listened to the complicated before-starting checklist. He could hear the ground crew ready the jet for towing and the sound of the hangar doors opening.

## 0015 WEDNESDAY / 3 NOVEMBER 1999
## KADENA AIR BASE / JAPAN

The sound of a massive jet engine startled Jason.

He guessed that they had already towed them out to the launch pad and now were at "engines start." The start was loud, and promised to get louder. The Space Diver rocked lightly back and forth as the Blackbird taxied to final.

As he listened in to the pilot's radio for the tower's lineup call, Jason's stomach tossed and rolled with anticipation. Tower released Habu, and in the next moment sixty-five thousand pounds of thrust from two Pratt and Whitney engines howled to life. The pilot released the breaks and Jason held on tight to the hand braces as the bird screamed down the runway, then lifted off into the night sky.

For five minutes the noise was almost unbearable, then Jason didn't feel any particular sensation—other than that of being in a coffin. The engines vibrated the hull, and the noise leveled off to just a notch below unbearable.

Hydraulic noises signaled an air-to-air transfer of fuel to the Blackbird from a KC-135 tanker. Separated, the engines once again came to life for a short period, and then throttled back to a tolerable hum.

NSA pilot Dash Roberts, code-named Casper, finished his Cruise Altitude Checklist, then pulled the circuit breaker, disabling the Cockpit Voice Recorder (CVR). "Hey, Froto, you on?"

"Roger, Casper."

"Good. I hear you have a partner."

"His name is Alice. Say hi to Casper, Alice."

"Hello, Casper."

"Hi, Alice, welcome aboard Habu. They call me Casper because I say I fly with the spirits of all the pilots who've been in this seat. We're going to be flying at about two thousand miles an hour, at about one hundred and twenty thousand feet. At this height and speed, the skin of my bird is somewhere around nine hundred degrees, or more.

"Nice to have you on this very unique flight. After we level off, I'm going to air-refuel again with another KC-135 tanker a couple of times. Then I'm going to do a toboggan maneuver to get us up to altitude. After that we're going to skirt the Chinese and Russian airspace and drop weather sensors that will plot your drop angles. Before we get too far we're going to accidentally on purpose develop engine trouble, and then I'm going to activate an automatic program and pass on some code words. After the info goes out, every Commie for thousands of miles around will know that I'm turning around and returning to Kadena for maintenance. Once I've turned around I'll do the same thing. But I'll drop you at the first weather sensor I dropped, you'll be gone, and I'll land back at Kadena, less you guys. Can you handle that?"

"I'm a big boy," sighed Jason.

"Unless you have any questions, I'm going to reactivate the CVR and you won't be able to speak anymore."

"No questions," Jason said. He was sure that if his

knees could touch each other they would probably knock louder than the engines.

"A-okay," said Kelly.

"Good luck to you guys; you'll be punching out at one hundred and twenty thousand feet." Dash reactivated his CVR.

The basic mission was to electronically probe and photograph the activities of the North Koreans, Chinese, and Russians: border skirmishes, military movement, and anything else that needed furtive observation.

Dash and all the other NSA reconnaissance pilots had been working double duty since the crash of the NIMA computer system. He knew that the "cargo" he carried was headed to solve *problems,* among other things.

Reaching final altitude, Dash turned on his autopilot, reported his position, and then pressed a button on his console. Everything was on automatic as the program flawlessly made all the designed moves. Dash had no real idea what was happening with the automatic program; he was there to take over in case something malfunctioned.

At a certain point the forward bomb bay shell retracted into its body and several small air sensors, called dropsondes, were ejected into the thin air. As the dropsondes fell they sampled and mapped two hundred miles of an atmospheric trail to an area just beyond the Zond stronghold.

Suddenly one of the plane's engines made a popping sound and just about scared the hell out of Jason.

Dash quickly radioed engine trouble to Kadena on an unsecure channel and was told to immediately return to base for maintenance. Smiling, he deftly maneuvered the SR-71 around to a reverse course.

Show the false. Hide the real. It was the top and bottom line of any successful tactical deception. The goobers on the bad side monitored the spy plane's every move. Engine trouble was a shrug-off—everyone gets that—so they quit looking as hard at their radar screens as they normally did—not taking into account that the route the SR-71 flew back was exactly the same one it had come by. Dash once again pulled the CVR circuit breaker.

"How you guys holding up?"

"Just fine, if you like riding in a sardine can."

"Shit, Jason, this is fucking awesome!" said Kelly.

"Yeah, but you can't *see* anything."

"Just wait."

"I'm reading two minutes before you guys get ejected." Dash turned the valve that switched them from the SR-71's oxygen system to the Space Divers' system.

"Ten seconds."

Jason could hear whines from hydraulic systems opening up the cargo bays.

"Good luck, boys," the pilot said.

## 0215

Jason's body went weightless; he was barely aware that he was falling at two thousand miles an hour. Heat began to build on the belly of the pod. If Mike's design was wrong, he would soon fry in the nine-hundred-degree Fahrenheit heat.

The cross section on radar looked like pebble-sized meteors entering the atmosphere. Boringly common. At fifty thousand feet they would disappear from the screen, vaporized. In reality the makeup of the hull's stealth would be fully operational.

"Alice, how you holding up?"

"Hot, but fine."

"We're going through one hundred thousand feet."

Jason would breathe easier when he got to an altitude he knew. *Relax. You're almost there.* Suddenly he heard a ripping noise that made him yipe. A front layer of the Space Diver peeled away, leaving a clear shield through which Jason could see the curvature of Earth. He could see the separation of the light and darkness and look down upon Earth like a god.

"Pretty cool, huh?" Kelly asked. "I told Mike not to tell you so you would be surprised."

Jason was speechless. Though he was falling at the terminal velocity, it felt as if he weren't moving at all. The sun was setting, creating hues of red and blue that he would never forget.

"Jason, we are about to enter our own atmosphere and it's gonna get really rough, so hang on. Jason?"

"Oh, roger, get rough," he answered, still mesmerized by the sights.

Now he could hear air rushing past the Space Diver. Then it got bumpy and rough. It quickly turned into a ride beyond bizarre as the diver's flight probe followed the path of the dropsondes. Negative and positive g-forces almost pushed him through the skin of his compartment. It got blacker the closer the Space Diver got to Earth and over Siberia.

At five thousand feet, if the Space Diver didn't split, then he would be a three-million-dollar dirt dart.

Suddenly the pod exploded into a billion pieces and Jason spun in the darkness. Something was wrong. He tumbled out of control. The equipment pack was partially detached and rolling him out of control. If he didn't do something fast, he would pass out from the centrifugal forces.

Gyrating and doing back flips, he did everything he could to straighten out. Finally, in a flat spin, Jason pulled his ripcord. The chute popped open, and he barely had time to flare the chute before he landed hard, losing his breath in the process. He lay senseless on the cold ground.

## 0220
## BRIEFING THEATER / MISAWA AIR BASE / JAPAN

Every seat in the theater was filled. The C-130, JSTAR, AWAC, and RC-135 Rivet Joint aircrews sat together, positioned according to their weapons systems. They listened to the briefers, but they already knew the drill: a made-up war intell scenario, mission profile, weather, radio frequencies, and a host of other information. They were politely interested. This was the fighters' ORI, not theirs. They were there just for support, but would give the best they had anyway.

Halfway through the mission profile a man in a strange-looking wheelchair rolled in, followed by a giant black Marine general and a spastic Air Force general.

Catching everyone by surprise, Tom Chain excused the cadre of IG inspectors and briefers. Looking confused, they beat a hasty exit when Colonel John Carrillo, the wing commander, entered and waved them out.

"Lock the doors, thank you," Tom said. He waited a few moments, then addressed the aircrews. "So much for IG games. This briefing is classified top-secret—real world, folks."

He watched as people sat up straight in their chairs or opened their eyes wide. He had their full attention.

# CHAPTER 19

**0235 WEDNESDAY / 3 NOVEMBER 1999**
**SIBERIAN TUNDRA / RUSSIA**

**A**LICE, ALICE, ARE YOU OKAY?"

Opening his eyes, Jason saw the concerned face of Froto. "I think so. Hard landing. Damn. We actually made it."

Slowly sitting up, Froto helped Jason remove the pressure suit and put on his helmet and battle gear. Pulling down the night vision visor, Jason took in the environment he had landed in. Stunted hills and a mostly flat terrain surrounded them. The temperature gauge on the visor read fifteen below zero, but he felt warm in his gear. "Let's check in."

Froto nodded and turned on his communicator. "Belly."

No response. Rabid's team was supposed to be five miles away at the Dance checkpoint.

"Well," Froto said, checking his watch, "we met our time. No changes. We stay on schedule." Linking up with Rabid was secondary—it came *after* they planted the bomb.

They wrapped their space suits and parachutes in netting that made the whole deal look like a clump of dirt, then Froto helped Jason strap on the bomb. They checked their gear, making sure that they hadn't left anything lying around, and brought down their clear visors, which gave them a heads-up display of the direction in which they needed to go. Jason glanced back at the netting—they were abandoning equipment over half a million dollars.

Light winds blew as the tundra crunched under their feet, leaving telltale footprints on the ground. Even though they were in bad-guy territory Jason wasn't nervous, just hypersensitive. The only difference from training was that this time the bullets were real and any mistakes would be fatal.

Jason could barely walk under his heavy load.

"Can you handle the weight?" questioned Froto.

"Me? No problem. Go."

Froto took off at a trot.

Jason knew the trail well, having marched it several times in mock-up simulations. But this time there would be no breaks. There was no turning back.

"Stop, Alice. Activate your cape," came Froto's urgent voice.

Slipping on the cloak, Jason kneeled down against a small berm and waited.

"See it?"

Jason adjusted his amplified hearing until he heard a distant humming sound.

"What is it?"

"From what I could see, it's a hovercraft of some sort. Fuck. That's how they move around here. It's heading straight to an entrance. We got to be careful. We didn't count on them using hovercraft—they don't have to stay on any roads and can glide over just about everything." Froto once again switched on his radio and tried to warn the insertion team, but got nothing.

Jason shook his head. Somehow everyone had thought that the Russians would use only wheeled vehicles. Know your enemy. *Mistake one.* He got to his feet and moved out.

Froto waited for Jason near a large mound.

"Not much to report," commented Froto. "There

are people out there near the blockhouse. I can't say if they are extra-alert or what. I can't really tell anything."

"The shaft?"

"I already checked it out. It's the air shaft we believed it was, twenty feet in diameter. But get this—it has a safe-way ladder; miners use them as escape passages. It has steel ladders that lead down in seventy-foot increments. It had a simple alarm on it, but I disabled it."

"We don't use the magnets?"

"No, but we'll bring them along just in case we need them."

Carefully hiding their MOLLE packs, Jason waited until Froto crawled to the top of the berm and disappeared. Then, following, Jason felt for the side of the ladder and carefully edged over the side.

"How ya doin'?" Froto asked.

"Doing." Testing the rungs—they were solid, not rusted. The next rung held, then the next. "This ain't too bad," Jason whispered. "Better than the magnets. It'll cut our time down to nothing." Little victories.

"Then let's get to work."

Silently as they could, they climbed ever lower.

Jason concentrated on each step, trying not to think of how far they had to descend, or what would happen if they came across any people.


THEY HAD BEEN IN THE ESCAPE SHAFT FOR LESS THAN AN hour before sounds began filtering through, but they couldn't identify what those sounds were. They could smell oil and something else, stale vodka? Climbing down further, they reasoned that it was the sounds of generators and machinery.

"Hear that?" Froto asked.

"What?"

"I'd bet it's the sound of big generators winding up. It's what Greg said happens as they bring the EMP on line. My guess is that they're getting it ready to fire. We gotta hurry. If they fire it while we're in here we'll probably fry to death from the hot exhaust."

"Damn!"

"What?" Jason squeaked.

"I'm at the bottom. It leads only one way. You got just one more level to climb down. Hurry!"

Silenced pistols at the ready, and using night vision with infrared lights, Jason felt as if he were in the movie of H.G. Wells, *The Time Machine*. Who could get used to living underground? He followed Froto, who seemed to have an unerring direction or sense of purpose. Quietly, but quickly, they neared their objective.

The tunnel was still wide, ten feet or more. They had yet to come across any fan system. With as much area as they were in, it had to be a huge system. Coming to an area where many smaller air shafts came together, Froto stopped.

"This feels wrong. Alice, wait here until I check out one of these air shafts."

Jason nodded, grateful for a break. He sat down and took a drink of water from his camelback waterbag that hung from between his shoulders. They told him it would be a few degrees warmer underground, but right now it felt like he was in a sauna.

Froto slipped into the tunnel. Looking at the grates, he realized that he was in an access tunnel. He stopped at the first grate and tested the knob—unlocked. Opening it slowly, he sent out a *ping*. It took ten seconds before anything came back. *What in the hell?* What came back was immense.

Cautiously peeking around the door, Froto was shocked. It was a giant cavern, a city. Men in uniforms raced back and forth, assembling for muster. They were mobilizing for some kind of attack. "Oh, fuck me," he gasped. Shit! If intell was wrong about the size of the place, and the readiness of the Russians, then they might be wrong about the generator.

Turning on his radio, Froto keyed it. "Lavender. Repeat, Lavender." The code word meant that the infiltration was successful but that something was wrong and to stay away. Nothing. He was too deep for any transmissions to go out.

Jason sat quietly listening to the underground sounds. No one sound quite registered. But mixed in with all the grinding electric and metallic noises was something even more out of place. Was that the sound of children singing?

"Alice."

"Christ, Froto. Cut that out!" Jason was startled by Froto's return.

"We're going to get as close as possible. Then you leave. Get the fuck away from here and send out the Lavender code."

"Froto, what's going on?" Jason was nervous again.

"I got this real bad feeling that someone knows that we're coming, that we're already here. You got to go and let the team know, then you guys get the fuck outta here."

"No, Froto, plant it and we'll get out together."

"No good; if they know about the team, then they might already have people out looking for us. With these guys on alert there's too much of a chance they'll find the bomb before it blows. One of us has to make sure it blows. That's me. You know it and so do I. It's what I came here for. You're the backup, and now I don't need you anymore. You go and warn the team."

There was no arguing with the little man when he made up his mind.

The howl of turbines and generators stopped them for a moment.

"See, they're getting close to being on line, real close," hissed Froto. "I have to wait to make my move and then get out of this shaft if I can. Now help me arm my bomb and get outta here."

Jason took the bomb off his back and laid it on the ground. "Froto, I'm telling you, plant the thing and we'll get out of here together."

As he knelt and unpacked the weapon, a strange look came over Kelly's face. "This is what I came for. You understand? Help me set the thing and get out of here before they fire the thing and fry us both. It's got to be me, just me. Don't take away my distinction of becoming the ultimate sapper."

Jason kept trying. "Okay, I'll help you set it, but are you going to get out after you plant it?"

"If I can." He looked up at Jason. "We've been friends for a long time, but now your job is to warn Rabid and let me do my thing. Now help me prime this fucker."

Kneeling next to his friend, Jason went through his memorized procedures and codes for arming a priority "A" munitions. Just like in the classroom, it was a two-man operation, but this time the weapon was real. Jason pressed his arming switch at the same time Kelly pressed his. On the panel, a small red light blinked on. It was a live nuclear weapon.

"Hey, bud, this bomb's for you," Kelly smiled. "Now get the hell out of here."

Jason grabbed Kelly and hugged him.

"Listen," Kelly said, squirming away. "Tell Mac to find some fresh pussy for me and put it on hold. Thanks for getting me here. Now go, and—"

"I know: 'Don't do anything stupid.'"

"No. I was going to say watch your back. I might not be there to cover you."

Jason turned and left without looking back, heedless of the need for quiet. He wanted to get out of the shaft fast, before Froto was discovered and set off the nuke or the EMP was fired and sent searing radioactive heat exhaust through the tunnel. Hitting the base of the ladders, he wasted no time climbing, not even thinking about slipping and falling.

**0350**
**ZOND HEADQUARTERS / SIBERIAN TUNDRA**

Draped in his cape, Jason moved cautiously but rapidly toward the blockhouse. He knew the trail from hours of map study and endless practice scenarios. This was no longer a game. *Now* he was getting nervous. In a short matter of time a nuclear blast was set to obliterate the ground he walked on.

He hadn't heard from Rabid or any of the team since he had gone into the escape shaft—just static. No one had acknowledged the Lavender code. Someone had to be jamming the frequencies.

The sky was black and overcast. A chill wind blew. The cold front was coming, just as predicted. In another few hours a "Siberian Express" would roll through, bringing freezing fifty-mile-an-hour winds. Fortunately, the gear he wore was designed to withstand such an onslaught and even more on the hard frozen tundra.

Jason could waste no time. He had to be gone before the bomb blast, with or without the team. He would have to find Kurgan on his own.

Turning on his GPS, he ascertained that he was at the insertion point, but there was no one waiting, or any markers that said they had already been there. "Where are you guys?" he asked the wind. "Nervous" graduated to "scared." Were they compromised, or maybe captured?

He checked his watch—time was wasting. *You're on your own, pal.* Even without backup, Jason decided to get into the command center and take out Oleg Kurgan the moment he saw him. It was suicide, but there was nothing else he could do. If somehow Kurgan survived the blast, he could start building another weapon. It would be just a matter of time before someone would have to find the EMP and blow it up again, and by then it would be even harder to get to him. Without the Brothers around, Jason decided that Kurgan had to die.

Jason removed his MOLLE pack and stored it at the designated collection point, then crawled toward the blockhouse. It was open and exposed. A single road led to a small guardhouse with just one guard. Was he bait?

The Russian launch was in about ten minutes, thousands of miles away. The EMP was probably up to full power, ready to protect their launch from any cruise missiles or from anything else trying to stop the launch.

There was no time to ponder his actions; time had run out for stealth. One silenced shot. The guard fell. No one was in the guard shack.

Jason ran to the blockhouse, opened the door, flipped up his NVV, and just walked in. No one even noticed him; everyone was intently watching computer screens and monitors. *Where's Kurgan? Where's Kurgan?*

Suddenly there were soldiers with guns everywhere, and then Lucas and the team burst in behind him and the shooting started.

For a moment, Jason stood in disbelief as time slowed down. The Russians started yelling and pointing at the team; then there were screams of surprise, anguish, and pain as the Brothers opened up with their weapons. The sounds of bullets zipping and snapping around him made him realize that if he didn't move for cover he would be hit.

Jason jumped to the side as Pia took the point and let loose with his automatic rifle.

"No primary!" Jason yelled. Though he was hyperalert, his eyes taking in everything, he hadn't ID'd Kurgan, so the team restrained their shooting until they had their man.

They fought as one, covering one another's move or countermove. Pick a target. Drop a target. Bob, weave, and watch your teammate's back. Control the action. Don't let the situation get away. Do your assigned duty without delay. Keep the fight moving.

The Brothers advanced through the gun smoke that clouded the room. Jason searched frantically for any sign of Kurgan. All the plans and training were going to be wasted.

"He ain't here! Extract!" Rabid called over the noise.

The team immediately began the retrograde maneuver, covering each other as they backed out of the low building.

Jason was angry and frustrated. All he had done to get to the battle, and now he was headed out the door without meeting his objective. He had come for one man and was leaving without him.

A Russian soldier tried to cover the exit door but Pia turned his rifle on him and sprayed him with lead. The man flew back into a metal locker. As his body crashed into the locker door, a man fell out from inside it. Surprised, he jumped up from the floor and ran toward a group of soldiers who were returning fire. The profile: Kurgan! Jason sprinted, heedless of the lead in the air, and tackled him. Holding him on his back, Jason saw that he had the right man. "Pia, where are you? I got Kurgan." Not waiting for a response, he hammered Kurgan as hard as he could in the temple with his closed fist, knocking him unconscious.

Pia appeared next to him, then threw Kurgan over his shoulder and raced toward the door, with Jason right behind him.

"Ming, light it up!" commanded Rabid.

Ming reached into a pouch and pulled out two silver canisters. He grabbed a short lanyard and threw it against the far wall. It immediately exploded, hotter than the sun, sucking oxygen from the room and giving off toxic fumes at the same time.

"Out! Out! Out!" ordered Rabid as he covered the door.

Jason scrambled through the door, then turned and took a defensive position to let Rabid back his way out, followed by Puma, Zorro, and Ming.

Rabid nodded, and Ming threw in his last heat bomb. Then Zorro lobbed in a cyanide gas grenade over Ming's shoulder.

"Now let's get out of here." Rabid calmly ordered.

Resetting their NVVs, they sprinted for exactly four hundred yards, then ran into Pia, kneeling over a bound-and-trussed Oleg Kurgan.

Gathering his team together, Rabid asked, "Is anybody hit or injured?" They had only seconds to grab their gear and get out of there.

"Remind me to kiss Dennis when this is over," heaved Zorro.

Everyone had taken hits, but their body armor had

held up. Bruises in the body beat the hell out of holes; the team was fine.

**0420**
**SIBERIAN TUNDRA / RUSSIA**

Jason was shocked and puzzled. He had taken hits, but had been too hyped to realize it during the fight. Now he was too full of adrenaline to feel sore. After taking a gulp of water from his pack, he shined his mini-flashlight to get a closer look at Kurgan. Kurgan looked just like his pictures. Jason reached out and touched the still-unconscious man, as if to demystify a ghost. He then searched Kurgan for any concealed weapons. Kurgan wore a quilted suit made of wool; it looked like it could keep him from freezing on the tundra. He wore silver cuff links with the Zond insignia on his shirtsleeves. Jason removed the cuff links and dropped them into his pocket. Finding no weapons, he sat back on his haunches to put on his gear.

"Alice, where's Froto?" Rabid asked.

"Back at the generator. I think he's going to hand-blow it." Jason couldn't see Rabid's eyes through the gray NVV. "Where were you guys and how come our communications don't work? I tried to warn you that they might be onto us."

"You're right; somebody *is* onto us. And I don't know what happened to our communications. We had to slip by a fucking brigade of security, which I'm sure is right behind us—so much for stealth. Let's move out."

Gear donned, they started to leave. That's when night turned to day. Powerful area lights and illuminating flares shot into the sky.

Kurgan suddenly got to his knees and started screaming frantically at the top of his lungs.

"He's calling for help," said Puma.

With lightning speed, Pia crashed his fist against Kurgan's temple. As Kurgan fell to the ground, Pia jammed a gag in his mouth.

"Ooooh, fuck me," Ming moaned. "Man, we're attracting *lots* of unneeded attention." In a matter of moments he put together his UAV and launched it into the air.

From a short distance thousands and thousands of men came swarming toward them.

Rabid flipped up his NVV and then, calmly taking in the scene, he asked, "Ming, you think you can transmit our info? Tell them we're surrounded and looking for a breakout."

"It's ready to go."

"Then do it," Rabid said, looking back at the smoldering blockhouse. "There's nothing here to defend and we didn't carry in enough firepower for a breakout. We can't go back to the blockhouse—it'll be hours before the cyanide fumes are gone. Any suggestions?"

"Suicide?" Puma offered.

"Forget it," Ming said.

"Fight our way through," Zorro said.

Puma looked at the oncoming horde through his night vision binoculars. "It looks *real* bad. Tell me this don't make you wanna shitsky in your pants."

"See any way out?" Lucas asked Ming.

Looking through his Dragon eyepiece, Ming shook his head. "If you're going just by the amount of radiant heat on infrared, we're fucked."

"No surrender, gentlemen. We gotta keep the attention away from Froto. If we spread out we might be able to confuse them a little. If we split up now, I think that some of us might even get through to the rendezvous point," Lucas observed as the soldiers got into firing range. "Anyone say different? Guys, I was wrong—I didn't think that this would happen. We're out of time."

Only the vein pounding in Lucas's temple gave away the fact that he was apprehensive and nervous.

*Now what?* Jason's only thought was of how to get out.

"Yeah, let's do it," Puma said. "Like NOW."

"Activate your capes. In pairs, get moving." Lucas

ripped off his helmet and grabbed Jason. "If you're lucky and get out, *don't* make the rendezvous. You and Kurgan are targets now," Lucas hissed into his ear. "Take Kurgan with you. Pia's going with you too. You got to get out of this fucking place on your own with Kurgan. Now you know why I wanted you on this mission: Only a PJ with skills like yours can survive in this environment with a hostage. Stay alive. *Survive!* Good luck, pal." He grabbed Pia for a few seconds and gave him orders, then set out on his own toward the advancing Russians.

"Pia, this way," Jason called over his shoulder.

Hoisting the still-unconscious Kurgan over his shoulder, Pia took out after Jason.

Jason led the way up and over many short hills, not knowing where they led, but not caring—it was away from the Zond soldiers. With everything gone to shit, Jason resolved that the first moment he got, he was going to put a bullet in Kurgan.

They stopped in their tracks when the darkness Jason was heading for turned into day. Lights lit up the surrounding area for miles.

"Oh...no." Jason sighed.

"Now where?" Pia asked.

"Up there." Jason pointed to a ridgeline.

They scooted up the hill, Jason leading the way.

Bullets flew everywhere, and Jason fell into a hole. Looking back, he yelled for Pia. Then Pia's helmet exploded.

"Ah SHIT!" cried Jason, running low from the hole until he reached Pia. There was no question that Pia was dead; his head was almost gone. Grabbing Kurgan's limp body, Jason dragged it toward the shallow hole and pushed him in first.

The impact of something smacking his head threw Jason into the hole after Kurgan. Feeling his helmet, he was surprised to come away holding an intensifier tube. Shit. Someone had gotten a head shot on him, missing a direct hit by less than an inch! Split and cracked, the helmet was just about useless—but had saved his life!

# CHAPTER 20

**A**ND THAT'S IT," JASON SAID. "THAT'S HOW WE GOT here. I don't care if you understand the whole thing, because I'm probably a dead man anyway. Now it's just you, me, and thousands of your Russky comrades with all their guns pointed at this little hole."

He felt strangely elated. He had accomplished the impossible: After having come halfway around the world to one of the most inhospitable places on Earth, he now had the man he'd vowed to kill at his feet, just a trigger pull from death.

He knew he couldn't sit in this ratty little hole forever and that the Zond soldiers weren't going to wait much longer, but there was no way he was going to peek over the pit. "I ain't going nowhere," he said to himself. "It's out of my hands, pal," he said aloud, and grinned at Kurgan. He decided that he would just sit and wait for someone else to make the next move.

Suddenly the ground began to rumble.

"Froto!" Jason hit the ground and pulled Kurgan on top of him.

Kelly had done it! He had blown the generator and

set off a nuclear explosion. "Better hold on, Kurgan. We're all about to die!"

The concussion almost blew out Jason's ears. The shock wave tossed Pia's body directly into the hole with him. Then came the dirt and heat. Eyes tightly shut, Jason tried to claw his way deeper into the hole.

## 2005
## PENTAGON / ARLINGTON / VIRGINIA

The room was located in a lower basement among wet floors, leaky pipes, and stained walls. In the dark room several men in suits sat or stood watching a flat screen. On the screen was an overhead close-up of the Zond stronghold. A supersecret satellite known as a Superconducting Quantum Ultraviolet Device (SQUID) delivered the image. The satellite was so far out in space that it actually went backward to circle the Earth.

Men avoided eye contact as they wrote on notepads or Palm Pilots.

A cellular phone rang. Quiet voices conversed at the back of the room. But the somber atmosphere changed in an instant.

"We got the data and the video's clear. They did it, and they got Kurgan, but they're surrounded."

"Look!"

The men in dark suits watched slack-jawed as a portion of the Siberian ground collapsed, then mushroomed into the night sky. Almost instantly the phone rang again.

"What's the signal? What's the reading?"

One man held up his hand to silence the others. After speaking into the cellular phone in intense whispers, he addressed the room. "The DSP readings say it's not at nuclear levels. After the dust settles we can attribute the explosion to a huge pocket of natural gas. I have people ready to plant the story in the media."

Audible sighs filled the room.

"I can't tell about the team there, or Kurgan. They

could have been consumed in the blast. Either way, there's a lot of work to do to keep this project quiet."

"Then get on with it," a man wearing a black leather trench coat said, as he rose from his chair and left the room. As he walked up the mildewed hall, there were a lot of things on his mind.

Now the Russian rocket launch meant nothing to him. Without the EMP generator, the reflector was useless, though he still had a point to make with the Russians. The team on the ground in Siberia meant nothing to him either. As a matter of fact he was glad that his chances of seeing Jason Johnson again were slim. He would have to deal with the loss of Kurgan. The game was about over. Now was the time to tie up loose ends and cover his trail.

"Mister Black!" an aide called.

Boris turned around.

"Sir, I think that you should come back here and have a look at something."

## 0430 THURSDAY / 4 NOVEMBER 1999
## SHRIEVER AIR FORCE BASE / COLORADO

Doug Jones sat watching the atomic clock on the wall. He had already input the checklist data into the computer and was just waiting for the clock to match the checklist before he put the periphery card in the laptop. He snapped it securely in place and got the green light to proceed with the final instructions.

Time. He had two minutes to type in the last instructions. The instructions had to be perfect. Confident of his ability, he was done in less than a minute, giving him a minute to check his work. That done, he hit the enter key and placed his checklist in a small tub of water sitting beneath the computer table.

The instructions were microburst by a small transmitter connected to the computer. Doug looked at the tub of water.

The checklist was water-soluble and dissolved away

completely. The computer screen suddenly went black.
Done. The periphery card had zapped the computer and
transmitter with an electromagnetic pulse. No one could
ever use the devices again, or figure out what the units
did. Jones found it ironic that the same periphery card
that had started the mission had killed it.

"Damn!" Jones spit. His wristwatch stopped. He'd
been sitting too close to the computer and the card had
zapped the watch too. Like the computer, it was now forever useless.

His mission was over.

Jones stood up as he heard the tumblers on the door.
The door opened and he walked out of the room. The
man in the black suit stood back to let him pass, whisper-
ing into a cellular phone as Jones left. Jones had a good
idea of what he had just done, but would never reveal his
knowledge—one of the reasons that he had been selected
for the job. If any information about what he had just
done in the vaulted room was ever leaked, he would not
live to tell anyone anything.


## 1040 THURSDAY / 4 NOVEMBER 1999
## NORTHEASTERN SIBERIAN TUNDRA / RUSSIA

Like something out of a cheap horror movie, first a hand,
then an arm, and then the rest of the body struggled from
the shallow grave.

Coughing and hacking, Jason didn't care if anybody
was around. Everything was dark and the dust choked
him. But no one was shooting at him. All around him
was a thick and blinding fog of dirt. The explosion had
actually blown away the wind. But it would be back.

Digging around, he pulled Kurgan's head out from
the dirt and removed the gag. "Hey, you still alive?" He
felt the neck for a pulse; it was weak and rapid. Jason
pulled him from the hole.

He'd have to wait on killing the man now that he
was his ticket out of here. Pia lay dead just inches away,

covered in dirt. Rooting out Pia's body, he removed his ammunition clips, water pack, and all his MREs. It was difficult looking at the space that had once been the head of Marine Gunnery Sergeant Nicholas Pia. "Semper fi, Brother."

It was time to move. He had to put ground between him and what was once Zond. It was time for the two-minute drills. He could barely see his hand in front of his face. Standing, he took a deep drink from his camelback, heedless if any radiation had contaminated it. He had to head somewhere. There was no telling if anyone around was still alive. And there was no telling when a Russian might show up to investigate the scene.

As Kurgan lay on the ground without moving, Jason said, "I know you're awake. Get up, fucker; I ain't carrying your ass no more. I got you this far. You want to go any farther, then your happy feet will have to carry you. Bye." Jason turned to go.

"Wait. Please, I'm an old man."

"Hey, I know a few things about you. You're fifty-eight, and a former marathon runner. You can probably outrun me. Unless you've gotten lazy in the past years, you can walk." Jason could barely see his face.

"You seem to know a lot about me, mister."

"Alice."

"May I have some water?"

Jason cut Kurgan's bonds—he could take the man if he tried anything. Then he tossed him Pia's camelback. "When it's gone, don't ask for more. We got to get going. Hurry!"

"Mister Alice, then what *can* I ask you for? You monsters just killed my city. There were a lot of people who lived there, over twenty-five thousand. I had many friends. My family! My wife!"

Jason stopped, stunned. "That's a lie. You can't be right. No more than a few thousand support personnel were there—it was a military target."

Kurgan's head hung low. "You have been lied to, to

get you to kill us!" Looking up at Jason, he gritted his teeth. "You know I'm telling you the truth! You murdered thousands of innocent women and children."

"No. It can't be true," Jason gasped. But he wasn't talking to Kurgan as much as to himself. The man was right. Those *were* children's voices he'd heard in the shaft. A lifetime of rescues and lifesaving as a pararescueman had been eclipsed the moment he'd become a mass murderer.

Though Jason had thought he was in control, he'd been played like a wooden violin from the very beginning. All the time he was playing it cool, the Doors were stringing him along, as long as he played their tune. The song over, the mission accomplished, now he was expendable.

"In all the building efforts of the world, none could match ours. We had discovered how to create endless cheap energy. It could have changed the world. And you have destroyed it all."

Lied to, betrayed, and abandoned, Jason had no idea what to do. The vendetta no longer mattered. The mission no longer meant anything to him. He felt empty. In one instant, everything good he had ever done was gone. Blinded by his own agenda, he had allowed himself to be used by others—so much so that he was a primary target for a rubout.

But now what? *Stay alive! Survive.* Lucas had said it. That's what PJs were best at. He would have to deal with the pain later. Kurgan was stalling for time. If anyone alive was around they were probably just coming to their senses. Time to go. Right now there were few options. Lucas was right—he wouldn't bring Kurgan to the extraction point. He was sure that they would both be instantly killed. He was suddenly grateful for all the time he had put in studying the coast of Siberia.

Get to a port and Kurgan might be his ticket out of this mess. He had to get Kurgan to go with him. *Try a bluff.* "Kurgan, I had a mission to do. I did it. You can go back and be counted among the dead, or follow me and

live. I am the best survival specialist in the world." *Man,
I have no idea where to go.*

Kurgan rose unsteadily to his feet.

Jason pulled out his compass. It went haywire. He
couldn't see two hundred feet through the dust. He
flipped down his NVV; it had only two operable NV
tubes and was very fuzzy, so he turned it off.

Quickly checking his weapons and gear, he lost what
meager hope he'd had. The rescue radio was dead; he figured
that the EMP given off during the nuclear blast had fried it.
There would be no talking to anyone, even if he wanted to.

There was no telling how long he would have to
evade, so he'd have to conserve his rations. Except for
what he was carrying, he had to assume that any water
he came across was polluted with radioactivity. Once
again he was in a world of shit, a world he knew quite
well. It was time to move out.

Which direction? *Away from the blast.*

Jason heard Kurgan's footsteps crunching on the
ground behind him. Suddenly the man's pace quickened.
Jason sidestepped as quickly as he could, but was hit
across the helmet by a rock, Turning his head, he rolled
with the strike and threw a blind left uppercut that
struck Kurgan on the chin, dropping him to his knees.

"Asshole! I'll fucking kill you right here. Is that what
you want?" Jason yelled.

"You don't know what it took to do all this. And
you, you killers, you spawned-from-hell murderers, come
here and take it all away! My wife. My work. My life."

"Away? You're the son of a bitch who shot down shit
with your fucking ray gun. You killed my friend, so I came
here to kill you. I can still do that. Is that what you want?"

Grabbing his M-9 bayonet from his survival vest, he
held it to Kurgan's heart, no longer caring about any
vendetta or promise to Lucas. Upon Kurgan's answer he
might very well plunge the blade through his heart until
it came out his back.

"So this is what it is all about, who killed whom,

yes? Well, Mister Alice, you Americans have it all and
you still want more. Destroy my country and still you
want more. Kill thousands and you still want more
blood." Kurgan pressed close to the blade. "I tell you
what. After all you have murdered, *you* decide whether I
live or die. I will tell you true: We knew you were coming
and we know where you are going. You got through, but
Zond will not let you get away!"

The blade wavered, then lowered. Jason turned and
walked away. Kurgan followed.


## 0615
## MISAWA AIR BASE / JAPAN

No one spoke in the Door Operations Center. DSP satellite data went off scale. Tom, Ben, and Twitch wordlessly
stared at the screen for several minutes.

"Any word from the sub?" Ben asked.

"It's in place and the extraction team is on the ice,"
an airman answered.

"Do you think anyone's left?" Twitch asked.

"I don't know." Ben sighed. "I think something happened and Froto probably dialed up the nuke to its highest power."

"Who else is monitoring this?" Tom asked.

"Everyone," muttered Twitch.

"Mission objective complete," commented Tom.

"Bullshit!" exploded Ben. "This ain't over until I get
my team back here. God, what went wrong?"

"It doesn't matter." Tom circled Ben. "The incident
occurred on *Russian* soil. *We* got to let it drop. I'm bet-
ting that nothing will happen, nothing at all. It wasn't
*that* big of an explosion. Let's just sit back and see what
happens."

"And my team?" Ben asked. "What are you trying to
say?"

"Try and locate them, of course, then bring them

home. Nothing's changed, nothing at all. The Brotherhood completed the tasking. That's all I'm saying."

"Tom, what the fuck is wrong with you? This is family. My boys are out there. *Our* boys are out there. Now I'm gonna get them the fuck back. Are you in or out?"

Tom hung his head. "You're right. I'm sorry. What can I do to help?"

"Contract all the time from that commercial satellite we've been using and look for them."

"But they won't sign a security clearance."

"Fuck it. Fake it. You know how. Tom, I hate to pull rank on you, but this is an order. Get a rescue team ready, wherever you can, and have it prepared to go in after them after we pick up their signals."

Twitch said, "You realize that sending in a rescue team would show U.S. complicity. Ben, *I* outrank *you*, and I'm as sorry as it gets, but I have to say no. The extraction portion of the plan remains the same. If any of the team is left, we'll know then."

"Ah FUCK!" screamed Ben. "This ain't right. I can't stand it in here. I'm gonna find out where my boys are at." Ben stormed from the room.


**2130**
**PENTAGON BASEMENT / ARLINGTON / VIRGINIA**

"I'm *telling* you what the DSP satellites detected, understand? A massive natural gas explosion has occurred in the Arctic Circle region of Siberia. That's all I want circulated," Boris said.

"Yes, sir, the readings were all within the range of a natural explosion, a real big one," the assistant confirmed.

"Make the explosion footprint look more irregular," Boris ordered.

The assistant manipulated a joystick and mouse, and the imager made the satellite picture of the explosion take on an oblong shape.

"That looks better, but you better take this to the geology shop and make sure it's accurate enough for them before you release the official photos for selected distribution, *and* for a controlled leak to the media," said Boris. "Decker, I got a job for you. It's time for you to collect some dues owed to me."

## CLASSIFIED DEBRIS LOCATION / 23,000 MILES INTO SPACE

The instructions were received from Jones's computer. The unit came to life. A small gasp moved the stealth SAINT hunter-killer antisatellite away from the debris field. It gasped one more time and began a slow descent as its internal targeting system computed its solution. Ready for battle, it waited patiently for the Lucifer Light to come into view.

It didn't have to wait long. In less than a second, the Lucifer Light appeared just over the horizon and the SAINT fired all its jets unerringly toward it. Colliding at over forty-two thousand miles an hour, the SAINT and Lucifer Light shattered into millions of pieces as its combined debris flew away from the Earth.

NEWS REPORTS OF A LARGE NATURAL GAS EXPLOSION IN Siberia attracted very little attention, as did the intense Leonid meteor storm, a cloud of pebble-sized rocks from the Tempel-Tuttle comet. The rocks, moving at 155,000 miles an hour, threatened only a few satellites. The Air Force Technical Applications Center reported to the news media that only one inoperative Russian satellite in a Molniya orbit was struck and had exploded, the pieces tumbling into deep space. Coincidentally, a new Russian-launched satellite failed to achieve orbit and plunged back to Earth, burning up on reentry into the planet's atmosphere.

# CHAPTER 21

**1530 FRIDAY / 5 NOVEMBER 1999**
**SIBERIAN TUNDRA / RUSSIA**

THERE WAS NO REASON TO TALK, JUST AN ENDLESS process of putting one foot in front of the other. Jason followed the sunrise. The flat horizon stretched forever. The air was still dusty and probably radioactive. If what Kurgan had said was true, the rendezvous with the Brothers was out, if any were still alive. Right now Jason's only thought was to put distance between him and the explosion.

Jason pulled out his compass, which pointed to north fairly well. Little victories. They could head northeast and be at the Bering coast in a couple of days. Jump a ship or freighter. It might work. Having a direction, some kind of option, made things seem a little better; besides, it was the only thing he could think of at the moment.

Kurgan was doing his best to keep up. "Mister Alice, please slow down. I am hungry and tired. *Please.*"

Right now Jason didn't care if Kurgan lived or died. The simplest thing to do, Jason realized, would be to turn around and put a bullet in his head. Baggage dropped. But something told him to reconsider. Deep in his heart, he felt that he owed Kurgan something, having taken a direct hand in destroying—if not ending—the lives of thousands in his city.

It was just rolling mounds and mounds as far as he could see. There was no place to build a fire, or anything to fuel a fire, so Jason sat on the ground. His clothing was impervious to the cold and wind. Reaching into his vest, he pulled out two Meals Ready to Eat. He tossed one to Kurgan. "It tastes better than seal blubber, and it better last you at least three days."

Sitting close to Jason, Kurgan inspected his pack. "Ham? Is good?"

Jason shrugged and cut into his own MRE, spaghetti.

"Is good!" Kurgan smiled.

"Make it last."

"Last for what? Are your men coming to get you?"

"Us."

"Yes, us."

For the first time since he could remember, Jason had time to think about what had happened. He had survived a nuclear explosion unscathed. The primary mission had been met: The EMP generator was dead. The secondary sat next to him. He had no idea which members of the team were alive, dead, or captured.

Froto had to have been vaporized in the blast. As for the rest of the team, who knew? It looked as if those who were going to rub out the team wouldn't have to waste their time. *We rubbed ourselves out. And I killed everyone else.*

Bracing himself against the cold, Kurgan looked back the way they had come. "You know that there will soon be others out looking for survivors. If they find me, they will kill you."

"No. If they find me, I will kill you first. Besides, they're all dead."

"You think so, mister spy? I think not. Tell me, Mister Alice, why did you save me? Why did you not let me die?"

Jason said nothing as he ate his spaghetti.

"You are taking me back to your side, are you not?"

The drab sky grew dark. "How cold does it get here at night?"

"Cold enough to kill us." Kurgan laughed derisively. "So show me the high-technical device you have to get us away from all this. The nuclear blast burned up any electronic devices for many kilometers around. How far do you think we have gone? Ten miles? Twenty?"

"In a matter of hours there will be planes all over the sky. Do you know who the EMP you destroyed belonged to?"

Jason shook his head.

"The man next in line to succeed Boris Yeltsin. This was his secret weapon. He was the one who funded our city. Did you know that? Do you know you have changed the balance of power in Russia? Without his secret weapon, he is as vulnerable as anyone else trying to gain power."

Kurgan seemed talkative. There was more Jason wanted to know. "So Zond is just a political tool."

"Ah, no. Zond has been with the Soviets from the beginning. While you Americans raced to beat us in space, I never saw it as a race. It is like...how to say? Mastery of space. That is what I was after. Yes. That was our goal."

Kurgan looked in the distance over Jason's shoulder and then, like a shot, jumped to his feet and began to race away before Jason could react. He was fast. Jason sighted his rifle on him, but did not fire.

"Shit!" He jumped to his feet and ran after Kurgan.

A hovercraft in the distance glided to a stop, and four armed men jumped from the cab.

Running toward the craft, Jason saw bullets pocketing around Kurgan, who then suddenly dropped to the ground and crawled away, struggling toward a rock boulder.

The men sauntered toward Kurgan and surrounded him.

Jason tried activating his cape, but it would not function. He would have to use old-fashioned stealth.

The driver sitting behind the controls didn't even know he was dead as his brains splattered on the windscreen. Jason quickly got off six more equally fatal shots.

Kurgan writhed and rolled on the ground, his leg covered in blood.

As Jason grabbed Kurgan's right leg, the man's howls of pain could be heard above the wind. The obvious assessment was that he had taken a round through his lower right calf. The bullet hole entrance from the shin was small, but the exit wound had torn away most of the calf muscle. Arteries were ripped and torn, and blood from the exit wound pumped everywhere. Jason had to stop the bleeding, but didn't have time to do a thorough job—they had to get the hell away from where they were, fast. More men were probably on the way.

"Oh, don't be a wimp!" Jason chided. Ripping open his medruck and pulling out a tourniquet, he tied it above Kurgan's knee and tightened it until the bleeding stopped. It needed to hold until Kurgan could be properly attended to. The damage done by the bullet was not overly serious—requiring amputation, maybe—but without immediate treatment, Jason knew, a shock like this to an older man's system could kill him.

"Listen, you wouldn't listen to me and now you might die. Do you really want to die?"

Kurgan shook his head through the pain.

"Good. You're listening to me. I'm going to shoot you up with some drugs and take away some of the pain. Then we're going to try and get the fuck out of here. You got to hang on. Understand?"

Jason fixed up a morphine syringe, then injected the morphine into the vein on Kurgan's right forearm. He passed out immediately. The PJ checked and found that his heart still beat strong.

Dragging Kurgan over to the hovercraft, Jason dumped him into the front passenger seat and checked to make sure that the man's leg wasn't bleeding, then went back to the dead men and removed their water canteens and weapons before climbing into the truck.

Putting the gear into the backseat, he discovered several bottles of vodka. *Well, well.* He tossed a few of the bottles at the dead men, sure that whoever found them would not let them go to waste and maybe the liquor would slow down their pursuit a little. He pushed out the man and got behind the steering wheel, then ripped out the radio before taking stock of the controls.

It didn't looked like a hovercraft at all. Checking the outside, Jason found there was no bellow skirt, or driver fans. What the hell was he sitting in? He flipped what looked to be a battery switch and pressed a prominent black button. The vehicle lifted noiselessly off the ground.

"Holy shit! What in the hell is this?" Oh well, he would figure out the various gauges and switches later. Right now he had to put as much ground between the four dead men and himself and Kurgan as possible. He pushed a lever forward, and the vehicle started moving.

It was a smooth ride, and almost noiseless. A gauge on the dashboard showed a needle halfway into the green and moving toward the yellow. He would keep the thing moving until it got in the red and ran out of power. After that, opportunity would have to present itself again. In the meantime he would head northeast.

Kurgan seemed to be taking the pain well—he was just a little groggy now—but there was no time to stop and check him out. "Just keep your leg still and I'll take care of it as soon as I can. Let me ask you something. What is this thing we're in?"

"It's called a glider. It rides on an electromagnetic cushion and is battery-powered. It used to run on a radio frequency that supplied power to the battery, but you destroyed the relay station, along with everything else."

Jason wouldn't have believed the man if he hadn't at that moment been at the controls of this... "glider." Froto had mistaken the thing for a hovercraft. The steering was not unlike that of a hovercraft, but it was quicker and more responsive. "Let's say that I destroyed everything at Zond but this glider. Are there copies of your work somewhere that would enable you to do it all over again?"

Kurgan gave Jason a wary look. "*Maybe*. It is encrypted."

"Maybe, shit." Jason laughed, "How much you want to bet that they have your work decrypted by now?"

Kurgan squinted his eyes as if he was focusing on the past. "I used to have a dacha in Moscow. I was a *respected* man. I had connections. I put together the whole program. I fought the political battles. It was me, damn it! I am the one that brought Zond my directed energy program." Looking down at his leg, he muttered, "And this is my reward." He looked at Jason. "You have saved my life, but you killed everything else."

"Right now you're not the one I'm concerned about." Jason didn't want to hear it. He pulled the throttle back until Kurgan shut up and hung on to his seat to keep from being thrashed against the wall.


## 2130
## RALEIGH / NORTH CAROLINA

"The SQUID's picking something up. I got thermal movement on the ground," the imager said.

"Moving in what direction?" Boris asked.

"Northeast. It might be a vehicle of some sort, possibly a scout vehicle. We're moving out of camera range."

Another imager ran in from the next room. "There are four bodies five miles away."

"How do you know?" Boris demanded.

"Their thermal signature is fading, but the oscilloscope color frequency definitely ID'd them as human."

"Damn," the lead imager spit. "We won't have anything else until thirteen hours from now."

"I want you to patch a feed to me," Boris said under his slouch hat.

"That'll cost you," the imager replied. A private company owned the supersecret SQUID satellite. Every request cost money, no matter who asked.

A white envelope landed on the desk in front of the imager.

"My man here will take care of the details. You just do what he asks for." Boris turned and walked out as the man flipped through the stack of hundred-dollar bills.

"I want your codes," Decker said. He had learned hundreds of Boris's codes, and memorizing a few more would be no problem.

## 1630
## TYRIAN AIR BASE / RUSSIA

Two Su-27 Sukhoi Flanker jets roared off the runway flying at over Mach 2, headed in an easterly direction. More were being prepped for flight. Due to the devastation of the Russian military and the unavailability of tankers, air-to-air refueling was impossible, so it would take two landings to refuel the jets before they reached their target. The Russian Mafia provided the fuel, so it was virtually guaranteed to be there. The pilots were confident they could reach their target in time and destroy it.

## 1631
## ON AN RC-135 RIVET JOINT AIRCRAFT CIRCLING OVER THE SEA OF JAPAN

"Sir, I got a clearance heading for one or two fast movers," the Russian linguist, Technical Sergeant Bob Hazelwood, called over to the tactical coordinator. He was following the progress of the 35th fighters going through their inspection paces, while keeping one ear on Siberia, as ordered.

"Is that unusual?" John Sheman, the tactical coordinator, asked.

"Very. Unless you can tell me what's going on over a vast tundra that jets have to move faster than the speed of sound."

"Shit." John bit his lip. "I got a feeling that these are the 'unusual happenings' that we've been told to be alert for. Mike, can you get me a fix on those radio transmissions?"

"I'm on it," said Mike Perry, the mission supervisor, dialing up his range finder.

## 1945
## SIBERIAN TUNDRA / RUSSIA

It was like sliding on an ocean of ice. The uneven wind picked up and blew on their tail, making the steering hard and causing a bumpy ride. But as long as they kept gliding northeast, it was fine with Jason. However, the ride was rough on Kurgan, who slipped in and out of consciousness. In a short time the tourniquet would cause irreparable damage to his leg.

Kurgan mumbled in Russian. Jason wondered what the words meant. Were they secrets Boris would kill for, or endearments to his dead wife and family? Whatever he was saying, Jason felt sure, had probably been made necessary by the bomb he had placed under the man's city. *Would I have done it if I had known?*

Jason slowed to a stop, turned off the power switch, and then grabbed his medruck. The wind howled and shook the truck, piercing through gaps in the doors. The heater vents offered little warmth against the cold.

Cutting away the blood-soaked pant leg, Jason was gratified to see that the main artery was only cut and not severed. The shinbone was chipped, but not broken. The calf muscle was another story; it would take surgery to reattach it.

Working quickly on the unconscious man, he sewed up the artery, bandaged the wound closed, and then released the tourniquet. No seepage. Kurgan jerked and screamed in unconscious pain.

It was time to move. Scratching his chest, he felt a small bump. Unbuttoning his shirt pocket, he reached in and pulled out a small liquid vial. It was Lucas's ninja potion to get Kurgan to talk. "What the hell." This was what the Doors wanted done. It would be interesting to see what happened. He drew the entire potion into his syringe and injected Kurgan with it.

Jason kept one eye on the terrain and one on Kurgan as they continued northeast. The battery gauge was in the yellow and almost to the red. He would keep driving until they ran out of power, and try to make it to Omersk. The last ships would be pulling out before the harbors finally froze over. If he and Kurgan could stow away on one of them, he could figure out what to do next. His only concern was whether or not Kurgan could travel. If not, he would kill Kurgan in the glider before he left.

Suddenly Kurgan became alert. Looking around, confused, he eyed Jason. "Are you Death?"

"What?"

"Death. I know you, do I not?"

*Oh shit.* Jason kept silent. Kurgan was probably hallucinating and in a world of his own.

"You *are* Death. I know. You killed thousands. Killer!" Looking wildly around, Kurgan snatched a weapon from the backseat. Getting his hand on a Makarov pistol, he tried to shoot Jason, but the PJ was too quick and grabbed Kurgan's wrist.

The noise of the gun going off was deafening inside the cab. Jason swung the steering handle hard to the right, then let go and punched Kurgan's calf. The glider spun in circles. Kurgan quickly turned the gun on himself, and Jason tried to wrestle it away. This time he hammered Kurgan's leg with all his strength.

Dropping the weapon, Kurgan screamed as he clutched his leg.

Grabbing the pistol and the Russian AK-47s, Jason tossed them out the door. Now the only weapons in the vehicle belonged to Jason. He started to grab the remaining vodka bottles and toss them also.

"NO!" Kurgan cried.

Jason shrugged and jumped back onto the driver's seat. Switching on the power and slamming the glider back into gear, he lurched away as Kurgan nursed his throbbing leg.

Jason figured that mixing the morphine and Lucas's drug had been a real bad idea. He chided himself for being a first-class fuckup, but then tossed the last vodka bottle to Kurgan, who sucked it down like a man dying of thirst.

Since he was a kid Jason had always screwed up trying to do his best. It was dumb luck that he had gotten as far as he had. His luck had to be just about at its end. How far? He didn't know. Looking up at the dark gray sky through the windshield, he shook his head.

## 0300 SATURDAY / 6 NOVEMBER 1999
## SIBERIAN TUNDRA / RUSSIA

The heater sort of worked. The ride was still relatively smooth and the headlights illuminated the ground enough for Jason to move along at a moderate speed, fifteen miles an hour.

Glancing over at Kurgan, he saw that he was docile now and staring at nothing. Jason knew his thoughts. It was a face he had seen countless times, in many places around the world. The thousand-yard stare. A little girl named Pat had it when she lost her dog. Vivian had the look when she lost Toby. Kurgan had lost more.

"I remember. You did death's bidding," Kurgan mumbled.

"I did my job."

"Do you have family, Mister Alice?"

"No."

"Then it was no problem for you to murder so many and destroy a most amazing work."

"I told you, I didn't know."

"Of course not," Kurgan said simply. "I was not just making 'death rays,' as you call them. My city was an experiment that would've helped my country and changed the world. No more polluting gasoline engines. Free power."

Jason had no desire to get into any political discussions with Kurgan. Crosswinds began to buffet the glider.

"Do you know who Nikola Tesla is?"

"A friend of yours?"

"No, no." Kurgan smiled. "Well, yes, a spiritual mentor. He died in 1943."

"Wait. I remember. Wasn't he around during Edison's time? He was an inventor."

"This world would be a different place if his ideas were adopted, very different. Radio frequencies would power the world. There would be no gas engines, or wires and plugs that power electrical things. Think about it. Rather than gasoline to power cars and such, all we would have to do would be tune in a frequency and electromagnetic power would be there. You're driving on it right now."

Jason wouldn't have believed him if not for the fact that something other than a gasoline engine was moving them at the moment. "I don't think that the big oil and electric companies would support it," he said.

"No, they didn't. It would have ruined your Rockefellers', Gettys', and other capitalists' profits. So they conspired to destroy him. Your oilmen killed him. They ran him down with a car as he was crossing the street. Ironic—he died penniless in a flophouse.

"He was ridiculed, and still is. They called him a stupid Croatian. I have studied all there is to know about Tesla. He proved his theories by making enormous electromagnetic transmitters. Free power for the masses—is there any purer communism? My city ran on this power. No wires. No pollutants for you Americans to analyze, except when we fired the EMP. With this power we could have reflected it around the world, bringing power to places that never had it. Alice, it wasn't just about the destructive power we held."

Holding his fist toward Jason, Kurgan spit. "Peace through unlimited energy. That was the promise. That's what we had. Fifteen years of building Tesla's dream, a chance to change the world. But, thanks to you, it is not to be." Kurgan nodded over his shoulder. "Back there I had many of Tesla's original papers—in his hand, original; his diary written in his own hand. Gone. All gone.

"You Americans could have had this power long ago."

"What?"

"Yes, but you ignored him, ignored the most important invention of all time."

"Bullshit."

"No. No 'bullshit,' Alice. Tesla had it all figured out in 1934: an inexhaustible source of energy that could circle the world. Everyone in the world with access to free power, but you *Americans* would not let it be. With that power came a weapon that could rule the world, and during World War Two everyone ignored him—but not the Soviet people.

"We bought his invention for twenty-five thousand dollars—twenty-five thousand dollars. You paid us how much for Alaska? *We* got the better deal! After we were in possession of his information you Americans tried to kill him, but not before we got all he had to offer.

"You think that you have destroyed Tesla's legacy back there?"

Kurgan looked at Jason, his eyes smoldering as he tapped his temple. "But not here. I have it all here. I have memorized all his work, word for word. I *know,* Mister Alice, and I can do it again. Magic—that is what those who don't understand call it. *Black* magic.

"Tesla's work taught me well. *My* magic is made from a red mercury shell, a plutonium core, and high explosives. The energy from my explosion passes through a supercooled magnet, and *water* is the capacitor—a whole lakeful. That is the secret your physicists missed.

"Simplicity. NASA spent millions inventing a pen that could write in space. We took pencils!"

Kurgan gripped his hands closed as if he was holding unlimited nuclear power in his hands. "Many think that it is all over, but it is not true. There will be those in your country who will be waiting for me to start it all over again. And I will. I will because you will take me there. Is there a choice?"

"I could stop and throw your ass out right here. You would freeze to death."

"Oh no you would not, Mister Alice. Not yet. I have not told you enough. There is more. You are not interested in how we knew that you were coming?"

Jason remained silent, waiting for Kurgan to continue.

"You have a natural gas generator in Alaska called the HAARP program."

"So?"

"So your country made a field of antennas, acres of them. Firing up a generator powered by a natural gas pocket, they beamed the power to bounce it off the aurora borealis, the ionosphere, and other concentrated masses. Nothing will work as well as a man-made reflector. A reflector costs billions to make. An American mole kept me informed of the reflector's progress. I told Zond when it was time to go after your Godspeed reflector. I pressed the button that blew up the Titan. Me. I chose all the targets. I directed our weapon. I killed the mole on the jet that tried to reach you."

"You pulsed the Canadian helicopter."

"The mole had evidence that needed to stay unrecovered."

Jason could barely breathe.

"Zond stole your reflector and we put it into space. I blinded your eyes in the sky by attacking your ground computers, and then I gave you back your sight, *and you looked through my eyes*!"

"What are you talking about?"

Kurgan leaned back in his seat and folded his arms. "There is a commercial imagery company in America that contracts one of our satellites. I gambled that by striking at the heart of your spy satellites, your intelligence world would eventually use our product. And they did! They were misled by one of your own. We prepared and waited for you, but you did get through, did you not?"

Jason gripped the steering handle, knuckles white. *The sellout has to be the same one who ordered the rubout!*

"So do you want to know more?"

Jason shook his head. "Why? Why are you telling me this?" He had heard enough.

"You are a typical American who fears the truth. You, the murderer of thousands, are afraid of what a simple Russian tells you."

Kurgan misread Jason. The last link to everything he'd believed in before the explosion broke. He'd been manipulated, fooled, lied to, and made to feel like he was somebody, then set up to commit murder and be cast aside.

But there was no one to blame but himself. Everyone had used him because he was a guaranteed fuckup. But that period was about to end. Looking at the power gauge, he laughed. "I'll tell you what. Tell me all you want, because we ain't gonna make it to the coast. We're almost out of power. Is there any way you can use one of your Tesla experiments to keep us moving?"

He would keep moving until the glider stopped.

*Now* he felt like giving up. He had reached the point of believing everything and nothing. What happened after the glider stopped was out of his hands. In a hurry to nowhere, he opened up the throttle.

## 2130
## CLASSIFIED LOCATION / EAST COAST / USA

"On line! We got it all back!" Maria Duran cried. The mainframe computers were back and the imagery was clear and detailed.

Colonel Doug Jones put his fists over his head and triumphantly yelled, "Quick, process the FLASH requirements and get them out. OUT!" No one knew that he had memorized the data of the SAINT's final trajectory and plotted out its target location. That same day he read the papers and came across a small article about a meteor destruction of the two Russian satellites—Russian, not American. Taking the measurements and studying the data, he understood that he was only a small compartment of the Big Picture. A lot more was going on, and he knew that what had gone on in space was probably going on below. Where, he didn't know, but he had to do something.

## 1530
## DOORS OPERATIONS CENTER / MISAWA AIR
## FORCE BASE / JAPAN

There were three different views of the same area over Siberia: a thermal image that showed the moisture content and approaching weather, a hyperspectral image detailing color differences, and a real-time JSTARS feed that had been in a surveillance orbit for over twelve hours.

Steve Leath followed an unidentified vehicle headed in a northeasterly direction. Looking over his shoulder, Ben Cadallo peered closely at the screen.

"All I can see is a blob," Cadallo said. "How can you tell it's a truck, or anything?"

"Lots of practice," Leath answered. "You can barely see it, or make it out, but it's there, moving. My bet is that it's at least one or more of your people."

"Sir, look at the screen, say fifty miles to the west—there's a bunch of other craft also headed east," another imager called out.

"More scout vehicles?" Ben queried.

"No, it could be a pursuit."

"Who else knows about this?" Cadallo asked.

"Just my team."

"Mister Leath, until I tell you otherwise, do not tell anyone—I mean *anyone*—about this," Cadallo cautioned. "Get the rest of your team here and keep them here. Don't let anyone in or out. Understand?" Grabbing a pen and sticky note, he leaned closer to Leath. "Now who else is on your team?"

"Wolff!" Cadallo yelled as he barged from the room.

"Yes sir!"

Thrusting the paper into the lieutenant's hand, he grabbed his shoulder. "You done a good job, son. Now you got to do a little sneaky stuff. Find out where these people are and quietly get them here. Don't tell anybody, even them, what you're doing. Just get them here. Understand?"

"Yes, sir."

"Good." Cadallo raced out to his car and headed for Security Hill. He had some very fast work to do.


**0600 SATURDAY / 6 NOVEMBER 1999**
**SIBERIAN TUNDRA / RUSSIA**

The glider was dead. Out of power. The wind screamed around them. The sun was low in the sky. It would stay low and set early. It was cold in the cab, but there was no reason to go anywhere, as the land was flat forever.

Jason watched as Kurgan shivered. Without complete

medical treatment or cold-weather gear Kurgan would die on the tundra in a short time. Without power there was no heat. After destroying Kurgan's world, Jason pondered whether to just leave the man and go on his own or to try to get him through.

He wondered what kind of people wanted to speak with the man. What would they talk about? The concepts that Kurgan dealt with only a few men in the world could understand. What would it be like for trailer trash like himself to kill a genius like Einstein, or Tesla? Killing. He'd had enough of it.

Pushing hard against the wind, he opened his door and stood up and searched the flat surroundings through a pair of binoculars left in the cab. Far in the distance he could see something moving in his direction. "Shit." It was a convoy of trucks. The men that he had killed had probably been discovered. How had they tracked him across the frozen ground?

Sighing deeply, he fell back into the cab. There weren't any more options left. The Russians looked to be about five miles or more out. There was no point in running; it was nothing but flat out there. At the moment the glider offered the most relative safety and warmth for miles around. No help was coming. A cold loneliness settled over him.

Hope. It was what Mac had told him to search for. Well, hope wasn't with him in the cab, if it had ever been on this journey at all.

"I think the game's over." Jason looked at Kurgan. "I know you want to live, but I won't let them take you alive. You won't feel a thing." There were a lot of things he wanted to say. "Look. I don't expect you to believe me, but I didn't know that there were women and children in your city."

"And if you knew, would you still have killed them?"

He couldn't answer the question, and it scared him to his core. Froto wanted to pop the nuke for the thrill. Is that what it was all about—the thrill, not hope? The thrill of cheating death—is that what had really brought him to Siberia? Not a vendetta. Not revenge, not duty, not a double cross, and for sure as fuck not hope. "I actually thought I could beat the odds."

Jason started laughing to himself. "I took this covert mission to come and kill you. I thought that I was the cool one, the insider. Instead I killed all those people and then left my comrades in the heat of battle. Nobody used me—I used myself." Once again, a strange calm came over him.

Suddenly, a high whine overrode the howling wind.

Jason climbed back out of the vehicle. Turning on his amplified hearing, it seemed to work, and he caught the high whine of . . . jets? Coming out of the west. Russian. "Hey, Kurgan, think you can get away from this glider?"

"Why?"

"Some of your jets are coming and I would bet that there are some dead-for-sure rockets that have our name on them."

"No!"

"Yeah." Then, from the east, he felt a low-pitched rumble. It sounded like one he knew. But it couldn't be. Impossible. He flipped down his NVV. It partially functioned. He looked to the east. At first it was just a dark speck on the horizon. Then slowly, the closer it came, the specter began to take shape. "I don't believe it!" The return of the Messiah seemed suddenly more believable.

## 0605
## SIBERIAN TUNDRA / RUSSIA

The Russian fighter pilots were less than five minutes from their target acquisition. They would fry the target and then hopefully have enough gas to make Omersk to refuel.

"Sergi, what is that on screen?"

"It's big and it's coming in from a reciprocal heading at two hundred and fifty knots. Looks like it's flying at possibly twenty meters. Do we have anything in the area?"

"I do not know but do not like this. Go to afterburner!"

In seconds they would overrun the bogey.

Sergi almost laughed when he saw what was below him. "It's an American C-130. What is a C-130 doing here?"

Olaf did not answer and made his missile run on the target on the ground. He released his missile the moment he got a tone. The missile flew wildly into the ground, missing the target completely. "This is very wrong. The plane must somehow be jamming our signal. Shoot it down!" He could not afford to waste a single shot.


"DON'T DARE ROCK A WING OR WE'RE DEAD; PULL UP IN-stead!" ordered the C-130 aircraft commander.

"Got it. Lower, bad. Higher, good," translated the left-seat pilot at the controls.

The C-130 bounced along, thirty feet above the Siberian tundra floor. An abrupt turn, or a downdraft, and the plane would strike the ground and cartwheel into a million pieces of flaming wreckage.

To bring the helicopters covertly into Siberia, the C-130 functioned as refueling escort and electronic suppressor for two H-60 Blackhawk choppers. Its mission suddenly changed when the tactical coordinator on the Rivet Joint made an emergency call to the Siberian rescue package. They said that two AWACS-pinpointed Russian jets were on the same intercept course as the rescue package.

Quickly plotting the difference in airspeeds, and realizing that the trailing choppers would not make the pickup before the jets waxed Jason, the commander of the faster prototype HC-130JX decided to take the lead and race for their objective. The two choppers set down on the tundra coast to wait for the arrival of the *precious package*, or to beat feet in the event the package was lost.

Mac Rio hung on for dear life in the cargo compartment as the plane climbed to 250 feet, exposing their position for the first time to enemy air defenses. They had no choice; Jason's life depended on it.

Ingressing over one hundred miles undetected into Russian airspace had taken an incredible amount of crew coordination and one super C-130XJ model. Equipped with more electronic gadgets than a James Bond car, the electronic warfare operators had not relaxed one second the entire flight.

Targeting radar, Meconning, passive ELINT, a Directed Infrared Countermeasures (DIRCM) laser missile blinder, and a host of other classified systems, two electronic warfare wizards flipped switches and turned dials trying to discover and stay ahead of any detection systems that would give away their position. Now they had to let the pilot and loadmaster complete the mission, staying alert to jam any further missile launches.

"Heavy Equipment Drop Checklist," Steve Lacy, the flight engineer, said.

"Roger," acknowledged Mac Rio as he unstrapped from the crew bunk he had been clinging to and made his way to the rear of the plane. He began a final inspection of the load as he worked his way forward. This was his last chance to fix anything that might be wrong. Any misses at this point would mean that not only Jason, but the aircrew as well, would perish.

"Drop checks complete," keyed Mac. He had been nervous the whole trip, but wasn't anymore; now he was terrified.

"Slow down in thirty seconds," cautioned Jackie Powell, the navigator.

"Climbing through two fifty to three hundred and fifty feet," said Darwin Hall, the pilot, as he pulled back on the yoke.

"Oh, shit!" yelled Mark Midden, the EWO. "We're getting illuminated like a fuckin' Christmas tree. Got two bandits, close, danger close."

"Crew, y'all stay on the drop," ordered Hall from the right seat. "Navs, y'all fire up your weapons and be ready for a dogfight."

"Slow down. Slow down now," keyed the navigator.

"Airspeed," said Steve Lacy, the flight engineer.

"Two hundred and fifty. Set flaps at fifty percent," said Bill Scarboro, the copilot.

"Ramp and door coming open," said Steve.

Mac ran to the aft edge of the platform, made his left-side lock release checks, then got behind the emergency release handles. "Doors opened and locked, slow-down checks complete, loadmaster."

"I got the lead jet coming out of twenty-five," cried the nav.

Hall held them to their course. "Stay on the run."

"Ten seconds," called Powell.

Mac was so scared that he could barely breathe.

"Green light!" she cried.

Mac watched as a fifteen-foot extraction line dropped from a bomb shackle and then swung out into the slipstream. The moment it inflated it ripped the load out from the plane.

"LOAD CLEAR!" screamed Mac, as he climbed up to the plexi-glass bubble at the center wing to set up for the second portion of the mission: trying to stay alive by calling out overhead Mig attacks.

"We're divin', boy. Goin' low. We're in a knife fight and we got to do some serious flyin' to keep our asses goin'!"

## 0615
## SIBERIAN TUNDRA / RUSSIA

Jason watched as an extraction chute ripped something from the tail end of the C-130. A parachute bloomed. The load oscillated twice, then struck the ground.

"Come on! I ain't waiting on you!" Jason cried as he jumped from the useless vehicle.

"What is it?" Kurgan coughed as Jason pulled him out of his seat.

"Hope!"

The cargo chute separated from the load. Jumping to the top of the load, Jason pulled a release lever and all the restraint and suspension lines fell away from it. "Shit, it looks like the hovercraft back at the PJ section." Peering closer, he was astonished to see that it *was* the hovercraft he drove in his section—a GPL Air Commander AC3, the Ferrari of hovercraft—and that it was almost ready to fly. Jason rudely dumped Kurgan into his seat, heedless of any pain he may have caused the man.

In the driver's seat, Jason flipped on the power switches, turned on the key, and gunned the twin engines to life. Compared with the glider, the hovercraft was *loud*, and smelly. He couldn't stop smiling when he saw a handwritten message taped to the dash:

*Jason,*
> *Don't do anything stupid,*

> > > > *Mac*

"Hang on, we're cruising!"

The hovercraft glided from the pallet and flew across the ground.

Doing his best to man the controls, Jason plugged his helmet into the comm cord and keyed the button. "This is Alice, and who are you guys?"

"This is Lightningbird," radio operator Rene Rubiella answered. "Take a heading of one-two-zero. We're a little busy right now. I'll get back to you."

Jason turned toward the indicated heading display and twisted the throttle to its maximum travel. Looking up, he saw the C-130J dive toward the ground as a rocket plume flew over him. The C-130 flew in between him and the jet, chaff and flares popping from the airplane like popcorn to decoy Russian missiles. The missile suddenly went vertical and exploded.

"I got a tone. I got diamonds: Missile!" warned the navigator. "Setting the DIRCM."

"Flares, flares, FLARES! Ah, shit, there's another launch," said Mac, who was in the bubble over the center wing watching the two Russian jets circle above. "Ready, ready, break right!"

The pilot pulled hard on the joystick and the plane pitched to the right in a three-g turn as Jackie hit the missile blinder button on the DIRCM.

Mac pressed the flare button. "Flares away! Missile still locked on."

"Lock on break!" cried Jackie. "The DIRCM nailed it."

"Missiles going vertical." Mac watched with frightened relief as the missile flew blind and exploded.

"Seven high, what do you see?" the nav queried Mac.

Looking up and to the right, Mac saw one of the jets roll onto its back. "It's going to try to get on our six. It's going for a tail shot." He watched until he saw the pilot committed to the run. "Now, bank right."

The pilot rolled the plane into an eighty-degree, three-g left turn. "I got him. I got him," confirmed the pilot.

"THE FUCKER!" CURSED SERGI, THE RUSSIAN PILOT. "THEY keep jamming my shots with something I've never seen. Olaf, go get the target. I'm going after the one-thirty." Trying to get a shot resolution, he had to maneuver into a ten-g turn, trying to get on the 130's tail. It was no good. He flipped on his gun switch.

"HE'S LEADING HIS NOSE, GOING FOR A GUN SHOT. READY, ready, bunt!" Mac said. Fright had changed into exhilaration. A C-130 was no match for a jet fighter, or was it?

"He said bunt, boy. Bunt!" spit Darwin to the copilot.

"Guns, guns, guns!" Mac watched with white-knuckled terror as a line of fire reached out from the jet, and then arced away from them.

"I got it at twelve high," cautioned Jackie.

"SHIT!" THE C-130 JUMPED OUT OF SERGI'S TARGET DISPLAY the moment he fired. He broke off his run to make another pass. "It's just a matter of time, American. I *will* get you," he vowed. It didn't matter that he was low on fuel. He no longer cared about the primary target on the ground. No bumbling *transport* plane was going to outmaneuver him.

"GOT HIM," CONFIRMED DARWIN. "WE'RE GOING RIGHT after him, right on his nose. Mac, where's that shooter?"

"He's going vertical."

The pilot pushed the throttles and aimed at the jet.

*HE'S JOKING!* THE C-130 FILLED THE MIG'S WINDSCREEN. The C-130 was playing chicken! The Russian pilot pulled hard to the right as it zipped past the plane.

"DAMN!" GASPED MAC AS A BLUR FLEW OVER HIS HEAD. "Gone to the left."

"I lost the jets on the radar," said the nav.

Heads inside the C-130 bobbed frantically as they scanned for the fast movers.

"Five o'clock at maybe three miles, and here they *both* come!" cried Midden.

"Got them!" Mac said. "Hold. Hold steady!"

"I got a lock on. Diamonds. Two locks. TONE! They're gonna fire." Jackie kept a close watch on her missile warning gear, ready to dispense chaff and flares to try and decoy the missiles or to strike back with the DIRCM laser.

"I got the plume. Two plumes. It's yours. Oh shit!" Mac grit his teeth.

The plane pulled hard to the right as flares and chaff popped from the tail and wing wells.

Jackie closed her eyes tight and hit the DIRCM. The missile dove toward the ground.

"Hit to kill." The light from the self-destructing missiles almost blinded Mac.

"Hit the deck!" Darwin ordered.

The turns and g-forces made Mac sick. He quickly pulled out a barf bag from his flight suit and vomited into it as he kept his eyes locked on the jets. Wrapping the bag closed, he dropped it onto the floor beneath him. The jets got bigger. "They're going on afterburner."

JASON FELT THE HOVERCRAFT SHUDDER AS THE TWO Russian jets flew at supersonic speed just feet above the tundra. The C-130 flew valiantly, keeping the fighters from zeroing in on the hovercraft. Looking back, he pulled away from the Zond ground pursuers, putting a cushion of space between them. A little longer and he might lose them altogether. *God, I hope you know what you're doing, Mac.* It was only a matter of time; Jason realized that a C-130 was no match for fighters.

"SERGI, BREAK LEFT AND GET A HEAD-ON VECTOR WITH IT. I'll flank them, then push them into a trap."

"Breaking left."

Olaf was tired of playing with the stubborn plane. He was running foolishly low on fuel, but he wanted the C-130 as badly as he would have any fighter. It was now a matter of pride. Besides, until they got rid of the C-130 they wouldn't get a clear shot on the ground target.

DARWIN'S CREW WAS JUMPY, BUT TIGHT. LIKE ANIMALS about to be cornered, they were waiting, just buying time until the endgame maneuver.

"Got 'em both. One at our twelve and the other rolling to the six," cautioned Jackie.

"Six is on his run," said Mac.

"I've lost the lead. Don't know where he's gone."

"EWOs, you on it?" questioned Darwin.

"Standing by," Midden keyed back.

"He's level." Mac watched, almost in panic, as the jet began to get even bigger. "Break left."

"Shit!" keyed Jackie. "The second jet is at our five!"

"Got them both on our six. Damn, they're on us tight this time!" squealed Mac.

"I got a tone!" Jackie cried.

This time they were too close to try any countermoves.

"This is it, guys!" Darwin hesitated a moment, then leaned over Lacy, the flight engineer, and counted to three before he pressed the red button next to the autopilot.

"NOW THEY ARE OURS!" SERGI WAITED A MOMENT, SAVORing the feel of taking out an American plane, even if it was just a transport; it would be his first real kill. But the second he was about to fire his missile, the tail of the C-130 lit up and the plane began to pull away. "What the fuck?"

SIX JET ASSISTED TAKEOFF (JATO) BOTTLES FIRED ALL AT once. The added rocket ordnance put thousands of pounds of power into the full thrust of the throttles as the C-130 roared away from the confused Russians.

"I got my solution!" the EWO keyed.

"Then shoot, boy, SHOOT!" yelled Darwin.

Midden hit the fire buttons on his EWO panel.

THE RUSSIAN PILOTS WATCHED OPENMOUTHED AS TWO MISsiles came *backward* off of the C-130's wings. They were still in shock as the Aim-9X rockets impacted and blew the jets into just so many pieces of fiery shrapnel.

"HOLY CHRIST!" JASON YELLED. WAS THAT REAL? DID A C-130 just take out two Russian fighters? Watching the battle above, he almost lost control of the flying hover-craft.

"DON'T GLORY-GLOAT, GUYS, THIS AIN'T OVER," DARWIN KEYED. "We just announced ourselves to every damn Russky from here to China. Now let's see if we can help our boy home."

"Roger," the flight engineer answered. "Loiter Attack missile checklist."

Mac already had the loadmaster checks completed and was waiting on the rest of the crew. The C-130 turned around and headed back toward Jason. When the C-130 had climbed to six thousand feet, its spine opened.

"I got the Russian convoy on the ground. No surface-to-air missile indications," confirmed Jackie.

"The launch is yours, nav."

THE ZOND CONVOY ON THE GROUND WATCHED AS FIFTEEN small objects popped from the top of the plane. They stared in awe as seven missiles rocketed toward them. It was the last thing they saw before they and their vehicles were ripped apart.

The remaining flying missiles began a slow flight home. Kept aloft by inflatable wings, an electric motor, and a turbopropeller, the seven LAM (Loitering Attack Missiles) had an onboard GPS automatic targeting system. The flying munitions covered the C-130J's exit. Any more enemy jets or ground pursuit vehicles now had a very nasty surprise waiting for them as they tried to follow Jason's trail. The missiles were programmed to fly back to friendly territory and be recovered by ground teams for reuse.

## 1045
## SIBERIAN TUNDRA COASTLINE / RUSSIA

One Blackhawk helicopter sat on the ground and another circled in the air. Jason throttled down the hovercraft and landed while he checked out the scene. Recognizing the miniguns protruding from the windows of the Blackhawk choppers, he turned off the engine. If they wanted him dead, there would be no outrunning those guns.

"Come on, Kurgan, we got a date to meet."

Kicking open the door, Jason waited until he had Kurgan in front of him. The wind howled around him as he pushed the hobbled scientist along with his rifle. One man stood by the chopper. Jason knew that there had to be at least two more men flanking him somewhere on the tundra.

If this was a setup, it was an elaborate one. Flipping the rifle's switch to automatic, Jason was ready, if necessary, to call it quits and kill anything in front of his weapon, including Kurgan.

The closer Jason got, the more the man in front of the chopper began to look familiar, and big. He raised his Gau-5 in front of his chest and shook it back and forth in a familiar star pattern. "Hurry up, dude!"

He knew that move—it identified PJ team members in an unfamiliar environment. "Lance!" Jason answered with his own rifle move, then ran to his radio operator, dragging Kurgan with him.

"Dude, we gotta go!" chattered Lance.

"We're outta here!" Jason yelled. To his left and right two armed men stood up and ran with him to the chopper.

He threw Kurgan onto the chopper like a sack of rice and jumped in after him, then the other three men piled in behind Jason. The chopper lifted into the sky. Looking back, he saw the second chopper land and quickly pick up the air commander. Little evidence of any American presence had been left behind.

The moment they were airborne the C-130 extended two hoses from each wing and the choppers fueled simultaneously, then disconnected and tucked close beneath the wings to draft off the plane.

Jason watched with surprise and awe as the helmets were removed. Dan Murray gave him a shy smile.

Alex Abbey gripped his shoulder. "We're going home, Brother."

The pilot leaned back and smiled. It was Sunshine Hannon. "We're on our way back to Kansas, Alice, and your little dog, Toto, too."

Dan handed him a white paper flight lunch made by an Air Force chow hall. It wasn't gourmet, but no better feast in the world was in a box. Two roast beef sandwiches, chips, a Pepsi. *Damn!* Jason didn't wait to check out the rest of the contents as he began to ravage his food. An orange and candy were gone in moments.

They raced with the wind, flying the nap of the earth, over the ice floes and then over the cold, blue water. No one was out of danger yet, but they felt that victory was close. Carlos Gonzales handed Jason a headset. Sunshine told him it would be about a two-hour ride to the safe air space ADIZ where ten F-16s from Misawa were on station, armed and ready to fire on any Russian pursuit jets that appeared on their radar.

Once back in friendly airspace, the choppers would air-refuel with Darwin's crew and climb to altitude.

"Who's the guy?" keyed Sunshine. "No one told us about a second pickup."

Alex handed Kurgan a box lunch. They smiled at each other. To Alex, Kurgan looked like a nice old man.

"The biggest secret in the world," Jason replied.

"Oh?"

"He got shot in the right calf by an AK-47 and lost a lot of blood. Look, right now I can't even keep my eyes open. You guys check him over and make sure he won't fucking die."

Dan Murray nodded.

He didn't care where they were headed; anywhere was better than where he had been. "Hey, Sunshine, mind if I rack out, like now?"

"Spoken like a true PJ," Hannon said as he and the rest of the crew laughed.

Jason took off the headset and was about to lie down next to the right door, but stopped. Pulling himself over to Lance, he said, "That guy belongs to me. If anything happens before we make it safely back, put a bullet in his head."

Lance looked astonished, then grinned. "No problem, dude."

*Sleep. Wait. I got to know something.* "Hey, Alex, how'd you do it? How did you guys know where I'd be? How'd you get in? How did you know?"

The PJs looked at one another.

Alex leaned over. "Mac Rio."

"What?"

"He brought your letter to the PJ building and showed it to us. He said that a pilot named Darwin Hall was working on some sort of experimental C-130J rescue program. Darwin put the thing together with your General Ben Cadallo. We weren't doing anything at Misawa at the time. Fuck, once we found out that you were in trouble there were almost fistfights in the unit to get on your rescue mission. Everyone in the whole goddamned group tried to get in on it!"

Lance unzipped his flight suit and reached inside. "Dude, this is yours—you left it in your locker back at Patrick."

Something landed in his lap. Jason picked it up and peered through the darkness. He'd come thousands of miles, been fooled into killing thousands of innocents, and lost all hope, thinking his own had turned their backs on him—but here they were once again saving his ass. He'd been looking for hope in the wrong places. What he had been searching for had never left him.

As he put on his worn maroon PJ beret, hot tears began flowing down his face.


**1200 SATURDAY / 6 NOVEMBER 1999**
**OVER THE SEA OF JAPAN**

All aircrews were released from their stations. The mission was over. The wing commander had placed all of his assets at the disposal of Operation Lucifer Light. The ORI was over and the 35th Fighter Wing had passed with flying colors. It was a done deal.

Upon landing, the aircrews were locked behind closed doors and debriefed. They had participated in an ORI. Period. Nothing out of the ordinary had happened. A simulated war had been fought and a *victory* had been achieved. Any rumor of strange things occurring while they'd performed their mission was just that: rumors. After the debrief a few crew members were kept behind and given specific details on how to quickly squash anyone from talking about a top-secret mission that had gone down in a foreign country. The final message was: Thank you very much for your help. Now go home and keep your mouth shut.

---

# CHAPTER 22

**H**EY, MISTER, ARE YOU A REAL PJ?"
Jason whipped around, arms open wide, and ran to the voice. Embracing Mac, he hugged him with all that he had.

"Jason, you stink," Mac said as he held his friend.

"When did you know that I was in trouble?"

"The moment you turned your back to get on the jet at Patrick to go on the mission," Mac said with a laugh. "I called Darwin, then flew out to see him. He put the whole thing together. He called Cadallo to get the mission specifics."

"But how'd you find me?"

"We got it from Cadallo. You had a GPS locator chip injected into you. Shit, they knew where you were all along. He told Darwin it's good for thirty days before it deactivates."

Jason unconsciously rubbed his arm, remembering the painful shot he'd received before the mission began.

Even though he was back in American territory, he felt less than secure. "Where's Tom Chain?"

"Don't know, but Cadallo came to the PJ team and

flight crew personally and told us not to tell anyone about the rescue mission, especially Tom. We launched the rescue while the IG at Misawa was going on. Nobody was the wiser. Funny, huh? A top-secret mission hidden behind an IG inspection."

"And the Brothers? Any word on Lucas or Kelly?"

Mac held out his palms and smiled wide. "Jason, we're rescue. Who's gonna update us on a mission that never existed? Hey, you got a story to tell me?" The smile dropped when he saw the pained look on his friend's face. "That bad?"

"Worse."

The sound of a low-flying jet drowned out all voices. Turning to final, landing gear extended, the C-21 jet touched down, taxied to the choppers, and shut down engines. The crew door opened and a man in a black trench coat and slouch hat appeared.

Jason couldn't believe his eyes. "Ah, *fuck*! How did he get here? How'd he know?"

Boris stepped down from the plane like a Roman emperor. Haughty and taunting, he had come to claim his prize. Like dogs on the hunt, his black pajama guys poured from the plane and surrounded the rescue team. The combat rescuers quickly turned into CIC hostages.

Decker was not beside Boris. Jason looked around, but did not see him anywhere.

"Y'all want sompin'?" Darwin asked Boris.

"Are you the A code here?" Boris asked. "A code" signified the man in charge.

Jason spit. He knew what was going on and didn't like it one bit. Did Decker have him in his sights already? The hair rose on the back of his neck.

Boris handed Darwin a paper. "This is a presidential NSR order. I know you know what that is. Are you going to question my authority to take possession of that man in the litter?"

Reading the document, Darwin put his hand on Jason's shoulder and whispered, "I've seen these before.

He's got the authority to shoot anyone trying to stop him from takin' what he wants. I gotta comply—sorry."

Boris took back the paper and dangled it in front of Jason and grinned. "Did you have a nice trip and kill lots of people?" Pointing at Jason's arm, he said, "I followed your progress on my own locator net."

Boris was on his back before he knew it. Mouth bleeding, he stared at the muzzle of a silenced pistol.

"Don't do it." Darwin's voice was quivering.

"Jason, listen to him," Mac cried. *"Don't do it!"*

The sound of pistols being drawn and rifle slides racking filled the air. Once again Jason felt like a target, but he didn't care. It was nothing new.

Staring deep into Boris's frightened eyes, he saw the truth. "You *knew*. You knew what was there. You knew what I was going to do. You were the one behind it all. You *evil* son of a bitch." A hand slowly wrapped around his pistol. Looking up, he saw the face of Dan Murray, who nodded over to their chopper.

Lance was behind the minigun. "Don't none of you dudes move."

Jason jerked the muzzle of his gun against Boris's mouth, making sure that he had knocked loose his front teeth, then slowly stood up and backed away with Darwin and the PJs.

"Just say the word, Jason." Lance moved the deadly minigun from side to side. "After I'm done we can feed these dudes to the sharks."

Jason sighed, then chuckled at Boris and said, "Got the drop on you, finally." He watched as Boris's men picked him up off the ground. Punching the man had felt great. The blood running down Boris's mouth made Jason feel even better. Having Lance cut the fucker to pieces with thousands of bullets would be best of all. But he knew that there was nothing more he could do. Frustrated, he'd nailed Boris just because he was mad. "Take your prize."

Lance lowered his weapon.

Boris's men quickly disarmed Jason of his pistol and rifle and then scrambled to get Kurgan and take him aboard their jet, but Kurgan stopped them and motioned to Jason.

"I want to speak alone with him."

Waiting until everyone else was out of earshot, Kurgan leaned forward and whispered to Jason, "You want to know the darkest secret I have?"

"I'm all ears."

"Then come closer. Nikola Tesla died a bitter man. I have his diary and journals in my head, memorized word for word, page for page. Even though you have destroyed my work, even though Z has my disks, they don't have Nikola's last and greatest invention.

"I tell you how it works. You make the same contained, controlled nuclear explosion. So much power, the same I used on all our attacks, *but* with the flick of a switch I tune that power into a radio frequency pulse, anywhere from one to fifty hertz." He stopped and looked at Jason. "Do you know that our brains function on those hertz?"

"No."

"It does. Yes. Now think of what would happen if the beam touched you. Your brain would overload in less than a second and you'd drop dead."

Jason's jaw dropped. "A death ray."

"Absolutely! I've already done it," he said with enthusiasm. "Six hundred prisoners dead at the same instant.

"I was working on the weapon long before Reagan started Star Wars. We used many research facilities to hide my project from your spy satellites—Semipalatinsk, Sary Shagan, and Sarova, to name a few. I built giant facilities at those places and diverted the attention of your spy satellites while I began constructing the real nuclear-pulse generator."

Jason was speechless.

"*You*—you have come and killed my city. This I promise you, Alice. I will kill ten times, a hundred times those you have taken away from me. You think you have done a service to your country?" Kurgan nodded, eyes full of hatred. "You have delivered Lucifer into the Garden."

Looking up, Kurgan saw Boris standing over them.

Mister Black and Kurgan locked eyes for a few moments, like sharks sizing each other up. Boris's men picked up the litter as Mister Black held out his hand to Kurgan. They shook hands and smiled—two devils meeting.

Kurgan turned toward Jason. "Good-bye, Mister Alice. Remember what I have told you. Remember that wherever you live or go."

After a glance at his blood-soaked rag, Black narrowed his eyes at Jason. "His name is Jason Johnson. I can tell you where he lives. He lives in Florida in a cheap apartment. I will tell you more about him on the plane."

Boris was the first to board the plane, followed by Kurgan on the litter. The jet engines started and they were gone in minutes.

As the jet lifted off the runway, Jason felt a hand on his shoulder.

"Come on, Jason, Darwin's one-thirty is just about refueled," Mac said. "Let's go home. It's over."

"Is it? Is it really?"

# CHAPTER 23

**1600 TUESDAY / 9 NOVEMBER 1999**
**PATRICK AIR FORCE BASE BEACH / FLORIDA**

JASON SAT LOST IN THOUGHT ON THE RETAINING WALL overlooking the beach in front of the Patrick Officers' Club. Once again, everyone had won while he lost. If he stayed a PJ for a hundred years he could never make up for the thousands he'd helped to kill. In his mind he saw the face of a little girl holding her little black dog.

A lifetime of showers would never wash away the dirt from the Lucifer Light. Lies, half-truths, conspiracies, betrayals, and illusions were the staples of the dark world. A "military complex" was how they described it. "A valid and sanctioned target." Set up and spit out, Jason now carried his gun wherever he went. The Brotherhood of Death had been torn apart by the mission. "Fuck. I'm the reason they got involved in the first place."

"The reason who got involved?"

"Shit!" Jason exclaimed. He whipped around, his hand gripping his pistol. "How do you do that?"

"Do what?" Lucas asked.

"Show up." How could he draw on Lucas? There

was no way he would ever know Lucas's part in the rubout.

"Ninja." Lucas laughed. "No. You were so lost in thought that a tank could've rolled up on you." He crouched down next to Jason. "So how ya doin'? You never came back to us."

"What, as a target? Shit, I'm trying to stay lost here."

"I asked how you're doing."

"Just...doin'. Are you the only one left from the mission?"

"Maybe."

"Maybe, shit!" Jason gripped his gun tighter, ready to pull and fire. "Are you behind the rubout?"

"Not me."

"Then how'd you get out?"

"After I sent you off, we activated our capes and tried a diversion to keep them away from you. All hell broke loose. Rusty covered our exit, but he stopped; I never knew why. Zorro and Ming got trapped in a berm. They fired off the remote high explosives that we planted. Then everything stopped, and the nuke went off. I thought I was the only one left. I found Rusty's body. I never saw Ming or Zorro again; I hear that their locator chips went dead. Zond was blown, and Kurgan captured. I walked to the recovery point and came home. Mission complete."

"Mission complete? You're lying. You sent Kurgan with me as a diversion for *you*. What about the rubout? Come on, man, if you don't know how bad we got used, then you're on their side. I set myself up like a chump, and the Doors chumped me."

"You think I lied to you?"

"I...I don't know. I don't know a lot of things. I just know that I don't want any part of the Doors. I'm a PJ. I can jump into any situation and take over to keep life going. I work with what I got. I train my boys to lay down their lives to save another, if they have to. It's simple and all out in the open. Not like you guys. Now I realize that

I was never after the thrill of the game. Can you tell me why this deal got laid on me?"

Lucas shrugged his shoulders. "The Doors did what they had to do."

For the first time since the mission began, he saw things the way they stood. A thought came forward. "Where's Tom?"

"Gone."

"You do him?"

"No. Me try and hit Tom? No. He just disappeared. Jean too. You know how we do it."

"I'm still learning. So it was Tom who set us up?"

"Maybe, but I can say with all confidence that it wasn't Ben. He was the one who directed the mission from Misawa. Tom was back here. He disappeared the moment you landed at Attua. I can't say for sure if he crossed us, but believe me when I tell you that I'm trying to find out."

"I think Boris is behind the rubout."

"True, but Boris is no longer a player in *anybody's* game." Lucas gave one of his rare grins. It was like looking at death's smile. "Yeah, we might be expendable, but we're not trash. Boris is out of the game and will never be seen again, by anybody."

Was Boris really gone? He had to trust someone. Lucas had been straight with him, as far as he could tell. "John, I brought back a guy with the knowledge to make a real working death ray. I saved his life. And—and here's the real kicker: That fucker plans to turn the weapon on us. And it's my fault. Shit, I'll be drowning in blood."

They sat quietly for a while.

"So what are you going to do, John?"

"Rebuild. There's nothing else I can do. This was my last field operation. Yours too."

"What?"

"I'm cutting you free. You've more than paid for all the kinds of deeds you have done—hero deeds, black and dirty deeds, you know? I'm sorry. You can go your own way." Lucas put his hand on Jason's shoulder. "You're right: You're a lifesaver. If you would've known about Kurgan's city, you wouldn't have popped it. You're going to have to believe I'm telling you the truth when I tell you that the Doors didn't know about the civilians being there.

"This ain't a goody-goody world. It's pretty nasty. But you have to know that without *your* kind in the world it would be a lot worse. Think about how many other people could've died if you hadn't set the nuke.

"Anyone can take a gun and kill, destroy life. Some of us are better at it than others. But to put your life on the line to keep life going—that takes the kind of heart that few have."

Jason frowned. "I don't understand. You still want me with the Brotherhood?"

"More than ever, but like I said, you're a free man. It's your choice."

"First I gotta find out who's after me. I have my ideas."

"Need help?"

"No. I think I can handle it, but I'll call you if I need you. What do you think about Kelly? Dead?" He sorely missed his little friend.

"I count him among the missing. But you never know about Froto. He has this eerie way of turning up."

"Like you?"

"Yeah. I hope the little fucker's not dead." Lucas handed Jason a newspaper.

"What's this?"

"Today's paper. I like to read the local crimes, especially the obituaries. You'll never know who'll turn up in 'em." Standing, he added, "Think over what I said, and leave me a message either way. I'll see you around, friend."

This time Jason actually saw Lucas get into a blue Ford and drive away.

Opening the newspaper to the obituaries, he saw one obit highlighted. It was a John Doe report about a man with a bullet wound to the right calf found dead in an alley in South Beach, Miami. The height, weight, and age were the same as Kurgan's. He'd died of a massive cerebral hemorrhage.

A paper slipped from the next page. A note was written on it:

> *Jason,*
>> *Once again you held up the honor of the Brothers—you delivered Kurgan alive.*
>> *A second mission commenced the moment Boris got him.*
>> *What he knew made him the most dangerous man on Earth to certain people who saw him as a liability. Boris too.*
>> *Your vendetta's been served,*
>>>>>> *Lucas*

Jason watched in amazement as the light-sensitive paper crumbled into dust.


**1730**
**CAPE CANAVERAL AIR FORCE BASE / FLORIDA**

The plan, if you could call it one, was simple. Drive to the Skid Strip. Make the turn on the runway he remembered from the day the Titan exploded. Find the CIS building. Park the car. Get out, knock on the CIC's front door, and start shooting at anyone pointing a gun at him.

Jason figured that he had already been made the moment he drove onto the base, but he wasn't about to run. It was time to end it. If a hit team was after him, then he would make it a public show.

Reaching the Skid Strip gate, he turned the car around and tried to remember being in the shuttered CIC van. Looking to his right, he was astonished to see King George sunning himself on the canal bank. Jason turned off the car and got out. He would say good-bye to an old friend before the gunfight.

The giant alligator lay sleeping in the sun. Jason creeped in from behind the alligator's blind eye, getting as close as he dared. Strangely, he felt safe for the first time in months. The Skid Strip was void of people. It was just King George and him.

"Hello, old man," he greeted. "I haven't been sleeping very well. I was hoping it was all over, but I've been having bad dreams. George, I can't see their faces, but they're there, every night, every fucking night. I didn't know that there were women and children there. Now I see blank faces almost every night." He reached out and touched the alligator's tail.

"Like the one I woke you from?"

Grabbing his pistol and spinning around onto his stomach, Jason had a "dead bang" shot on a man carrying an alligator-skin suitcase.

"*You?* Decker, the CIC asshole, or do you work for Zond?" Jason resisted the overwhelming urge to blow him away right then and there.

Decker stood calmly watching the alligator. "I saw you on a surveillance camera. I've been waiting for you. Listen, I don't work for anyone anymore. You got a license to carry that thing? Why don't you put it down before it causes.... *problems.*"

"Funny thing, I figured *I* was looking for *you.* I still owe you from the last time you were here, asshole, and for a lot of other things. After all I've been through, putting a bullet in you would be the least of my problems."

"The name's Mike. I worked for Mister Black, but he's disappeared. You know anything about that?"

Jason raised the pistol to Decker's heart and pulled back the hammer. "Mister Black? Isn't this the place where *he* makes people disappear? I got no problem killing a guy like you. My buddy here could turn you into alligator shit."

"Jason, be *real* careful. A word or gesture from me and you're dead."

"Maybe, but I'll get the last shot off," Jason told him.

Mike smiled, then chuckled. "Oh, you could. But I think that you should hear me out before you pull that trigger."

"Keep talking."

"I used to run a Protective Team. A few months ago somebody tried to hijack my load and my whole team got wiped out. Fucked up. Black gave me an opportunity to find those responsible for the attack. He gave me access to a lot of his secret files. Too much didn't add up. Remember when we met during the Titan explosion?"

"And a few other places, like when your boys tried to take me out at the Doors."

"No they didn't." Decker smiled. "I just wanted you ready for Siberia, inspired."

"They got close."

"I wanted them to. It was all part of the plan."

"Plan?"

"See, I discovered that Black was hiding something, and he was *very* paranoid about it. He totally freaked when he found out that you were with the Brotherhood of Death—you were my bait."

"Bait?" Jason felt like squeezing the trigger.

"Bait. That's right. To get to all Black's files I had to have him believe that you guys were running an operation against him. He bought it. He wanted your team dead to hide his dealings, so he convinced a top-secret ad hoc Senate committee about the need for a rubout of the insertion team. I was there when he did it."

"Who was going to do it?"

"Me."

Jason's finger trembled on the trigger.

"And what was his operation?"

"A guy with that much power and pull...think about it, Jason. Here's a guy making a couple hundred thousand a year while he honchos a secret organization worth billions in secret money, *untraceable* money. He got greedy and stole billions, but forgot about all of it when he realized you could put Kurgan in his hands."

"What? How?"

"It wasn't so hard. He drew up the contracts for his satellites, and when the parts came in he'd use dummy stuff for some of the satellites and then condemn good parts, sending them to the military junkyard. Black had the recycle system under his control. He had people buy multimillion-dollar parts for pennies for dummy businesses that he secretly owned, and then he'd buy back the genuine parts for millions in pure profit. He also collected insurance money on bad satellites that he himself had screwed up.

"He triple-built satellites and then secretly warehoused them. He made billions off the sale of them. He kept imaging satellites in orbit longer than planned." Decker laughed. "He also had this great scheme going. He had all these major corporations—and I mean *major* companies—pumping money into what he called ultrablack programs. The corporations thought they were landing contracts worth billions. Here's the catch: He had each company sign nondisclosure statements promising not to tell anyone that they were connected to the program or they would lose his support and he would throw them in jail. Can you believe it? They all fell for it—greedy, dropping millions, hoping to make billions. He took in millions and gave back nothing. No contracts. Nothing. What a guy!"

Decker pointed his finger at Jason. "He got *real* paranoid when you suddenly showed up—he thought that the Brothers of Death were onto him. He had to trust somebody."

"You."

"Me. I played to him that you guys were about to uncover his whole operation. So I got his trust by volunteering to take care of the Brotherhood. Oh, I tipped off Lucas to the rubout. Boris had to hide his money deeper, and needed me to start moving it to other secret accounts. Once he gave me his code I discovered that it was basically the same for all his other accounts.

"He forgot all about the money when he realized that Kurgan was alive and with you. Suddenly you became very important to him. His mistake. The smell of power made him slip up."

Jason shook his head. "I'm losing you."

"Rich as he was, it was ultimate power that he was really after. He would use Kurgan and the stolen money to re-create the EMP weapon and then become the power behind it. This guy's scum. What could I do? I was after the bad guys. I didn't know they were us."

"What did you do?"

"I made a money deal with the government, but didn't tell them about Kurgan."

"Yeah?"

"It's called the False Claims Act. Anyone who can prove fraudulent deals made against the U.S. government can get up to a thirty percent reward. I turned him in to friends I have in the Secret Service. The deal I made was for twenty-five points from one hundred of whatever I recovered. Tax-free.

"I had gone after the guys who took out my team, but it turns out that you were doing that for me. So while you were gone, I used the time to dig up all his deals and make the case against him. After you came back and the dust settled, I turned over some of my findings to Bruce Davis. U.S. Marshalls and the IRS went to arrest him, but he's gone. I came here to tell you that the rubout's off. No one is after you. Especially me. Jason, you think Boris is going to be hard to find?"

"Very." Jason lowered his pistol, but kept it between them as he rose to his knees.

"You know that I could've dropped you sitting next to that gator at any time. You're close to the place where people disappear." Turning to leave, Decker put the suitcase down and said, "It's over. You're clean and clear. Well, I got to go. I just thought I'd tell you that I used you and that I'm sorry. We're a lot alike. Maybe we could have been friends, alligator man."

A bittersweet smile crossed Jason's lips. "No. I don't think so."

"No? Oh well." He took a few steps, then stopped,

turned around, and walked over to Jason. "Oh," Decker said, pointing to the suitcase. "That belongs to you. And this." He held out a scrap of paper.

Carefully taking the paper, Jason read a series of numbers written on it. "What's this?"

"It's a federal bank account number and a telephone number to reach them. I couldn't have gotten to Black without you. I cut you in for five points of my twenty-five."

Jason was astonished. "How much you recover?"

"About two billion, so far. There's a lot more out there. I'll turn in more when I'm ready. You'll get your cut."

Jason's gun dropped to his side as Decker held out his hand and helped him to his feet. Then they shook hands.

"I'm rich. So are you. Ironic, isn't it? We were the expendables, played by puppet masters, but you and I are the ones that get to walk away. See you around." Decker turned and left.

Jason stood there in shock until Decker was out of sight. Then, picking up the suitcase and opening it, he discovered it was full of hundred-dollar bills.

**0600 THURSDAY / 11 NOVEMBER 1999**
**CANADIAN FORCES BASE / GREENWOOD / NOVA SCOTIA**

THE C-130 TOUCHED DOWN ON THE RUNWAY IN THE cold, clear predawn and pulled off onto the taxiway. Engines running, the plane came to a stop in front of Hangar Ten. The crew door opened and a lone figure wearing a maroon beret descended from the steps and walked in the snow toward the hangar. The PJ removed his earplugs and entered the hangar through a side door.

Two Labrador helicopters sat under the bright hangar lights, crew and cargo doors open for instant boarding. The floor was waxed and spotless. Rescue gear was neatly stored for quick access. The double doors to the right led to the SARTech alert facilities where the alert and maintenance crew slept. At a moment's notice a rescue call could come, and the choppers and crews would be in the air.

Quietly stepping aboard the closest chopper, the PJ took the left scanner's seat where his friend used to sit. The seat was not overly comfortable, but it had probably been designed that way; stay alert. The PJ folded his hands together, almost in prayer, and looked around, trying to see what his friend would've seen.

Slowly and carefully, the PJ removed his old beret and ran his hand over the worn creases, gently rubbing the pewter flash of the rescue angel, symbol of both the pararescueman and SARTech. He placed the beret on the right armrest next to the observation window and then pulled out a photograph from his flight suit and studied the picture.

Two men stood side by side, holding fishing poles, proudly displaying two small fish. The PJ grinned, remembering the circumstances behind the picture. Fifty miles had been hiked in the Canadian wilderness to the SARTech's secret fishing hole, and over a thousand dollars had been spent on the fishing gear. The result of all the time, money, and effort was two fish, both tiny. But the trip had formed a friendship that lasted for years and turned into an annual event to see who could catch the smallest fish.

The PJ took a deep breath and set the picture on top of the maroon beret. There would be no more fishing trips. No more stories and lies to swap. A Brother was gone, and the PJ felt hollow inside. All that he had done, all the lives he had saved, had been wasted in one angry moment in an effort to avenge the loss of his beloved SARTech friend.

"I'm just a little fish," he whispered to the picture. "I never meant to hurt anyone."

Rising from the seat, the PJ laid the picture over the beret, walked out of the hangar, and looked at his solitary footprints in the snow. He had traveled a lifetime to make them, and was still alone. He was a good man who had done a bad thing, and the only way he knew to right the wrong was to continue to save lives wherever he could, the same way his friend Toby Wiler would have.

Looking around, Senior Master Sergeant Jason Johnson decided that all things considered, it was a beautiful day. He climbed back aboard the C-130, and Mac Rio closed the crew door.

The airplane taxied back to the runway and the pilot applied full power to its engines and released the brakes. Then the C-130 raced down the runway and climbed toward the rising sun.

## ABOUT THE AUTHOR

MICHAEL SALAZAR is an Air Force loadmaster instructor with over nineteen years
of service. He is considered one of the Air
Force's most experienced persons in search
and rescue. Currently assigned to the
920th Rescue Operation Group at Patrick
Air Force Base in Florida, his primary mission is to provide combat rescue for fighter
pilots. His group also acts as a rescue support for all NASA space shuttle launches,
and he is regularly called on for civilian
search and rescue.